"Behind you!" Hámund shouted, drawing his bow.

Geirmund dodged aside as the arrow whistled past him, heard a thunk and a whimper, but he had no time to turn and look. The fourth wolf leapt upon him before he could raise either of his weapons, and he went down under its weight, the snapping of the animal's teeth in his ears, its rancid breath in his nose. Geirmund put his sword arm up to keep that mouth from his throat and the wolf seized it. Its fangs sank into the meat of his arm, puncturing leather, wool, and skin, and he knew those jaws would shatter his bones.

Geirmund had not yet regained his feet when a fifth beast charged that narrow gap in their defenses. He scrambled to get up, bleeding and slipping in the snow, but couldn't reach his brother in time.

"No!" Geirmund cried. The wolf flew at Hámund, yanking him to the ground.

ALSO IN THE ASSASSIN'S CREED® SERIES

ASSASSIN'S CREED
VALHALLA

GEIRMUND'S SAGA

MATTHEW J. KIRBY

ACONYTE

UBISOFT

First published by Aconyte Books in 2020.
This paperback edition published in 2021.

ISBN 978 1 83908 060 9

Ebook ISBN 978 1 83908 061 6

Cover art by Jung Gi Kim

Distributed in North America by Simon & Schuster Inc, New York, USA
Printed in the United States of America
9 8 7 6 5 4 3 2 1

ACONYTE BOOKS

An imprint of Asmodee Entertainment Ltd
Mercury House, Shipstones Business Centre
North Gate, Nottingham NG7 7FN, UK
aconytebooks.com // twitter.com/aconytebooks

For Josh.

PART ONE

A Common Knife

1

The wolves appeared almost as soon as the red deer fell, and Geirmund wondered how long the beasts had been stalking them. His brother's arrow had not been well placed in the stag's side, and the wounded animal had bellowed and bled a vivid trail, leading them on a lengthy chase before it finally collapsed in the early snow with one last grunt and sigh. The sounds and smells of its death had doubtless reached deep into the surrounding valleys and over the hills, as loud to the wolf pack as the summoning of a blown battle horn.

"How many do you count?" Hámund asked.

Geirmund peered into the woods, which were already twilight-dim that late in the afternoon and darkening still. The open lowland groves of oak had long since given way to dense mountain forest in which all manner of beasts could hide. Black trunks of pine and birch stood in silent vanishing array, the posts of a hall into which Geirmund and his brother had not been invited. No hearth or soapstone lanterns burned there, and if such a hall had a king or a chieftain, be it troll or spirit, that ruler would offer them no protection.

"I count five," Hámund said.

And those were only the wolves that wanted to be seen. Geirmund drew his sword and pulled his axe free. "There could be twice that many held back."

"Held back?" Hámund frowned. "You credit these wolves with the battle cunning of a raiding party."

"That is what they are, in their way." Geirmund had glimpsed their leader as she skulked between the trees and paused in open view as if to look into his eyes and make certain that he realized she knew all about him. Her hackles bristled, her coat the colour of wet driftwood, and though she was large, there were others in her pack that were larger. That meant she did not rule by strength alone. "They may not sail by longship, but these wolves have come a-viking."

Hámund continued to scoff. "Next you'll tell me they'll attempt to flank us."

"They'll certainly try."

Now Hámund scoffed at him, and Geirmund's temper flared.

"Perhaps if you had spent less time drinking ale and flattering jarls with Father, you would know how wolves hunt."

Hámund stopped laughing but made no reply. Geirmund measured his older twin's silence and knew he would have to answer for the insult later, however true the observation might have been, but not in the danger of that moment. Several of the pack had openly advanced a few paces towards them, heads down, lips curled, with low thunder in their throats.

"They want the deer," Hámund said. "Perhaps we should let them have it."

Geirmund glanced down at their kill, a young buck that had not yet fought and claimed his own herd of hind-wives. That early in the winter he still had his antlers, and though they were no trophies, they were large enough for carving something useful, and his unblemished red coat still held a silken shine. His meat would make good eating.

"You would let them take what is yours?" Geirmund asked.

"You would die for a deer when there's a full larder at home?"

The bluntness of that question caused Geirmund to stop and reconsider. They were three days out from their own hall at Avaldsnes. What had started as a short hunt for small game had quickly become something much more ambitious. Finding larger prey scarce nearby, they had followed the Ålfjord north-east, far into the uplands that rose south-west of the village of Olund, near the border with Hordaland. But they were still more than a day from that place, their only refuge should the battle go ill for them. Geirmund smelled no smoke on the wind, no cookfires. Only the fragrance of the trees and the musk of sodden ground beneath the snow.

"We came this far because you wanted a hart," Geirmund said.

"But not at the cost of my life. Or yours."

Geirmund was leaning towards agreement with his brother when the pack's leader suddenly reappeared, as cold and silent as a mist out of Niflheim, and closer to them than any of the other wolves in her pack. Then, just as quickly, she loped out of sight, her head high. But Geirmund had seen the embers of Muspelheim in her yellow eyes, a burning and fearless defiance, a hunger for more than deer meat. This wolf knew of hunters, and she had hunted them. Geirmund had felt her ruthless hatred for the two men trespassing in her mountains, her forest hall.

But these were not her mountains, and this deer was not her kill, and she must be made to know it.

"If we run," Geirmund said, "they'll track us and rip out our throats as we sleep."

"Surely not," Hámund said, but without conviction.

"I'd also wager the people of Olund are well acquainted with this wolf."

"And if they are?"

Geirmund turned towards his brother, frowning. "They are of Rogaland and loyal to our father. They are our people. And you will one day be their king."

Hámund straightened at the accusation that Geirmund had stopped just short of making, his honour now at stake and his fate decided.

"Come, brother." Geirmund grinned and raised his weapons. "Do you want to fight? Or would you rather try to negotiate a trade agreement for the deer?" He nodded towards the wolves. "They'd be glad to offer terms, but not in our favour."

Hámund slipped his yew bow around from his back. "It might surprise you, brother, but I have learned some useful things in my travels." He pulled an arrow from his quiver and nocked it. "For example, I've learned you can't negotiate with the sea, no matter how many offerings you make, and I don't think it takes a hunter to know the same is true of wolves."

Geirmund stepped closer to his brother. "Aim truer than you did with the stag."

"Keep them off me so I can."

Then Geirmund turned and set his back to Hámund's, and they planted their feet for the fight to come as the wolves began to circle, searching for a weakness or opening in their defences. They huffed clouds of breath-mist into the air, the cold afternoon light having waned further in the last few moments, giving their wolf eyes an advantage.

When two of the beasts finally charged, they did so as one, from opposite sides. Geirmund heard the twang of his brother's bow over his shoulder, followed instantly by a yelp, and then he ducked and swung his sword at the second animal lunging for his axe hand. His blade caught the big male's left foreleg, and when the beast retreated it did so limping, its dripping paw hanging on by little more than skin.

Geirmund glanced over his shoulder at his brother's target, which lay folded on itself, head beneath its body in the snow, an arrow protruding from the space between its neck and shoulder. A killing shot and a quick death.

"Well done, brother," Geirmund said.

"What of yours?"

"Out of the fight. But we–"

The next snarling wolf-wave rushed towards them, four in number, with another three or four beasts already circling, ready to add their teeth and claws. Hámund loosed an arrow and pulled another from his quiver while Geirmund swung his axe at the head of the first wolf to come within striking distance of his brother. The arrow found its mark, but not fatally, and the injured wolf tumbled, staggered to its feet, and fell again, while the animal Geirmund had struck rolled away and lay still.

"Behind you!" Hámund shouted, drawing his bow.

Geirmund dodged aside as the arrow whistled past him, heard a thunk and a whimper, but he had no time to turn and look. The fourth attacker leapt upon him before he could raise either of his weapons, and he went down under its weight, the snapping of the animal's teeth in his ears, its rancid breath in his nose. Geirmund put his sword arm up to keep that mouth from his throat and the wolf seized it. Its fangs sank into the meat of his arm, puncturing leather, wool, and skin, and he knew those jaws would shatter his bones.

He opened his eyes wide and roared into the wolf's ears, and then Hámund also roared, and suddenly the wolf convulsed and let go of Geirmund's arm. It leapt a few unsteady paces away, pawing at its face, an arrow sticking out of one eye. In the closeness of that fight, Hámund had stabbed the beast with it like a dagger, and so the shaft had not gone deep enough into the brain to kill it outright. Hámund drew another arrow to finish the job, his attention focused on the struggling animal.

Geirmund had not yet regained his feet when a fifth beast charged that narrow gap in their defences. He scrambled to get up, bleeding and slipping in the snow, but couldn't reach his brother in time. The wolf flew at Hámund, snatching him by the clothing and flesh in the pit of his drawing arm and yanking him to the ground.

"No!" Geirmund shouted. He had lost his sword but launched himself at the wolf with his axe, bringing it down in the middle of the beast's back with both hands, halving its spine. The wolf shrieked and tried to flee, dragging its useless hind legs, and Geirmund ended its misery quickly before turning to face the next assault.

But none came, and the battle was suddenly over. The pack seemed to have simply vanished, at least for the moment, leaving their dead and wounded behind. Geirmund picked up his sword and killed the two still twitching and suffering. That was when he noticed the familiar, nearly severed paw dangling from the foreleg of his brother's final attacker, a grievous wound that had not stopped that wolf from rejoining the fight with even greater bravery and ferocity. Or perhaps the wolf simply knew he was to die, and so decided to meet his fate with teeth bared. Geirmund considered either choice worthy of honour. He knelt next to the wolf in admiration, which quietly changed into a kind of regret.

"They've gone?" Hámund said.

Geirmund nodded.

"Will they return?"

"Always," Geirmund said. "But not today."

"How bad is your arm?"

Geirmund glanced down and noticed something pale protruding from his reddened and torn sleeve. At first, he thought it might be his arm bone, but realized in the next moment that it was merely a wolf's tooth. He pulled it out and held it in his palm, an ivory fang with a bloody root. "I will live," he said. Then he turned to assess his brother, who was staring at him, eyes still alight with the fading frenzy of battle, and he saw a red stain seeping down Hámund's side. "I fear your wound is worse."

Hámund broke his gaze from Geirmund's arm and looked down at himself. "I will live. The blood bodes worse than it is."

"You're certain?"

Hámund swallowed and nodded, then glanced over the battlefield. "We took six of them."

Geirmund laid a hand on the wolf's side and pressed his fingers into its thick fur, feeling the animal's ribs. "They're almost down to bones," he said, "and their teeth are loose."

They were not bloodthirsty, or evil, or vengeful–merely desperate; but Geirmund knew that changed nothing in the end, and closed his fist around the fang. Even if the defiance and rage he'd seen in the pack leader's eyes had been a figment, there simply wasn't enough land and prey in Rogaland to feed every belly. Fighting and death were inevitable.

Geirmund stood. "We need to make camp. Light a fire and clean our wounds, then skin the animals. We'll move out in the morning."

Hámund blinked and nodded, and they spent the last daymark before the setting of the sun clearing a spot of ground and cutting deadwood. Then Geirmund dragged the wolf carcasses closer to the firepit while Hámund bent to light the fire with the ornate strike-a-light he'd acquired in one of his travels with their father eastward to Finnland. It had a glinting bronze handle carved with two opposing riders on horses, but for all its decoration did not seem to make better sparks than Geirmund's plain steel. Hámund appeared to be struggling with it, his strikes with his fire-flint weak and ineffectual. Geirmund was about to step in when at last a few wisps of smoke curled up from the touchwood. Hámund was slow to rise from his task and seemed unsteady on his feet when he did.

"You do not look well," Geirmund said.

Hámund nodded. "I feel…" he said, but did not finish.

"Sit down. Let me look at your–"

Hámund dropped to the ground as if suddenly robbed of his bones.

Geirmund rushed to his side. "Look at me," he said, slapping his brother's pale cheek. "Look at me!" But his brother's eyes simply rolled behind half-closed lids.

The layers of clothing at Hámund's side felt heavy and sodden. Geirmund sliced through them with his knife and discovered a deep wound still pouring blood from under his brother's arm. He sucked air through his teeth at the sight of it and leapt towards the firepit. There he set the head of his axe in the growing flames, then filled a soapstone cup with snow. He left that near the fire to melt and heat up while he returned to his brother's side and did his best to staunch the flow of blood with the pressure of his hands.

"Hámund, you fool," he whispered.

A few moments later, he retrieved the soapstone cup and poured its steaming contents over the wound to clean it. Then he took up his axe and tested its heat by dropping some snow onto the metal that sizzled and disappeared.

"I don't know if you can hear me," Geirmund said, standing over his brother, "but shore yourself up. This is going to hurt."

With that, he bent and grabbed his brother's wrist. Then he lifted that arm to fully expose the wound and pressed the flat poll of his axe against the torn flesh. Hámund groaned but did not flinch as the hot metal seared his skin, sending the smoke and aroma of cooked meat into Geirmund's nose, making him gag for knowing what it was.

After some moments had passed, Geirmund pulled away the axe, which peeled gently from his brother's skin, relieved that the evil-looking wound appeared to have stopped bleeding. Geirmund hoped the flow had not turned inward to fill Hámund's belly and ribs, but he could do nothing about that if it had. He rolled up a strip of cloth and soaked it with the last of the mead he had left in his skin. This he wedged under his brother's arm, against the wound, and tied that arm down at Hámund's side to hold the dressing in place and keep pressure on the injury.

"Now I just need some way to bear you from this place," he said, and turned his attention to the dead wolves.

He chose the two largest, one of those the wolf with the severed paw, and strung them up to skin them by firelight, proceeding carefully but as quickly as he could with the crude work. Usually he would have slit the bellies and legs open to splay the pelts and lay them flat, but for his present plan he needed the fur to remain of a piece, which took time, care, and strength. He began at the legs, making minimal slices through the skin, and peeled the fur upon itself down the body, as if removing wet leggings that had tightened and shrunk. At times he had to use the weight of his body to rip the pelt downward, away from the carcass, sweating from the work even in the cold, but eventually he had two soft barrels of fur. He then used his axe to fell two young birch trees, each with a trunk as thick as his wrist, and he cut these down to half again, his brother's height in length. He laid out the wolf pelts nose to tail, and passed the two poles through them. Once the birch trunks had been braced apart, they stretched the furs tight, creating a sled that was at once tough, soft, and insulating to the cold air and snow beneath it.

Geirmund pulled this moveable bed alongside his brother and gently rolled Hámund onto it, and after strapping his brother's body to the sled along with his bow and other weapons, they were ready to depart.

It would be dangerous to travel at night, but Geirmund worried it would be more dangerous to linger there, not only because of the wolves but because of the risk to his brother. Hámund needed the cunning of a healer back in Avaldsnes, one who possessed the skill to prevent that wound from turning putrid, and he needed that care quickly. To delay would almost certainly mean Hámund's death.

Geirmund lowered the wolf carcasses to the snow and left them for their pack, should they return, for he knew that wolves would sometimes eat their own, but if not, they would find the body of the red deer waiting for them. He cut a few large pieces of meat from the buck's haunches, just enough to feed himself and his brother on the return journey, and left the rest behind.

Then he took the cord he'd used to truss the wolves and tied it around the birch poles in loops that he could cross over his chest and shoulders. This would allow his back to carry most of the burden, leaving his hands free to steady the poles and keep the sled level. But as he hoisted the load for the first time, the combined weight of his brother's body, the wolf pelts, and the birch poles took his breath and caused him to stumble before he'd even taken his first step.

"Thór grant me strength," he whispered, straining to regain his footing.

A moment later, he set off.

2

After a night, a day, another night, and another day had passed, the muscles in Geirmund's shoulders finally went numb where the merciless cords pressed like axe blades into his flesh. His feet had also numbed from the weight pressing his heels into the ground and from the snow and ice that received them, and his stiff back creaked like an old oak one storm away from falling. The poles had scraped his hands raw through his gloves, and his chest burned, deep inside, where the icy air he inhaled met the fire of his lungs.

It was past dawn on the third day, and during the night he had finally come down out of the rocks and snow of the mountains, into the lowlands where the open fields and meadows gave him less trouble. In some places the long grass, wet with rain, offered soft and slippery ground over which to drag the sled, which made the going easier for a time.

But that did not last, either.

As the sun approached its midday mark, the pain that had been his enemy was replaced by a far deadlier opponent. The muscles in Geirmund's legs and arms quavered with exhaustion, and his joints and ligaments felt loose and frayed. Where pain had been a direct assault against which he could rally and throw himself, fatigue was an endless siege, content to wait until he had used up every store he had in reserve and so depleted fell at last. To withstand it, he knew he needed sleep, but he had hoped to reach Avaldsnes without stopping, thus far allowing himself only the briefest of rests to assess Hámund's condition, cook the deer meat, and chew a few bites of it, only twice closing his eyes for a span shy of dreaming. But he realized now he did not have a choice. His body could take no more.

He sighted a stand of hazel trees near a small pond some acre-lengths ahead and decided it would do well as a resting place. Having attained it, he lowered his brother to the ground and then collapsed into the wet leaves and ruined nutshells, enveloped by the dank, sweet scent of mouldering vegetation.

Before he allowed himself to sleep, he checked Hámund for colour and fever, and though his brother's dun face still looked pale, his forehead was not hot to the touch, which Geirmund took for a good sign. His brother had seemed lost in a fitful sleep since falling senseless, mumbling at times and calling out at others, but never with his full wits. Geirmund thought his present state a kindness, given the pain and discomfort he would surely feel otherwise, and so long as it did not bode ill for him. For that reason Geirmund hadn't tried to rouse him and didn't do so now as he finally raised the anchor on his own mind and let the tide take him where it would. When he opened his eyes again, it was night, and he was shivering.

Pain had returned, but Geirmund welcomed it, and he now possessed a will renewed to confront it. With gritted teeth he climbed to his feet and gathered wood for a small fire, planning to examine his brother by its light and warm himself before attempting the final effort of his journey. But he was surprised to find Hámund's eyes open and watching him.

"How do you feel?" Geirmund asked, crossing to him.

"Itchy. These wolf pelts have fleas." Hámund attempted a grin. "I'd also feel better if I could take a piss and a shit."

Geirmund chuckled and loosed the straps holding his brother to the sled, then helped him to his feet. "Mind your arm. Don't try to raise it."

"I'm not sure I could, even if you hadn't tied it down."

Hámund hobbled just beyond the reach of the firelight, and Geirmund waited a while before calling to him. In reply, Hámund returned wordlessly and lay back down on the sled with a groan of pain. Geirmund offered him the last few bites of cold deer meat that he'd roasted the day before, or the day before that. It was hard to remember.

"Where are we?" Hámund asked.

Geirmund sat down across the fire from him. "I hope to reach the hall before nightfall tomorrow."

His brother stopped chewing. "You've carried me all this way?"

Geirmund tossed another length of hazelwood onto the flames, sending up sparks and a plume of deep and nutty smoke. "What else should I have done? You were too lazy to walk."

"That I was." Hámund laughed, winced, and took another bite of meat. "I'm afraid I'm still feeling lazy."

Geirmund could see the pride and concern in his brother's eyes and knew his thoughts as well as he knew his own. Hámund didn't have the strength to walk, but also didn't want to be a burden. Geirmund shrugged. "Another day is nothing to me."

"But it's something to me," Hámund said. "I'm the one getting flea-bitten."

"You were already flea-bitten. Your clan of fleas and the wolf clan could hold an Althing."

Hámund chuckled, then winced again. "Don't make me laugh."

"I doubt you'll have any cause for laughter once we set off." Geirmund rose and scooped up a clump of wet leaves with both hands. He dropped this onto the small fire and stamped out the flames, plunging the stand of hazel trees into darkness. "Are you ready?"

Hámund looked up at the night sky and its stars, as if trying to determine how close they were to dawn. "Now?"

"Yes. I think we must." Geirmund brushed the leaves from his hands and his voice grew weighty without his intending it to. "You need a healer with skill greater than mine."

Hámund nodded, slowly. "Then I suppose we must."

Geirmund moved to strap his brother to the sled once more, for the last time, but this time, Hámund was awake enough to groan in pain. The sound of his suffering roused Geirmund's pity, but did nothing to change what must be done, and for Hámund's part he gave not a single word to any complaint he might have offered, simply closing his lips and his eyes tightly through his ordeal. But as Geirmund finished, he did make a request.

"Give me my sword."

Geirmund paused. "Your sword?"

"To hold in my hand."

Geirmund realized then the meaning behind his brother's desire and tried to wave away his fears. "Fate isn't done with you. And neither is Father. He'd go to Valhalla himself to fetch you back from–"

"Please, brother." Hámund opened his hand near his chest. "My sword."

Whether it was necessary or not, Geirmund could find no

good reason to refuse his brother the honour of having his sword in his hand should he reach the end of his life's thread before they reached Avaldsnes. Inwardly, he swore that he would outpace the Norns and their shears as he untied Hámund's sword from where he had secured it and pulled it from its scabbard. The weapon had a blade of fine steel from Frakkland, a gift from their father before Hámund's first sea voyage that, as far as Geirmund knew, had never tasted the blood of man or beast. It had a grip wound with leather cord, and a hilt and pommel inlaid with intricate wheel patterns in silver and gold. The ripples and whorls that curled through its cold length shone like a river in the starlight.

"If you drop it, I'm not going back for it," Geirmund said with false severity.

"I know."

He stuck the end of the blade under one of the straps near his brother's knees to hold it somewhat in place, should his brother's grasp fail, and placed the hilt in his brother's open hand.

"Thank you." Hámund tightened his fist around it and pulled it close to his heart.

Geirmund nodded and moved to his position near the head of the sled, then knelt to slip the cords over his shoulders. When he lifted his brother, the weight on those cords cut into his shoulders with fresh ferocity, and he wondered if he would even be able to row an oar after this, when the time finally came for him to sail on his own ship.

"I think you're lighter," he said. "My thanks to you for having that shit."

Hámund chuckled behind him, his laughter quickly smothered by a moan, and his groans did not cease when Geirmund leaned into the cords and the sled lurched forward.

He did his best to seek the even ground as he followed a stretch of lowland between the Álfjord to the north and the Skjoldafjord to the south, but it was still dark. Jostling and bumping were inevitable, and with each jolt Hámund seemed to groan louder. For much of that night Geirmund used the stars to stay on course, but lost those guides just before dawn behind a thick bank of cloud that brought thunder and rain. Hámund fell silent then, even though Geirmund's feet slipped more often on the wet ground, causing him to tip the sled. He stopped to make sure his brother hadn't taken a turn for the worse and fallen senseless again but found him simply stoic.

"Can you at least cover my head," he said through clenched teeth, his face aimed skyward, eyes closed, with raindrops trapped in his lashes.

"Of course, I should have–" Geirmund pulled the hood of Hámund's cloak up and over as far as he could, reaching the end of his nose. "That's the best I can do."

Hámund nodded, but barely, the knuckles of his sword hand white.

Geirmund sighed and took up his yoke again like an ox. The rain fell hard and cold and it soaked through his cloak, leather and furs at the seams, but he came at last into a farming country with roads. To the south-east a swell of rocky land rose bald and grey, but he aimed his path around it to the south, near the shore of the Skjoldafjord, and as the morning wore on, the rain eased, and a mist rolled down from the heights to gather in the low places and on the water. Geirmund followed the shoreline of the fjord, and after that the edge of a lake.

The roads should have made the going easier, but rain had turned them into mires that sucked at Geirmund's boots and grabbed the ends of the sled's poles, caking both in heavy mud. His pace slowed even as his body strained at the limits of his strength, and his heart felt ready to burst. Twice his legs simply went out from under him, dropping him and his brother into the muck, and on the third time he simply lay there, unsure whether he could even get to his feet again.

"Is there a house in sight?" Hámund asked. "Or a place to seek shelter?"

"Not yet," Geirmund said, hand at his chest as he struggled to catch his breath, though he did smell woodsmoke. "And even… if there were, I would– I would still… need to fetch a healer and… that would take too much time."

Geirmund found his knees, and from there he got to his feet.

"I can wait for a healer," Hámund said. "Find a place to leave me and go."

Geirmund yoked himself once more. "I'm not leaving you anywhere."

"But you can't–"

"I said, I won't–" Geirmund had tried to raise his voice, but the effort only robbed him of breath. "I'm not leaving you."

He thought about taking the sled off the road to seek easier terrain, but the surrounding barley fields had been harvested and looked even more impassable than the way ahead. There was nothing for it but to keep moving. Nothing other than the road and the mud and the fathoms and rests he had yet to trudge, even if he fell a thousand times more. He soon lost track of the distances between far-off hillocks and trees, his awareness honed to only the stretch between each step, and he thought about nothing beyond the reach of his weakening stride. He ignored even his growing certainty that he would not, could not, last much longer, and they would not reach home. He kept moving.

Eventually, the rain clouds scattered, and sunlight set the wet world a-shimmer. When they arrived at the northern spear point of the Førresfjord, they turned south-west and followed its shore towards the Karmsund strait and home. Though perhaps less cold, Geirmund gained no strength from the change in weather, and found he now had to squint against the glare that struck his eyes from the many puddles in the road.

"Do you hear that?" Hámund asked.

"Hear… what?"

"Horses. Riders."

Geirmund stopped and tried to listen over the deafening roar of exertion in his ears. Hámund was right. There were travellers ahead of them, just around the next bend, by the sound of it. Their voices carried over the mired roads, cursing the mud and the rain.

"Too loud to be outlaws," Hámund said.

He was right again. Outlaws did not travel the roads except to wait in hiding in lonely places for travellers to murder and plunder. But before Geirmund could muster his senses to decide if it would be prudent to avoid them anyway, the travellers appeared. A moment after that, the riders called out, having seen them, and Geirmund thought he recognized the rough and familiar voice of Steinólfur. He wondered if a madness or delirium had taken him as the riders rushed towards them, but when they drew near Geirmund saw not only Steinólfur but also his young charge, Skjalgi, a lad with an unmistakable scar over his left eye. They rode with four other men from Avaldsnes, and they covered the stretch of road between their company and Geirmund as if it were no more than a homefield. Geirmund nearly swayed on his feet with relief at the sight of them.

"Hold!" Steinólfur called, pulling up his reins a few paces away. "Geirmund, is that you?"

"It is," Geirmund said. A trembling seized his arms.

"What is that sled you're dragging?" Steinólfur dismounted and strode towards him. "Where is Hámund?"

"That sled *is* Hámund," Hámund said.

Skjalgi had also dismounted, and the two men rushed up to take the sled poles from Geirmund's hands. They had to pry the staves loose, not because Geirmund refused to let go but because he could not make his fingers open. Skjalgi then took the weight of the sled with his arms while Steinólfur lifted the cords from Geirmund's shoulders.

"By the gods," he whispered as he looked into Geirmund's eyes. "What happened to you?"

"Wolves," Hámund said.

"Wolves?" Skjalgi slowly laid the sled down on the ground. "Where?"

"Perhaps a hard day's ride from here," Geirmund said. "Near Olund."

"Olund?" Steinólfur shook his head. "You were meant to be hunting squirrels. Your father has parties out searching for you, but none as far as Olund."

"We wanted more than squirrels," Hámund said.

"Steinólfur, listen to me." Geirmund had finally found the words to say what needed to be said. "My brother is injured, badly, under his arm. He needs a healer."

Steinólfur looked down at Hámund. "Can you ride?"

"I can," Hámund said. "But it would be a very short ride."

"He'll need someone to hold him steady," Geirmund said.

One of the company spoke up, a man called Egil. "My horse can carry the Hel-hide."

Geirmund ignored his use of that name, though he hated it, for no one who used it meant it as a true insult.

Steinólfur nodded and said, "Egil's horse is the strongest." He motioned the rider over and called for Skjalgi to untie Hámund from the sled. Then he turned back to Geirmund. "And what about you? That arm does not look well."

Geirmund glanced down. He had forgotten about his own injury, and by now his blood had dried in the layers of his sleeves, mixed with mud where the fabric and leather had torn. "I haven't tended to it yet."

"Let me," Steinólfur said, "after your brother is on his way."

Geirmund then watched as Egil approached on his powerful horse, a stallion with a golden coat and mane, and then several men gathered to lift Hámund into the saddle in front of the horse's rider. When he was settled, Steinólfur addressed the others in his party.

"Skjalgi and I will come behind you with Geirmund. You must see that Hámund reaches King Hjörr's hall before the sun sets."

The riders all nodded in assent, and a moment later Geirmund watched them gallop away bearing his brother, mud flying high into the air from their horses' hooves.

"I must go with him," he said. "We must–"

"You're not going anywhere until I've looked at your arm." Steinólfur led Geirmund off the road into the shade under a large ash tree, and Geirmund was too exhausted to protest. "After that," Steinólfur added, "you can tell me why you didn't just leave Hámund to die."

3

Geirmund straddled a root of the ash tree, his back against its trunk. Its bare branches reached high and stretched far, having shed their golden leaves, which surrounded him and the tree like a fallen crown upon the ground. On his left the Førresfjord shone in the sun, its shore perhaps a hundred fathoms distant, while farmland and pasture covered the low hills to his right.

Next to the tree, Steinólfur went about laying a small fire. The older warrior moved with a rigidity that spoke of past battles and their scars, and it often seemed to Geirmund that the fifteen summers between their ages held more life-skein than would naturally fill that time. Steinólfur already had grey in his brown beard, and if his skin were leather, it would not be fit for new use. He could speak to Geirmund as both friend and adviser, sometimes in the same breath. Once, when drunk and lost in his memories, he had mentioned a time at the oar, and that had caused Geirmund to wonder if Steinólfur had been a thrall. But it wasn't right to ask a man about something he'd said after drink had wiled away his wits and his tongue was not his own, so Geirmund had kept that question to himself.

"You don't look fevered." Steinólfur pulled a pinch of black touchwood from his tinder pouch, along with his fire-strike. "How much pain is that giving you?"

"Only a little," Geirmund said, but that was a lie. Relieved of his brotherly burden, he now noticed a tight swelling in his arm, sharp pain when he moved, and a dull throbbing when he held still. But he wouldn't complain to Steinólfur about that. He wanted to return to Avaldsnes and finish seeing to Hámund first. "We don't need a fire. There isn't time for it."

"It is no longer a matter of time." The older warrior struck sparks into the tinder, then blew over the flames through tight lips until the fire could live on its own. "Your brother will reach a healer and he will live. Or he will not, as fate wills it. Nothing you can do now will change that, and we need to dress your wounds."

Geirmund said nothing aloud but whispered an inward appeal to the Norns who would determine the outcome of his brother's healing, if it had not already been decided.

"There." Steinólfur nodded at the fire, satisfied with it, and glanced at Geirmund. "But I know you're not worried about your brother. You're worried your father will be angry."

Geirmund scowled. "I do worry about my brother."

Steinólfur stood and folded his arms, waiting until Geirmund nodded.

"But I worry about my father, also," he admitted.

The warmth of the fire had reached through his clothing on his left side, nearest the flames, but the damp and cold still clung to the other, and a Ginnungagap shiver ran down his spine, between his halves.

"When my father sees Hámund," Geirmund said, "he will look for me, and he will blame me."

Steinólfur relaxed his arms and stepped towards him. "He

will blame you whether you are there or not."

Skjalgi returned then, carrying two skins of cold, fresh water from the fjord. "Who will blame you?"

"My father," Geirmund said.

"What will he blame you for?" Skjalgi asked.

"For prying into matters that don't concern him," Steinólfur said. "Now put some stones in the fire, boy."

Skjalgi glanced at Geirmund and they exchanged grins. Then he went about gathering rocks of the right size, which he tossed into the flames at the fire's edge to heat them.

"Well, let's have a look at you," Steinólfur said.

He and Skjalgi pulled Geirmund's leather tunic over his head, then his wool, taking care as they peeled both layers away from his arm. Geirmund winced as the fibres tugged at his wounds, but both outer garments came away without reopening his skin. His linen undertunic would prove more challenging, however. Its weave had been saturated with his blood and become one with his torn flesh. To soften it, Skjalgi pulled the hot stones from the fire and dropped them into the water skins, which bubbled and swelled with steam. Then he dribbled the scalding water over Geirmund's arm as Steinólfur rubbed and loosened the tunic as best he could. Geirmund grunted and gritted his teeth against the pain, which lasted for some time until they could finally remove the tunic and look at his injury.

"A lot of blood and fuss over a scratch," Steinólfur said.

Geirmund looked at his arm, almost gasped, then laughed. Much worse than a scratch, the wolf's teeth had left a vivid arc of punctures and rent skin, the flesh around the bite black with hot, festered bruising. "I'm sure you've seen worse," he said.

"I've given worse," Steinólfur said. "Even the boy here has given worse."

Skjalgi said nothing, his face stolid as he took in Geirmund's wounds, for he had clearly done no such thing. But the deep and twisted scar over his eye proved that he had seen such injury, and worse. The tree that had almost taken his sight had crushed his father as it fell. He was old enough to carry a spear, but as yet had no beard, though unlike Geirmund he would one day grow one when his hair decided he had come of age.

"I suppose he is Hjörr's son, after all." Steinólfur sighed and nudged Skjalgi, trying to rouse some mirth in the boy and quell his unease. "That means we'll be expected to nurse him along like a runty pup and take the blame if anything should happen to him."

"I suppose so," Skjalgi agreed, but quietly.

"Now," Steinólfur said, frowning at Geirmund's arm. "I assume you want to keep this limb?"

"If I can," Geirmund said. "My sword would miss it."

"Would it? A sword needs feeding, and I wager your sword would be glad of finding another limb that could take better care of it."

"Like yours?" Skjalgi asked, grinning now.

Steinólfur shrugged. "Perhaps. But I have a sword, and I'll do my best to keep Geirmund united with his." He then let the jeer slide from both his eyes and his demeanour. "But like your brother, you should also see a healer when we return."

Geirmund nodded. "Perhaps that will cool some of my father's anger."

"Perhaps." Steinólfur turned to Skjalgi. "Fetch more water. And some mayweed, if you can find any."

Skjalgi emptied the stones from the skins and hurried off, and Geirmund waited until the boy was out of earshot before speaking.

"You didn't keep me here just to mend my arm. You have something to say."

"I do." Steinólfur tossed the stones from the skins back into the fire. "And it is this: no one else would have thought ill of you. No one else would have blamed you."

"For what?" Geirmund asked it as a challenge, because he knew very well what Steinólfur meant.

The older warrior rubbed his forehead and sighed. "People die. It is the way of things."

Geirmund leaned towards him, the heat of the fire on his cheeks. "He's my brother."

Steinólfur nodded, poking at the stones and embers with a stick. "Brothers also die. In the south, where I come from–"

"This is Rogaland." Geirmund's throat tightened. "You are not in Agðir any more, and you would be wise to remember that before you speak."

"I am your oath-man, Geirmund. If I can't speak plainly with you, then who can?"

Geirmund looked into his eyes and saw no guile there, a rare quality in those who surrounded him in his father's hall. "Speak plainly, then. But take care."

Steinólfur hesitated, like a man about to cross spring ice. "Years ago, when you were even younger than Skjalgi, I happened to see you sparring with Hámund. I watched you both for a time, and afterwards I went straight to Hjörr and asked his leave to become your oath-man."

Geirmund remembered the day his father had introduced Steinólfur to him. Though he had since come to value the company of the older warrior, he'd resented Steinólfur at the time, assuming he was there to spy on him and keep him out of mischief, and there had been many days when it seemed Steinólfur resented the duty as much as he did. That he had volunteered for the job had never occurred to Geirmund. "Why?" he asked.

Steinólfur chuckled. "Why, indeed. Your arms were thin as saplings, and you could barely wield a wooden training sword. But even so." Steinólfur grinned and wagged his finger at Geirmund. "You frightened me. I saw hunger in your eyes, and I saw rage, the kind that never burns itself out. I knew you were meant to be a king. I did not see that in Hámund's eyes. Not then, and not now. That is why I am your oath-man and not his. It is your fate to be king of–"

"Enough," Geirmund said, and then he sat quietly, weighing his next words. The older warrior had filled him with sudden pride and hidden shame, his quarters pulled in all directions by opposing loyalties, and as this turmoil subsided, he began to shake, in anger and in pain. "I thank you for speaking plainly," he said.

Steinólfur nodded.

"And now I will speak plainly with you. You will never again say such words, neither to me, nor to anyone else. Hámund is more than an oath-man. He is my brother." Geirmund made his voice sharp and dangerous. "Never again will you speak to me about what you see in him, or what you find him lacking. You will never know the battles we have fought, side by side, inside our own father's hall."

The older warrior stared, struck dumb. Geirmund knew that Steinólfur had heard the story of how the brothers had begun their lives in the straw with the dogs, which meant he knew but a fraction of the whole.

"You do not know my brother's hunger and rage," Geirmund said. "Neither do you truly know mine."

Steinólfur dropped his gaze to the ground and nodded, apparently sensing that he had gone as far as he could in his purpose without incurring a permanent cost.

A moment later, Skjalgi trotted back huffing, cheeks as red

as his hair, and Steinólfur grabbed the water skins from his hands. The boy flinched a little and looked back and forth between them, clutching a few dried stalks of mayweed left over from summer. He seemed to sense that something had taken place in his absence, but he knew better than to ask about it. Steinólfur went to the fire to retrieve the stones and added them to the skins, and then he took Geirmund's injured arm in his hands.

"Try not to squeal," he said.

Geirmund set his teeth hard together, refusing to make any kind of sound or complaint, though the pain blinded him. Steinólfur poured hot water over his wounds and rubbed them with a clean strip of linen to clean them as best he could. Some of the punctures reopened, oozing foul pus and blood. Steinólfur squeezed them until the blood flowed pure and dark, and then he boiled the mayweed to pack the wounds before binding them.

"I think your arm will heal well," the older warrior said as he finished.

Sweat ran down Geirmund's forehead as he nodded. "Thank you."

"I wish I'd brought ale or mead," Skjalgi said. "To ease the pain."

"You couldn't have carried enough for that," Geirmund said.

They pulled Geirmund's tunics back over his head, and once he was dressed they set off towards Avaldsnes. At Steinólfur's insistence, Geirmund rode Skjalgi's horse while the boy trudged in the mud alongside, but they kept a pace the boy could match with an easy stride. The earlier disagreement between Geirmund and Steinólfur remained between them, unspoken but ongoing, and they travelled in silence broken only by the occasional remark from Skjalgi on the land or the changing season. Eventually, the boy asked if either of them had heard of a Dane called Guthrum.

"I have heard my father use that name," Geirmund said. "He is a jarl, I think."

"Why do you ask about him?" Steinólfur asked.

Skjalgi squinted up at him. "Some men from a trading ship mentioned him."

"And why do you think of him now?" Geirmund asked.

"No reason." The boy placed his hand on the head of the axe that hung at his side. "They say Guthrum is gathering ships and men under the Dane-king, Bersi. Not just his Danes, but Northmen also. Perhaps even Geats and Svear."

"For what purpose?" Steinólfur asked.

"To join with the army of Halfdan and conquer the Saxon lands."

"Which Saxon lands?" Geirmund asked.

Skjalgi shrugged. "All of them, I suppose."

Geirmund glanced over at Steinólfur. The older warrior stared at the road straight ahead as though holding his tongue, but Geirmund knew his thoughts. Steinólfur had often spoken of the sons of Ragnar Loðbrok, praising their successes across the sea. No longer content with summer raiding, they had begun to seize Saxon crowns and kingdoms, and were Steinólfur not sworn to Geirmund, he would no doubt have crossed the seas long ago to join the battle and win his own house and homefield.

Geirmund looked down at Skjalgi. "I hear eagerness in your voice. You wish to join this Dane?"

The boy hesitated, glancing past Geirmund at Steinólfur. "I might, yes."

"I do not blame you," Geirmund said. "In truth, I share some of that eagerness."

"Then let us go," Steinólfur said in a low voice. "Ask your father for a ship."

"You know he won't give me a ship. Not for raiding."

"Why not for raiding?" Skjalgi asked.

Geirmund shook his head, unsure of how to speak the truth without sounding disloyal.

"This isn't raiding, and you know it." Steinólfur turned in his saddle and looked Geirmund in the eye. "Hjörr knows it also. He has the blood of his father and grandfather in him, even if he has chosen a different path. There is nothing traitorous in asking. This is what a second son must do to make his own way."

Now Geirmund turned and fixed his gaze on the road ahead, and for some time he made no answer. Steinólfur spoke the truth, and Geirmund could not deny it. It was also true that Geirmund had long wanted his own ship to sail from Rogaland and meet his fate, wherever it might find him. But he was a man divided and could not yet bring himself to leave his brother behind.

"I'll think on it," he finally said.

After a pause, Steinólfur nodded, but added, "Think on it, then. But ask yourself if you know your own mind. I believe you do and thinking more won't change that. All that's left is to act."

They spoke no more about it as on they rode and walked, eating smoked fish along the way, and soon came into familiar country. As the sun set before them, they passed through the farms and holdings of Avaldsnes, and they could have sought shelter at one of them for the night if they so wished, but Geirmund wanted to reach his brother's side. So, after the sun set, they travelled onward in the dark, the road lit only by a thin moon and distant hearthfires, until they reached the black waters of the Karmsund.

From Avaldsnes that narrow strait reached nearly twenty sea-rests south to the enormous Boknafjord, while in the other direction it opened into the North Way of whale roads and trade routes. On the other side of the Karmsund lay Geirmund's home on the long shield island of Karmøy, whose ancient kings traced their lineages from the gods. The ferocious seas beyond that island forced almost all northbound ships to take the Karmsund fairway, and the tides ensured they would stop at Avaldsnes for supplies and repairs. Therein lay the strength and wealth of his father's hall.

They approached the Karmsund at its narrowest point and passed under five ancient stones that stood in wide formation fifty fathoms from the shoreline, all of them white and thin as rib bones in the moonlight. No one could remember what people had raised them, or whether they might even be the work of giants, or the gods, but the power in them could be plainly felt. They stood near the place where Thór was said to have crossed the Karmsund, and where a ferry now carried travellers to the island. The advance party bearing Hámund must have given word of Geirmund's coming, for they found a boat waiting to carry them across.

As they drew near the opposite shore, Geirmund could see the distant black silhouettes of his ancestors' burial mounds against the night sky to the north, the largest of which belonged to his father's father, Half. Upon reaching the island, they turned south and followed the road for a rest, and on the other side of a small cove they came at last to Avaldsnes.

Bright torches burned at the city gate, which opened almost as soon as they came in sight of it, the guards no doubt having been alerted to keep watch for them. Once they had entered the town, the gate closed behind them and Geirmund found the main road similarly lighted. A procession of torches ran the length of the main road eastward from the gate, through the town, up the rise, to the ridge where his father's hall dominated the Karmsund.

"It seems we are looked for," Skjalgi said. "That's a comfort."

Geirmund felt the beginning of dread in his chest, but he managed a chuckle. "Or a warning."

"Best wait for your welcome to decide," Steinólfur said.

They followed the torches through town, and several familiar faces emerged in the doorways and windows they passed, many of them calling blessings on Geirmund and his brother. The smell of woodsmoke and the aromas of cookfires surrounded them, as did the muffled sounds of laughter and even music from inside a few of the houses.

As they approached the climb to his father's hall, Geirmund sighted movement above them, a shadow among the standing stones that had been raised on top of that hill long before any of his ancestors had built a dwelling there. Unlike the stones they had just passed on the Karmsund, these towered three times the height of a man and leaned close together, like the claws of a dragon reaching up out of the ground. The long bow-roof of his father's hall rose out of the ridge nearby, taller than the stones and somehow caught between reverence and defiance of their presence. When Geirmund and his companions reached the summit of the hill, the figure amidst the stones stepped out into the firelight.

"Geirmund Hel-hide," she said, approaching them as they dismounted.

Geirmund knew that voice. He recognized the antlers jutting from the völva's hood of goat and cat skins, and he could imagine the woman's unsettling eyes of icy blue, though he could not see them in the darkness. "Yrsa," he said. "My father summoned you?"

"No, he did not." The seer strode towards them, the silver rings on her bare toes glinting in the grass, until she stood near enough for Geirmund to see the blood she wore on her linen shift and her face, hopefully that of an offering and not his brother's. "I was already here when Hámund returned," she said, seemingly unaffected by the chill of the night air. "I knew I would be needed, and I was waiting."

"Of course you were." Steinólfur folded his arms and regarded the woman with the same wary mistrust in which he held any practitioner of magic who claimed to come between him and the gods, or to speak for them. "But if you knew Hámund would be injured, why did you not warn him before he left on his hunt?"

The seer smiled, a cold grin, and poor Skjalgi shrank into Steinólfur's shadow.

"I only knew I would be needed," she said. "I did not know why."

"Even so," Steinólfur said, undeterred. "How many reasons are there that a king might need a witch?"

"I'm sure my father was grateful for your presence," Geirmund said, hoping to silence the older warrior. Geirmund also had doubts about some seers and sorcerers, whose prophecies seemed shrewdly vague and self-serving, but he had no doubt of Yrsa's powers. "How is my brother?"

"He will live, and he will mend," she said.

Skjalgi took a brave step forward. "Geirmund is also injured. Will you see to him?"

The völva turned towards Geirmund and glanced down at his arm. Then she moved closer to him and looked up into his eyes. He did not know her age. At times, she seemed older than his mother, at other times, younger. But her eyes were ageless. "There is no need," she said.

Geirmund wondered if that meant he would heal, or if he was doomed and nothing could be done to prevent his death, but Steinólfur spoke before he could seek clarification.

"Why do you say so?" he asked.

Yrsa had not taken her eyes from Geirmund's, nor he his from hers. "Because his fate is tied to his brother's," she said. "Their life-threads are interwoven for many years to come. If one is to live, then so is the other."

Steinólfur scoffed. "And if one of them is to die?"

Now the seer swung her blade-gaze and plunged it into the older warrior, who took a small step back from her in spite of himself. "I see greatness achieved before I see their deaths," she said.

Steinólfur coughed and nodded. "At least we are agreed on that."

"I thank you, Yrsa," Geirmund said. "For being here."

She nodded, and then she turned away, but before she descended the rise, she said, "One day, Ægir will swallow you, but he will also spit you out. It is time to travel the whale roads, Geirmund Hel-hide." Then she was gone.

Skjalgi paled. "How did she know?"

"Know what?" Steinólfur said.

"That you told Geirmund to ask for a ship."

"But that's not what she said, is it?" Steinólfur took the boy's shoulder in a firm grasp and pulled him close. "Listen to me now. When soothsayers speak, they count on you to patch the leaks in their words, but you mustn't add any wood or pitch to make them seaworthy. A true seer wouldn't need your help. She said what she said knowing it would be time for any son of any king at Geirmund's age to take command of a ship. Nothing unnatural about it. Do you see?"

Skjalgi nodded, frowning now.

"Good." Steinólfur let go of the boy's shoulder. "Now go and see to the horses."

Skjalgi nodded again, then took the reins of both animals and led them towards the stables.

"Is that what you believe?" Geirmund asked. "Is there nothing to what she said?"

Steinólfur grumbled and growled before speaking. "I believe everything I just said to that boy. But I also believe that woman frightens me, and I don't like to be frightened."

"'Show me a man who is never afraid and I'll show you a fool.' Those are your words, in case you'd forgotten."

"I've always been a fool."

Geirmund smiled. Then he looked down at his injured arm. "You may be a fool, but you have my gratitude. And I hope you won't be offended when I have a healer take a look at your handiwork."

Steinólfur laughed. "Not at all. I insist on it."

Geirmund nodded and turned to go inside and face his father, but the older warrior held him back.

"Another word or two from this fool," he said, looking past Geirmund at the hall door. "He may blame you. He may be angry with you, and he may upbraid you. But pay no mind to it. Rest tonight knowing that you saved your brother's life, and there is honour enough in that to cover any mistake he might lay at your feet."

Geirmund inhaled, then nodded again. "Rest tonight knowing you almost surely saved both our lives."

"I'll expect an arm-ring in the morning," Steinólfur said.

Geirmund chuckled and led the way to the door. Before opening it, he straightened his back and lifted his chin. Then he and Steinólfur stepped inside his father's hall.

4

The hall was warm and brightly lit with many lamps. What remained of a pig hung upon a spit over the cookfire at the far end of the hearth, the bones and last shreds of meat crusted dark brown and sizzling, filling the hall with its aroma. Dogs barked as Geirmund entered, and several men and women left their benches to greet him, clasping his arms, his shoulders, his hands. The people of his father's hall were his father's kin, and his oath-sworn, but many were traders and merchants, and some had been sent by kings from other lands. All expressed their relief and joy at Geirmund's safe return.

He acknowledged them, not wanting to offend, but he winced when they bumped or gripped his injured arm and he did not want to linger there among them at the door. Steinólfur knew his thoughts without having to hear them spoken aloud.

"That's enough now," he said to the gathering after a few moments had passed, and he pushed his way through the press to clear Geirmund's path. "Let him through. His mother will want to kiss his beardless cheek."

Geirmund gave the older warrior an appreciative nod and

made his escape, striding the length of the hall, past the heavy smoke-stained beams that supported its high rafters and roof, and past the woven tapestries his father had brought back from Frakkland. Those visitors who had not felt it their place to approach Geirmund at the door, lacking in familiarity or status, stood to the side and bowed their heads as he passed, and he greeted them with nods in return.

One of them captured his attention, a woman his age, or perhaps a bit older, and dressed for battle, a shield-maiden with a scar across her left cheek and neck, and golden braids turned to bronze by the firelight of the hall. He had never seen her before, but she stood near a man Geirmund knew to be Styrbjorn, a jarl from Stavanger to the south. They both stood with Bragi Boddason, the ancient skald from Götaland, and the three of them acknowledged Geirmund with nods as he passed. He recognized in the woman's green eyes the curiosity that many felt upon seeing one of the Hel-hide sons of Hjörr for the first time.

He returned a nod to the three of them, wondering who she was, and continued to the end of the hall, past his father's high seat, then around the carved partition that separated the great room from his family's private chambers.

He found his brother in the council room, where his father received smaller delegations and conferred with his advisers. Hámund lay upon a pallet, covered in furs taken from his bedcloset. Geirmund assumed he had been situated there on the floor, rather than in his bed, so the two læknar women standing at his side could more easily tend to him. He appeared to be sleeping a heavy sleep, his chest rising and falling like the tide, slow and even. Sweat glistened across his brow.

Hjörr and Ljufvina stood at Hámund's feet, near to one another, their backs to Geirmund, but his mother turned to look over her shoulder as if sensing his presence.

"Geirmund!" she cried out, rushing to him, and pulling him into a tight embrace. "I thank the gods for your return."

Geirmund put his arms around her and held her for a moment before asking, "How is he?"

His father answered. "Yrsa says that he will live. But he is fevered. Thyra læknir says that he bled much. But we slaughtered a pig and he ate a cake of its blood, as she said to do. Now he rests."

"His wound?" Geirmund said. "I did the best I could, but–"

"We have dressed it," Thyra said, gesturing down at his brother, where he glimpsed fresh wrappings under the furs. "Inga helped me. But you did well, Geirmund. I believe it will heal, and he will still have full use of his drawing arm."

Something loosed inside Geirmund when she said that, a barb of fear he had been unaware of that had been pulling on the meat of his heart. "Thank you," he said.

"But what of you?" His mother looked him over, then gently lifted his arm. "When Hámund was awake, he said you had also been injured."

"I was. Steinólfur saw to it."

"Steinólfur?" Thyra said. "That old Egðir?" She crossed the room as though marching to battle. "Please, Geirmund, allow me." But she wasn't truly asking his permission. Instead, she hustled him into his father's chair at the head of the room's long table, where she laid out his arm and checked the work that Steinólfur had done. "Oh, mayweed," she said with approval. "But this wrapping is filthy. Inga, bring some new linen."

Steinólfur's wrapping did not look dirty to Geirmund's eyes, but he knew better than to protest as Thyra's daughter brought a basket to the table that held the tools of her mother's trade.

"This will be better," the older læknir said. "New, clean linen." She applied some of her own salve to his wounds, a sticky substance that burned his raw skin, and then went about rewrapping his arm.

"That is no minor injury." Ljufvina stood next to her son and laid her hand on his shoulder.

Geirmund looked up at her and noticed redness in her eyes, from crying or from sleeplessness, or perhaps both, and it seemed the lamps in the room caught more threads of silver in her raven hair than had been there before the hunt. "I'm sorry to have troubled you," he said.

"As you should be," his father said.

Hjörr stood a few paces away, arms clasped behind his back. He too looked tired and worn, his skin pale against the dark brown of his beard, though Geirmund did not feel the same remorse over his fatherly distress, for the larger share of it had no doubt been for his brother. Nevertheless he managed to say, "I do regret what happened, Father."

"What matters now is that you are both here, and you are well," his mother said, her voice firm, her words the terms of a temporary truce to which his father merely offered a grunt.

A few moments later, Thyra finished binding Geirmund's arm. His mother thanked the læknar and led them back to the main hall to find them a bench and blankets for the night. They would stay at least until Hámund's fever broke, and probably for longer, depending on the wishes of the queen and king. Geirmund remained seated in his father's chair and silent after they had gone, his arm resting on the table, waiting for his father to speak.

"Your brother sleeps now, but he told us what happened."

"Wolves." Geirmund nodded almost absently, his gaze buried in the table's deep wood grain. "Hámund fought well."

A moment passed. His father approached the table, and Geirmund almost rose out of instinct to offer the king his rightful seat. But some anchor of resentment and anger kept him moored there, and to his surprise his father simply sat in the chair next to him, slumped low and plainly exhausted. The king sighed, rubbing his eyes and his forehead, and Geirmund fortified his defences with the material Steinólfur had given him outside the hall.

"'Hámund fought well'," his father said. "Is that your full accounting?"

Before Geirmund could reply, the king went on.

"If my father were alive, he would tell you that the bonds of kinship are no protection against envy and treachery." He nodded in the direction of the great hall. "Do not doubt that there are men and women out there who think you were a fool to save your brother's life, especially at risk to your own. They think you honourable, yes, but a fool."

"And you? What do you think?"

The king's eyes narrowed. "I have never doubted your honour. It is patience, wisdom, and restraint that you lack. You are a fool, and you are reckless. You went into the mountains, into danger, completely unprepared."

Geirmund could not disagree with that, but neither would he allow himself to agree with his father's judgement. "Surely your sons may hunt, my king–"

"Be silent! Do not deny what is plain to every man and woman in this hall, including your oath-man. It would be one thing if you endangered only yourself with your witless actions, but you endangered your brother's life." He sat up and leaned forward. "You endangered the life of the future king of Rogaland."

The burning from Thyra's salve had begun to ease, replaced by a hateful itch, but Geirmund kept his arm upon the table, refusing to scratch it, and held himself still before his father. "I have long known what matters most to you, my king."

His father expelled a sharp breath and sat back, shaking his head. "Your words and your actions stand as proof that you were born in your rightful place. As a father, it wounds me to say these things to you, but as a king I must. You do not have the temperament or the wisdom to rule, but my greatest fear is that you will not learn to follow."

Geirmund's mother returned then, followed by her loyal dog, Svangr. The large moosehound loped into the room in a way that reminded Geirmund of the wolves he and his brother had fought but days before. It was only the devotion in the dog's eyes when it looked at his mother that marked the animal as tamed.

"Well," the queen said, glancing back and forth between Geirmund and his father. "I can see nothing is mended between you two."

The king looked at Geirmund. "I wish it were."

"And I wish it could be," Geirmund said.

Svangr padded across the room to Hámund's side, sniffed his shoulder, and then lay down beside him with a high, windy whine.

"He will be well," Geirmund's mother said to the dog. "Do not trouble yourself."

The dog swung his head to look at her for a moment, then settled himself as a warrior takes a watch at the gates. The queen smiled at the hound and then turned to Geirmund's father.

"Styrbjorn is waiting," she said.

"It is late," his father said. "Can I not speak with him tomorrow?"

"That depends on the mood you would like him to be in." The queen sat down in the chair opposite the king, with Geirmund between them. "He will wait if he must. But he knows Hámund and Geirmund are now both safely returned, and it is not yet midnight, so there is little in his mind to prevent a meeting."

Geirmund's father scowled but nodded. "Very well." He turned to Geirmund. "Go. Send in Styrbjorn."

As Geirmund rose to his feet, his mother tried to take his hand in passing, but he departed too quickly to allow it and stalked from the council room, back into the main hall. He found Styrbjorn where he had seen him before, now sitting on a bench with the shield-maiden, Bragi having moved elsewhere. The two of them looked up at his approach, and Geirmund hid his lingering anger as best he could to speak to the jarl with respect.

"My father will receive you now," he said.

Styrbjorn gulped down the rest of the ale in his horn and stood. He was a tall man, and broad-shouldered, but aged past the fullness of his strength. "Your father is fortunate to still have both of his sons," he said.

Geirmund suspected those words contained a hidden meaning, and possibly even an insult, but could not locate it with enough confidence to make a reply. Instead, he simply bowed his head and Styrbjorn left for the council room he knew well. Geirmund watched him go, feeling suddenly exhausted, aware that even when asleep and fevered, Hámund was included where he was not.

"You are the younger brother," the shield-maiden said, looking up at him. "Geirmund Hel-hide." She motioned towards Styrbjorn's vacated place on the bench to her left. "Sit."

Though tired, Geirmund remained curious enough about her to do so, and together they faced the end of the cookfire that sat perpendicular to the hall's long, central hearth.

"Does it bother you?" she asked.

"Does what bother me?"

"Being called Hel-hide."

He did not have the patience for such questions. "That is the name my father gave to my brother and me."

"That doesn't answer my question."

Geirmund turned to look at her. She was older than him by more than just summers and time. She smelled of smoke and the sea, and something in her eyes felt familiar to him, a kind of kinship that drew him to her.

"Who are you?" he asked.

Her smirk said that she knew he had still avoided her question, but also that she had decided to allow it. "I am Eivor."

"I am honoured to meet you." Geirmund bowed his head. "I didn't know Styrbjorn had a daughter."

"I am not his daughter, though he has raised me as one for the past eleven summers."

"You are fortunate," he said. "And where is your father?"

She looked away suddenly, down the length of the hall towards its doors, and he thought his question might have offended her. "Forgive my boldness. I am tired and not in my right mind. You needn't answer–"

"My father is dead. It is no secret." She gave him a fleeting smile that held no mirth. "I'm sure some here would know of him if you were to ask. Perhaps that Egðir you came in with."

"Steinólfur? Why should he know?"

She took a long drink from her ale horn. "Because it was Kjötve, king of the Egðir, who murdered my father."

Geirmund swallowed, finding words scarce.

"Kjötve came to my father's hall to kill Styrbjorn, who was our guest. He failed in that, but took my father's life."

"What was your father's name?"

Eivor frowned into her ale and shook her head. "It doesn't matter. He died a coward."

The insulting way she described her own father stunned him. "You speak very freely."

"I speak the truth," she said. "There is a difference between a loose tongue and an honest one. I only have patience for one of them."

Geirmund sat for a moment with that, thinking that he had discovered what made her seem familiar to him. Like him, the rune stone of her life was already a haunted place, beset by the ghosts and carved with a past she could not escape. Her honesty inspired him.

"It does bother me," he said.

"What does?"

"Being called Hel-hide."

She passed him her ale horn. "Then I won't."

Geirmund accepted the shared vessel. "Can you also speak the truth about why you are here?" He knew Styrbjorn's hall at Stavanger lay on the other side of the Boknafjord, and that Styrbjorn's lands included much of Rogaland's southern reaches, at the border with Agðir. The jarl may have even thought of himself as a king in Rogaland, but such a claim had no weight or power behind it. As ever it had been, Rogaland belonged to the one who controlled the Karmsund waterway, and that was Geirmund's father.

"Styrbjorn wants to discuss the matter of Harald," she said.

"Which Harald?"

"The king of Sogn."

Geirmund nodded. Sogn lay to the north of Rogaland, on the other side of Hordaland. There were rumours moving about that a matter of honour had come between Harald of Sogn and Eirik, the king of Hordaland, creating tension at their border. "Why Harald?" Geirmund asked.

"Styrbjorn does not trust him. Too many warriors have gone

to England. Hordaland is weak. Agðir is weak. Styrbjorn believes that something must be done, now, before Harald's ambition grows too large to contain."

"Is this not a matter for the Gulating?"

"Harald controls the Gulating."

Geirmund returned her ale horn. "So, it is war you speak of."

She shrugged. "Of course."

Her ease with the subject agreed with her warrior's clothing, her leather and ringmail that bore the signs of heavy and frequent use. "You have the bearing of one who has fought many battles," he said.

She turned and made a show of looking at him anew, at his face, his hands, his knuckles, and his injured arm, as if appraising him for purchase. "And you have the bearing of one who has fought a battle or two but would like to fight more."

"Your tongue remains honest," he said.

"What of your raiding? You have a ship and men from your father, surely?"

Geirmund made no answer, but that was answer enough. Eivor frowned at him in confusion, then drained the last of her ale and several moments of silence followed. The heat of the cookfire and the smell of slowly charring pig bones turned his stomach, and he began to feel dizzy with fatigue. She was a stranger to him, and she was the ward of one of his father's rivals, but something about her made him feel as though he could trust her. He wanted to trust her, reckless as that would be.

"I have no ship," he said at last. "I am of age, but my father has not given me one."

She said nothing, but she waited for him to go on.

He leaned forward, and something jabbed him in his hip. He felt to see what it was and remembered the wolf fang still in its pouch at his side. "There isn't enough land and prey to feed every belly," he half whispered.

"People think I am a fool for saving my brother's life. Perhaps you agree. Perhaps I am. But if I too speak with an honest tongue, then I say there is nothing for me here in Avaldsnes."

"Then you must go elsewhere," she said. "Why do you have no ship?"

Geirmund stared into the flames and embers of the cookfire. "My father does not believe raiding can make a kingdom that will last. He says a kingdom cannot be built on plunder alone. That is why he has strengthened Rogaland and Avaldsnes through alliances and trade. He has many dealings with Frakkland, and he sees the way of things there, where they build their kingdoms without raiding."

She snorted. "In Frakkland they simply call it war."

"I know it." His eyes had begun to water and burn. He closed them against the fire in the hearth and the fire in his chest. "It does not matter."

A moment went by and he heard Eivor stand. He opened his eyes to find her looking down at him, her face softened by an expression of pity.

"Styrbjorn and I will leave with the morning tide. I am tired, so I will find a place to sleep now. But I have enjoyed talking with you, Geirmund. You should also know that, even though I speak the truth, I do not betray what is said to me in confidence."

"I thank you." Geirmund bowed his head. "I have also enjoyed speaking with you, Eivor. I will ask the gods to grant you and Styrbjorn safe travel."

She nodded and made as if to leave, but hesitated and then turned back. "If there truly is nothing for you here, then think on what I said." Her smile was gentle. "You must go elsewhere." Then she was gone, and Geirmund watched her walk away until he lost sight of her in the crowd and the shadows.

Before he could rouse himself to seek his own bed, Steinólfur and Skjalgi stood before him.

"How did things go with your father?" the older warrior asked, gnawing at what was left of a burnt joint he had twisted from the pig.

"As you would expect," Geirmund said. "But I am not in a mood to talk about it."

"As you wish," Steinólfur said. "Should we leave you?"

"Not yet." Geirmund lowered his voice. "I need you to gather men."

Skjalgi's good eye widened a bit, but he said nothing. Next to him, Steinólfur spat something and tossed the joint aside, where it would soon be found by Svangr. "What sort of men?" he asked.

"Men who can row and fight," Geirmund said. "Men who would leave my father and Avaldsnes for the promise of silver and gold."

"Men like that are common enough," Steinólfur said. "But you don't want oath-breakers at your back. What you want are men free and willing to swear to you."

"Can you find men like that?" Geirmund asked, though Steinólfur had long hinted he could do exactly that, should Geirmund require it. "Enough to crew a ship?"

Steinólfur looked at Skjalgi, whose wide eye and grin held both fear and excitement, as though he had been waiting a long time for this moment to come.

"It will take time," the older warrior said. "But I believe we can."

"Do it," Geirmund said. "But quietly."

"You have a ship, then?" Skjalgi asked.

"Not yet," Geirmund said. "But I will."

5

Geirmund's arm healed well, and so did Hámund's shoulder, though more slowly.

Winter came and brought with it the seasonal storms that kept most ships tucked into their harbour beds. With fewer ships plying the whale roads, there were fewer travellers and guests in Avaldsnes, and a quiet peace fell over Hjörr's hall. Despite this, Steinólfur made headway gathering a crew that stood ready to swear to Geirmund and sail with the summer, so long as Geirmund had a ship to carry them.

Thus far, he did not.

He had gathered all the wealth that was his, but it wasn't enough to buy or build a ship, even if he could somehow have a ship made without his father hearing of it, which was unlikely. He had several times considered enlisting his mother's help. She had silver and gold, and he thought she might be sympathetic to his cause, but he could not be sure enough of her to ask. That left Hámund as a possible ally, but Geirmund had felt reluctant to speak to his brother about his plans. He told Steinólfur and Skjalgi it was because he wanted to let Hámund heal fully before he troubled him, and that was true, but what he left unsaid, almost even to himself, was that he had begun to doubt if he could trust his brother.

It had started with the wolf pelts.

After having them cleaned, Hámund had made a public gift of them to their father in his great hall, dedicating his victory over the beasts to King Hjörr's honour. That Geirmund had slain several of those wolves and supplied the very pelts did not merit inclusion in Hámund's speech, nor had Hámund mentioned his plan to Geirmund beforehand. Though angered, Geirmund had remained silent, but he had since questioned his brother's loyalties.

When winter's tyranny over the sea and the wind came to its natural end, ships returned to the sail-roads, and word of Guthrum reached Avaldsnes. The Dane was coming to Hjörr's hall, calling on Northmen to join Bersi's fleet for the conquest of England. At this news Geirmund decided he had to act quickly, if he was to have a ship, so he invited Hámund to go fishing with him, the first time they had gone after any kind of prey or game since their last fateful hunt.

They did not go far, merely to a small bay on the other side of the island, two rests westward from their father's hall, where trees were sparse and redshanks piped and picked between the rocks with their long beaks for food. They travelled on horseback, and neither spoke much on the way, nor for some time after they had reached their destination. The waters in that cove were deep blue and calm, sheltered by several islets that broke up the sea, and though fish were abundant in its waters, they had hooked none on their lines by midday.

"It seems Ægir is against us," his brother finally said. His body remained wasted from his wound and his time abed, but his brown skin had regained some of its red life.

"But perhaps the gods are not," Geirmund said.

Hámund turned towards him, perplexed.

"The sea offers other opportunities," Geirmund said. "There are riches to be had. In England."

Hámund laid down his line as a sudden wind blew in from the north, smelling of brine and carrying tales of lands where the ice and cold never retreated. "What are you speaking of?" he asked.

"You've heard of the Dane Guthrum?" Geirmund said.

"Of course I have. What of him?"

Geirmund now looked out to sea, to the west beyond the rocks, to the open and wild ocean beyond. "What if you and I were to sail with him?"

Hámund now turned and regarded Geirmund askance. Then he smiled, as if suddenly catching a jest, but that grin faded when it was not returned, and he seemed to realize that Geirmund spoke in earnest.

"There is honour to be found in Bersi's fleet," Geirmund said. "In England we will make our names known, like our grandfather Half. The sons of Hjörr and Ljufvina will bring back riches and reputation to Avaldsnes."

The northern wind gained in strength, pushing its own waves against those that found their way into the bay from the sea. It pulled hair from Hámund's braids as he looked up at the sky, where a shield-wall of clouds pressed in. He crouched and began to pull in his fishing lines. "We should go before the storm reaches us."

"No, brother, listen to me." Geirmund bounded over the rocks to his brother's side. "Guthrum is coming to Father's hall. I have men who will swear to us. I need only a ship, and then we can sail."

"You have men?" Hámund held still, the wet fishing line in his hands. "What men do you have?"

"Free men. Men who want what I can offer."

Hámund said nothing until he'd finished pulling in and coiling his empty lines, and then he stood. "And what do you offer these men?"

"I offer them what I'm offering you. What Guthrum and Bersi offer us. Saxon lands and wealth."

"And yet you have no ship." Hámund pushed by and crossed to Geirmund's fishing lines, which he also proceeded to pull in, wincing a bit at the pain from his still stiff arm. "I understand now why you asked me to come fishing with you."

"Yes," Geirmund said. "I need a ship. And I need your help with Father to get it. He will listen to you."

"So, you would take one of Father's ships, and you would take Father's men? Men from Rogaland?"

"I told you, they are free men."

"And they will be your oath-men?"

"Yes."

The wind now raged around them, and the clouds had advanced far enough across the sky to block the sun. Having finished coiling the last of the lines, Hámund moved towards the horses and Geirmund followed.

"They will be your oath-men also," he said. "If you come with me."

Hámund packed away their fishing gear, his eyes on the sky, and untied his horse from the stubby pine to which he had tethered it. Then he mounted. "If we ride fast, we might be able to outrun the rain. But this storm–"

"Brother," Geirmund said, taking hold of the bridle to Hámund's horse. "I feel this is my destiny. My fate calling to me. Do I have your word you'll help me?"

Hámund raised his chin. "I will do what I can."

"I can ask no more than that," Geirmund said. He went to his horse and they set off for home at speed, whipped by wind and then by rain that found them just as they reached the Avaldsnes gates.

Six days later, Guthrum arrived with a longship of Danes.

They feasted in the hall, the hearth ablaze. Geirmund's mother, draped in silk from Frakkland and clad in gold and silver ornaments, passed the mead horn, first to Geirmund's father and then to Guthrum. Seated next to Hjörr, the Dane looked like a very different kind of ruler, with numerous rings upon his arms and fingers, furs across his shoulders, embroidery in his tunic, and jewels upon his belt, no doubt the spoils of his many raids. In age he appeared to have seen some forty or more summers, many of them hard by the measure of his scars, and he ate and laughed with a passion equal to the fury that Geirmund imagined he brought to battle.

"The tales of the friendly lady of Rogaland are all true," Guthrum said. "Your beauty and grace are renowned, Queen Ljufvina, though now I see for myself that the stories do you scant justice."

His mother bowed her head. "I thank you, Jarl Guthrum."

Geirmund knew well that every man who came through Hjörr's hall felt honour-bound to express admiration for Ljufvina, even while secretly disliking and distrusting the colour of her skin, the texture of her hair, and the shape of her eyes. But Guthrum's praise seemed to be sincere.

"If every woman of Bjarmaland is as beautiful as you," the Dane continued, "I wonder that your sons haven't already sailed there in search of wives."

Geirmund's mother laughed. "If you flatter the women of every hall in this way, I wonder that you still need ships, Jarl Guthrum."

He grinned. "Then you know why I have come?"

"Of course we do," King Hjörr said, sounding slightly insulted. "But discussion of that matter will wait until after we've eaten."

The Dane gestured towards the open hall. "I believe the men and women of Rogaland would wish to hear what I have come here to say–"

"No," the king said. "We will speak in private."

The Dane picked at something in his teeth, then bowed his head. "As you wish."

At the mention of Guthrum's purpose Geirmund looked at Hámund and gave him a slight nod to affirm their understanding. Hámund glanced quickly at their father, and then he returned Geirmund's nod.

Bragi, the skald, sat near Geirmund and leaned towards him. "When ring-breakers speak, they change the weather of weapons."

Geirmund turned to look at the old man, whose beard was already white when he came to Hjörr's hall fourteen summers ago. His watery eyes and distracted grin led some to believe that age had dulled his wits, but Geirmund knew him to be as cunning and clever as ever he had been, and that his eyes missed nothing. He liked Bragi and would always be grateful that he had come to Avaldsnes.

"And what sort of weapon-weather do you foretell?" Geirmund asked him.

"I am no seer," Bragi said. "But I think of war as I think of farming. Come winter, neither king nor thrall can expect to harvest anything other than what they sowed in summer."

"I'm not convinced of that." Geirmund finished the last bite of pork on his platter and used some flat barley bread to sop up its fat, which tasted of nuts and the dark forest floor. "War can find a king whether invited or not."

"That's true." Bragi took a drink of ale. "Weeds aren't invited, either, but the careful farmer knows how to prevent them from destroying the crop."

"What about floods? Or famine?"

"Ah! But now you speak of the gods. You speak of fate."

"And what is to be done about fate?"

"The coward believes he will live forever if he avoids the battle, but there can be no truce with death." Bragi put a hand on his shoulder. "When you see your fate, there is but one thing to be done. You must march to meet it."

Geirmund laughed, and the night deepened. The guests of Avaldsnes emptied trenchers of food as quickly as they were served, and the ale and mead fell down both throats and beards like waterfalls, but the time soon came for talking. The king rose from his seat and led the way from the great hall towards his council room, followed by Geirmund's mother, then Guthrum, then Hámund. Geirmund was about to go with them when Bragi took hold of his arm and held him back.

"As a younger man," he said, looking in the direction the others had gone, "I was included in such things."

Geirmund was still a young man, and he was anxious to join them. "Do you want me to ask my father to–"

"Bah, no." Bragi let go of his arm. "As a young man, I also had interest in such things. But I no longer do."

Geirmund frowned. "Then what is it you–"

"I want you to meet me at your grandfather's burial mound. At sunrise tomorrow."

"Meet you?" Geirmund shook his head. "I don't understand."

"It's quite simple," Bragi said. "I wish to speak with you, but not right now. I wish to give you something, but not here. And I wish to do it before your grandfather's burial mound. At sunrise."

Geirmund nodded, still confused. "Very well, I– I will be there."

"Good." Bragi waved him off. "Now, go and talk about the weather."

Geirmund left him, perplexed and frowning but curious, and went to the council room. He was prepared to object if his father should try to send him away, but that proved unnecessary. Guthrum was speaking as he entered, seated at the opposite end of the table from the king, but the Dane stopped talking when Geirmund entered.

"I'm sorry to interrupt," he said.

"No apology is necessary," Guthrum said. "Please, join us. It is better that both sons hear what I have to say."

Geirmund took a seat next to his mother on the other side of the table from his brother, and then his father asked the Dane to continue.

Guthrum stretched out a hand as though to reach for his ale, obviously a mindless movement of habit, but there was nothing upon the table, so he simply placed his empty hand on the linen cloth that had been laid over it. "It seems the reason for my visit is no secret," he said. "I wish to speak of England. Danes there, with a few Northmen, have won great victories over the Saxons in Northumbria. Halfdan Ragnarsson has secured Jorvik, from which he has just conquered East Anglia. He will soon take Mercia, and that will leave only Wessex."

"We have heard news of their victories, of course," Geirmund's father said.

"Mercia and Wessex will not fall easily," the Dane added. "Wessex has a strong king in a man called Æthelred. That is why my king, Bersi, is gathering a fleet, larger than any ever seen, to sail and join with the Danes of Jorvik. Together, the forces of Bersi and Halfdan will conquer all Saxon lands, including Wessex."

He looked at Hámund, and then at Geirmund. "Warriors from Rogaland who join with us will gain reputation and wealth as well as lands."

Those were the riches Geirmund wanted. If Avaldsnes was to be Hámund's, then Geirmund would have to seek other lands and fields, or he would never have anything to call his own. But he knew Guthrum would demand more than just his sword. A son of Hjörr would be expected to bring with him a ship with men to crew it and fight, but Geirmund was reluctant to speak out of turn and give his father a reason to dismiss him from the council room. So he waited.

"Mercia and Wessex are strong, and I know there are riches to be won from raiding." King Hjörr motioned around the room. "This hall was built with silver from raiding the East Way, in Kurland and Finnland."

"The deeds of Half and his company are renowned," Guthrum said. "Your father's reputation is well known even among Danes."

Geirmund straightened his back and lifted his head in pride.

"Those deeds were accomplished many years ago," the king said. "That was a different time. You speak now of much more than raids and silver. You speak of crowns. You and I both know that even if every Saxon kingdom falls to Bersi and Halfdan, the crowns of England will sit on the heads of Danes. Not the heads of Northmen."

"You presume much, King Hjörr." Guthrum unfolded his arms and held up his hands, the gold on his fingers glinting. "Bersi and Halfdan are men of honour. They reward those who live and honour those who die as befits their battle deeds. I swear to you, there will be both land and silver in measure equal to what you offer Bersi's fleet."

"And if the Danes fail to defeat the Saxons of Mercia and

Wessex?" the king said. "The vanquished will be left to squabble over Northumbria and the fens of East Anglia, will they not?"

"Your doubt is an insult to all Danes." Guthrum's jaw and mouth tightened, but not quite to a frown. "We *will* defeat the Saxons."

"It is possible you will." Geirmund's father paused. "Perhaps it is even likely. But Rogaland will not send our ships or our warriors with you. They are needed here."

"For what?" Guthrum scowled openly now, and his voice turned harsh. "To guard your fish and your sheep? Or perhaps to guard your wharf where you cheat passing ships in need of repairs?" He pointed a finger at Geirmund's father. "Do not think your tactics here have gone unnoticed."

Geirmund wondered how his father would reply to that, but it was Hámund who leaned forward. "And *you* should not think your disrespect has gone unnoticed, Jarl Guthrum. Need I remind you that you are here as my father's guest?"

"I have not forgotten," Guthrum said. "But it was your father who first showed disrespect to the Danes."

If Guthrum's sudden hostility disturbed Geirmund's father, he did not show it, and maintained calm in both his voice and his demeanour. "It is said that Harald of Sogn plans to make war on the other kings of the North Way. That is why I now deny the call to join Bersi's fleet. Rogaland cannot spare any warriors or ships until the threat to our lands has passed."

"Ah, of course," Guthrum said. "King Harald would want Avaldsnes for the same reasons it made your father and grandfather powerful." He raised his eyebrows and softened his voice in false concern. "But what will you do? If your lands are in danger, surely you mean to make war on Harald. You must attack first, before Harald grows too strong, or you risk being overrun."

It was rumoured that Styrbjorn had proposed a similar strategy during his visit at the beginning of winter, but Geirmund had heard nothing about it since the night he had talked with Eivor, and he knew that King Hjörr would never be the one to start a war. As Geirmund listened to Guthrum now, he thought about what Bragi had said out in the great hall about fields and weeds, and he wondered if the Dane had it right.

"Surely you must delay no longer," Guthrum said.

The queen cleared her throat. "I mean no offence when I say this, but why would we take counsel from a Dane on this matter? These are not your lands, or your people, and Harald is not your concern."

"I am a Dane, it is true." Guthrum stood and leaned over the table, both fists planted before him. "But we Danes have not turned soft in our halls. We are familiar with war. When King Horik died, old grudges and ambitions returned, and much blood has since been spilled." He began to tremble with remembered fury, and he made no attempt to conceal it. "I have known nothing but war for fifteen summers, and that is the reason I am going to England. If I must make war, then I would rather kill Saxons than Danes. If I must fight, then I would fight for lands and peace that I hope to secure long enough to bequeath to my children, and they to their children."

"I admire your aims." Geirmund's father now stood, as poised and rigid as a standing stone. "I have the same desires. I also want to leave my children and grandchildren a strong and lasting Rogaland. That is the very reason I will not send ships and men with you."

"And what if Harald defeats you?" Guthrum asked. "What will you have left to leave your children when Avaldsnes is taken from you?"

Geirmund expected his father to deny the possibility of victory for Harald, but he said nothing, and Geirmund wondered what agreement had been struck between Avaldsnes in the north and Stavanger to the south. He looked to his mother, who was watching his father as though also waiting for him to speak. When he didn't, she turned back to Guthrum.

"I believe I have already made it clear that Harald is no concern for the Danes."

Guthrum shook his head. "You do a disservice to your sons–"

"I will decide what is right for my sons!" Geirmund's father glared, having finally reached the end of his patience. "Not some landless Dane with war fever."

Guthrum slammed the table with his fist and Geirmund leapt to his feet by instinct, ready to fight. Hámund rose also, and so did his mother, her hand at the dagger she wore on her belt. But almost immediately the Dane leaned backwards, palms upraised.

"Forgive my temper," he said, still red-faced and chewing his cheeks and lips. "I came here to seek an alliance, not to create new enemies."

"We are enemies to no Dane," Geirmund's mother said. "And our refusal of men and ships should not make us so."

Guthrum's chin fell to his chest and he shook his head. "I regret to say that King Bersi may not see it that way, Queen Ljufvina. He will take your refusal as an insult. I hope you are prepared for the consequences of that, with Harald to the north and Bersi to the south."

Geirmund saw Hámund's body tense, his hands clenched, and he could feel his brother's anger at the Dane, but he was surprised to find that he did not share it. Guthrum had not lied to them, so far as he could tell. Bersi needed ships, and Guthrum was simply carrying out the orders given to him by his king. If Geirmund were tasked with the same duty for Rogaland, he believed he might speak in much the same way, and he agreed that it would be a disservice to him if his father should prevent him from sailing to England.

"Jarl Guthrum, you strain my hospitality." The king's calm had returned, but it was now the stillness of a coiled viper. "Does Bersi know you threaten a king of the North Way in his name?"

Guthrum laughed. "Tell me, if you meet a fellow traveller on the road who tells you of dangers ahead, does he threaten you with that danger? No, he does not, because there is a difference between a warning and a threat, and my king would not have given me this errand if he didn't trust me to speak for him. But I will strain your hospitality no longer, King Hjörr. I have your answer, and I see you will not be moved from it. My men will sleep on my ship tonight, and I with them, and we will sail from Avaldsnes in the morning."

"In which direction?" Hámund asked.

"Why?" The Dane grinned. "Do you worry I will sail to Sogn? Do you wonder if Harald will answer King Bersi's call?" He tugged on his beard in exaggerated contemplation. "Let us consider. If Harald sends warriors to England with the Danes, that will mean fewer warriors for Rogaland to fight here." He paused. "But if he sends warriors to England, he might gain enough Saxon silver to buy the ships and warriors he needs to seize all the North Way."

"Hámund asks because of the tides," the king said, "and no other reason. You must sail where your king commands."

Guthrum bowed his head, but there was mockery in it. "And so I must." He turned to Hámund. "I sail south, Hel-hide. I was in Agðir before I came here, and like your father, Kjötve fears Harald of Sogn. It now seems pointless to continue to Hordaland until the Northmen find the courage of their fathers. I do not see the sons of Half here."

Before anyone could make a reply to that, he turned and stalked from the council room. Hámund followed after him, and a moment later the Dane's voice could be heard roaring an order for his men to depart the hall. They must have complied almost instantly, because Hámund soon returned and gave a nod to say they had gone.

"Should we send men to watch their ship?" Ljufvina asked.

The king, still standing, put one hand on the table and thought. "Two men, as a precaution. No more. A large company of warriors might anger him further, and I doubt he will cause any mischief."

"Will you see to it, Hámund?" the queen asked.

His brother turned to leave the room again.

"Hámund, wait," Geirmund said. He needed his brother's support to ask what he was about to ask.

Hámund paused and turned, waiting for his brother to speak. Then he seemed to realize what Geirmund intended and lowered his voice. "No, now is not a good time."

"You gave me your word," Geirmund said.

The queen stepped closer to them. "Now is not a good time for what?"

"Nothing," Hámund said, his brow low, eyes locked on Geirmund. "Right, brother?"

A storm ravaged the sea of Geirmund's mind, battering him with waves and winds of doubt, but he had his bearing and knew his destination, so he pressed ahead. "I will go with Guthrum," he said loudly. "I will join with Bersi and go to England."

Hámund's eyes closed and his shoulders fell, while Geirmund's mother and father simply stared at him. Then the king shook his head and looked at his wife, mouth partly open in disbelief. "Do my ears deceive me?" he asked.

"Geirmund," the queen said, her voice quiet and exhausted. "You have had too much ale. I think we should leave this until tomorrow."

"No," Geirmund said. "I have not had too much ale. And I will go to England, where I will take Saxon lands for—"

"You are going nowhere," his father said, "except to your bed like the child you are."

"Father, I am a man of my own mind, and it is a different mind to yours." Geirmund spread his arms wide. "You know I am not meant for this. There is nothing for me here. You don't trust me with duties of any importance. You give me no tasks, no responsibilities—"

"I give you only the commands you have shown me you can fulfil," his father said. "If you want more, you must prove that you—"

"But I don't want more of your commands. I no longer wish to prove anything to you. Instead, I will seek my own fate."

"How?" his mother asked.

"With a ship. I have men who will swear to me. If you but give me a ship, I will ask for nothing more." Geirmund swallowed and glanced at his brother, who was now staring at the ground. "Hámund supports me in this. Perhaps he would even choose to sail to England with me."

Now Geirmund's father turned to Hámund, eyes wide. "Is this true?"

Hámund looked up at the king, then at Geirmund, then back at the floor, and Geirmund felt ice in his chest.

"I did support Geirmund in this," his brother said. "He deserves a chance to seek his destiny. I know we need warriors and ships in Rogaland, Father, but I believed we could spare one vessel for him." He looked up at the queen. "But now that I have met Guthrum, my mind is changed. He insulted you, Father, and he threatened our kingdom. I refuse to give him or the Danes anything of Rogaland, especially my brother's service."

The queen sighed and nodded, as if in gratitude.

"You are wise, Hámund," the king said, "unlike your brother. Geirmund, you will have no ship and no men. This matter is settled."

It was far from settled, but for a moment Geirmund felt too stunned by his brother's betrayal to say anything, and he stood there, disbelieving. Then a rage rose within him, and he knew it would lead to terrible violence if he stayed in that room much longer. "You are an oath-breaker, Hámund," he said, and then he shouted, "Look at me, you coward!"

Hámund flinched and lifted his head.

"After all we have been through together." Geirmund stabbed his finger in the direction of the king and queen. "After everything they did to us, everything they did to you, you now turn your back on me and take their side?"

"Brother, I–"

"Do not dare to call me that. You are no longer my brother."

The queen gasped. "Geirmund, you cannot mean that–"

"I do." Geirmund now rounded on her. "And you were never my mother."

At that the king bellowed in rage and charged at him, aiming to strike him with his fist, but Geirmund ducked his blow easily, and could have returned a strike of his own but instead he backed away. His mother had begun to weep, half reaching towards him with shaking hands, and his father went to her side. Hámund hadn't moved, but the hatred in his eyes exceeded that which he had shown for Guthrum.

"I see now this was inevitable," Geirmund said. "I have been a fool to hope for anything different. Fate made me a thrall's child. Then it made me the second son of a king. I go now to find what it will make me in England."

Then, like Guthrum, he left the council room without waiting for a reply.

6

In the deep-water light just before dawn, Geirmund rode north from Avaldsnes towards his grandfather's burial mound. Only the brightest of the night's remaining stars could still be seen, the last fading embers of Muspelheim. Steinólfur and Skjalgi had insisted on riding with him, but they agreed to stop and wait when the burial mound came in sight, since it seemed that Bragi wanted Geirmund alone.

The three of them rode in silence. There was little to say after Geirmund had described the events of the night, because nothing could be gained by dwelling on a past that was no longer a part of Geirmund's fate. Steinólfur actually seemed more relaxed than he had been for some time, as though relieved that something he had long dreaded had finally happened and was over. It was Skjalgi's anger at Hámund's betrayal that had surprised Geirmund. The boy's easy nature tended towards good humour and quick forgiveness, but he had cursed Hámund with words Geirmund had never before heard from his mouth, though he had cooled to a simmer in the hours since.

Steinólfur looked across the Karmsund, towards the hills on

the eastern horizon. "We shall need to be at the wharf before the sun is fully up, if you mean to sail with Guthrum."

"We have no ship," Geirmund said. "Guthrum is our only way to England."

"Then we can't let the Danes sail without us."

"Will any of the men you gathered still join us?"

"As you said, we have no ship. And word will have spread that the king wants the warriors of Rogaland close at hand."

"Then we are alone."

Steinólfur said nothing for a few moments. "Any idea what Bragi wants with you?"

"None," Geirmund said. "He mentioned that he wanted to give me something."

"Bragi is strange," Skjalgi said.

Steinólfur chuckled. "He's a skald. Strange is to be expected."

Two rests from Avaldsnes they came to the ridge where burial mounds of past kings rose above the water, visible to any ships travelling the fairway. A distant fire flickered at the base of Half's grave, and the three halted at the sight of it. Then Geirmund broke from his companions and continued onward until he reached the light, where he found Bragi seated on the ground, wrapped in bear fur near a lit brazier. The skald had set up a hnefatafl board, with its pieces of coloured stones and bone, on a flat rock in front of him, and he motioned for Geirmund to join him on the other side.

"I regret I don't have time for a game," Geirmund said.

"Then I will defeat you quickly," the skald said. "Sit."

Geirmund sighed and dismounted. When he sat down, he found the grass cold and already wet with dew. "Which side will you play?" he asked.

"You shall be the king." Bragi winked.

"You're thinking of my brother." Geirmund took the first move, an opening feint to make Bragi believe he intended for his king to escape to one of the bottom corners, when he aimed his true strategy towards the upper right.

"I did not say you would be king at Avaldsnes." Bragi made his first countermove, but it was tentative, and Geirmund couldn't tell whether the skald had taken the bait. "Perhaps you will be a king of Saxons," Bragi said.

Geirmund looked up from the board. "Who have you been talking to?"

"No one. I went to my bed after you and I spoke last night. But you are going with Guthrum, are you not?"

Geirmund made his second move, then his third, and with each of Bragi's turns, the skald placed his warriors as if he knew Geirmund's true, hidden strategy. As the game progressed, and it became clear that Geirmund would lose, he wondered about something he had wanted to ask since he was a boy, and he realized he was unlikely to have another opportunity.

"Are you a seer, Bragi?"

The skald's eyes seemed to flicker with the flames in the brazier. "The gods and the Three Spinners do not speak with me, if that is what you mean. I have simply lived long enough to read the weather."

"And long enough to read the hnefatafl board."

"I promised you a short game." Bragi moved a warrior into position, suddenly trapping Geirmund's king on two sides. "If I am reading the weather correctly, your father refused Guthrum because of his fear of Harald."

As angry as Geirmund was with his father, he did not like hearing the truth that the king was afraid, especially from a skald who would tell stories, and in frustration he made a reckless, aggressive move.

"I mean no offence or dishonour to your father," Bragi said. "Hjörr is right to fear Harald, and he is not alone in that. It is what he does with that fear that will determine the fate of Rogaland." The skald then moved a warrior and closed off a third escape route for Geirmund's king. "But I do not think the fate of Avaldsnes is your fate. You are leaving with the Dane?"

Geirmund moved one of his warriors to clear a path for his king's retreat. "I am."

"I anticipated that, which is why I summoned you here." Bragi paused before taking his next turn and twisted to look up at the burial mound. A thin mist had risen around it, and a raven cawed somewhere nearby. "What does your father say when he speaks of his father?"

"Very little," Geirmund said.

Bragi nodded slowly. "That does not surprise me. Your father has even forbidden me from telling the story of Half inside the hall that Half built." He inhaled the cool air deeply through his nose. "But right now, we are not inside the hall."

"Tell me," Geirmund said.

So Bragi continued. "Half was younger than you are now when he first took to the whale roads. The tales say he chose his crew only from the men who were strong enough to lift the millstone from a large quern, and that he and his warriors had their swords shortened so they would have to get closer to their enemies. When their ship rode too low in a storm, each of Half's warriors fought for the honour of throwing himself overboard to save the others."

"Is that true?"

Bragi smiled. "It is true that Half and his men were very brave." From within the bear fur Bragi produced a knife in a leather sheath. "It is also said that Half and his warriors killed no women or children on their raids, and if a warrior wanted to bring back a woman for himself, your grandfather made the warrior marry that woman and bestow generous gifts upon her."

Bragi pulled the knife from its sheath, and Geirmund was surprised to see it had a thin bronze blade. Other than that, it was a common knife with a wooden grip and a simple copper heel.

"Half raided for eighteen summers, gaining much silver and a fearsome reputation. During that time, his stepfather, Åsmund, ruled Rogaland in his place. When Half returned to reclaim his seat, Åsmund welcomed him with a warm embrace and held a feast in honour of Half and his heroes. They ate and they drank late into the night, singing songs and telling tales. Then, while Half and his men slept, Åsmund barred the doors to the hall from the outside and set it afire."

"What? His stepfather–"

"Yes, Åsmund murdered your grandfather. Only two warriors survived that bloody night, a man called Utstein, and another called Rok the Black. They gathered an army and slayed Åsmund, avenging their fallen king, and they took back Avaldsnes for young Hjörr, the son of Half."

Geirmund had long known that a great betrayal had led to his grandfather's death, but he had never heard the details of what happened, and he had never dared ask his father. It was a story with the power to alter how a man sees himself and is seen by others, and that may have been the very reason the king had never shared it. Geirmund wished his father had talked more openly about it, but it was too late for that now.

Bragi slid the blade back into its sheath and offered Geirmund the knife. "This is my gift to you."

"Oh." Geirmund accepted it but struggled to hide his confusion. "I'm... grateful."

"You are not," Bragi said.

Geirmund looked down at the board, where the skald's warriors had surrounded his king on three sides, and he knew he could not lie to the old man. He doubted anyone could. "It's a good knife," he said.

"And yet you think it is a common gift."

"I do."

"Because it is common. It isn't made of steel. I've had it for many years, and I've sharpened it countless times. I used it to cut my meat last night. I give it to you now *because* it is common."

"I don't understand."

"As you leave your father's hall, and leave you must, take with you the memory of your grandfather. Though I did not know him, there are still some in Rogaland who remember him, and they see much of him in you." Bragi reached across the hnefatafl board and laid a hand on Geirmund's arm. "Before you enter any door, it should be looked around and spied out, to know for certain where enemies are sitting in the hall ahead. A common knife is worthless against an axe or sword on the battlefield, but it becomes the most lethal of weapons when wielded from the shadows or, worse, by someone close whom you should not have trusted."

Geirmund tightened his grip on the knife's handle, beginning to understand. "I am grateful, Bragi."

The skald released his arm and looked down at the game. "It is my turn."

"It is, but I think the victory is plainly yours."

"I haven't won yet," the skald said. "But I will end the game here and leave your king with one path open. That allows him to go out and meet his fate, while possibly preventing a blood feud. I would rather consider no man my enemy."

Geirmund nodded, and just then the first rays of sunlight reached over the horizon to crown the crest of Half's burial mound in gold. Steinólfur would be fretting, wondering what was taking so long, and Geirmund still had one more visit to make before boarding Guthrum's ship.

He stood and tied the skald's knife to his belt. "I have often wondered what my life would have been if you hadn't come to my father's hall."

Bragi shrugged. "The Norns will not be denied. But I am proud of my part in your story."

"It saddens me that our paths will likely not cross again."

"They will not." The skald stood slowly under the weight of the bear fur. "I will also leave Rogaland, very soon."

"Where will you go?"

Bragi looked eastward. "It feels as if the World Tree is shaking, Geirmund. The wars we now fight are not just between Northmen and Danes and Saxons, but between gods. I would return to my people and my land at Uppsala."

"May the gods protect you as you travel," Geirmund said.

"I offer the same prayer for you."

He gave the old man another nod and went to his horse.

"One more piece of advice," Bragi said.

Geirmund climbed into the saddle. "I welcome it."

"Watch out for sea men. Half's father, Hjörrleif, once caught a sea man in his net, and the creature gave a prophecy that later saved the king's life."

Geirmund had questions but no time. "Farewell, Bragi Boddason."

A few moments later, Geirmund rejoined Steinólfur and Skjalgi, and the three of them set a brisk pace south towards Avaldsnes. The sun had almost fully risen before they reached the town, and Geirmund could see distant movement on the wharf around Guthrum's ship.

Steinólfur leaned in his saddle towards Geirmund and lowered his voice. "Do you still plan to go to her?"

Geirmund nodded. "Ride ahead and tell Guthrum I am coming."

The older warrior opened his mouth as if to object, but nodded.

"Tell him I will be there soon," Geirmund said.

"See that you are." Steinólfur then spoke to Skjalgi. "Come on, boy."

They kicked their horses into a trot down the road, and a few fathoms on Geirmund took a path that led west towards a small grove at the base of a grassy hill. When he reached the treeline, he dismounted and walked his horse inward along the track, feeling his stomach tighten with each step. He worried it might be too early in the morning for such a visit, but the smell of woodsmoke reassured him that someone had awakened to rouse the hearth.

The building that soon came into view was a humble house set into the hill behind it, with a steep peaked roof covered in soft turf. Geirmund led his horse to the empty stable that extended from the south side of the house, and as he tied its reins to a post, Ágáða came outside carrying a sack of feed for her chickens. She jumped in fright and dropped the sack at the sight of him, then held a hand to her chest with a sigh and a smile.

"Geirmund, you awful boy," she said, her voice almost a whisper. "You startled me."

"I'm sorry." He kept his voice low to match hers. "Is Loðhatt–"

"He's sleeping." She walked over to him, tossing her long, thin braid of yellow hair over her shoulder. "Best we don't wake him."

Geirmund hadn't visited this place since the previous summer, before the fateful hunt with Hámund, and he felt as much unrest over his absence as he felt when he thought about seeing her. She wore the same apron-dress she had worn the last time he was here, its red now faded almost to brown, but the silver brooch he had given her gleamed, free of any tarnish. The wrinkles around her storm-coloured eyes seemed deeper.

She took one of his hands firmly in hers and led him away from the house. "Are you well? I heard you were injured."

"I was," he said.

"I made an offering to Óðinn, asking for you to be healed."

"I was healed."

"Then I will make another offering of thanks." She smiled and let go of his hand. "What brings you here this morning?"

Geirmund felt awkward, as he always did in her presence, unsure of his words, and even his reasons for coming. He knew only that it had to be done. "I'm leaving Avaldsnes, Ágáða."

"Oh?" The muscles in her slender throat tightened. "Where are you going?"

"To fight the Saxons," he said.

"You–" She swallowed. "You will be gone for some time, then."

"I will. I am here to say goodbye."

She nodded and clutched herself tightly. "You honour me."

"No, Ágáða." Geirmund stepped closer to her. "The honour is mine."

Tears wet her eyes. "Is Hámund going with you?"

"No." He didn't know when she had last seen or heard from his brother, but it had to be a silence of years, and he didn't have the time or the desire to burden her with the full truth, so he simply said, "He will remain here, with King Hjörr."

"And with his mother," she added.

Geirmund hesitated. "Yes, and the queen."

"As it should be." She shook her head, blinking away her tears. "When do you leave?"

"Today," he said. "This morning."

"So soon?"

"It was only decided last night." That was another matter he didn't want to explain, so instead he pointed towards the stable. "I'd like you to have my horse."

"What?" Her eyes widened. "Geirmund, I can't accept–"

"You can. His name is Garmr, but despite that he is even-tempered. If you don't have a use for him, you can sell him. And here." He pulled a small bag full of silver pieces from his belt and pressed it into her hands. "Take this."

She looked down, then shook her head, trying to push the bag away. "Geirmund, I don't want–"

"Take it," he said. "Please, take it. I wish I could do more for you. You deserve so much more, for what my mother did to you."

"She didn't do it to–" Ágáða pulled away, leaving the silver in Geirmund's hands, and smoothed her apron-dress. "That was all settled long ago. The queen made it right."

But there were some injustices and some injuries that no weight of silver or gold could heal, no matter the price the Althing gave them. "Then accept these as gifts," he said. "This silver and Garmr are not to make things right. They are to honour and show my gratitude to my first mother."

"Geirmund!" She glanced around as if to make sure they could not be overheard. "You mustn't say such things."

"I am saying just what I came to say." Though Geirmund had only now realized it. "You did not have to treat us as your sons, Ágáða." He gestured towards the house. "Loðhatt saw us as dogs, and I don't blame him. But you did your best for us, and I stand here as I am because of it."

She bowed her head and was silent for several moments, as if measuring her words. "The pride I feel when I see you is the same as a mother's pride in her child."

Geirmund felt his own tears rising, and he realized that he had not gone there only to speak, but to hear. "I will continue to make you proud," he said.

"I know you will."

He tried again to place the bag of silver in her hands, and this time she accepted it.

"May the gods watch over you," she said.

"And you, Ágáða."

Geirmund turned away and returned along the forest track, waiting until the house was far behind before he broke into a run. The effort was intended to speed him towards Guthrum's ship, but the pounding of his boots and his heart also helped to beat back the waves of grief and pain that threatened to swamp him, and the wind dried his eyes. The harder and faster he ran, the greater the distance he placed between himself and everything that had come before. All that mattered now was what lay ahead.

He reached the wharf and found Guthrum's ship still moored, but nearly ready to set sail. Steinólfur and Skjalgi had sent their horses back to the stables and were standing on the dock nearby, waiting for Geirmund, laden with heavy packs containing all their gear. Steinólfur held a familiar sword.

Geirmund's boots drummed the wooden planks as he approached them. He looked at the sword in the older warrior's grasp. "Was Hámund here?" he asked.

"He was," Steinólfur said. "He asked me to give you this."

Geirmund accepted the sword without much surprise, assuming Hámund had given it to him out of shame over his betrayal, the same shame that had compelled him to leave the weapon with Steinólfur rather than waiting to give it to Geirmund himself. "Did he say anything?" Geirmund asked.

"No," Steinólfur said. "He must have forgotten. But if I might speak for him, I think he meant to say that he knows you'll feed it better than he ever will."

If Hámund had waited and offered it in person, Geirmund might have refused the weapon, because no gift would ever erase his brother's betrayal. But since Hámund had left the sword behind, Geirmund could hardly abandon it on the wharf. He had envied the weapon since the day his father had given it to Hámund.

"It's a king's blade," Steinólfur said.

"It is a fine weapon," Skjalgi said.

Geirmund looked down at the boy. "I think it's time you had a sword to call your own." He unbuckled his own weapon, a plain blade of good steel, and presented it to Skjalgi. "This is not a king's blade, but it has served me well, and it will serve you well, if you let Steinólfur show you how to care for it."

Few warriors could afford a sword until after their first raid, and Skjalgi received the weapon as though it were made of gold. "Thank you, Geirmund," he said.

One corner of Steinólfur's mouth lifted in a grin, and he gave Geirmund an approving nod.

"Hel-hide!"

Geirmund turned towards the ship, where Guthrum stood on deck. Behind him, the crew raised the mast and stepped it into place.

"I hear you wish to sail with me!" the Dane said.

Geirmund moved closer but did not yet board. "I do, Jarl Guthrum."

"I admit I am surprised to see you," Guthrum said, "after the offence your father gave me."

"I am not my father," Geirmund said. "And I will not apologize for him."

"Good. No man should apologize for another. Each must make an answer for his own actions and his own honour." Guthrum nodded towards Steinólfur and Skjalgi. "But you come to me with no ship, and but one oath-man and a boy."

"We have swords," Geirmund said, "and I now swear them to you."

"Can you use that sword?" the Dane asked, nodding towards Hámund's blade.

"I am trained to use it, but I have yet to take another's life with it. Is that enough?"

Guthrum shrugged. "It is enough. But before you take any lives, you will take your turn at the oars, and make no mistake, Hel-hide. You may be a grandson of Half, but you will lead no Danes until you have proven yourself."

"I expect nothing more," Geirmund said. "But make no mistake, Jarl Guthrum. One day, even you will fear the warriors who follow me."

The Dane laughed and waved them aboard. "I await that day as a stone awaits moss."

Geirmund crossed the plank from the dock to the ship, followed by Steinólfur and Skjalgi, and the three of them found places to sit among the crew on the deck towards the bow. Geirmund looked down the length of the vessel and counted sixteen oars to a side, with the first company of hole-men already seated upon their sea chests, ready to pull as the ship's commander ordered. The helmsman stood at the steerboard, surrounded by an additional dozen men ready to take an oar when those already seated reached their thousand strokes, while the lookout took his position at the prow. A moment later, Guthrum gave the order to depart.

The commander took up his position at the mast and bellowed commands at the linemen, who moved down the length of the ship, untying the walrus-hide rigging and pushing the vessel away from the wharf with long poles. Then the hole-men dropped their oars into the water and the commander directed their movement, easing the ship away from the wharf into the currents of the Karmsund, where the water sloshed against its thin skin of wooden strakes.

The hole-men rowed them west and south, around the peninsula where the hall of King Hjörr stood, and though the ship passed under the building's gaze, Geirmund felt out of its reach for the first time in his life. He felt free.

Guthrum poured an offering of costly wine into the water and called on Rán to give them a safe journey, and then he crossed the ship's deck to stand near Geirmund. "I won't mock you if you want to wave goodbye," he said.

"Yes, you will," Steinólfur said, grinning at the Dane. "And I'll join you."

Geirmund laughed and said nothing. Neither did he wave, but instead he bade a silent farewell that was the closing of a door he accepted might never open to him again. With Avaldsnes behind, and the shores of the Karmsund to the east and west, Geirmund felt penned in on three sides, but he fixed his eyes on the one path left open to him. Not long after that, the commander ordered the sail raised to catch a wind out of the north. The hole-men pulled in their oars, and the ship sped southward.

PART TWO

The Crossing

7

The goddess Rán gave them calm seas for most of the journey from Rogaland to Jutland, and the wind filled the ship's sail so fully that Geirmund had to take only a handful of turns at the oar. Those were enough to strip his hands of skin and strain the muscles in his arms, shoulders, and back. When he complained, Steinólfur told him he knew nothing of the ocean's true rage and brutality, the storms that reached into the ship and stole the man at the oar next to you, the waves like rolling mountains that would twist and wring ships like wet rags.

Guthrum's vessel was named *Wave Lover*, but sometimes called *Wave Humper* by the men, depending on their humour and the temperament of Rán's daughters. The ship's crew viewed Geirmund with suspicion. He would catch them casting wary stares at him, and they rarely spoke to him, but as they journeyed he managed to learn a few of their names.

The ship's commander was called Rek. He had a scar across his scalp that mangled the hairline of his brow, as though someone had tried to take the lid off his skull. The curses and complaints he sent Geirmund's way whenever he sat his turn at the oar, and often when he was doing nothing at all, spoke to an instant and unexplained hatred. The commander had a brother onboard, a giant of a man with a broad back and powerful shoulders, who seemed to have a less violent temper than Rek. His name was Eskil, and he was a mere hole-man, although the other hole-men seemed to defer to him and, unlike them, Eskil would nod when Geirmund caught him staring, rather than look away.

On their fourth day under sail they arrived at Ribe, on the western shore of Jutland, where they joined a fleet of some two hundred ships or more. The regular tides along that coastline shoved the shallow seas there up against a shore of grass and reeds, then pulled the water far away, carving channels and exposing wide flats of sand and silt. Geirmund had never seen anything like it, and Guthrum said that if they were to sail southward to the end of that mud-sea, the journey would take another three days of sailing at least and carry them all the way to Frisland.

They idled in deeper waters just off the Jutland coast until they could use the evening tide to carry their ship inward, to anchor nearer dry land with the rest of the fleet, and then the tide retreated, stranding *Wave Lover* with the other boats like a beached whale.

They disembarked down a plank that flexed under their weight, then trudged through clumps of seaweed and splashed across a saltmarsh that bubbled with buried crabs and shellfish. Proud white storks strode that land, feasting on prey they pulled from the mud with their beaks and tossed in the air. The wind there smelled of fish and brine, and even that soft ground seemed to resist their feet after the days they had spent riding the unstable seas.

"How long do you suppose we'll stay here?" Skjalgi asked.

"That depends on whether the expected jarls are all here," Steinólfur said. "But the Danes will wait for favourable winds and waves, at least."

Skjalgi glanced over his shoulder, back towards the ships. "The seas seem favourable now."

"Sailing south, yes," Geirmund said. "But from here we travel west."

At the boundary of the tideland the sand beneath their feet dried out and became shifting and pale, windblown into dunes. The three of them scrambled up from that beach onto higher, grassy ground, where they found the fleet's encampment spread out over hundreds of acres, almost as far as Geirmund could see. The noise of it rumbled like distant and unceasing thunder.

"Now there's a sight," Skjalgi said.

"Hel-hide!" Guthrum stepped up onto the plain from the beach and motioned for Geirmund to follow. "Come with me."

Geirmund nodded, but before he left he told Steinólfur to find a place to camp near Guthrum's men, but as far from the water as he could manage, so as not to wake up swimming in the sea if a storm swell should come in the night. Then he followed Guthrum to a wide thoroughfare that ran through the encampment towards what seemed to be its centre. They passed blacksmiths hammering near makeshift forges, craftsmen of leather and wood, sewers and weavers, butchers and firepits, and the deeper they went, the more the encampment smelled of life and its refuse, a moveable city much larger than Avaldsnes.

There were many shield-maidens among the warriors that they passed, and Geirmund searched their faces, wondering if Eivor was among them. The warriors there all bowed their heads at Guthrum, whereas Geirmund's passing attracted stares from the tents along that makeshift road, and Guthrum seemed to notice it.

"They've never seen anyone so ugly before," he said.

"Have they not seen Rek?" Geirmund asked.

Guthrum's laugh was like a single blast from a goat horn. "I'd mind that tongue when Rek can hear you. You'll be in his company for the time being."

Geirmund had feared as much.

"I understand why they stare," the Dane said. "You don't look like a Northman."

"So I've been told."

"Is Hjörr your father?"

The bluntness of the question stopped Geirmund from answering right away, and it almost stopped him in the camp road.

"Or were you already in your mother's belly when she left Bjarmaland?" Guthrum said.

That did halt Geirmund's feet, and he fought to keep his hand from seeking the grip of his new sword. "You will take that back, Jarl Guthrum."

The Dane stopped, turned, and stood up taller, his head cocked to one side. "Will I?"

"You will. Insult me if you must, but you will not insult my mother."

A tense moment passed, and then Guthrum nodded. "Fair enough, I withdraw what I said about your mother. But what about Hjörr?"

"He is my father." Geirmund resumed his march through the encampment, catching the odour of livestock on the air from wherever the animals were penned. "My brother and I take after my mother's people."

The Dane seemed to accept this. "After the manner of your leaving, I wondered if you still call him father. If he is still your king."

Geirmund had not asked that question of himself, or, at least, not in those words. "Frankly, I don't know how to answer."

"It took courage, what you did," Guthrum said. "Coming to me like a beggar, with no ship and no warriors."

"I didn't beg," Geirmund said.

"I meant no insult. I admire your courage. But courage and honour are not the same thing. Even traitors and oath-breakers can show bravery. I am simply wondering where you place your loyalties."

"I suppose that's fair." Geirmund noticed a large tent in the distance and assumed that to be their destination. "But I would say that loyalty and honour are not always the same thing. There are times when honour calls for the end of loyalty."

The Dane frowned, as if doubting the truth of that. "Perhaps," he said.

"But I have sworn to you," Geirmund said, "on my honour."

Guthrum looked at him for a moment and nodded, then pointed down the lane towards the large tent. "You are about to meet my king. You will say nothing to Bersi until asked."

"Yes, herra."

They reached the tent and found its entrance guarded by two warriors in ringmail, armed with spear, sword, and axe. They recognized Guthrum and bowed their heads, but they stepped in front of the opening to block Geirmund's path.

"Who is this, Jarl Guthrum?" one of them asked. The other kept his attention on Geirmund, weapons at the ready.

"This is Geirmund Hjörrsson," Guthrum said. "A son of the king of Rogaland."

The two guards exchanged a glance, then moved to allow entrance.

Geirmund followed Guthrum and they came into a dim enclosure. A fire burned in a hearth near its centre, blue smoke rising lazily up to the vent at the peak of the tent. Geirmund noted several tapestries and rugs from distant Serkland and Tyrkland, while tall folding screens of ornately carved wood set a few smaller rooms apart from the central chamber. A half-dozen men sat or stood around the fire, some with gilded ale horns, and judging by their furs and rings they were all of them jarls.

"Guthrum!" one of the men bellowed as he lumbered across the room to grip arms. He was loud and red of beard and cheek, and his presence dominated the tent. He towered over Guthrum and most of the other Danes, likely not a swift or agile fighter, but powerful and strong. Geirmund knew him instantly to be Bersi. "I thank Óðinn for your safe return," the Dane-king said. "How many ships have you brought me from the North Way?"

Guthrum bowed his head. "None, I regret to say."

"None?"

"The Northmen are consumed with their own troubles. In every hall I visited they spoke of war with Harald of Sogn."

"All the more reason to join with us and seek new lands."

"I made that same argument, but they could not be persuaded. With one exception." Guthrum gestured towards Geirmund. "This is one of the sons of Hjörr Halfsson and Ljufvina."

"One of the Hel-hides?" Bersi looked down at Geirmund and his mouth split into a broad smile that revealed two gaps in his teeth. "Which are you?"

"I am Geirmund."

"And how many men have your brought me, Geirmund Hjörrsson?"

Geirmund hesitated and looked at Guthrum before answering. "Two."

"One and a half," Guthrum said.

Bersi's smile vanished into his beard and his eyes narrowed.

"I defied my father to join with you," Geirmund went on. "That is the reason I have nothing from him."

The other jarls stood waiting, as silent and still as winter pines, as Bersi looked Geirmund over from heel to hair. "He gave you a fine sword by the looks of it," the king finally said.

Geirmund thought better of correcting him. "It thirsts for Saxon blood," he said.

Bersi's smile reappeared. "And it will be sated. Your sword will bathe in Saxon blood, if that is what it wishes." Then he turned and addressed his jarls. "With Guthrum returned we can look to the crossing." He strode to one side of the room and stepped up to take his seat upon a raised dais, the chair groaning under his weight. "Halfdan now marches through Mercia, to a place called Readingum on the River Thames, and we will use the Thames to bring our ships to that same place. If the gods are with us, Halfdan will have taken it before we reach him. But our ships will be vulnerable on the river." He called on an older jarl with grey hair who wore a stubby Saxon sword at his side. "Osbern, what is the latest from your men at Thanet and Lunden?"

As the jarl answered him, Guthrum leaned in close to Geirmund. "My men will be situated at the south-west corner of the encampment," he said. "Go and find them. Eat, then rest."

Geirmund wanted to stay and learn more of what lay ahead, but he nodded and slipped away from the gathering, then from the tent.

Outside, the sun had set, and dusk descended over the encampment, which was now lit by the scattered glow of fires and torches. Geirmund returned the way he and Guthrum had come, heading west towards the sea, surrounded by the sounds of revelry and the frenzy of warriors eager for war and plunder.

Near the edge of the encampment, the mud-sea came into view, spread with the dark humps of the waiting ships, and he turned south, wandering through and around the clusters of tents.

He searched the firelit faces of the warriors he passed, looking for men he knew from Guthrum's ship, and he eventually spotted Eskil seated before a small bonfire in a circle of twenty or more Danes.

He approached the warrior and asked if he had seen Steinólfur. Eskil looked up at Geirmund, then nodded and pointed to his right without saying a word. Geirmund thanked him and moved in that direction.

"Hel-hide!" a rough voice shouted from across the circle.

Geirmund turned towards it, recognizing the voice. "What is it, Rek?"

The ship's commander got to his feet, leaning a bit with ale. "Tell me something. Are the men of your mother's people fighting men?"

"I cannot say," Geirmund said. "I have never been to Bjarmaland. Why do you ask?"

Rek stepped inside the ring of Danes and came around the fire towards Geirmund. "I'm just wondering what– what kind of man you are. Because it is plain that you are no Northman."

"That's enough, brother," Eskil said from behind Geirmund.

But Rek continued his advance. "It's not enough until I'm satisfied, brother."

"Satisfied of what?" Geirmund asked, refusing to lift one boot or give any ground.

Rek came near and stepped right up to him, face to face, staring into his eyes with ale on his breath and the bonfire at his back. "Satisfied of your mettle, half-breed."

By that point some of the other Danes were also on their feet, ready for whatever was coming. But Geirmund knew well what was about to happen. It had happened before. Many times. "Do you mean to test me?" he asked, as the pounding of his anger reached his ears. "Because if you do, I will–"

"You! Rek!" Steinólfur stepped into the circle then, arms outstretched. "Perhaps you wish to test my mettle?"

"Enough of this." Eskil sounded irritated as he also stepped into the circle. "All of you, sit down," he said, glowering at the Danes around the fire.

The warriors settled back as they were, but reluctantly, and Geirmund wondered how it was that a hole-man had such authority. Only Eskil, Rek, Steinólfur, and Geirmund remained on their feet as the same north wind that had brought Guthrum's ship to Jutland whipped through the encampment, stirring sparks and embers in the fire.

The commander pointed at Geirmund. "You are an ill omen, Hel-hide," he said, and murmurs of agreement moved through the circle. "I would be rid of you."

Steinólfur took a few steps and placed himself in front of Geirmund, arms folded. "He's an ill omen for you if you continue to speak that way. I could easily be rid of you."

"Can he not speak for himself?" Rek asked. "Or does he always hide behind his–"

"Enough!" Eskil shouted, and Rek flinched.

"Brother, I only–"

"You have drunk too much ale," Eskil said to him. "I suggest you go to your tent while you can still find it."

Some of the Danes laughed at that, and Rek's face reddened. He glared at Geirmund, shaking with murderous rage, but eventually he turned and stalked away from the circle into the darkening night. Eskil shook his head, and then he returned to where he had been sitting, leaving Geirmund to feel the weight of the other Danes' stares.

Steinólfur glanced around the circle. "Come," he said. "The boy will be wondering where we are." He nodded in the direction from which he had appeared.

But Geirmund still felt ready for a battle, as if armed with spears and arrows that needed a new target. He swung around and looked again at Eskil, who in turn stared only at the fire, and then he searched the faces of the other Danes for a new challenger. When it seemed that none would meet him, he cursed and followed Steinólfur, who led him through the tents and leather sleeping sacks towards a large growth of buckthorn.

"You'll want to stay clear of Rek for a time," the older warrior said. "Like all men of the sea, he looks for signs, and he always finds them."

"How can I stay clear of him?" Geirmund asked. "He's the commander."

"On the *Wave Humper*, yes, but I've been talking with the Danes. Rek is a skilled shipman, but it is well known that his brother is the better warrior. At sea Eskil chooses to pull an oar with the crew, but on land his authority is second only to Guthrum's."

They arrived at a small campfire, around which a restless Skjalgi fretted and paced.

"Who's second to Guthrum?" the boy asked.

"That explains much," Geirmund said, remembering the way the other hole-men had deferred to Eskil, and how his brother had obeyed him just moments ago. "How many warriors has Guthrum gathered for the Dane-king?"

"They say he has forty ships." Steinólfur sat near the fire and motioned for Skjalgi to do the same. "Settle yourself, boy, you're agitating me."

Skjalgi blinked, but clamped his mouth shut and sat, and then Geirmund joined them. Steinólfur handed out food from their provision store, a few strips of dried and salted meat, some crisp rye bread, hard cheese, and dried fruit. As they ate, the older warrior went on.

"Most of Guthrum's ships are snekkja like *Wave Humper*. But some are skeiðar with sixty oars."

Geirmund reckoned the number of warriors that many ships could carry. "So Guthrum has an army of at least two thousand."

"He does," Steinólfur said. "Why do you ask?"

"I'm trying to measure his standing with Bersi and the other jarls."

"Making sure you've sworn us to the right Dane?" The older warrior tossed another piece of wood on the fire.

"Guthrum is the right Dane," Geirmund said, though he couldn't explain yet what made him so. He only knew that fate had put him on Guthrum's ship. "We should get sleep now, while we can. We sail soon, I think."

They unrolled their sleeping bags of walrus hide, one for Geirmund and one for Steinólfur and Skjalgi to share, though each húðfat was sewn large enough to accommodate two grown men. There hadn't been much dry wood left near the encampment to gather, but Skjalgi threw the last of it into the fire before climbing into the sack with the older warrior.

"Hold your farts until morning, boy," Steinólfur said, lying on his back, eyes closed, with his hands folded across his chest.

Geirmund grinned at Skjalgi to let the boy know he was aware who would be more guilty of that crime. Then he climbed into his own sleeping sack, but he didn't fall asleep right away. He looked up at the stars, thinking on what Bragi had said about war between men and gods, and he imagined the stars going out like snuffed lanterns after the final battle and destiny of Óðinn, and Thór, and all the other Æsir and Vanir, leaving the sky a gaping abyss, a new Ginnungagap into which everything would fall. Geirmund drifted in that oblivion until he was almost asleep, but then Skjalgi whispered his name and brought him back.

"What is it?" he asked the boy.

"Why do we make war on the Saxons?" he asked. "Is it a blood feud?"

Geirmund sighed. "Some might call it that. The Saxons have murdered farmers and their families. Danes trying only to settle and live in peace."

"Why did the Saxons murder Danes?"

"Because Danes murdered Saxons," Steinólfur said with a growl, awakened by their talk. "Yes, it's a blood feud, boy. Neither side will ever agree who started it. You can let that keep you awake if you want, so long as you stop talking about it and give the rest of us some peace."

Skjalgi went silent after that.

Geirmund closed his eyes, warm in the walrus hide despite the wind that scoured that coastline. He slept well, though his body and his dreams remembered the rolling of the ship on the waves of the past few nights.

They spent the next day, and two days more, training Skjalgi in the use of his new sword. Though thin, the boy's strong arms and legs learned quickly, and he could strike with the speed of a hawk. During that time the three of them kept mostly apart from the Danes, and in that way Geirmund avoided a second confrontation with Rek. But he knew that to be only a delay of the inevitable, unless he was willing to ask Guthrum to put them on a different ship, and he wasn't willing to do that. Geirmund saw little of Guthrum, who spent most of his time in council with Bersi and the other jarls. Each day the tides brought a few last straggling ships and warriors, but the joining of their spears to the host was like the joining of a single barley stalk to an acre-field of grain.

On their fourth day at Ribe Geirmund went out into the encampment to see if he could find shields for purchase, which the three of them hadn't taken from Avaldsnes. He spent the morning asking around and following fruitless leads. The encampment was enormous and chaotic, and it wasn't until midday that he finally found a Frisian willing to sell.

The shields he had on offer were used but strong and made of fir. The leather sewn around their rims was tight, the iron straps oiled and free of rust. Geirmund had expected to pay too much for any shield he managed to find, but the Frisian seemed to have no intention of joining Bersi, wanting only to sell his wares before the fleet departed those shores, so Geirmund managed to buy all three shields for two pieces of silver.

On the way back to Jarl Guthrum's section of the encampment, he passed several tents in which women offered themselves for less than silver. One of them waved and called to him, and for a moment her blond hair and red cheeks enticed him. But he now carried three shields, one on his back and another in each hand, and he had too much silver with him to risk its theft by one of the woman's friends, so he made the safer choice and continued on his way.

The next day, he and Steinólfur had planned to show Skjalgi how to stand in a shield-wall, but they had barely begun their instruction before word went through the encampment that the fleet was to sail. Then Guthrum appeared among them, smelling of mead, and gave the official command to make their offerings to the gods and load his ships for the invasion of England.

8

The fleet enjoyed calm seas for two days, but on the third a storm roared down from the north without sign or warning. The howling winds and ferocious waves scattered the ships, leaving each to fight its own battle for the life or death of its crew. Rek ordered *Wave Lover*'s sail lowered to save it from tearing free, and every man pulled his thousand strokes at the oar.

Geirmund took his turn rowing, then his turn with the bailing bucket, then back to the oar, until his legs and his arms felt as useless as sodden reeds, and he could barely see through the wind and rain and saltwater spray that tore at his eyes. Without the sun there were no daymarks, and the storm seemed endless. Geirmund soon lost himself to the rhythm of the oar and couldn't say whether days or hours had passed.

Wave Lover was well built and rode high in the water, whether atop a swell or in a trough so deep it turned dark as night until they climbed out of it. But there were times when the waves and currents twisted the ship until its prow and sternpost seemed to point in opposite directions, and that flexing wrenched gaps between the strakes and let water in. When Guthrum learned that

Steinólfur had spent time at sea and knew something of boats, he gave the older warrior the task of packing the leaks with tarred wool. Skjalgi worked with him, and the boy soon learned the method of it, after which Steinólfur left him to it and went back to rowing and bailing. But it was a futile cause, for as soon as Skjalgi stopped one leak, two more would open.

As Geirmund worked next to Guthrum, bailing the water that poured in, Rek staggered over to them and shouted.

"Ægir and Rán want to swallow us! They want us dead!"

Guthrum laughed. "Ignore them! Óðinn is with us!"

Rek looked at Geirmund. "Will Óðinn save the ship that carries a child of Hel?"

That question seemed to change the direction of the wind. Geirmund could see doubt splitting the strakes of Guthrum's courage, and that split spread almost instantly down the length of the ship's crew.

"I say we offer the Hel-hide to Ægir!" Rek said. "Let the jötunn have him!"

"No!" Steinólfur left his oar and struggled across the pitching deck. "You'll have to kill me first, and I swear I'll take Danes with me!" He pointed at Rek. "Starting with the coward!"

The altercation had attracted Eskil and Skjalgi, and Geirmund did not need to be a seer to know how this would end.

"Brother, stop this!" Eskil shouted.

"No!" Rek's eyes bulged as he pounded his chest. "I give the commands aboard this vessel!"

"Surely Jarl Guthrum gives the commands!" Steinólfur said, but Geirmund could see plainly that the crew sided with Rek.

Guthrum looked at Geirmund, water pouring off his brow, and Geirmund knew what had to be done. He could see that the jarl felt fear enough, of the storm and of his own men, that he would not refuse the ship's commander's challenge. If that led to a fight, then Steinólfur and Skjalgi would die alongside him, even if they managed to kill a few of the Danes, for the crew outnumbered them ten men to one. To spare the lives of his companions, Geirmund had to prevent the fight, and he knew Rek would only be satisfied with one outcome.

"It is said that Half and his men were each willing to throw themselves into the sea to save the others." He turned to Steinólfur. "Farewell, my friend," he said, and he leapt over the side of the ship.

The sea rushed up to snatch him in its icy grip, and then all went quiet as he plunged beneath the waves. The fury returned a moment later as he fought his way up and breached the surface, where Steinólfur screamed his name and reached down to him, leaning halfway over the gunwale. The older warrior made to leap into the water to save Geirmund, but Eskil held him back.

The swift current pulled Geirmund away from the ship. His hand reached for a passing oar in an instinctive attempt to stay alive, but he quickly withdrew his arm and let both the oar and the ship slip beyond his reach.

This was not the life-end he had imagined when he left his father's hall.

But, clearly, it was to be his fate.

Guthrum's ship had not even left Geirmund's view, and already the weight of his armour and clothes dragged him down. Seawater flooded his mouth and filled his nose. He gagged and gasped, but he had no strength left to fight the sea. Even if he had, it would make no difference, for no one could defy what the Three Spinners had decided.

When you see your fate, there is but one thing to be done. You must meet it.

A calm came over him then, an acceptance of what had been decreed. Geirmund pulled his knife free of its sheath, the only weapon he could hold to face his death as a warrior. Then he ceased to fight, took one last breath, and let the sea pull him down, down, down into the dark and endless void of a watery Ginnungagap. Down where there were no waves, and the storm couldn't reach him, where Ægir's cold and iron grip crushed all, whether Northman, Saxon, or Dane.

Geirmund held his breath, his unthinking body still unwilling to relinquish its desperate hold on life, but there would soon be no choice. The pressure of the sea squeezed his head and stabbed his ears. The burning in his lungs spread through his body, a kind of starvation in every muscle and joint. When he opened his eyes, he saw sparks in the frozen darkness, like the embers of Muspelheim drifting around him.

One of the sparks did not move, a speck of light beneath him that grew steadily brighter and larger. Rán was coming to witness him drown and claim her offering. He closed his eyes, but the light remained, bright enough to turn his vision red, and he shook with a roaring in his bones. When he could hold his breath no longer, he opened his mouth and inhaled the sea. Ice and salt filled his lungs with cold fire. He tried not to fight, but lost control of his limbs and thrashed against a god. The light brightened until it seared his eyes, blinding him and burning the thoughts from his mind until there was nothing of him left in his skull.

Then he saw nothing, and when he opened his eyes again he was lying in the middle of an enormous hall, its roof and its walls too distant and dark to measure, and he seemed to be alone. His whole body ached, as if every part of him had been bruised, and he sat up slowly, remembering himself. Only a moment ago he had been drowning, but his clothing was now merely damp, and his knife was back in its sheath at his belt.

The bed he rested upon appeared to be made of steel, with an impression in the shape of his body at its centre. Geirmund had never before seen or heard of a bed like it, and he couldn't understand why a smith would put so much good metal to such pointless use. The walls and floor that surrounded him were made from a dark stone, polished and hewn of a piece, as though carved into the heart of a mountain, and he could see no lantern, torch, or other source for the hall's dim light. He began to think he must have found his way to the house of a god, or perhaps a jötunn.

He assumed he was dead, but he knew he wasn't in Valhalla. He saw no other warriors, smelled no food for feasting, and heard no sounds of fighting, and he also knew he had not fought and died in a way that would please Óðinn, with only a knife in his hand. He next considered the possibility that the darkened hall belonged to the goddess Hel. It was surely cold enough to be the realm of the dead, but if it were, he wondered why it appeared empty, save for himself. If the hall didn't belong to Óðinn or Hel, he might have sunk into the realm of Rán, but this place did not resemble the stories of her coral caves. With no plain answer and no other guesses as to where he might be, he decided to go in search of his host.

As Geirmund rose from the metal bed, he found his legs and feet steadier than he had expected them to be. The pain and weakness in his bones had likewise begun to ease, but he had always thought the dead would feel no pain, and he decided that those sensations had been only a lingering memory of his death.

He peered into the reaches of the hall and glimpsed a distant doorway. As he moved towards it, he discovered it to be an arch, sharp and narrow like the tip of a spear, as high as three tall warriors and a bit wider than the span of Geirmund's arms. The opening led into a long tunnel, which he followed towards a gleaming light that flickered at the far end.

Some distance along the corridor, the polished stone came to an end, and beyond that point the walls and ceiling appeared to be made of a kind of crystal or glass. Geirmund would not have believed so much of the precious material could be gathered in one place, nor shaped by any being other than a god. As he admired its beauty and craftsmanship, he realized that the crystal was perfectly clear, and that what he had first taken for a dark hue within the glass was outside it. He stepped back from the wall to the centre of the tunnel and looked upwards, mouth gaping.

He was underwater. Under the sea. Rán had taken him into her realm, which meant he might not have died, after all.

Geirmund peered again through the crystal wall into the black abyss beyond, which seemed alive with enormous and barely glimpsed shadows. Along the seafloor he could almost make out the shapes of what he imagined to be standing stones, or the broken trunks of trees. And somewhere in that vastness the serpent Jörmungandr waited for his time to awaken and rise.

"Thór protect me," Geirmund whispered, and even that echoed loudly against the crystal walls.

He pulled himself away from the abyss and turned again to face the end of the tunnel with its glowing light, which he approached more cautiously now that he thought he might not have drowned after all, and could still die. He had left his sword on Guthrum's ship, which left him with Bragi's bronze knife as his only weapon. He drew it as he reached the end of the corridor, where he peered around its edge into a second chamber.

The room was smaller than the first hall, but made of the same stone, its walls and floor decorated with carvings and paths of inlaid silver. An altar stood against one wall, surrounded by a shroud of light that appeared to move and swing like a tapestry. Within that light, upon the altar, sat a golden arm-ring, which glinted and drew Geirmund into the room towards it, though he stopped a few paces away, wary of meddling with the god-treasure.

"You may take it, if you wish."

Geirmund cried out and spun round.

The voice had seemed to come from everywhere, loud and strong, and when Geirmund looked for its source, he discovered a man had appeared in a corner of the room behind him. The stranger stood taller than Geirmund by two hands, and he glowed with a pale light, like that of the moon. He wore a tunic of fine linen or silk, with plates of armour and a helm crafted from silver. He was obviously a god, but Geirmund refused to bow until he knew which god he would be honouring.

"Are you Ægir?" he asked the stranger.

"I am known by many names, but you may call me Völund."

Geirmund had heard tales of a man called Völund. He wasn't a god, but he did have dealings with gods and kings, for he was a smith of great cunning and skill, and his creations were the envy of all. "What is this place?" he asked, still holding Bragi's knife down at his side.

"It is my home," Völund said. "My forge."

Geirmund looked up, towards the ceiling. "We're under the sea?"

"Yes, you are. Long ago, mountains of ice covered much of the northern lands, and this place stood on dry ground. Your forebears hunted the mighty aurochs and gathered food in the forests that grew here. When the ice retreated, the sea swelled. It drowned those forests and my forge, and it drove your forebears to settle new places."

Such ice and floods existed only in stories. Búri, the father of Borr, who was the father of Óðinn, had been brought out of the rime by the cow Auðumbla as the ice of Niflheim also retreated, and it was Búri's descendants who had slayed the jötunn, Ymir, to fashion the world from his corpse.

"How did I come here?" Geirmund asked.

"You were drowning," Völund said. "So I summoned you." He moved closer, and Geirmund felt a chill through his body as he noticed that he could see through the smith to the wall behind him.

He raised his knife and backed away. "You are no man."

Völund shook his head. "I am not."

"Are you alive?"

"I was once alive."

"If you're not alive, then what are you?"

The smith paused. "Think of me as a memory."

"Whose memory?"

"The gods'."

Geirmund began to lose his grasp on himself, and whether he was where he was, or whether he was dreaming. "Am I alive?" he asked.

"You are alive."

"Why?"

"Why are you alive?"

"No. Why did you save me? Many ships are lost to storms, their crews drowned." Geirmund looked around the room. "I seem to be the only one you have taken into your hall. So I ask you, why did you save me and not others?"

"Now I understand your question." Völund turned towards the altar. "This ring is, in part, an answer to it."

Geirmund didn't lower the bronze knife, but he did allow his attention to fall again on the altar and the arm-ring, which was unlike any he had seen. It had been forged in seven pieces, each adorned with a different rune, and each rune seemed to shine with a different colour from within.

"This ring has a name," Völund said. "Your forebears called it Hnituðr."

Geirmund took a step towards the altar. "My forebears?"

"Yes." Völund waved his hand, and the tapestry of light that surrounded the ring vanished. "I explained that you have the blood of your forebears who lived on this land before the sea covered it. You are familiar to me. Your ancestor was familiar to me when I also saved him from drowning."

Geirmund had only one ancestor who had nearly drowned. "You speak of Hjörrleif," he said. "The father of my father's father."

Völund nodded.

"But that would mean... You're the sea man." Geirmund pointed his knife at the smith. "He caught you in his net."

"It would not be possible to catch me with a net."

"But you are the sea man in the story, are you not? You foretold the fate of Hjörrleif."

"I described the most likely of his possible fates."

Geirmund lowered the knife. "What does that mean? There is only one fate for each of us, and it is inescapable."

"Fate is simply a word for the result of choice and its consequence. It is consequence that is inescapable after a choice is made. Action will be met with reaction. Tell me, do you believe choices are inescapable?"

"No. I can always choose how I will meet my fate."

"Can you?" Völund smiled. "Could you have chosen to remain on land, rather than attempting to cross the sea?"

Geirmund considered that for a moment. "No, that was a matter of honour. I swore to follow Guthrum."

"Did you have a choice when you made that oath?"

"No, because that was the only way–" Geirmund knew that if he had not sworn that oath, Guthrum would not have taken him aboard his ship, and if he had not taken him aboard his ship, Geirmund would have remained trapped in his father's hall at Avaldsnes. For each of his choices there had been but one path forward, but that path had been determined by the choices before it, and they by the choices that preceded them. To make different choices would have made Geirmund someone other than who he was. But that did not mean those choices were inescapable, or that other choices had been impossible. They were simply more difficult to make.

"Consequence is law," Völund said. "Choice is in your blood, and it is in your blood that I see what lies ahead of you."

"You are wise for a smith," Geirmund said. "What do you see ahead of me?"

"Betrayal and defeat." Völund spoke as though he were listing the yield from an unremarkable harvest. "You will surrender to your enemy, but you will not know who your enemy is."

Geirmund scoffed. "You are confusing me with my father and my brother. I would never surrender to my enemy."

"You surrendered to the sea."

He was about to deny that but realized he couldn't, and he grew angry at the smith. He had surrendered to the sea, that was true, but that did not mean he would surrender to an enemy, regardless of who that enemy might be. "Perhaps you are simply not as wise as I thought."

"I speak the truth." Völund's face remained calm within his silver helm. "I feel no need to convince you of it."

Geirmund returned his attention to the ring. "Why is it called Hnituðr? What about it is planned?"

"It was so named because it is part of the fate of each who wears it. The ring is law. The choice to take it is yours."

The offer of the ring felt to Geirmund like the offer of bait in a snare, and he wondered if it was his fate to take it or his fate to refuse it, and even whether he had a choice, for who could refuse the workmanship of Völund the smith?

He slid his dagger back into its sheath, and he stepped up to the altar where Hnituðr lay, glittering and waiting for him to make his choice. But Geirmund had begun to see that he did not have a choice. He would not refuse it. The ring was a prize fit for a king, and if it was his forebearers who had named it, then Hnituðr was his birthright.

Geirmund reached out to take the ring, but when his hand touched it, the blinding light blazed again in his eyes, scorching his mind to ash.

9

When Geirmund's mind returned, he was lying with his face and belly in mud, and he could hear the lapping of water and the call of terns. He thought at first that he had returned to Ribe, and then he wondered if he had ever left that shore, and if the encounter with Völund had been a vision or dream. But when he opened his eyes, he saw that he wasn't in Jutland. He didn't know where he was.

He staggered to his feet, his clothing soaked in seawater, and became aware that he was clutching something. When he looked down, he saw Hnituðr, and knew then that he had not dreamed of that hall under the sea, and he concluded that Völund, or some other power, had brought him to where he now stood.

The mudflats extended many rests to the north and south, much like the coast at Ribe, but here the sea lay on the opposite side, to the east, which meant he had landed somewhere on England's shores. To the west, across hundreds of acres of vast, flat wash, he saw the edge of a marsh, which he assumed to be East Anglia's fenland. If so, he was in territory the Danes had conquered, but far to the north of Lunden and the River Thames, where Bersi had directed the fleet.

Any boats that survived the storm would have sailed there, leaving Geirmund to find his own way to the place called Readingum, where Halfdan's army and Bersi's ships were to meet. He knew Bersi planned to use the Thames to travel west, which meant Readingum would lie somewhere west of south. Geirmund did not know how long the journey there would take, but it was a journey he had to make, if only to reunite with Steinólfur and Skjalgi. They had come to England because they had sworn to him, and the memory of the older warrior's face on the ship as he had strained to reach for Geirmund pained him.

He looked again at the arm-ring, the way its gold seemed not only to reflect the sun's light but to possess a light of its own, and he decided he had to hide it. To wear such treasure openly would be to invite robbery by anyone he should encounter, whether Saxon, Northman, or Dane, with only his bronze dagger for defence. So he placed the ring inside his tunic, at his belt and out of sight. Then he turned south of west and set off across the wash.

England's air felt warm and wet, and the mudflats mired Geirmund's boots. Some of the pools and channels he encountered were shallow enough for him to ford, but others looked deep and treacherous, requiring extra time and effort to circumvent. The marshes would be worse, from what he had heard said of the fenlands. To cross them might take days, even if he knew the paths and byways, which he didn't. He needed to find a faster means of travel, or a guide to show him the best route.

As he approached the boundary of the marsh, he saw a gap in the reeds some distance to the north, where a river spilled onto the mudflats and dribbled towards the sea. A river would surely lead eventually to a village or town, where he might find a boat he could purchase with the remaining silver in his pouch.

He angled his path towards that part of the marsh, and when

he reached the river's mouth he found it a wide and sluggish waterway, but with embankments that offered his feet some firm land and a track into that country.

The deeper he travelled in the fenland, the heavier the air grew, laden with clouds of biting flies. In every direction he saw nothing but tall grass, reeds, aspen, and scrub trees in a maze of brackish waters, all clothed in a thin mist that never seemed to drift or lift. Geirmund grew thirsty as he walked, but stopped to drink from only the freshest waters he could find, usually streams that fed into the river, though even those tasted of peat.

When the sun eventually moved into his westward view and began its descent, Geirmund gave more attention to where and how he might sleep that night if he encountered no settlement before the sun set. He still had his fire-strike in its pouch, but he also knew without having to check that the sea had made his touchwood useless, and most of the fallen kindling he had passed thus far looked too damp to burn. He would also need to eat soon, but his wet clothing was the more urgent concern. He would spend a very cold night if he couldn't find dry tinder.

The evening daymark approached, but it was hard to guess how far he had travelled, given the twisting nature of the river and the land. What might have been six or seven rests on a straight road felt like twice that distance or more in the fens. He swatted without effect at the flies and myggs and scratched the welts they left behind, believing they might drain him dry of his blood if he stayed in one place for too long.

He was somewhat surprised that he hadn't yet met another person on the river, either Saxon or Dane, but neither did the land have a feeling of emptiness, as though Geirmund were the first to walk there. Rather, the fenland seemed to be holding still and keeping silent, in the manner of prey when danger is near.

It was when the sun touched the tops of an aspen line on the horizon that he finally smelled woodsmoke. But it was old smoke, from charred timber. The river widened there, blackened with ash and fouled by death. The first body he saw floating in the reeds belonged to a man, bloated and blue, and covered in flies above the waterline. His legs stuck out straight and swollen from inside his long robes, which fitted the descriptions he had heard of clothing worn by Christian seers and priests. His head had been split open by either an axe or a sword.

Further along the bank Geirmund discovered another corpse, and then another, then several, all of them wearing the same priest robes, all of them men, all of their bodies torn, opened, or divided. He saw parts of bodies alone, including the head of a boy who might have been Skjalgi's age.

Geirmund had never been a witness to that kind of death. Old age, sickness, and misadventure had all ended the lives of people he had known; he had never beheld the death that followed raiding and war. Though he had left his father's hall prepared to kill Saxon warriors, he had never taken a life or seen one taken by such violence.

He almost retched at the stench that filled his nose and the sights that filled his eyes and mind, and he was so overwhelmed and distracted that he was nearly upon the men ahead before he even noticed their voices. But he did notice in time to halt and listen.

They were Danes, by the manner of their speech, but Geirmund couldn't hear the words they spoke. He crept forward, staying low to spy them out, unsure of what to expect from them, and saw a small, wooded island surrounded by the river and the marsh. It was from that place that the Dane-speech had come.

A causeway of wooden planks connected the island to the

riverbank and the fenlands beyond. Geirmund saw no other way to approach the Danes, which meant he would have to announce himself before he knew them.

Something stirred in the reeds behind him, and he spun to face a Dane coming out of the marsh, carrying a basket. He was young, but older than Geirmund, his yellow hair braided over the top of his head. When he saw Geirmund he dropped his basket and pulled his axe free, but seemed to relax when he realized Geirmund had no other weapon than a knife.

"You're no Saxon," he said.

Geirmund shook his head. "I come from Rogaland."

"A Northman?" He squinted. "You don't look like a Northman either. Or a Dane."

Geirmund sighed. "I am a Northman. I am sworn to Jarl Guthrum."

The stranger glanced around, as if searching the trees and marsh for others.

"I'm alone," Geirmund said. "And I'm hungry. Is there room at your fire for one more?"

The stranger nodded and took a step back. "Of course. You can take the basket. I've carried it a great distance and my arms are tired." He pointed towards it with his axe.

Geirmund hesitated. To carry the basket, he would need to sheath his knife and use both hands, which would put him at a disadvantage, something the Dane had obviously thought about.

"I am Fasti," the stranger said.

"I am Geirmund."

"I will take you to Odmar," Fasti said. "He leads our company."

The sun had fallen even lower, and the marsh was growing dim. Geirmund could see few choices and decided it would be better to trust the Danes than spend the night in the open. If the Danes meant him harm, they would be a threat whether he went with Fasti or not, because they would know him to be close by.

Geirmund gave the Dane a nod, put his knife away, and bent to pick up the basket, which held several dozen oysters. A few of the rough shells bubbled at the seams, and as Geirmund lifted them, they rattled and scraped against each other. It truly was a heavy load.

Fasti nodded towards a break in the grass, intending for Geirmund to go that way first, but Geirmund did not like the idea of having the Dane and his axe behind him. "You lead the way," he said.

Now it was Fasti who hesitated.

"I carry no weapon," Geirmund said, holding up the basket. "Unless you think I could do you harm with these oysters, which have another use I'd much prefer."

A grin slowly spread across Fasti's mouth. "True enough. Let's eat them." He strode in the direction he had just pointed and Geirmund followed.

On the other side of the gap in the grass they descended to a stairway of flagstones set into the embankment, and then came to the wooden causeway that Geirmund had seen stretching over the river. It was about the length of a homefield, and the wooden planks felt almost as solid as dry land as he walked on them, without the hollow echo of a bridge or a wharf. Fasti glanced back and saw Geirmund looking down at the wood.

"The Saxons drive tall stakes into the river bottom," he said. "All close together, like a quiver of arrows. Then they build on top of it." He stomped his boot on the causeway. "It's sturdy, but still lets the river through."

"That's clever."

"The Saxons are clever, it's true." Fasti held up his axe. "But Danes are stronger."

They reached the island on the other side of the causeway, and Geirmund found it thick with thorny shrubs and trees. Fasti led him through the bramble to a path up a gentle rise, and as Geirmund crested it he saw a large field of cleared land. At its centre stood the burnt and smouldering ruin of a hall.

"What was this place?" he asked.

"The Saxons call it Ancarig. It was a Christian temple. A small one, made of wood." Fasti pointed to the west. "Upriver there is a place they call Medeshamstede, where the temple is much larger and made of stone."

The remains of several other buildings had also been put to the torch, and, intentionally or not, the fire had also claimed what appeared to have been an orchard. Fasti stepped through the wreckage and entered what was left of the temple. When Geirmund followed, he was greeted by another dozen or so Danes sitting around a fire in the middle of the building's bones. All looked at Geirmund when he entered, but one of them seemed to command the most attention, a stocky warrior with dark hair and blue lines etched across his brow, with a bearded axe at his side.

"Fasti, who is this?" he asked.

"I am Geirmund Hjörrsson."

"I did not ask you," the man said.

"I need no man to speak for me. You are Odmar?"

The man glared at Fasti. "I am."

"I found him lurking on the other side of the river." The younger Dane shifted his feet next to Geirmund. "He claims he is a Northman."

Odmar scoffed. "This is no Northman. He is Gyrwas. A swamp-Saxon."

"I am from Rogaland." Geirmund dropped the heavy basket to

the ground and the oysters clattered. "I was at Ribe, in Jutland, and I sailed with King Bersi's fleet."

"Oh?" Odmar looked to the left and right. "Where is he? Where are Bersi's ships?"

"At Lunden, I assume, on their way to Readingum. A storm took me overboard, and I washed up here."

"Then you must either have good luck or a god's protection. Or you are a liar." Odmar pointed at the basket. "Are those our oysters?"

Geirmund looked down at the shells. "They are."

"Dump them in the coals," Odmar said.

Geirmund paused, but then did as the man asked, tipping the basket's contents into the embers near the edge of the flames. Within moments they began to whistle and whine, and the Danes gathered around to pull them out of the heat as the boiling juices inside popped their shells open. The warriors grinned as they slurped the juices and used their knives to prize the shells open to carve out the meat inside. Geirmund stood by until Odmar motioned for him to join in while scraping the inside of a shell with his teeth.

The oyster juices scalded Geirmund's tongue, tasting of brine and the sea, and the meat inside was rich and fatty. Within moments all the oysters were gone, but Geirmund had managed to snatch six of them for himself, afterwards tossing the shells in the same pile as the Danes.

"Took me the whole day to gather those," Fasti said, looking down at the remains of his harvest.

"Don't despair." Odmar wiped his mouth and beard with the back of his sleeve. "You can always gather more tomorrow." A few of the Danes chuckled, and then Odmar turned his attention back to Geirmund. "I still say you don't look like a Northman."

"I haven't looked like a Northman since the day I was born," Geirmund said. "Do you suppose you're the first man observant enough to notice?"

That drew more laughter, including Odmar's, and he shrugged. "Then sit, Northman. Join us here. The smell of smoke and burnt temple keeps the myggs from biting."

"I thank you, Odmar." Geirmund took a place with them around the fire, no longer hungry and a bit more at ease.

"I see your sword must have stayed on the ship," Odmar said, and then glanced at the warriors to his left and right. "We are Ubba's men. Young Fasti is Ubba's kinsman. We were at Hagelisdun, where Ubba slew Eadmund, the king of these swamp-Saxons. He now marches to Mercia, but we have stayed in the fenland to keep the people here obedient."

Geirmund thought of the bodies he had seen in the river and wondered how those priests had been disobedient. Then he looked again at the burnt temple's surroundings and noticed that one outbuilding had escaped destruction, a small round hut of sticks and mud sitting near the remnants of the orchard, a solitary shadow in the dusk that had now fallen over the marsh. It had a single narrow window and no door, and those features alone would have set it apart, but its survival amidst the ashes suggested that it had been deliberately saved.

He nodded towards it. "What is that place?"

"It's a tomb," Odmar said.

Geirmund looked at the building again. "The Saxons put their dead in wooden tombs?"

"They are living dead," Odmar said.

The oysters turned cold and heavy in Geirmund's stomach. "A haugbui?"

The Dane grinned. "Go and see."

None of the other men spoke. They were all watching Geirmund, waiting, and his unease returned. Odmar played at some mischief, that was plain, but it wasn't clear whether the Dane intended humour or harm. After a few moments of hesitation, Geirmund decided to satisfy his own curiosity, without regard for Odmar's purpose. He left the Danes around their fire in the temple ruins and made his way in the darkness towards the hut, which smelled of shit and piss a dozen paces away. That lifted some of his dread, for the dead did not shit and piss in the tales Bragi told.

As he crept up to the building, he located the waste he was smelling on the ground outside the window, suggesting prison more than tomb. Geirmund approached that window from the side, leaning and stretching his neck to peer within, heard a sloshing sound, and caught a brief glimpse of a pale, wild man just as something flew at his face. He ducked out of the way, barely dodging a cascade of more shit and piss that splashed on the ground.

The Danes back at the fire burst into laughter, and Geirmund's face turned hot. At first he cursed himself for a fool, but soon enough he wore a grudging smile at the prank. The man inside the hut did not laugh, and he was unlikely to be smiling either as he shouted and cursed in the Saxon tongue, which Geirmund found he could mostly understand.

"Keep away, you pagan devil!" he shouted.

Geirmund looked at the quantity of waste the man had just thrown out of the window and doubted there could be more in reserve, so he risked a second glimpse.

The Saxon wore the clothing of a priest, though his robes were filthy, and his tangled hair and beard hid much of his face. When he saw Geirmund, he threw himself at the window, howling from dry, cracked lips, and Geirmund retreated again.

"Leave him!" Odmar shouted, still laughing, and waved Geirmund back to the temple.

He looked one more time at the strange doorless hut, and then returned to the circle. The Danes taunted and pointed at him, still quite amused, and Geirmund held up his hands, nodding his admission that he'd been well tricked.

"You're quick, Northman," Odmar said. "Several of these warriors had to go and swim in the river after talking to that dead man."

"Why do you say he's dead?" Geirmund asked.

"I told you. That is his tomb."

Geirmund frowned, still confused, and Odmar swatted Fasti on the shoulder.

"Tell him."

The younger Dane cleared his throat. "Some Christian priests will go into a hut like that to pray to their god, and then they are sealed inside. Then another priest prays over that priest to say he is now dead."

"The priests choose to go into the hut?"

Fasti nodded.

"Do they ever come out?"

"No," Fasti said. "Their god forbids it."

Odmar laughed. "Some of them come out when we light their tombs on fire."

Geirmund wondered how many of the charred buildings around them had been huts like the one left standing. "Why did you spare him?" he asked.

"I want to see if he is really dead," Odmar said. "No man can die twice."

"What about the priests I saw in the river?" Geirmund asked. "Did they die twice?"

"They left their tombs," Odmar said. "If it is some Christian galdur, maybe the priests lose their power if they come out. A haugbui and a draugr can be slain." He leaned towards Geirmund and pointed at the lone hut. "No food or water. If that one dies in there, then he was never dead, and there is no power."

The marsh had come alive with night-sounds all around the island: frogs and singing insects. Geirmund looked into Odmar's eyes. He saw fear there, and hatred. "What did the priests do?" he asked.

"What?"

"You said you were here to keep them obedient. How did they disobey?"

Odmar leaned back. "They refused to give us their silver."

"They had no silver," a Dane said from the other side of the fire. "We came here for–"

"All priests have silver!" Odmar shouted.

Fasti looked at the ground. "Not these dead priests."

Odmar leapt to his feet, spitting fury. "Does any man wish to challenge me?" He pulled his bearded axe free and pointed it at the circle of warriors in a long, slow arc. "Speak! Let us settle things between us right now."

When none of the Danes made an answer to him, he sat down again, and that put an end to all talk afterwards. The warriors drifted apart and settled for sleep, wrapped in their cloaks, and Geirmund laid himself down also. He knew that doing so was a risk, but if they had wished him ill, they could have killed him before he ate a share of their oysters, or at any time since, and he was glad for the fire to keep him warm.

He fell asleep quickly, but in deepest night a distant wail startled him awake. For several moments he lay there in the dark, a chill at the root of his neck, unsure if he had heard an animal, a man, or something else that haunted the marshes. It had been a sound of suffering and pain. Geirmund thought it might have come from the priest, and he couldn't sleep after that for wondering if the dead man had died.

It seemed none of the Danes around him had stirred at the sound, but Geirmund got to his feet and crept from their midst towards the hut. When he reached the outbuilding, he stood near the window to listen for signs of life within.

He heard whispering, in a tongue that he did not understand, and the dread he had felt when he'd first approached the hut returned, thinking perhaps the priest now worked some magic or curse. But the longer he listened, the less it sounded like galdur and the more it sounded like a prayer to his god.

That meant the man was alive, or at least as alive as he had been when he threw shit from his window. Satisfied, Geirmund moved away, but his sleeve caught against the hut's rough skin.

The priest's whispering ceased. "Is someone there?" he asked, speaking once more in the Saxon tongue that Geirmund understood, his voice hoarse and weak.

"Yes," Geirmund said, softening his voice. "But I won't harm you."

The priest chortled, but it was the pained laughter of the mad and the doomed. "Perhaps you should harm me. Perhaps you should end my misery the way you ended the lives of my brothers."

"I didn't," Geirmund said. "I'm not with these Danes."

"No? Who are you with, then? By your speech you are no Saxon."

"I am with…" Geirmund paused. "Other Danes."

The priest laughed again. "I am certain there are many kinds of devil, but none of them serve God."

Geirmund glanced back at the Dane camp to see if any warrior had awakened, but they all appeared to sleep. "Are you alive in there, priest?"

"What manner of question is that? I'm speaking with you, aren't I?"

"I ask because the Danes say another priest prayed over you as if you were dead when you entered your hut."

"Ah. That is a pagan's understanding." He groaned, and Geirmund heard rustling, and when the priest spoke again he stood near the window. "My body did not die when I became an anchorite. When I entered my anchorhold, I forswore the world outside it, forsaking all wealth and title, and that is treated as a kind of death."

Geirmund shook his head. Priests who forsake wealth and title will have no silver to steal, and Odmar could have known that if he had simply asked them. "That means you can still die in there," Geirmund said.

The priest sighed. "Yes, that means I can still die, and I hope to die very soon. I have asked God to release me from this torment, but thus far he has left me here, perhaps for some purpose I do not yet see."

"Why do you not end your own life?"

"That is a sin against the god I pray to."

"So you cannot leave, but you also cannot end your life? Your god dishonours you."

"How so?"

"He denies you the right to meet your fate in the manner of your choosing."

"That is a pagan's understanding."

Geirmund understood the situation well enough to know that he would never pray to such a god, but he pitied this priest in his prison who did. "Would your god let you accept water from a pagan?"

A moment of silence passed. "Yes," the priest said. Geirmund heard more movement inside, and then the priest extended his arm through the window, holding a plain wooden cup. "Will the other devils punish you for this?" he asked.

Geirmund took the cup and stalked away from the hut, and from the Danes, through a corner of the burnt orchard, towards the river on the opposite side of the island from the corpses of the other priests. The thorny bramble scratched him as he stumbled in the darkness, but he eventually reached the bank and filled the man's cup. Further along the river to the west he glimpsed several dark shapes on the water and knew them to be the boats that had brought the Danes to this place. Then he stood and looked down at the cup, hoping the water here was clean.

Back at the hut, he handed the cup through the window, then listened as the priest gasped and guzzled the water down. "Bless you, pagan," he said.

"Do you bless me?" Geirmund asked. "Or does your god bless me?"

"I ask my god to bless you," the priest said with a sigh.

Geirmund shrugged. "I will accept a favour or gift from any god. Or any smith."

The priest laughed as through clenched teeth. "I should not have accepted that water from you. It will only delay my death. But it was a balm, so perhaps you were sent by God."

"No god sent me, priest. I am here by my choice."

"Then I am grateful you chose to show me a kindness," the priest said. "My name is Torthred. What is yours?"

"I am Geirmund."

"I am pleased to have met you, Geirmund. Now I wish to pray and then sleep. But I would say one more thing to you." He stepped up to the window, his eyes and face barely visible in the darkness.

"I think you do not belong with these Danes. I think they would kill you with little reason."

Geirmund agreed with him. "I would also say one more thing to you. If your god wants you to stay and starve and die alone when you could leave and keep making offerings to him, then your god is a fool."

Torthred didn't argue. He simply smiled, bowed his head, and retreated into the deep shadows within his hut.

Geirmund turned and looked at the ruins of the temple, thought about Odmar and his Danes, and decided not to return to their circle. Instead, he went back to the river the same way he had gone to fetch the priest his water, and then he crept down the bank towards the boats.

It would be a simple matter to take one of them, and Geirmund quickly had the nearest vessel untied and ready to push off. But then he heard a footstep behind him and turned to see a figure advancing, someone set to watch the ships, though it was too dark to see who it was.

"What are you doing?" the Dane asked. The voice belonged to Fasti.

"The rope wasn't secure." Geirmund pulled his knife from its sheath, trying to keep it hidden, knowing he had only moments to avoid death at the hands of this Dane or Odmar. "I needed to tie it."

"Liar." Fasti was now only a pace away. "You were trying to steal it." He inhaled to shout and raise the alarm, but Geirmund lunged and plunged his knife into the warrior's throat, up to the handle, silencing him before he could.

Fasti seized Geirmund's wrists, and his eyes went wide enough for the whites to show. He gurgled and sputtered, and Geirmund's hand grew warm and wet with Dane-blood as he lowered Fasti to the ground. Then he jerked his knife free, trembling, heart drumming, and returned to the boats, aware that he needed to put distance between himself and the Danes. Odmar was not a man to let such an insult go unpunished. He would give furious chase, and he seemed to know the fenland well. But Geirmund had no axe to harm the other boats in a lasting way and refused to steal a dying man's weapon, and anyway, such noise would rouse the Danes.

Fasti twitched and kicked weakly in the grass as Geirmund went to each of the boats, gathered up all their oars, and threw them into his vessel, knowing Odmar would find it difficult to push upriver without them. Then he launched his boat and leapt aboard.

10

The river's current wasn't strong, but the boat was Saxon-built, both heavy and large, with three oarlocks to a side. Geirmund scrambled up to a forward thwart, dragging two oars with him, and the river had pulled him a short distance downstream by the time those wooden blades slapped the water.

For speed he rowed facing the stern, with his back to the river ahead, and watched the island where Fasti lay dying or dead. He listened for the shouting of Danes and searched the thorny bushes for signs of movement, but all seemed quiet near Odmar's boats until the fenland took them from Geirmund's view.

It was only then that he paused in his oarstroke to dip his hands and his knife in the river to wash away the blood. When he'd left Rogaland, he expected the first man he killed to be a Saxon on the field of battle, not a Dane in the shadows of a marsh, but now he wondered how much the difference between them mattered. The Three Spinners determined the length of every life-skein, which meant that Fasti had reached the end of his, whether at Geirmund's hand or by some other means. What mattered, then, was not whether Fasti had died, but whether Geirmund had needed to kill him. He knew that if he could have avoided killing Fasti, he would have, and decided then that, as a tool of fate, he could and always would choose honour.

Something moved in the reeds to his left, and though it vanished as he turned to look, he thought he had glimpsed the pale face of a woman, and he wondered if he'd seen a river-vættr. He didn't want the spirit to mistake him for one of the Danes who had fouled its water with corpses, but he had only silver to offer. He dropped a piece into the current to be safe, shivered, and then rowed hard, wanting to be away from that place.

In time the fenland lifted out of night into day, and Geirmund watched the sun rise dull and distant through the fog that overhung the marsh. Just past that first daymark, the river he travelled met with another wider waterway, and not far from that joining he arrived at a second town.

It was larger than Ancarig, but like Ancarig, it too had been put to fire, though not so recently. Geirmund assumed it to be Medeshamstede, the place Fasti had mentioned having a stone temple, but as he rowed the length of the settlement he saw that not every building had been burned, and not every Saxon had been slaughtered. A few round huts remained standing, off in the trees, and people moved about near the waterline, washing, filling jugs and basins, and taking to the river in boats. They looked up at Geirmund's passing, but their eyes were hollow, their empty stares too defeated to hold either interest or fear.

He soon came to a wooden wharf built in the same manner as the causeway at Ancarig, where it seemed traders and travellers landed when visiting Medeshamstede or its Christian temple. Geirmund decided to make a brief stop there, to buy food if the townsfolk had any to sell, and perhaps learn how he might journey to Readingum. He rowed up to the dock and tied his boat there, then felt for Völund's arm-ring beneath his tunic to make it secure.

A worn track led him from the wharf, through a wood of alder and willow, to a broad meadow, and over that place towered what was left of the stone temple. Its roof had burned and fallen in, but its walls, though blackened and scorched, rose high and firm upon the building's heavy foundations.

An encampment lay beside the temple near its arched doorway, and Geirmund recognized the men there as priests by the robes they wore. There were five of them, and three Saxon men who looked to be warriors of a sort, as well as a young fair-headed boy. One of the priests worked with hammer and chisel at a large block of white stone, filling the meadow with the sharp chime of his regular strikes, but Geirmund was too far away to see what he carved.

Another of the priests shouted an alarm at Geirmund's approach, and then a third stepped forward, flanked by two of the Saxons, both bearing cudgels. The priest approached Geirmund holding up his open, empty hands, but shook his head in anger, the hair of which had been shaved like a crown.

"No, no, no," he said. "The Danes have stolen all our silver. They have plundered our food stores and taken the lives of the abbot and every monk, save us few and that novice boy. What more do you want of us?"

"I am no Dane's mouthpiece," Geirmund said.

"What do you want?" the priest shouted.

"Two things. First, I would buy food and ale..."

The priest's mouth hung open. "You–you would..." He blinked, and then raised his voice. "Look around you, Dane! Look what your people did! And you come seeking trade and hospitality? We will sell you nothing!"

"You have nothing to sell?" Geirmund asked. "Or you won't sell to me?"

"The answer to either is the same to you. You are a pagan and a devil, and you will find no comfort here. Be off with you."

Geirmund was hungry, thirsty, and tired from rowing. "I can see you have lost much," he said. "But you could yet lose more, and you would be wise to mind your tongue." The Saxon warriors at the priest's side glared at him, and Geirmund wished he had more than a knife. "I come to you in peace, priest, to deal fairly. When I found one of your kind thirsty, I gave him water–"

"I care not." The priest pointed a finger at Geirmund. "The only water you will get from me is the water of baptism." He paused. "In fact, yes." He glanced back towards his encampment, nodding to himself. "If you renounce your pagan gods and become a Christian, right here and now, we will gladly share what we have with you."

Geirmund didn't know if the priest offered the bargain sincerely, or if he'd said it expecting Geirmund to refuse, but in reply he simply laughed and asked, "What does your companion carve in that stone?"

The priest stood up taller. "The image of Christ Jesus and his followers."

Geirmund glanced at the burnt temple. "Why does he honour your holy man that way? Your god failed to protect his own temple, and the lives of his priests. Why would I pray to such a deity?"

The man's face turned red. "We are few, but we can surely kill one swordless Dane, and we would be doing God's work."

Geirmund did not believe any of the priests there could kill him, but the warriors would surely try, and if he would get nothing from them, it would be foolish to tarry overlong in that place when Odmar might even then be pursuing him. He bowed his head and backed away, hands raised. "Calm yourself, priest. No more blood need be spilled."

The priest said nothing, but stood his ground, willing to let Geirmund go. So he left the meadow and returned through the wood. Before he reached the river he heard someone rushing up from behind in the trees and wheeled round, ready to fight. But it was only one of the other priests, holding out a piece of bread.

"It's hard as stone," he said. "But it is yours if you want it. I won't even demand that you become a Christian."

Geirmund peered into the forest and listened, but neither heard nor saw anyone else. He stepped towards the man and took the bread, which would need to be soaked before he could chew it. "Why do you give me this?"

"My god commands that I feed the hungry."

"My gods do not, but I thank you."

"You're clearly no Dane," the stranger said. "Are you from Finnland? Bjarmaland?"

"My mother came from Bjarmaland." Geirmund now looked more closely at the priest, somewhat surprised at his knowledge. He was a small man, with short brown hair, smooth cheeks and a nose like the edge of an axe. "How do you know of Bjarmaland?" Geirmund asked.

"I have read about it, as many have. Your features match the description of the people who live there, but also of the Finns."

"I am no Finn. I come from Rogaland."

"The North Way?" His expression darkened a shade. "Not a Dane, but as evil as a Dane, they say."

Geirmund grinned. "Worse."

"I am called John," the priest said.

That was a common Frakkar name. As Geirmund remembered the traders from the south that he'd met, he saw some of their features and manners in this priest. "And you are no Saxon," he said.

"I am Saxon," John said. "But I come from Frankia, so I am called an Old Saxon. What is your name?"

"Geirmund."

"Welcome to Medeshamstede, Geirmund of Rogaland."

"There is no welcome here," Geirmund said. "Even your god seems to have abandoned this place."

John tipped his head slightly, and though he made no reply, he smiled, as if enjoying the taste of his words rather than the sound of them. "Back in the meadow, you said you came here for two things. Firstly, to buy food, but what was the second?"

"I wish to learn the way to a place called Readingum."

"In Wessex?" John frowned. "You are nearly one hundred miles from there."

"You know the way?"

He nodded. "I do. If you follow this river west for another five miles or so, you will come to–" He paused, and then he looked over his shoulder, back towards the meadow. "Wait here. I'll return shortly." Then, without another word, he ran off, back through the trees.

Geirmund watched him go, somewhat bewildered. He saw no threat in this Old Saxon priest called John, but he had little patience to offer any Christian, even a friendly one, and resolved not to wait for him.

A few moments later, as Geirmund stood in his stolen boat, ready to push off, John came rushing from the trees for the second time, now carrying a leather sack. He called to Geirmund, waving as he ran towards the river, and then his boots thudded on the wharf.

"I asked you to wait for me," he said, panting. "I am travelling that way. I'll go with you and show you the road."

His offer surprised Geirmund, and he nodded in the direction of the temple. "They will let you go?"

"Let me go?" John turned to look, his brow furrowed. "Oh! No, they do not count me among their number. I am not a monk."

"A monk?"

"Yes, a monk. Those men at the abbey are monks. Think of them as priests who often live and pray together in the same place until they die."

That suggested the priests at Ancarig had been monks. "Then what are you?"

"I am a priest who may come and go wherever God sends me."

"And where does your god send you?"

"Often, it is not until after I have arrived at a place that I realize I have been sent there." He tossed his leather sack into the Saxon boat. "But at this moment I am sure he sends me with you."

Geirmund had wanted a boat and a guide when he first entered the fenland. Now he had both, so perhaps it was not the priest's god who sent him but fate. "Get in," Geirmund said.

John bowed his head in thanks. Then he stepped from the wharf into the boat, tripping as he clambered to settle himself on the middle thwart. "Your boat is in possession of an excessive number or oars."

Geirmund pushed off from the wharf, into the river's current. "A boat goes nowhere without oars."

"Quite true." John tipped his head to the side in the same manner as before. "Five days ago, a large company of Danes left Medeshamstede in several boats like this one." He looked at the rest of Odmar's oars. "It seems they go nowhere."

Geirmund set his arms and back to rowing. "Let us hope not."

"May I ask where have you come from this morning?"

"Ancarig."

"That is a holy place," John said. "How do those monks fare?"

"Worse even than here," Geirmund said. "All slain, except for one in a hut. He is called Torthred."

"Torthred? I've heard of him. A godly man, by reputation. He had a brother, I believe, Tancred, and a sister, Tova. Did you see either of them?"

"I saw no other priest," Geirmund said, thinking that if he had seen the sister, he had wasted a piece of good silver. "Torthred was alive when I left him, but I think not for much longer."

"Is he the thirsty priest you spoke of?"

"He is." Out on the open, wide river, Geirmund felt the heat of the rising sun on his brow. "But he is also a fool. He should have left his hut to be a free priest, like you."

John was silent, and then he sighed. "This conquest by the Danes is as the coming of an evil night. But there are candles burning in the darkness, casting what light they can to push it back."

Geirmund didn't know if the priest referred to Torthred as a light, or if he referred to himself, or even if he thought of Geirmund as one of the candles, but he didn't ask. "What is five rests from here?"

"Five…? Ah, yes." He pointed upriver, over Geirmund's shoulder. "The Romans called it Durobrivæ. It was a small walled city, and a fortress, but it is no more. Much of its stone was plundered to build the abbey at Medeshamstede."

"Why do we go there?"

"Because the Romans also built roads, and now the Danes use them. Durobrivæ is where you will meet with Earninga Street, which will take you south towards Readingum."

"I see," Geirmund said. "Thank you."

John glanced up into the sky, which seemed bluer and clearer to

Geirmund than it had been over the marsh, and as he rowed the land to the north and south of the river seemed to be drying out, opening into a country of heath and forest.

"It is I who should perhaps thank you," the priest said.

"Why?"

"Because I would like to travel with you."

Geirmund paused for a moment in his oarstroke, taken aback. "I have not been long in England," he said, "but I think it is rare for a priest to seek a pagan for a travel companion."

John nodded. "That is true. But this land is changing. I left Northumbria because it has become overrun with Danes, and by the time I reached East Anglia it also had been conquered. I fear Mercia will fall next, and then only Wessex will remain. I am beginning to think that one day soon the priest who won't travel with a pagan will travel alone." He tipped his head to the side. "But I would not ask to travel with just any pagan."

"Only the swordless ones," Geirmund said.

"Ah, yes, about that." John reached for his sack and fished around inside it. "I think you will make better use of this than I will," he said, and pulled out a seax in a leather sheath that was both long for a knife and short for a sword. It had a wooden handle and a simple pommel of iron. "The blade isn't Frankish steel, but it will cut."

With each moment Geirmund spent with this priest, the less he understood the man and the more he believed him possibly mad. "You would give a blade to your enemy?"

"I didn't realize you were my enemy." John rested the seax across his thighs. "Saxons and Danes might be enemies, but that does not mean John and Geirmund need be foes. I consider no man my enemy."

Those words struck Geirmund. John seemed younger than his

father Hjörr by many summers, but he spoke with the wisdom of an old man. "You remind me of a skald I know," he said. "Bragi Boddason is his name."

"Is he a friend?"

That was not the word Geirmund would have chosen to describe Bragi, but it wasn't wrong. "A kind of friend, yes."

"And what would Bragi Boddason advise you to do?"

Geirmund pulled a few strokes on the oars, considering his answer before giving it. "He would remind me that I have no sword, and that you are offering me one, and he would say you are likely a fool, but also that you mean me no harm."

"Most of that is true," John said, and then he nodded. "The seax is yours."

A small hawk lifted out of the grass to the south and shrieked at them before flying off. Geirmund watched it go, wishing he could see through its far-reaching eyes. "If you mean to travel with me," he said, "you should know I go to do battle with Saxons."

"I may be a fool, Geirmund of Rogaland, but I assumed as much. That is why I do not plan to go to Readingum with you. Two days south of here lies a crossroads at a place called Roisia, where you will take the Icknield Way to Wessex. I will continue south to Lundenwic."

"Lunden? What awaits you there?"

"A ship, I hope, that will carry me to my home in Saxony. Unless God has plans to send me elsewhere."

"I suppose you will know when you arrive."

"I usually do," John said.

The river curved and swung around several times in wide arcs, back and forth, before they came in sight of Durobrivæ, and the priest had been right about the state of it. From the river Geirmund could see that the city walls, which may have been impressive when first built, had been reduced to a height that wouldn't keep sheep in pasture. But as he brought the boat around the last bend in the waterway and landed it against the south shore, he saw that the useful Roman bridge, at least, had survived. They pulled the boat deep into the reeds and left it behind, then climbed the embankment.

They paused there in the shadow of the bridge, and chewed on some of the hard bread John had given him. Then Geirmund tied the seax to his belt, John slung his pack over his shoulder, and together they stepped onto the road.

To the right, the street crossed the river over the bridge and continued north–all the way to Jorvik, according to John. To the south, the road passed under a lonely arch, white as bone, that appeared to have been a gate in the city walls, and then it cut through the abandoned town, right down the middle, straight as a bowman's arrow.

"Have you seen Roman handiwork before?" John asked as they entered the ruins.

"Never," Geirmund said quietly.

Though none of the buildings remained whole, he could sight their foundations in the bushes and trees that had returned to reclaim the land. The lines and shapes of those walls almost seemed to form enormous runes in the ground, speaking of what had been in a tongue that Geirmund could barely comprehend or believe. It seemed that some of the Roman halls there had been larger than Hjörr's, supported by stone columns as thick as trees. The city covered at least fifty acres, and John had said it was small. Even the street they walked on was unlike any road he had travelled. It was six fathoms wide, made of crushed stone packed hard, and where there were ruts, they were shallow. As Geirmund moved through the city, he felt the vanished builders surrounding him, and in their presence he kept his steps light and his voice quiet, fearing to wake the dead that still dwelt there.

They walked for nearly half a rest before reaching the southern end of the ruin, and as they left through its gate Geirmund sighed, relieved of an oppressive and weighty dread, glad to leave that place behind.

"If you had been to Rome, as I have," John said, looking back, "you would see this for the small way station it is."

Geirmund wanted to call him a liar, but John did not seem like that sort of man. "It is a haunted place," he said instead.

"Do you believe the dead can harm you?" asked John.

"I do," Geirmund said. "Do you not?"

"No."

"But you said the Danes use these Roman roads."

"And so they do. What of it?"

"Then it seems the dead Romans do you harm by speeding your enemy closer."

John smiled and nodded. "So they do. And perhaps that should not be surprising, for the Romans were once pagans, too."

11

The Romans had cut their road along the western edge of the great fenlands, through a flat country of heath and forest. As they walked, Geirmund learned that his path through the marsh had been a fortunate one, for he had crossed the fenland north of its true vastness. If he'd gone directly south from the bay where he had washed up, he would have been snared for many days in a territory some forty rests in length. He saw this for himself as they travelled south, and the fenlands pushed their bogs westward, at times within sight and reach of the road.

To the east a lowland of green stretched as far as Geirmund could see, a country of thick woods, gentle rises, and endless open fields for planting and grazing, but he saw no houses, no halls, no crops, and no livestock. It was the sort of land Geirmund had come to England seeking, and it seemed to be lying there for the taking, unclaimed and unused.

"Does this land belong to anyone?" he asked.

"All land belongs to someone," John said. "We are west of the Ouse and the Granta, which means we are in Mercia. I know of no ealdorman here, so I suppose this land belongs to King Burgred."

"Ealdorman?"

"A kind of jarl. But we are near the border with East Anglia, which means there may now be Danes who believe they have claimed it."

Several rests from the Roman city, through the trees, a shimmer of water appeared to the west across the marsh, broad enough on the horizon to be an inland sea. John said it was called Witlesig, after a village on its far shore, and it was one of many such meres, shallow and full of fish and fowl.

They walked a full three rests before the shimmer of the Witlesig sea came to an end. Another three rests beyond that, cultivated fields appeared out of the forest to the west. Then Geirmund sighted a village ahead, at the edge of the marsh. He saw no smoke rising from its houses, and heard no sounds, as though it were as empty as the Roman ruin had been.

"Do you know that place?" he asked the priest.

"Not with certainty. But I made a study of the road before leaving Northumbria, and that may be called Salters Stream."

"It looks abandoned."

"Perhaps it is." He stopped in the road and turned to face Geirmund. "If we meet Danes on the road, then I am your captive. If we encounter Saxons or Middle Angles, then we are messengers on our way to Lundenwic."

Geirmund nodded, and they continued towards the village.

When they reached it, they found it empty, just as it had seemed from afar, with only a few chickens left pecking in the dirt. It was a small settlement, with several huts gathered around a modest hall, along with workshops, byres, and a few other outbuildings. The undisturbed condition of the place suggested it had not been long abandoned, nor had it fallen victim to Danes intent on destruction.

"The villagers can't be hiding in the fens or the woods," Geirmund said. "They took everything, even their carts and wagons."

"They must have gone west, deeper into Mercia. With Danes on the march, and Danes at their border, this place is hardly safe." The priest looked round. "But it will serve us well enough. We'll find no better quarters to spend the night."

Geirmund agreed, so they went to the hall, thinking it the most preferable of the buildings in which to sleep, and found it dry and comfortable inside, about the length that Guthrum's ship had been. A few old benches remained, but by the shape of the charcoal left in the hearth, Geirmund could see that someone had used another bench or two as fuel, rather than searching for dry wood in the nearby forest.

"We're not the first travellers to use this place," he said.

Unlike the hall at Avaldsnes, which was entered at the middle of its length, the door to this Saxon hall lay at one end. John moved past Geirmund towards the other wall, where the wall bore a kind of shadow where something had hung for a long period of time and changed the colour of the wood in the shape of a cross, like the one the priest wore around his neck, except larger.

"Was this a Christian temple?" Geirmund asked.

"No. But the people of this place were good Christians. I assume they continue to be, since they took their cross with them."

For food Geirmund went outside, snatched one of the chickens, and twisted its neck. After giving it a rough plucking, he cleaned it using water from a nearby stream and roasted it over a fire made from wood he gathered. As night fell, the aroma of sizzling meat filled the hall, along with the faint smell of burning feathers. Then a storm came, pounding the roof with rain and rumbling with distant thunder. Geirmund was glad they had stopped there for rest, and grateful the hall stayed warm and dry as he ate his chicken and sucked on the bones. He even felt contented there at Salters Stream. It was a humble place, but it had a fine house and good land, the sort of demesne he wanted for himself, and there it was, abandoned and empty.

"With a few good warriors and their families," Geirmund said, "I could settle this place and hold it."

"Against an army of Danes?"

"Against bandits and thieves, after the war is won."

The fire in the hearth cast a glow that touched the rafters and walls of the hall with red, as outside the rain turned the dark night to pitch.

"It is a good place," John said, looking around and nodding. "You can be sure that many have known it. Before this land belonged to Mercians, the Britons were here, and before their tribes there were the Romans, who conquered another people here before them. Wave after wave breaking on these shores."

"That is the way of things," Geirmund said. "Land breeds war."

"Must it be so?"

"Yes, if all land must belong to someone."

"I disagree. I believe that if all lands submit to the One True God in baptism and common Christian faith, there could be peace between kingdoms."

Geirmund scoffed at that. "Envy is the end of peace. No god or goddess, no matter how powerful, can deny the greedy man his nature."

"You are right, of course. It is we who must deny the temptations of our fallen nature and submit to the will of God."

"Then you Christians are nothing but thralls to your god."

The priest tipped his head in amusement. "If we are, it is a curious bondage, for I have yet to meet a thrall who is willingly bound."

Geirmund felt his eyes growing heavy. "Enough priest talk for now."

"Very well," John said.

As Geirmund fell asleep, he heard John praying silently, but that did not keep him awake, and neither did the storm. It was the sudden ceasing of the rain that woke him just before sunrise, and because he couldn't fall back to sleep, he left the hall and returned to the stream. There he stripped himself of his armour and clothing, careful of Völund's arm-ring, and washed himself in the cold water. The forest leaves around him continued to shed delayed rain, and birds came out from their shelters to sing.

Back at the hall, Geirmund found the chicken roost and recovered a few eggs, which he knew would be free of chicks, for he had not seen or heard a cock in the yard. He found a bucket that had been left behind, which he washed and filled at the stream, and he used stones from the fire to heat the water enough to cook the eggs in their shells. John didn't wake until the eggs were ready, and then he simply sat up and bit into his whole, crunching up the shells with his teeth as he stared at nothing. Geirmund peeled his first, and after they had both breakfasted they resumed their southward journey.

Though the storm had moved on, heavy clouds still held the battlefield of the sky, threatening rain for much of the day without sending more than an occasional fine mist. A road of plain earth would have been turned to mud overnight and become difficult, or even impassable, but the Romans' use of crushed rock let the water drain through, leaving the path firm and easily travelled.

The country they passed through remained much the same as the previous day, forest and field, though more of the land they saw had been put to good use. They also found a few more small villages and holdings, all abandoned as Salters Stream had been, but some had seen more destruction by travellers, or by those hoping to find hidden wealth left behind.

At mid-morning, after they'd walked almost four rests, the road turned slightly to the east, towards a gap between two low hills on the horizon. Geirmund smelled smoke.

"Is there a village ahead?"

"There is, yes, a place called Godmundceaster, but it is still some distance away."

They proceeded with caution after that, especially when passing through stretches of wood that had been allowed to grow close to the road, affording robbers easy concealment, and soon they could not only smell smoke but also see it rising from the trees. Dozens of campfires burned across the land between the two hills, but did not seem to belong to a village or town.

"Danes," Geirmund said.

"I believe you are right," John said. "But we are still in Mercia, where King Burgred rules."

"If they are Danes, then Burgred doesn't rule here. This is Daneland."

The priest paled but nodded. "Then we go into Daneland. I am hereafter your thrall."

Geirmund felt he had to be honest with the priest. "When Danes look at me, they do not see another Dane. They don't see a Northman. If they distrust me, this could go badly for us, but especially for you."

"Then I will trust in God that the Danes trust in you."

Geirmund sighed. "I did warn you, priest."

They walked another half a rest, but not so quickly as they had travelled earlier that morning, as if their feet were reluctant to tread that road, knowing who had claimed it. Geirmund believed that if he were alone he could overcome any suspicion and convince these Danes of his name, but the presence of the priest, thrall or not, would give them pause and make Geirmund less convincing. He began to plan what he could say in his defence, wondering if he could safely claim that John belonged to Guthrum, and that the Christian was important to the jarl somehow.

"Ho, Father!" a voice called from the woods to the west.

Geirmund turned in that direction, weapon drawn, and saw a Saxon warrior approaching them through the trees, looking sodden and sullen, and not at ease with the armour he wore or the spear in his hand.

"Good day!" John said. He sounded quite overjoyed at the sight of the stranger, and Geirmund couldn't tell if the priest meant that to put the warrior at ease, or if he truly felt it at the sight of another Saxon. "How fare you this day?" John asked.

"I wish it were dryer, and I wish I were home instead of here." The warrior came up to the edge of the road, and Geirmund kept his seax unsheathed at the ready. "What business brings you this way, Father?" the stranger asked.

"Oh, I am but a humble mass-priest," John said, "travelling to Lundenwic."

The warrior shook his head. "I suggest you reconsider that plan. Danes lie to the south. They've fortified the area around Huntsman's Hill."

"Yes, we had noticed that." John nodded and gazed down the road. "It seems a great many Danes are now camped in Mercia."

"There is a peace," the warrior said. "King Burgred and King Halfdan agreed to terms. The Danes can move through Mercia, and they will cause no trouble."

"No trouble?" Geirmund said. "I think the monks at Ancarig and Medeshamstede would say otherwise."

The warrior looked hard at him, at the seax in his hand. "Who are you?"

"He travels with me," John said, "as my hired guard on the road. And he is in the right. We have come from Medeshamstede, where Danes slaughtered the monks and burned the abbey only days ago."

The Saxon looked over his shoulder, deeper into the woods. "We've heard reports of war-bands in the fens. Our border with East Anglia isn't always clear to the Danes. Mistakes have been made."

"Indeed they have," John said. "Deadly mistakes. Costly mistakes."

"Some mistakes can even cost a king his crown," Geirmund added. He knew well that Halfdan would have moved his army through Mercia regardless of any agreement, but he had likely received a payment of gold and silver to cause no trouble, if only for a time. Geirmund also knew the Danes would not be leaving Mercia now that they had a foothold, and Burgred had merely bought a delay in his downfall. "No agreement lasts forever," Geirmund said.

"That's why we're here," the Saxon said. "We're keeping watch over these Danes."

If all Saxons dealt with the Danes so foolishly, then England would surely fall. The man seemed not to comprehend that he had been appointed the task of watching over the very axe that would one day take his head.

John may have understood that also, for he was frowning. "And what do you watch these Danes doing in their camp at Huntsman's Hill?"

"They march," the Saxon said. "They come out of the fens and they turn south."

"Where do they go?" Geirmund asked, though he knew the answer. The Danes marched to Readingum. He simply wondered if the Saxon knew it also.

"They take the Icknield Way to Wessex."

"Does that trouble you?" John asked.

The man shrugged. "So long as they don't turn north or cross Earninga Street, it is not my concern."

"I hope for King Burgred's sake, and for yours, it remains that way." John gestured towards the distant campfires. "If there is a peace, why can we not travel on this road?"

"Oh, you may travel, Father," the Saxon said. "I simply advise against it. Unless you trust the pagans."

John looked at Geirmund. "I trust some pagans."

"Do as you will, Father." The warrior retreated from the road. "May the Lord protect you on your journey."

"May the Lord protect you also," the priest said. "May he protect all of Mercia."

The Saxon vanished back into the wood, returning no doubt to the hidden place from which he and his men watched the road. Geirmund sheathed his seax. "It is no wonder the Saxon kingdoms are falling if they are protected by warriors such as that."

"Most Saxon warriors are farmers," the priest said. "They fight with their ealdorman's fyrd when summoned but would rather be at home with their crops and their flocks."

"And why would your god protect these people from their own foolishness?"

John set off again, heading south. "If you saw a child about to put his hand into the fire, would you not move to stop him?"

"Of course I would. Are you saying that Burgred is a child?"

"No, I am saying that we are all of us God's children."

Geirmund laughed again at the priest's faith. He imagined

Valhalla full of children, all of them crying to Óðinn for milk instead of mead, and he couldn't help his amusement. Óðinn did not want children in Valhalla, and Thór would not grant strength to those who hadn't earned his respect and favour.

"You must think me foolish," John said, "walking into Daneland."

"I knew you were foolish when you gave me a sword."

"And yet you haven't used it to kill me. I would say the Lord has protected me, wouldn't you?"

"Fate has protected you."

The priest tipped his head. "Or perhaps your fate and my god are one and the same. I will have to think on that."

Geirmund found it difficult to consider that comparison. The closer they came to Huntsman's Hill, the more he worried that no deception would succeed. He could hear the distant sounds of the encampment, the loud voices, the animals braying, the trees falling, the iron ringing, but none of that seemed to frighten or disturb the priest. Foolish or not, John walked as though his god had removed his fear.

They saw the first Danes at another Roman bridge, which crossed a wide river John called Ouse. The encampment, Geirmund could now see, lay on the other side of the bridge, on a wedge of land created by a bend in the river. The arrangement reduced the need for extensive fortifications since the river protected it to the west, north, and south. The Danes had only to hold the bridge and defend the encampment's eastern edge. That location also gave the Danes mastery of the road and all who wished to travel it, leaving Geirmund with little choice but to approach the invaders as one of them.

"I am Geirmund Hjörrsson," he said. "I am sworn to Jarl Guthrum."

One of the Danes on the bridge stepped forward. He had two axes, and behind him stood half a dozen men similarly armed, and two bowmen. "Jarl Guthrum isn't here," the Dane said, looking at John. "Where do you come from?"

"I am a Northman of Rogaland. I was taken by the sea in a storm and washed ashore north of here. I travel to join Jarl Guthrum at Readingum, and I bring him a valuable thrall."

"A priest?" The Dane chuckled and looked back at the men behind him, who all joined in his laughter. "How is a priest valuable to Jarl Guthrum?"

Geirmund struggled to find an answer, but none came, and then John spoke.

"I read and write the Saxon tongue," he said, head bowed. "I can read messages that are not meant for the eyes of Danes."

That was not a skill Geirmund would have suggested, but it seemed to give the Dane before them pause. "Come with me," he finally said.

The other warriors on the bridge parted to let them pass, and the first Dane guided them through the encampment to a large open tent where several warriors sat eating and drinking. Two of the men sat in fine chairs and looked alike in their features, especially the pale blue of their eyes, but one of them had grey in his beard. Geirmund assumed them to be father and son.

Their bridge-Dane stopped a few paces from the tent and waited until the older of the two men waved him forward. "What is it?" he asked, eyeing Geirmund and John.

"This man claims to be a Northman sworn to Guthrum, my lord," the Dane said. "And he says the priest is his thrall."

"Does he?" The younger of the blue-eyes rose from his chair. "He does not look like a Northman."

"I am a Northman," Geirmund said. "I am Geirmund Hjörrsson,

and I can speak for myself." He then told what had happened to him, in much the same way he had told it to Odmar, and when he was finished the warriors in the tent were silent. "I ask that you let me pass, to continue my journey to Jarl Guthrum," he said.

The older man crossed the tent to stand before Geirmund. "I am Jarl Sidroc, and this is my son, Sidroc. I know of King Hjörr of Rogaland, and you are ugly enough to be one of the sons in the tales I have heard. But I must be sure."

"What can I say or do to convince you?"

"Nothing, for now," the old jarl said. "I march to Readingum tomorrow, with warriors for Halfdan. Guthrum will be there. You will march with us, and after we arrive at Readingum we will know the truth of what you say from Guthrum. If you have spoken the truth to me, all will be well. If you have lied to me, all will not be well."

Geirmund could accept that easily enough. Guthrum would back him. He had planned to go to Readingum, and with Sidroc's plan he would no longer be travelling alone as he'd expected to after parting ways with John. But John had not planned to go to Readingum, nor had he planned to march with Danes to battle. The priest would not be safe with Halfdan's warriors, and Geirmund did not know what Guthrum would do with John when they reached the end of the journey.

"What of the thrall?" he asked.

"The priest is for Guthrum, is he not?"

"He is."

"Then you will bring him. But he is your charge."

That meant Geirmund would be responsible for any harm John might do, but it did not deal with the harm that might be done to him. "Do I have your word he will remain unharmed until we reach Readingum?"

"Your property will be respected," Jarl Sidroc said, "as it would be for any Dane, and you will have the freedom of the camp."

Geirmund bowed his head. "You are wise and fair."

The old jarl waved him off and returned to his chair. The younger Sidroc stared at Geirmund a bit longer before he also sat, and then the bridge-Dane walked away without a word, returning to his post. Geirmund left the tent and looked for somewhere he and John could talk without being overheard, but also without raising suspicion, and eventually found a place near the river.

"I am sorry, priest," he said.

"For what?"

"You were going to Lundenwic."

"I was," John said. "Now I am going to Readingum."

"But I fear I have put you in danger."

The priest shook his head. "I was the one who ignored your warnings, so it was I who put myself in danger."

"Even so," Geirmund said, "danger is danger."

"And God is good." John smiled. "Think of it as fate, if you must, but know that my god has not stopped leading me since I threw my sack into your boat. Tomorrow we march to Readingum, Geirmund of Rogaland, come what may."

PART THREE

*The Great
Heathen Army*

12

Sidroc the Elder proved true to his word. The Danes had marched for two days, and during that time the jarl and his son had treated Geirmund as one of their three hundred warriors, whereas John had been tolerated or simply ignored, neither treated well nor badly. Geirmund knew that to be only a temporary truce, and the priest remained in danger.

Earninga Street had gradually climbed out of the fenlands and lowlands, and at a crossroads on the second day the Danes had turned westward onto the road called Icknield. That track followed the ridgeway along a range of chalk hills, up and down through wooded dales. Geirmund thought it good land, green and rich, and though it seemed little settled by the Saxons, it would surely be claimed by one of their ealdormen or kings.

At dawn on the third day into their march, Sidroc the Elder summoned Geirmund and John to his tent before the morning fog had cleared. The jarl hadn't brought either of them into his company since the day they'd met him at Huntsman's Hill.

"What do you suppose he wants?" the priest asked as they

made their way through the trees and the waking Danes.

"I don't know," Geirmund said. "But it troubles me."

"We're only a day's march from Readingum," the priest said. "Perhaps he means to limit our freedom for the last part of the journey, until we have been delivered to Guthrum."

"Perhaps," Geirmund said.

When they reached the jarl, they found him waiting with his son and several Danes, all of them fully awakened and armed. The mood in the tent felt as heated as stirred embers, and without knowing why Geirmund believed that he and the priest were in danger. Sidroc the Elder held a piece of parchment, and Geirmund could see that it had been written upon. The jarl stepped forward to face the priest.

"You can read and write, yes?" he said.

John bowed his head. "I can."

"You will read this and tell me what is written." Sidroc the Elder held the parchment towards him.

John hesitated, glanced at Geirmund, and then accepted it. "As you wish, Jarl Sidroc," he said, and then he examined the writing for a few moments. His eyes widened. "It is a message to King Burgred, sent by someone in Wessex to keep Mercia informed of what goes on there."

Jarl Sidroc began to pace. "Go on."

John cleared his throat. "It says the Danes are encamped at Readingum, and their fortifications are strong. King Æthelred of Wessex and his brother, Ælfred, attempted an assault there, but Halfdan had received fresh warriors from the River Thames. The Saxons lost many warriors and were driven back. Among the dead was an ealdorman of Bearrocscire, one Æthelwulf, who had recently defeated a company of Danes in a skirmish at Englefield."

"Is there more?" the younger Sidroc asked, but he wore the

slight smirk of one who already knew the answer.

"Yes, there is more," John said. "Æthelred and Ælfred are now at Wælingford. They hope to draw the Danes out of their fortifications for a battle on open ground at Ashdown." John handed the parchment back to Jarl Sidroc. "That is the end of the message."

Jarl Sidroc looked at John, then took the parchment and gave his men a nod. At that signal the warriors departed from the tent, and Geirmund found himself and John alone with the jarl and his son. The mood had cooled.

"You already knew what the message contained," Geirmund said.

Jarl Sidroc nodded, while the younger Sidroc went on smirking.

"My father is not a fool," he said.

John sighed. "Certainly not."

"I took the opportunity to prove you, priest," the jarl said. "I wanted to know if you would tell me the truth."

"What if I hadn't?" John asked.

"You would be dead." The elder Sidroc spoke as though that answer should have been obvious. "Or dying slowly. But now I shall keep you safe. You will stay behind with the wagons."

"Behind?" Geirmund asked.

"We march." The jarl held up the parchment. "This message was written days ago. The battle may have already been fought, but perhaps it will be today. If it is today, then we must be there for it. But it will be a long, fast march. If Æthelred has strengthened Wælingford, we won't be able to cross the river there. Instead, we will try to cross further south, at the Moulsford. If that is blocked, we will have to go even further south to cross at Garinges, and then travel north to Ashdown. I suggest you find something to eat now, while you can."

Geirmund and John bowed their heads and left the jarl's tent. They then went in search of a cookfire, where they received bowls of porridge with lard. They sat to eat away from the other Danes, and Geirmund asked the priest how he knew not to withhold the true contents of the message.

"Did you know somehow the parchment had been read?"

"No," John said.

"Did you think to lie?"

The priest seemed to consider that question as though he didn't know the answer straightaway. "Perhaps for a moment," he said. "But I thought firstly about my god, who asks me to be truthful, and secondly about what a lie would mean for you, who had vouched for me, and I decided to deal honestly with the Dane."

Geirmund shook his head and ate a mouthful of his porridge. "What do you know of this Wessex king and his brother, Ælfred?"

"I hear they are learned men."

"That does not make them clever."

"But they are said to be clever also, and I hear they are pious and fierce warriors for Christ."

"If they were clever, they would not be Christians." Geirmund chuckled to himself. "Are you a warrior for Christ? Can you fight, priest?"

"Alas, I spent my time learning to use a quill, rather than a sword."

"Can your quill write us to victory, then?"

"It can, even if you lose, but only after the battle has taken place."

Geirmund scoffed. "Your quill can change the past?"

"Only what is said about the past, which is almost the same thing."

As Geirmund finished his porridge, he thought about how different a Saxon tale of war would be from a tale of war told by the Danes, and he understood what the priest meant. When the oldest warrior who fought in a battle dies, and there is no one left who remembers it, the story of that battle can become the field of a new fight. Blood feuds had begun over such things, for tales could make or destroy reputation and honour.

"Can you fight?" the priest asked.

"I learned to fight," Geirmund said. "But I have never been in a battle."

"Are you frightened?"

"I know a man who would say that only fools are never frightened."

"The skald again? Bragi Boddason?"

"No, a man called Steinólfur. With luck we'll see him on the battlefield today." He grinned at the priest. "I'll try not to let him kill you."

"I would be grateful for that."

"Don't fear, priest. You will be safe with the wagons."

"I will pray nevertheless," John said.

The Danes also prayed. Word had spread through the encampment that they marched to Ashdown, and the warriors made offerings to Thór, Týr, or Óðinn, asking for godly favours and strength in the fighting to come. Sidroc the Elder sacrificed a horse before his men, the sight of which seemed to cause John great distress. He tapped himself, drawing a cross from his forehead to his waist, and then he kissed the cross he wore around his neck and clutched it in his hand.

"Did you forget you travel with pagans, priest?" Geirmund asked.

"I did not forget. I think I never truly knew it."

He seemed to almost tremble as he spoke, which Geirmund may have once seen as a sign of Christian cowardice. Having now travelled with the priest for several days, Geirmund knew he was no coward. His distress had another source that Geirmund didn't understand, and he felt a measure of pity for the priest as he bade him farewell.

Jarl Sidroc drove his Danes at a furious speed, and they made quick progress along the ridgeway. Several rests on Geirmund saw a river below, flowing towards them from the north-west bearing many ships up and down. A short distance from there, the Icknield Way and that river came almost together, but the road turned sharply southward and ran a parallel course along the hills above the waterway. Geirmund assumed the fortified town and bridge he saw near the river to be Wælingford, where Æthelred had retreated.

Several more ships had gathered there, and the Saxons could no doubt see Jarl Sidroc's Danes marching south. Geirmund wondered if they would attack or let them pass. To attack would require several hundred men to leave the safety of the walls, which the Saxons either did not have, or did not want to spare, for none emerged to stop them, and on they marched.

After midday they came to the Moulsford and found it unguarded. Directly across the river, at a distance of perhaps one rest, Geirmund could see two armies facing each other from the bald tops of opposing duns, forming human thickets over the land. An open valley lay between them, and it was clear that neither force wanted to give up its high ground to cross the valley and charge at its enemy uphill. The armies were too far away to discern banners or say which was Saxon and which was Dane, but Geirmund assumed the nearest, northern dun to be occupied by Saxons from Wælingford, while Halfdan's Danes held the southern dun, having marched up from their fastness

at Readingum. From their high vantages both would have seen
the arrival of Jarl Sidroc's warriors, and both sides appeared to
possess warriors numbering in the thousands. In such a battle the
appearance of even three hundred swords from a new direction
could change the outcome.

The Moulsford crossed the river near enough the Saxons to put
Jarl Sidroc in a flanking position, on the eastern side of their dun.
Halfdan and Æthelred would undoubtedly see that and move to
answer it, though it was not yet certain how.

Jarl Sidroc ordered his men to ford the river where it flowed
knee-deep over a flat bed of rocks that stretched for nearly fifty
fathoms of its length. Geirmund waded through, watching the
Saxons as the cold water soaked through his boots, and by the time
he reached the other side of the river the Saxons had apparently
chosen to divide their force.

A seam opened in the thicket of warriors, and then its eastern
half moved across the dun towards Jarl Sidroc's Danes, descending
its slope as if a shelf of earth had been loosed and now came sliding
and roaring down, appearing three times as large as Jarl Sidroc's
force. The western half of the Saxon army stayed behind, keeping
its claim to high ground.

Jarl Sidroc ordered his warriors to form lines and march to
meet the enemy, despite their greater numbers. Geirmund had
no shield to stand at the front, so he found himself at the rear
with the warriors who were similarly ill-equipped, or possibly ill-
trained, or perhaps only fearful. But reputation and reward were
not earned by warriors who avoided battle, and Geirmund wished
he could join the true fight.

Away to the south, Halfdan's Danes also divided their force,
to match the Saxons. The eastern wing charged down the face of
the dun, rushing, it seemed, to join Jarl Sidroc's warriors, while

the other half remained on the hill, holding the opposing force in place on their northern peak.

Jarl Sidroc ordered a quickening of his warriors' march over heath and scrub, and around a large thorn tree. Geirmund's feet pounded the ground, and his vision darkened at the edges, as though he ran through a tunnel. They closed the distance between Dane-shield and Saxon-spear, and then the elder Sidroc urged his warriors into a full and howling charge. Geirmund drew his seax and added his roar, his fear rising, but he grappled with it until it turned to rage and fire in his blood.

When the front ranks finally collided, Geirmund stood too far back to see the impact, but he heard it as a roll of thunder down the line, shield against shield, shield against spear, spear against armour and flesh. He readied himself to fight and kill any that might breach the shield-wall, but none came, for neither the Dane or Saxon line had broken on that initial charge.

With the size of the Saxon force, Geirmund thought Jarl Sidroc's Danes should have been overrun, but he quickly realized they only faced a part of the Saxon line. Away to the west, the enemy had formed a second front, creating a wedge to prevent the two Dane forces from uniting. As Jarl Sidroc's men pressed against one wing, the Saxons would no doubt be prepared to receive Halfdan's oncoming warriors at the other. The order went out by horn to push the enemy hard, perhaps to close the wedge and trap the Saxons between Jarl Sidroc's men and Halfdan's.

Despite their efforts, the Danes gained no ground, the ringing of their weapons and bashing of their shields an unceasing storm.

A few warriors closer to the fighting soon dragged the injured and dead from deep within the press, those who had fallen when sword or spear point found a gap between shields. The warriors who brought the wounded out carried them only far enough to prevent them from being trampled, laid their bodies on the heath, and dived back into the fray. Geirmund wasn't yet fighting, so he sheathed his weapon and rushed forward to see how he might offer aid to the fallen.

The first warrior he reached spat blood high in the air with a forceful cough as he clutched at the base of his throat, just above his breastbone. Blood leaked from that wound, but Geirmund knew the greater part of it poured into his lungs. The man heaved himself onto his side, facing away from Geirmund, and coughed again, spraying the ground with red. Terror opened his eyes wide, and Geirmund noticed he had let go of his sword.

He was a dead man, that was certain, and it would not take long. Geirmund could only stay with him until the end, so he grabbed the warrior's sword and reached around him from behind to force the weapon into the man's bloody, slippery hand. Then he pulled that hand close to the warrior's chest, and he held him in a cradled embrace as the warrior thrashed and drowned on dry land. Geirmund closed his eyes, remembering his own drowning, holding fast until the man went still.

A moment passed before Geirmund let go and rolled away. Then he noticed Sidroc the Younger nearby, watching him. The jarl's son was still on his feet, but bent over, holding his hand to a bleeding wound in his side.

"If you need a sword, use his," he said. "Keld would want that. You can always return it when we bury him."

Geirmund nodded. Then he reluctantly took the dead man's sword from his limp and lifeless fingers, wiped its bloody handle in the grass, and looked up to see Jarl Sidroc's Danes falling back. He scrambled to his feet.

The line had not yet broken, but it seemed fragile. The Saxons had somehow pushed the Danes onto their heels and now pressed the advantage, hammering and driving them east the way they'd come, back to the river. In the chaos of that plight Geirmund couldn't see what had become of Halfdan's force, nor the Saxons at that wing of the wedge. He could only draw his seax in one hand and raise Keld's sword with the other to face what was to come.

"Hold them!" he heard Jarl Sidroc bellowing. "Give no ground!"

But the Danes fell back, and sunlight pierced the widening gaps between their shields.

When they reached the large thorn tree, the Saxons finally broke the backbone of Jarl Sidroc's line against it. Shields fell and swung like doors thrown open, letting the enemy through in a snarling flood.

Geirmund shored himself and leapt at the nearest Saxon, swinging his sword and seax in a fury. The warrior took Geirmund's first sword-strike with his shield, but staggered under it, and Geirmund swung again. This time the Saxon blocked with his sword and threw Geirmund's blade and sword arm outward. Geirmund lunged forward, shouldered the Saxon's shield aside and drove the seax backhanded into the man's neck.

Before he had hit the ground, another Saxon charged into Geirmund like an ox, striking his chest with the heavy boss at the centre of his shield, throwing him off his feet. Geirmund stumbled and fell hard on his back, gasping for air as the man came at him with an axe.

Geirmund rolled aside, dodging the blade as it bit into the ground, then swung his sword blindly at the man's legs. He missed, but the Saxon leapt out of the way, which offered Geirmund time to gain his feet. Then he rushed at the warrior, striking high so the man would raise his shield. Then Geirmund dropped and swung low, slashing the man's knee with his seax. The Saxon's leg buckled, and in that moment of imbalance Geirmund swung his sword hard at the man's neck. The cut didn't take his head, but it released his blood in a torrent.

Geirmund wheeled to face his next enemy, only to find Jarl Sidroc's Danes in full, disordered retreat, fleeing towards the river. He caught a distant glimpse of Halfdan's Danes and the Danes on the southern dun, and both now faced their own Saxon onslaughts.

He didn't want to run, but he had no choice. The Saxons had routed them on this front, and to stand and fight there would mean death to the last Dane. But Jarl Sidroc had mentioned another river crossing further south, which might offer a way to circle around, join with Halfdan, and stay in the battle.

Geirmund sheathed his seax and gripped Keld's sword, then turned and charged towards the river with the other Danes.

The Saxons pursued them, cutting them down as they caught them. Spears and arrows struck the water around Geirmund as he ploughed across the ford, dragging his feet through the current. When he reached the other side, he looked back and saw dozens of Danes half submerged in growing blooms of red.

Most of Jarl Sidroc's warriors that made the crossing fled along the track to the south, but some ran northward, back towards Wælingford and death.

"Stop!" Geirmund shouted at them. "Stop, you fools! To Halfdan!"

A few heeded him, but most did not, and Geirmund left them to their fate.

For the next two rests the Saxons harried them, and those Danes that turned to fight were all killed. Geirmund felt the rage of battle subsiding within him, replaced by fear. His body weakened, exhausted by the day's march, fighting, and flight, but on he ran as the sun touched the tops of the duns to the west. When at last he came to the bridge at Garinges, there were Saxons upon it, and more Saxons battling Danes on the other side of the river.

"We must fight our way across!" Geirmund said to the nearest warriors, perhaps eight Danes, and together they charged the bridge.

The Saxons there stood ready to receive them. Geirmund tried with all the strength he could gather to battle his way through, but before he had made it three fathoms a Saxon bludgeon struck his head and sent him over the side of the bridge into the river below.

13

When Geirmund next remembered himself, he was half floating in frigid water, and it was dusk. He looked around, shivering, and discovered he was somewhere on the shore of the river, caught in the bony fingers of a low-hanging branch, surrounded by the sounds of distant fighting, weapons ringing, warriors shouting and crying out in pain.

He then remembered the battle and the retreat of the Danes, and then the charging of the bridge, but nothing after. He decided he must have fallen into the river, but he had no idea how far it had carried him.

When he moved to find his footing on the river bottom, a wave of disorientation crashed over him, spinning his mind, and turning his stomach. He thought he might vomit, but he relaxed back into the water and let himself float there with his eyes closed until the feeling of swimming inside his own head had passed. A painful throbbing on the side of his skull reminded him that he had been wounded.

He knew then that he was in no condition to travel by foot to Readingum. He doubted he could even stay upright for more than two paces, and he certainly couldn't defend himself from any Saxons that might find him. The river seemed to be his only means of escape, and since it had carried him that far, he decided to let it take him the rest of the way, if it chose to.

He wrangled himself free of the branch, and then the current took him, both pushing and pulling him downstream. He did his best to float with his feet first, and to avoid rocks and other obstacles, but he was largely at the river's mercy. His body also wanted to sink, as it had in the sea. He would sometimes sputter and gasp when the water covered his face, but the river was smooth and shallow enough to mostly keep his head above it, except for his ears, which heard nothing but sloshing inside them.

Dusk turned to night, and the river turned black. The chill in the water reached Geirmund's bones, and his mind drifted. He lost track of daymarks and distance, balancing at the edge of wakefulness and dreaming. When he looked up into the sky, he saw the stars and a moon halfway to full. He saw Steinólfur looking down at him from the ship, and the trees along the riverbank became the pillars of the drowned trees outside Völund's hall. Then the moon was gone, and Geirmund wondered if it had already set, or if a cloud had covered it, or if it had simply gone out.

He bumped into things in the darkness, some of them immovable and bruising, some of them floating corpses, both Saxon and Dane, carried by the river just as it carried him, because the current made no distinction between the living and the dead.

The stars eventually faded, replaced by dawn's first light in the sky, and Geirmund wondered how it could already be a new day. He heard voices nearby, and splashing, that were muffled by the river in his ears.

Then something seized his left arm, and his head came fully out of the water. "This one's alive," a voice said. "But not for much longer by the look of him."

"Dane or Saxon?"

There was a pause.

"I don't know."

Geirmund heard more splashing and felt himself dragged against the current. He opened his eyes and saw the dim shapes of two men standing over him.

"He's no Dane," one of them said.

"He doesn't look Saxon either."

"He's got a Saxon knife."

"What should we do?"

"Same as the others. Take what we can use and let the river have the body."

They were Danes.

Geirmund opened his mouth. "Northman," he said.

"Did you hear that?"

"I don't know; he–"

"Not Saxon," Geirmund said, as forcefully as he could, but still barely a whisper. "I am... Northman. Geirmund, sworn to... Guthrum."

There was a pause.

"Better take him to the tent," one of them said. "Find out who he is."

"Right. You take that side?"

Geirmund felt himself lifted, and his head lurched violently. Hearth-sparks and embers flashed in his eyes, and a pain assailed him as though some cursed blacksmith used his head as an anvil. He squeezed his eyes shut, and, when he opened them, he caught glimpses of an encampment, and then he was inside a tent.

"Lay him down there," a new voice said.

The world tipped, and then Geirmund felt firm ground against his back instead of the soft river.

"I'll tell Jarl Guthrum," a voice said, and then one of the shadows moved away.

"Will he live?" another asked.

Geirmund felt someone touching the side of his head, reigniting the searing pain there.

"I don't think his skull is cracked. I'll bind the wound, but, yes, he should live."

Those words were enough for Geirmund to finally release the weak hold he still had on his mind. He closed his eyes and fell into a vast and empty nothing.

When he awoke, the ferocious full light of day struck his eyes. He brought his hand up to cover them and felt a wrapping of linen around his head.

"It's you," a familiar voice said. "How are you here?"

Geirmund peered up, squinting, and saw Guthrum standing over him.

"When last I saw you," said the Dane, "you had stepped into the sea. And now we pull you from the river. How?"

"That tale will–" Geirmund's voice felt as though it dragged sand through his throat, and it sounded too loud in his head. "That will take some time to tell."

"You should not be alive." Guthrum looked at Geirmund just as he had when they were last on his ship, but with even greater doubt and suspicion, and even fear. "You should be dead, Helhide. So, I must ask, what are you?"

Though they were no longer at sea, Geirmund still faced the same mistrust and danger, but his ragged mind struggled to find the words to explain himself. His head pounded against the bindings constricting it, and he wanted only to keep sleeping. He had to do something to prove himself to Guthrum. He had to win the Dane's trust.

"I have…" He reached into his tunic and pulled out Völund's arm-ring, which he held out to show Guthrum.

The Dane said nothing, but he took the arm-ring and looked closely at it.

"I have a gift," Geirmund said.

"A fine gift," Guthrum said. "Never have I seen an arm-ring like it." He turned it over, the light of its gold shimmering across his face. "I accept this gift, Geirmund Hel-hide, and I look forward to the tale of how you came by it."

"I–" Geirmund had not meant the ring as a gift for Guthrum. He had only meant to say it was a gift to him from Völund, but now the Dane had it and believed it to be his, and Geirmund could think of nothing to say to change that without causing confusion and dishonour. "I–"

"Rest now," Guthrum said. "Heal. I will tell your oath-man of your return."

That meant Steinólfur was alive, at least. But then Guthrum left the tent, and Geirmund didn't know how he would get his arm-ring back, or whether he should try, or whether he wanted to. The gift had seemed to change Guthrum's mind towards him somehow, so perhaps there was a reason of fate why Geirmund had thought to present it to the Dane.

He could think no more about it. His mind frayed, and he closed his eyes again. When he next awoke, he felt more himself. The sun had gone down, and Steinólfur and Skjalgi knelt on the ground next to him.

"Did you enjoy your visit to Valhalla?" the older warrior asked. "Or were you in Hel?"

"Neither." At the sight of his friends, tears of exhaustion, relief, and joy formed in Geirmund's eyes. "I'm very glad to see you both."

Steinólfur placed a hand on Geirmund's shoulder. "I'm glad to see y–" His voice started to break, but he grunted it back into place and paused for a moment. "Welcome back, Geirmund Hjörrsson."

Skjalgi took Geirmund's hand and squeezed it hard. "I can't believe my own eyes."

"I thought Guthrum must be lying." Steinólfur shook his head and wiped one of his eyes with his stubby thumb. "Or mistaken somehow."

"How did you come here?" Skjalgi asked.

"I… don't think I can tell that tale yet," Geirmund said. "Not properly. My skull is afire. I don't think I can even sit up."

"Don't try. You took quite a blow." The older warrior gestured towards the right side of Geirmund's head. "The swelling has gone down a bit now, but for a day or two you looked like you were sprouting a second head."

"A day or two? Where am I?"

"Readingum."

"How long have I been here?"

Skjalgi gave Geirmund's hand another squeeze and let go. "They pulled you out of the river four days ago."

"What?" Geirmund tried to remember the passage of that much time, but all was night and mist between the present moment and the battle at Ashdown. "Four days?"

"You were here and there," Steinólfur said. "In and out. Lucky for you, your stubborn head refused to crack, or we might have known for certain whether you've a brain in there. I'd still wager you don't. Why else would you have thrown yourself into the sea?"

"You know why," Geirmund said. "There would have been a fight, and none of us would have lived to speak of it now."

"So be it," the older warrior said. "Or are you confused about what it means to be an oath-man?"

"I'm not confused about what it means to you," Geirmund said. "That's why I didn't ask your permission before I jumped."

Steinólfur looked truly angry with him, but it felt like the frightened anger of a parent towards a reckless child, and Geirmund didn't know if the older warrior wanted to shout at him or embrace him.

Skjalgi spoke instead. "No matter why you jumped," he said, "we thank the gods for your return."

Though Völund had not claimed to be a god, the boy's gratitude did not strike Geirmund as misplaced. "What has happened in the last four days?" he asked. "What occurred at the battle?"

The boy looked at Steinólfur, who clenched his teeth. "The Saxons held the field at the end of the day. The Danes slew many of them, but also suffered great losses." He paused. "Bersi is dead."

"What?" Geirmund found that hard to accept. The Dane-king had seemed a mighty warrior and had only just begun his war. "How did he fall?"

"He led the charge," the older warrior said. "But the battle was disordered. One of Halfdan's jarls came late to the field."

"Jarl Sidroc."

"Yes. How did you know?"

"I fought with him," Geirmund said.

Steinólfur looked puzzled by that, but he went on. "We weren't there. But from what has been said, Halfdan divided his army. The jarls took one force to join with Sidroc, while Halfdan and Bersi led the second. They believed the Saxons would break quickly, having easily defeated them just days earlier."

"Where were you?"

"Here," the older warrior said. "One of the jarls had to stay behind to defend the ships and the encampment. That task fell to Guthrum and his warriors. Many of the jarls who went to the battle were slain."

"Who?"

"The elder Sidroc, and also his son. Osbern, who was at Ribe. Jarl Fræna, and others. It was an evil day."

Steinólfur's account struck Geirmund silent. Jarl Sidroc and his son had met their fates with courage and honour, of that Geirmund would swear. Their sudden presence on the field had altered the shape of the battle, but their warriors could not have changed its outcome. The Three Spinners and the gods had decided that. He only hoped the priest had found his way to safety.

"What now?" Geirmund asked.

"Now?" Steinólfur said. "You mend. And we wait. Ships from Bersi's scattered fleet still come up the river, bringing fresh warriors. The fight is far from lost. I hear we will attack the Saxons again soon, and we need you ready for battle."

Geirmund wanted to nod in agreement, but his head ached, and his eyes fought to close again.

"Sleep," Steinólfur said.

So Geirmund slept, and awoke, and ate, and slept again. For a week he rested, each day regaining more of his strength, until he was finally able to leave the tent to go and stand before Guthrum. As he crossed the encampment, he saw that it was smaller than Ribe, but much larger than Huntsman's Hill, and, like the latter, it had been built on a wide plain at the wedge where two rivers met. Those waterways, lined with many dozens of ships, guarded the encampment to the north and south, and a wall of earthwork and wood had been built to the west. When Geirmund entered Guthrum's tent, he saw Völund's ring gleaming on the Dane's arm.

"Geirmund Hel-hide," he said. "I am glad to have you on your feet."

"I am glad to be on my feet," Geirmund said, bowing his head.

With him in Guthrum's tent were Steinólfur and Skjalgi, while Eskil stood next to the jarl. "But now we come to the question I have waited patiently to have answered," Guthrum said. "How is it you are here?"

Geirmund had already told the story to Steinólfur and Skjalgi several days prior, as soon as he'd recovered enough of his wits to do so. He now related the story to Guthrum, exactly as it had happened. Geirmund's honour, and the evidence of the arm-ring, gave him little reason to lie about it, and he would suffer no man to deny it or call him mad.

Guthrum did neither, nor did Eskil. Instead, the jarl took off the arm-ring and studied it again, as if it had somehow changed in material and quality. "Hnituðr," he said, "forged by Völund the smith?"

"Yes, Jarl Guthrum," Geirmund said. He hadn't yet come up with a way to ask for the ring's return, and Steinólfur had said he would be an utter fool to try. The ring had bought Geirmund's way into Guthrum's favour, and that was not worth the risk of losing again.

"If you were not a true Hel-hide before," Guthrum said, "you are now. Returned from the water as if from the land of the dead. And I hear you fought at Ashdown?"

"I did," Geirmund said. "But I only slew two Saxons before retreating across the ford."

"Then you achieved more than many of the frightened Danes

who were there from what I hear. They say the Saxons fought like wolves."

Next to the king, Eskil frowned, but said nothing.

"They fought hard," Geirmund said. "The Saxons–"

"We will not suffer such a defeat again." Anger flashed across Guthrum's face as he put the ring back on his arm. "Are you ready to fight for me, Hel-hide?"

"I am," Geirmund said. "But I have a question."

"Ask it."

"What became of my sword? It was stowed on the *Wave Lover*, but Steinólfur said it disappeared sometime during the journey."

The king looked at Eskil, who nodded. "I know where it is. My brother has it. He claimed it after you went into the sea."

"There." Guthrum looked back at Geirmund. "You have your answer."

Geirmund had never liked Rek, but now he had one more reason to hate him. "Then your brother is a thief," he said.

Eskil took a menacing step towards him. "Be careful with your words, Hel-hide. My brother believed you were drowned, as did we all."

"But I am not drowned," Geirmund said, "and that sword belongs to me. Rek must be–"

"Enough." Guthrum frowned in irritation. "You know where your sword is. If you want it back, then you must claim it. I will hear no more about it."

Geirmund turned to Eskil, resolved to do exactly what Guthrum said. "Where is your brother?"

"Rek is with the rest of our company," he said. "Near the ships on the south riverbank. But Hel-hide, you–"

"Jarl Guthrum," Geirmund said, "know that I remain sworn to you."

Guthrum nodded. "I welcome your service."

"May I take my leave?" Geirmund asked.

Guthrum looked at Eskil as he answered. "You may. But be mindful of the peace, Hel-hide. In this encampment are Danes, Northmen, Jutes, Frisians... All are here as allies against the Saxons, despite our previous disagreements."

Geirmund bowed his head. Then he, Steinólfur, and Skjalgi left the jarl's tent, but they had not put it far behind them when Geirmund heard Eskil call his name. He ignored him and marched towards the south riverbank, but the Dane hurried to catch him up.

"Hel-hide," he said. "What do you mean to do?"

"I mean to reclaim my sword." Geirmund stared straight ahead. "Just as Jarl Guthrum suggested."

"And if Rek won't give it up?"

"Why wouldn't he?" Steinólfur asked. "It belongs to Geirmund."

"I don't always understand my brother's reasons," Eskil said. "But I do know him."

He said nothing more, but he walked with them now as they crossed the encampment, and when they approached the circle of tents belonging to Rek's company, he strode ahead of Geirmund, calling for his brother. Rek heard him and stepped forward, surrounded by Danes whose faces Geirmund knew from his time at the oar aboard *Wave Humper*. When the crew saw him, their eyes and mouths opened wide, and none could speak, but Rek's eyes held more hatred than disbelief.

"The Hel-hide is with us once more," Eskil said, looking at each of them in turn. "Jarl Guthrum has welcomed him back. As should we all."

Geirmund knew those words would not be the last heard or said of his return, but for now he moved towards Rek and his purpose there. "I am told you have my sword," he said.

Rek rubbed his chin with the saddle of his thumb. "I do."

"I am here to retrieve it."

The Dane shook his head. "No. You abandoned it."

"Abandoned it?" Geirmund's blood roared in his ears. "Only a weak man without honour would make such a claim–"

"You accuse me of being without honour?" Rek said. "You, the cursed Hel-hide who nearly sank my ship?" He moved towards his brother. "I must be allowed to answer this."

"No," Eskil said. "There is a peace in the encampment. None may slay another between the wall and the rivers."

"Then let it be to first blood," Rek said. "Only let us fight. I would teach this little shit a lesson in honour."

Geirmund raised his voice so all could hear him. "And if you lose?"

Rek glared at him, then glanced at the warriors that surrounded them. "I will return the sword to you."

Eskil looked down at his brother as if considering his request, and then he turned to Geirmund. "If I allow this, will you consider the ownership of your sword to be settled at the end, regardless of the outcome?"

Geirmund did not believe he should have to fight to reclaim his own sword, but the disagreement over it had become a matter of honour between him and Rek, so it seemed a fight had become unavoidable. "I will," he said.

"Good." Eskil motioned to the warriors around them. "Make the square!"

The Danes obeyed, spreading themselves out to form a four-sided wall, with nine or ten warriors to a side. Geirmund strode towards one corner of the opening battleground, and Steinólfur and Skjalgi walked with him.

The older warrior leaned in close. "Are you well enough for this?"

"I am," Geirmund said, though he wasn't sure of it. He pulled the blood-stained linen wrappings from his skull and tossed them in the dirt, trying to ignore the sudden swimming in his head. "Skjalgi... fetch me a shield and a sword."

Skjalgi nodded and ran away through the gathering men and the tents. The air felt cold against Geirmund's scalp, the sky overhead a grey and tattered shroud. He could hear the river nearby, and above the heads of the Danes he could see a long row of prows, the many ships pulled up onto the shore.

"Geirmund," Steinólfur whispered, "perhaps some patience would serve you well in this moment."

"How so?" Geirmund asked, watching Rek arm himself with a shield and Geirmund's own sword. The Dane intended to use the blade against its rightful owner, a further insult Geirmund would soon punish.

"This fight can wait until you are healed," Steinólfur said. "There would be no dishonour in asking for a delay so you–"

"No." Geirmund could not abide the thought of returning to his tent while Rek carried his sword openly among the other warriors. "I will settle this now."

Steinólfur looked as though he remained worried, but he ceased his objections, and then Skjalgi returned with the blade Geirmund had given the boy back at Avaldsnes, as well as one of the shields bought at Ribe. Geirmund took both in hand and turned to face his opponent, and Eskil stepped into the middle of the square.

"This fight will end when first blood touches the ground," the Dane said. "If either man keeps fighting after that mark has been called, the same will forfeit his silver, his freedom, or his life, according to the judgement of Jarl Guthrum." Eskil looked back and forth between them. "Are you both readied?"

"I am," Rek said.

Geirmund nodded, but it felt as though his sight lagged behind the movement of his head.

"Begin." Eskil stepped back and joined the wall of men behind him.

Rek charged at Geirmund with surprising speed, yelling and snarling. Geirmund barely had his shield raised in time to deflect the Dane's repeated and savage sword blows. Each impact jarred his bones and made his head reel with pain and disorientation. He wondered if Rek was truly that much quicker than him, or if he remained too weak for combat and should have heeded Steinólfur's cautions. Neither mattered now that the fight had begun, and he dodged out from under Rek's assault and blinked, trying to steady his sight and his mind.

When the Dane charged again, Geirmund was better prepared, and used his shield to push Rek's strike aside, then attempted to land a blow of his own. But the Dane brought his shield up, blocked Geirmund's blow, and shoved him backwards.

Geirmund staggered and almost lost his footing. The pain in his head had become blinding, and he knew he would not win this, but also knew he would not surrender. He dropped his shield and flew at Rek wildly, wielding his sword with two hands.

His sudden attack put Rek on his heels for a moment or two, but the Dane recovered quickly, and after Geirmund made a desperate swing that sliced only air, Rek used Geirmund's imbalance against him and threw him to the ground.

Geirmund hit the earth hard, and his sight went black. Then he felt Rek kneel on his chest, and he saw the Dane leaning over him. Then Rek used his sword to slice Geirmund's cheek.

"First blood," he said. "But know that I could have killed you."

The weight on Geirmund's chest eased, allowing him to breathe again, and then Rek moved away. Geirmund laid there until Steinólfur and Skjalgi came to his side, helping him to his feet and to stumble back across the encampment to his tent, where he collapsed in exhaustion, pain, and shame.

14

Geirmund's defeat cost him more than his pride and his sword. It set back his healing, and he returned to his bed for several days. Then Steinólfur came to tell him the Danes were marching to battle with the Saxons at a place called Basing.

Upon hearing that, Geirmund sat up. "We must go with them–"

"You must stay where you are," the older warrior said, pressing him back down. "I will not be ignored again."

"But I must–"

"There will be other battles. If you wish to fight in them, you will wait until you have your strength."

Geirmund ground his teeth together, causing pain in his head. "The coward believes he will live forever if he avoids the battle."

"And the wise man knows which battles to fight," Steinólfur said.

"You sound like my father."

"Your father has his flaws, but he is no fool. Every warrior receives wounds, and every warrior must heal from them."

Geirmund closed his eyes, accepting that Steinólfur would have his way this time, for he could also admit, if only to himself, that he wasn't yet ready to wield a sword. "Where is Skjalgi?" he asked.

"With a woman."

Geirmund sat up again, this time in surprise. "What?"

"Not in that way," the older warrior said. "Her name is Birna, a shield-maiden, one of Jarl Osbern's best warriors. She tells me Skjalgi reminds her of her brother who died several summers ago. She's been helping me with his training, and I think the boy could be in love with her if he wasn't also frightened by her."

Geirmund met Birna the day after Halfdan, Guthrum, and the other jarls had marched. She was older than him by half a dozen summers, tall and strong, with tangled red hair, green eyes, and a nose that seemed to have set a bit crooked after a break. Geirmund stood with her, watching Steinólfur train Skjalgi in the uses of a spear, the way a high backhand grip is good for attacking over a shield, or throwing if necessary, and a low reverse grip is good for defence, how the ground can be used to brace the end of the weapon.

"You were sworn to Osbern," Geirmund said. "Who do you fight for now?"

"Most of Jarl Osbern's warriors now fight for Halfdan," she said. "The ones who are still alive anyway."

"Then why did you not march with Halfdan?" Geirmund asked her.

"The king doesn't know us. We were ordered to stay behind with some of the others to guard the encampment and ships." She glanced him up and down. "And to protect the wounded and the sickly."

Geirmund touched his chest. "I will surely sleep better knowing you are here."

One of her eyebrows went up, along with one corner of her mouth. "Are you mocking me? Because from what I heard about your fight with Rek, you do need protecting."

Geirmund heard the humour in her voice, so he took no offence, even though his shame called for it. "Perhaps you should train me when you're finished with the boy."

"Why wait?" She walked to where Skjalgi had laid his sword and shield, picked up both, and brought them to Geirmund. "I'll go easy on you."

He laughed as he took them, but he stopped laughing as soon as their bout began. Birna proved to be an agile and formidable warrior, which was not surprising, considering her reputation. She moved with quick and brutal efficiency, wasting no effort on strikes intended only to intimidate or dominate. Geirmund didn't know how easy she went on him, but he knew she beat him easily, and he wasn't sure he could blame that entirely on his wounded head.

"I'll sleep better knowing you are here," Geirmund said once again as he collapsed onto the dry ground, struggling to catch his breath.

"And I'll await your recovery." She sat next to him, also breathing hard. "Even wounded, you fight well."

"I was trained well," Geirmund said, nodding towards Steinólfur.

"Yes, your oath-man is good. He doesn't fight with his pride."

"What do you mean? Steinólfur has more honour than–"

"No, not honour. Pride. The two are not the same."

"What do you mean?"

"A warrior with honour will act with honour even when the gods alone will see it." She pulled a sharpening stone from a pouch at her belt and went to work on her sword, honing the notches caused by their bout. "Honour unsung is no less honourable for it and will still gain a warrior entry to Valhalla."

"And pride?"

"Pride needs an audience." Her sword sang with each stroke of the sharpening stone. "Pride is honour that a warrior wants others to see, and pride makes a warrior weak. Some warriors fight with their pride, as if it's a weapon that will help them win. But pride in battle is more often a burden that makes warriors careless and witless. Steinólfur knows this."

Geirmund nodded. "He wanted me to delay my fight with Rek."

"Perhaps you should have heeded him." She sighted down the length of her sword, inspecting its edge. "Pride is a common weakness. Even Halfdan marches to restore his pride after his loss at Ashdown. The Saxons know this, I think. They taunted him into battle."

"Where is Basing from here?"

"South. A day's travel."

"South?" Geirmund puzzled over that. "But Wælingford lies to the north. The Saxons must have marched a great distance out of their way to avoid us."

"So it seems."

That seemed a poor strategy to him, for the Saxons had cut themselves off from the safety of their stronghold. If the fight at Basing turned against them, they now had a Dane encampment blocking the path of their retreat. Geirmund assumed that if the Wessex king and his brother were clever, as John had claimed they were, they must have taken that risk for a reason, and he pondered what that reason might be.

He thought about what he had seen of Wælingford from a distance, its defences, its many ships, and its bridge over the Thames. He had floated down that river after falling from the bridge at Garinges, and he realized the Saxons could easily do the same in their ships to attack the encampment, especially with most of the Danes now drawn a day's march away in the opposite direction.

"You believe the Saxons taunted Halfdan into battle?" he asked.

"Perhaps. They surely provoked him, appearing the way they did so close to this place."

Geirmund rose to his feet.

"What is it?" she asked.

"I think we must prepare for an attack."

"What? Where?"

"Here." He pointed at the river. "I think the Saxons might try to take the encampment by ship."

"Are you sure?"

"No. But I saw many boats at Wælingford, and I think it likely enough that we need to prepare."

"How?"

They had no time to build a bridge or a sea-gate, but Geirmund remembered the wharfs made from wooden stakes that he had seen in the fenlands. "I know a way," he said.

The commander left in charge of the encampment was a man named Afkarr, a capable but unambitious warrior who had served Jarl Osbern. He needed some convincing, but he trusted Birna, and he chose to be cautious and prepared after hearing of the many ships Geirmund had seen at Wælingford.

"But how can you build a wall across the river?" the Dane asked.

"The Saxon boats sit heavy and deep in the water," Geirmund said. "I've rowed one. The stake-wall would only need to stretch across the width of the river's channel."

Afkarr seemed not to fully understand the plan, but at Birna's urging he shook his head and put Geirmund in charge of building the defences, ordering all the Danes in the encampment to work.

Geirmund quickly found a suitable place for the wall where the waterway narrowed, just one rest to the west, distant enough to keep the encampment safe, but near enough to respond quickly if the enemy attacked. The riverbank there fell into deep water very close to the far shore, while on the near side the current flowed over a wide, shallow bar of sand and rock.

Geirmund set some of the Danes to cutting and sharpening young trees into long stakes, while the rest worked from the decks of two anchored ships, pounding the stakes deep into the river bottom and lashing them together with leather and rope to bind their strength. Though Geirmund's head still swam and his body felt weak, he worked hard alongside the Danes without slowing or showing his struggle.

The building of those defences used up the rest of that day, and when the stake-wall was finished it resembled a thick and impenetrable bramble. It blocked the middle channel completely and butted up against the steep riverbank on the northern shore, but it left the southern shore open. Saxon boats rowing downriver would have only one path forward, and if they tried to push around the edge of the wall, they would be driven aground, stranded and vulnerable. The finished stake-wall did nothing to dam the river but made it impassable for any boats except the light and swift Dane ships that could easily traverse the shallows.

As the sun set on that day, Geirmund stood on the shore near the wall with Steinólfur, Skjalgi, and Birna, exhausted but satisfied.

"You have either saved the encampment," the older warrior said, "or we have wasted a day of hard work for nothing."

"The Danes were bored," Geirmund said. "Their hands needed something to do."

Birna nodded. "Even if the Saxons don't attack, this wall is a good thing."

"Let us hope Halfdan and Guthrum agree," Steinólfur said.

"Let us hope the wall won't be tested," Skjalgi said.

The Danes set watchers and returned to the encampment,

where they ate and drank Saxon wine that Afkarr gave them to reward their efforts. They sat easily around their fires telling stories, and for the first time since leaving Avaldsnes, Geirmund felt truly welcomed among them. Even the Danes who had balked at the beginning of the task now seemed pleased with what they had accomplished, in agreement with Birna that it was a good thing.

Before long, Geirmund felt his eyes closing against his will and bade a good night to Steinólfur, Skjalgi, and Birna. Then he drifted away from the fire to his tent, where he fell into his bed utterly drained. When distant horns blared, it seemed his eyes had only been closed a few moments, and he rushed from his tent in confusion to find the encampment quiet and waking with him.

"Saxons attack!" he shouted. "To the river!"

Then the Danes charged forth with spear and axe, bow and sword, ready for battle. They raced along the waterline to the wall, where they found four or five boats already pressed up against the stakes, their Saxon crews shouting in alarm. Another dozen boats still came down the river, but they seemed to have slowed, confused by the horns and unknown peril ahead.

"Arrows!" Afkarr shouted.

Bowmen fired a volley by moonlight upon the Saxons at the stake-wall, and warriors screamed and splashed in the darkness. Enemy bowmen attempted to return a volley of their own, but their arrows were few and in the chaos of their tossing boats hit no mark. The nearest enemy ships also received hurled spears, and some of the Saxons leapt into the river to escape. Those that tried to push through the stakes became entangled in the wall and the Danes filled them with arrows. Those that swam along the wall towards the shallows, perhaps thinking to fight their way free, found axes and swords waiting for them.

Then the Danes lit torches, revealing their numbers along the riverbank, and by that firelight the oncoming boats saw the stake-wall, and their slain countrymen, and they knew their plan had been thwarted. The Saxons then had to choose whether to turn back or to press their attack, and though Geirmund felt unsteady on his feet, he readied himself should they decide to fight.

Instead, the Saxons dropped oars and retreated, rowing upriver, and the battle was over almost within moments of its beginning, and without the loss of a single Dane. Afkarr sent bowmen after the boats to harry their escape and insure they would not turn back and make a second attempt, and then the commander came to Geirmund.

"You were right, Hel-hide," he said. "You and your wall may well have saved the encampment. King Halfdan will know of it."

Back at the encampment, as the first birds sang with dawn and the sun rose, many Danes sought Geirmund out to pay him similar honours. Several of them had been sworn to the slain Jarl Osbern, like Birna and Afkarr, and now found themselves far distant from their homes and without a loyal leader to reward them. There was Aslef, a man who was Geirmund's age but generally regarded as much more appealing to the eye. There was Muli, a warrior closer to Steinólfur in age whose only son had died fighting the Northumbrians a few years previous. Then there was Thorgrim, a boulder of a Dane in form and temperament, and lastly were Rafn and Vetr, companions of long standing, the former an enormous man named for his black hair, the latter a sinewy warrior called after his nearly white hair and pale skin. Geirmund found he got along well with all of them.

Two days later, Halfdan returned, having defeated the Saxons and scattered the armies of Æthelred and Ælfred from the field of battle, though many Danes had fallen at Basing. Shortly after

Guthrum came to fetch Geirmund for a meeting with the king.

"You have made a name for yourself," the jarl said as they walked towards Halfdan's tent. "Are you ready for what comes next?"

"What do you mean?"

"You are soon to know that reputation brings cost as well as reward."

"What kind of cost?"

"The king–" Guthrum looked around them, as if to see who might overhear. "Halfdan's power and reputation have been weakened by his loss at Ashdown. The jarls who sailed with Bersi are angry, and Halfdan's control over this army is faltering."

"You sailed with Bersi," Geirmund said. "Are you angry?"

"I am displeased. Just as Halfdan was displeased when he learned of the attack on the encampment in his absence."

"But we defeated the Saxons–"

"Yes, you did, and your reputation has grown considerably as a result." Halfdan's tent then came into view, and Guthrum lowered his voice almost to a whisper. "Tread carefully, Hel-hide. The king and the other jarls understand very well the disaster you prevented, which has earned you their respect. But some see it as another failure for Halfdan, and you are a reminder of that failure, especially for the king."

They reached the tent then, and Geirmund could ask no more questions before they both entered. Guthrum crossed to where the other jarls stood at hand, while Geirmund went before the high seat and bowed his head.

"I am pleased to finally meet you," Halfdan said. He was a dark-haired Dane with eyes the blue of Frakkland steel. "You are the son of Hjörr Halfsson, king of Rogaland. Afkarr has told me that were it not for you, I would have lost this encampment and all my ships. It has even been said that you drowned and returned from the land of Hel itself. I have heard much of you, Geirmund Hel-hide."

The way the king said the name Hel-hide made Geirmund think he meant it as praise, not as an insult. "I do not make those claims for myself," he replied.

Halfdan left his seat and stalked closer to him. "But it is true that you built that wall in the river, yes? It is true you guessed rightly that the Saxons would attack with boats down the Thames?"

"That is true," Geirmund said.

"How did you guess that?" the king asked.

Geirmund sensed that danger had just entered the room, and he did his best to explain his thinking without suggesting that Halfdan's march to Basing had been part of a Wessex trap. From what Geirmund had been told the Saxons had fought in earnest, and the battle had been hard won, and was therefore no mere diversion but a second front. "Credit is owed to Birna and Afkarr for trusting in me," Geirmund said. "And the wall could not have been made without the hard work of every Dane in the encampment, so honour goes to them also."

"That may be true," the king said, "but none of it would have been accomplished without you. You will have silver for it, and my gratitude."

Geirmund bowed his head. "I thank you, King Halfdan."

"And you will have warriors." Guthrum now stepped forward. "A company of your own. Several Danes have asked to fight for you."

Geirmund had not expected to be made a commander of Danes that day, not so soon. He had seen little actual battle, and his loss to Rek would surely be known to both Guthrum and the king. "Who has asked to fight with me?" he said.

The king folded his arms. "Many of them were Jarl Osbern's warriors. They built your wall with you."

"They honour me," Geirmund said.

Guthrum came to stand beside Halfdan, Völund's ring gleaming on his arm. "I told you before we sailed from Avaldsnes that you would lead no Danes until you proved yourself. You have now done that."

Geirmund bowed his head again. "I thank you for this, Jarl Guthrum, King Halfdan."

"Go, gather your warriors," Halfdan said. "I may have a task for you soon."

Geirmund bowed his head one last time, and he left the tent somewhat bewildered, but eager to share the news with Steinólfur. He found the older warrior working with Birna to train Skjalgi to fight with an axe, and when he informed the three of them of what had just occurred not one seemed surprised.

"You have been the subject of much talk," the older warrior said. "I'm not sure what else you expected when you returned to us like some draugr."

"And saving the encampment has only helped your reputation," Birna added. "I was one who asked Halfdan if I might join you."

"You?" Geirmund looked at her in surprise. "But surely you could lead Osbern's warriors better than–"

"I could. And I will one day, if that is to be my fate. For now I would fight for you."

"Why?"

Her eyebrows creased together, as though Geirmund should already know the answer to his question. "Because Halfdan has not yet given me that honour. He does not yet favour me. In this moment he and Guthrum favour you. To fight with you is to share in that honour and gain favour. Perhaps now I will not be ordered to stay behind to guard the encampment when they march to battle."

"I see," Geirmund said, smiling. "Your wish to fight for me has nothing to do with your faith in me."

"Remember what I said about pride, Hel-hide." She clapped him on the back. "You have impressed me a little. Be content and lead well, or I will seek honour and riches elsewhere."

"We should gather with your warriors," Steinólfur said, "as Halfdan suggested."

Geirmund agreed with him, so they moved their tents to where many of Jarl Osbern's warriors had already camped. There they were joined by several more warriors, all previously sworn to other jarls who had fallen at Ashdown, all now wanting to fight for Geirmund. He knew most of their faces from the day spent building the river-wall, and he was pleased to see Aslef, Muli, Thorgrim, Rafn, and Vetr among them. All told, Geirmund now had a company of more than twenty warriors looking to him to lead them, and though that was an honour he had long wanted, the sudden weight of it fell heavy on his shoulders. Later, as they all ate their night-meal together, he stood to address them.

"I am the son of Hjörr Halfsson," he said. "The deeds of my grandfather are well known to both Northmen and Danes. We here are twenty-three, which is the same number who swore to Half when he first took to the whale roads. I see fate in that, and though I do not have a ship, if you fight with me there will be honour for you, and riches, and land, and one day there will be a fleet of ships."

Geirmund looked into the eyes of each warrior before him, thinking of what Bragi had told him about his grandfather.

"I will not ask you to swear to me alone," he said. "Like Half and his heroes, each of you here will swear to fight for all, not upon my sword, but upon your own. And I will make the same oath to fight for each of you that you make to fight for me. But before we make our oaths, know this. In my company we will harm none but warriors who raise weapons against us. If you can abide this rule, then your sword is welcome. If you cannot abide it, you are free to leave now."

Geirmund paused, but none of the warriors moved.

"Then let us make our oaths," he said, and he went first, swearing to always lead them in honour, to wrest glory and silver from the enemies they would face, to never flee from battle, to fight and die for each warrior in his company, and to avenge them if they were slain. Those words then passed over the lips of every Dane in that circle, until they were all bonded by the same oath, and after that they all drank together.

Geirmund spent the next few days speaking to each of his warriors in turn, to learn their names, where they had come from, and what skills they possessed. All claimed to be dangerous and deadly fighters, but some were more deadly when wielding their weapon of choice.

Aslef claimed to have the eyes of a hawk when using a bow. Thorgrim and Muli both fought with bearded axes and seaxes. Rafn carried two swords, one of them a common Dane-blade, the other an odd single-edged weapon he said came from Miklagard, far to the east. Vetr fought well with his spear, which he had named Dauðavindur, for with it he said he brought death like the wind.

Some warriors in the company had seen many battles and bore the proof of it in scars, while others had seen no more fighting than Geirmund. For several days he ordered the most hardened warriors, including Steinólfur, Birna, and Muli, to train in the uses of weapons and the shield-wall, and when Halfdan and Guthrum came to speak with Geirmund, they seemed pleased by what they saw.

"You have established order quickly," the jarl said. "That is good."

"They are strong warriors," Geirmund said.

"Let us see how strong they are," the king said. "I said I would have a task for you, and I do."

Geirmund nodded. "Say it, and it will be done."

"If we are to defeat Wessex," Halfdan said, "we must control the Icknield Way and the River Thames. I want you and your company to take Wælingford."

15

Geirmund didn't understand what Halfdan was asking of him. "You are marching to Wælingford?"

The king shook his head. "I am not marching. I am sending your company alone."

Geirmund hesitated, unsure of what to say to Halfdan because he was still unsure of what Halfdan was saying to him. "Wælingford is strong. I would need an army to take it, but I have only twenty-three warriors—"

The king held up his hand, silencing Geirmund. "The Saxons of these Berkshire lands have suffered great losses, including their ealdorman. Æthelred and Ælfred have moved south, where they are stronger and can call up new warriors to replace those that have fallen."

"I see," Geirmund said. "How many warriors did they leave behind to hold Wælingford?"

Halfdan frowned. "Not many."

Geirmund did not expect that Æthelred would make it easy to take such an important place on the river. "But more than twenty-three, I think," he said.

"Perhaps." The king's blue eyes narrowed. "Perhaps not."

Geirmund looked at Guthrum, who stood a little behind Halfdan and said nothing either for or against the wisdom of the plan.

"You know Wælingford," Halfdan said. "You knew they would send ships–"

"I saw that hold from a distance," Geirmund said. "That is all."

"Nevertheless, Geirmund Hel-hide." Anger sharpened the king's voice, and his gaze hardened. "I have given you this task, and you will see it done. Are you not Geirmund Hel-hide who built a river-wall and defeated a Saxon attack? Are you telling me I was wrong to give you a company to lead?"

"No, you were not wrong." Geirmund realized then he had no choice but to follow Halfdan's order, despite its seeming impossibility. "I will see it done. But I would ask one thing."

"What?"

"I keep any silver we find there. If the hold is mostly emptied, as you say, there won't be much. But it will mean at least some reward for my warriors."

Guthrum smiled at that, but Halfdan did not, and he was silent for several moments.

"Very well," he said at last. "You and your men will depart tomorrow at first light. And may the gods be with you." He then turned and left.

Guthrum stayed a moment longer, and it seemed he had something he wanted to tell Geirmund but he left without voicing it. Steinólfur, however, had much to say when Geirmund told him and a few others of the task Halfdan had given them.

"It is a fool's errand!" the older warrior nearly shouted. "Does he want you dead?"

"That seems likely," Birna said.

"Guthrum warned me about this," Geirmund said. "He told me my reputation would come at a price."

"Your life?" Steinólfur said. "That is a heavy price."

"If that is my fate," Geirmund said.

Vetr and Rafn sat nearby, and the white-haired warrior spoke up, his voice as sharp as the cracking of ice over a pond. "Halfdan can't kill you. You saved the encampment, and everyone knows it. But your reputation is a threat to his, so he has found another way to get rid of you, by using your reputation against you."

"What are we going to do?" Skjalgi asked, quietly.

Defeat seemed imminent, but Geirmund remembered the future that Völund had foretold, that he would surrender to his enemy, and he resolved to defy it. "We have no choice," he said. "We must take Wælingford."

"How do you propose we do that?" Birna asked. "We are too few to take such a hold by force."

Rafn spoke up then, nodding towards the river. "We have Saxon boats. We could take the Saxon clothing and armour from the dead."

"You suggest we use guile," Steinólfur said, but Geirmund couldn't tell whether the older warrior disapproved.

Rafn shrugged. "It might get us inside their defences."

"But if they are fifty," Geirmund said, "or one hundred, and we are twenty-three, being inside their defences will give us no greater chance of success."

"Do you have a better plan?" Vetr asked.

Geirmund thought for several moments and considered everything he had learned about the Saxons, searching for weaknesses he could make use of to attack them. "Saxon warriors are mostly farmers," he finally said. "Almost to a man, they would rather be at home than fighting here, and I think we should allow them to leave."

"Allow them to leave?" Steinólfur said. "I didn't think we were stopping them."

Geirmund shook his head. "I mean that we should give them reason to leave. Æthelred has gone south. He has abandoned Wælingford with Danes almost at its gates, and I don't imagine the warriors there are happy about it, especially after the defeat we dealt them at the river-wall. If they believe they are doomed, perhaps they will simply leave."

"Why would they believe they are doomed?" Rafn asked. "We are hardly an army."

"We don't need numbers," Geirmund said. "We only need them to think their Christ has abandoned them."

"How?" Steinólfur asked.

"We use their fear of our pagan ways," Geirmund said.

Though his warriors seemed doubtful, they did as he asked and made three large crosses, which they fitted to three of the Saxon boats likes masts. Geirmund then ordered three of the dead Saxon warriors to be doused in oil and hung from those crosses, and rather than waiting until dawn to depart, they left with the setting sun.

They took a total of six boats, three with crosses and three that rowed with the rest of the company from Readingum to the Moulsford, where the scent of rot and death at Ashdown still hung in the air. Most of Geirmund's warriors halted there and disembarked for a land march while he rowed on, alone in his boat with a dead Saxon looming over him, pallid and raven-pecked. Rafn and Thorgrim came in the other two cross-ships, having volunteered for the task, for the heavy Saxon boats needed strength to row, and Wælingford still lay five rests to the north.

It was in the deep-night when they and Geirmund finally approached the hold. He knew there would be watchers set upon the walls, so when the three boats came in sight of the town, he lit his dead Saxon afire upon his cross. Rafn and Thorgrim did the same, and the light of those flames spread across the river and blazed through the darkness. Almost instantly Geirmund heard cries of alarm coming from the walls, and he could imagine the terror caused by such a sight at that time of night.

He rowed his boat to the shore near the fortifications before the flames could consume the wood of his ship, and Rafn and Thorgrim did the same. The three of them tied their boats in a row and left them burning where they could be seen from the walls and as a signal to the rest of Geirmund's company in the woods to the south. Then the howls of many Dane-horns shattered the night's quiet, blaring from east to west, as though a vast army had appeared from nowhere and now waited in the darkness.

Geirmund stalked towards Wælingford's gates, and after the Dane-horns quieted, he bellowed at the watchers on the wall. "I am Geirmund Hjörrsson, called Hel-hide! I defeated you on the river, and I have now come to take this place! You are outnumbered, and it will be mine! Your king has abandoned you! Your god has abandoned you!"

He paused, allowing fear to build within the walls of the hold.

"But I am prepared to be merciful!" Geirmund shouted. "I give you until sunrise to leave Wælingford! I see no reason for you to die here! Go back to your families! Return to your farms in peace! If you leave your silver and weapons behind, I swear to you that we will not harm you or pursue you!"

He paused again.

"But if you are not gone by sunrise, I will show no mercy! We will burn alive every Saxon inside these walls and sacrifice you to our gods!"

He stared up at the walls a moment longer, at the many shadows he could see there, and then he turned away. Rafn and Thorgrim followed him south, away from the hold and the burning boats, into the darkness towards his waiting company.

"Well done," Rafn said. The Dane's clothing and black hair became one with the night, leaving his face a faint and bodiless wraith.

"If that doesn't scare the Saxons away," Thorgrim said, "perhaps they deserve to keep the cursed place."

"They will leave," Geirmund said.

"Are we truly letting them go in peace?" Rafn asked.

"Yes, if they meet my terms. That is what I swore."

Rafn nodded, but in the darkness Geirmund couldn't tell if the Dane had simply heard his answer, or if he approved of it.

They lit no fires for the rest of that night, but let the darkness keep them and their true numbers hidden. A daymark later, when the sun finally rose, they marched from the wood through a thin morning fog, across fields and pastures, until they reached Wælingford.

Skjalgi pointed as it came in sight. "The gates are opened!"

"It seems you were right, Hel-hide," Thorgrim said. "The Saxons left."

It seemed that way, but the Danes nevertheless entered the hold with caution, weapons drawn, prepared for a trap.

They found none. The town, it seemed, had been empty for some time. The ground in the livestock pens had dried out, and the blacksmith forge had gone cold, but when they reached the secondary fortifications near the bridge, they found the campfires still smouldering, as if abandoned in great haste. The Saxon warriors had left some silver behind there, as well as their axes and swords, fourteen blades in all not counting the many spears, pitchforks, and other makeshift weapons lying about, hardly enough to defend such a hold if Halfdan had descended in force.

"Æthelred truly did abandon them," Rafn said.

Geirmund's Danes simply stood there, as if disbelieving of their easy success, surprised into silence.

Geirmund raised his voice to address them. "Wælingford is ours!" he said, holding up his seax, and at that his warriors finally roared with a sudden cheer. "Bring me any gold or silver you find to divide equally among you, but you are free to claim anything else in the town."

The Danes cheered again and separated to explore. Geirmund sat down upon a wooden stump before one of the cookfires as the sun rose above the roofs and walls of the town. Skjalgi went off to see what he could find, but Steinólfur and Birna sat down next to Geirmund.

"Warriors will be flocking to you after this," the older warrior said.

"I take no honour from it." Geirmund sheathed his seax without having to clean or hone its blade. "This victory was too easy."

Birna rolled her eyes at him. "You're thinking with your pride again, Hel-hide. Must honour be a struggle?"

"No, but honour must be earned," he said.

"Look around you!" Steinólfur spread his hands wide. "You have earned it. Twice now you have led these Danes to victory by use of your cunning, and without the loss of a single warrior. But if you'd rather have a fight, I'm sure you could go find the Saxons and invite them back."

"You have made your point," Geirmund said. "Now I must send word to Guthrum and Halfdan that we have taken Wælingford."

"I'll go." Birna stood. "I want to see Halfdan's face when he first hears of it."

Geirmund nodded. "Go, then. But tell Guthrum before you tell Halfdan. I am his oath-man, so if there is honour to be had here, he shares in it."

She nodded and strode away, and then Steinólfur leaned in closer to him. "Do you know that you have already achieved more than your father? He has never taken a town or a fortress."

"He never had to."

"Perhaps this place could be yours. It's a good place. Strong walls. A river for trade. Not unlike Avaldsnes." The older warrior looked around. "But Halfdan or Guthrum will likely claim it. And I suppose the Saxons will want it back, so even if the Danes gave it to you, you would have to fight to keep it."

"Do you think there are lands where that isn't the way of things?"

"What, where you don't have to fight to keep what is yours?" He rubbed his beard, almost tugging on it. "Perhaps there is. But I think no matter where you are, you would be wise to always be prepared to fight, even if it never comes to that."

"Do you think my father and mother are prepared?"

He dropped his hand from his beard to prop it on his knee. "I don't know."

Geirmund didn't know the answer, either, and it wasn't a question he wanted to dwell on. He rose to explore Wælingford with the Danes, and like Steinólfur he found it to be a good place, with workshops and warehouses arranged on two main roads that crossed each other at the centre of the small town. Aside from some food stores of grain, it seemed the Saxons had left little of value behind, only a few tools and some furniture in the buildings. But then one of the Danes found a small hoard of hacksilver buried in the corner of a stable near the smithy, and that increased the joy and reward for all.

Geirmund gave Steinólfur the task of dividing the wealth, allotting every warrior an equal share, and many of the Danes found new weapons among those the Saxons had left behind. Geirmund claimed an axe and an old Langbardaland sword with a narrow hilt the same width as its pommel, which allowed Skjalgi to keep the blade Geirmund had already given him.

At the mid-afternoon mark Halfdan and Guthrum came to Wælingford with a force of at least one hundred Danes. Geirmund met them at the southern city gate, and while Guthrum and Birna wore broad grins, Halfdan glowered and looked around as if he suspected some trick.

"The hold is taken," Geirmund said. "As you ordered."

"How did you do it?" the king asked.

"With cunning," Guthrum said, walking past Halfdan towards the gates.

The king made no reply, but he followed the jarl, and then Birna fell in beside Geirmund behind them.

"He called me a liar," she whispered. "He almost refused to come, but Guthrum would not be denied."

Then Geirmund shared in her grin as he showed Halfdan and Guthrum the town, the bridge, and the defences, which the king and jarl had only seen from a distance until that moment. The more Geirmund considered Wælingford, the more he realized its importance. The Danes could occupy it without weakening Readingum, while the river and the Icknield Way offered access to trade and fresh warriors, allowing the Danes to control that region almost indefinitely.

"Was there silver?" the king finally asked.

"There was," Geirmund said, wondering if Halfdan meant to go back on his word. "I have already divided it among my warriors."

"If you remember," Guthrum said, "you told Geirmund any silver would be his to–"

"I remember," the king said. "That silver is his reward for what he has done here today."

Geirmund bowed his head, knowing there would be no more wealth from the king.

Guthrum gestured towards the Saxon's secondary defences. "I will leave my warriors here, and I will send more. We must keep the Saxons from taking back this place. From here I might push north, to the riches of Abingdon–"

"No," Halfdan said. "You will hold Wælingford, but you will send no warriors north until we have put Æthelred to the sword. We cannot afford to lose even a single warrior unless it be in pursuit of that Saxon's crown. Wessex must fall, before all else."

"You sent Geirmund and his company here easily enough," Guthrum said.

It seemed that Halfdan's blue eyes turned to ice. "I sent them knowing they would succeed. The gods had given me a sign."

Guthrum paused for several long moments before he finally accepted that with a nod. Then Halfdan announced he would return to Readingum and departed immediately with some twenty of the Danes, while Guthrum and the remaining warriors stayed in the town. The jarl walked with Geirmund to the bridge where they could speak in private, and they stood in the middle of it, listening to the rushing of the Thames beneath their feet. A cold wind and sky in turmoil overhead threatened rain.

"Æbbe's Dun is a Saxon minster of great wealth." The jarl looked upriver, to the north. "A market town. Halfdan doesn't order me to stay here out of true concern over losing warriors. He doesn't want me to grow any richer." He turned towards Geirmund, and then towards Wælingford. "The king did not expect this. Neither did I."

"The king wanted me to fail," Geirmund said. "He wanted me dead."

"You may flatter yourself, but his sending your here was not about you. Do not forget that you are my oath-man."

Geirmund looked downriver, to the south. "He wanted to weaken you?"

"You fight for me, so, as your reputation grows, it adds to mine." He glanced down at Hnituðr on his arm. "He knows what is said of you, and he has seen the evidence. He knows that it was my warrior who came back from the land of Hel to save the encampment and the ships from his blunder." He chuckled to himself. "To think I almost refused you back at Avaldsnes. You offered me no advantage, no silver, no ships, no warriors. But I liked you, and so I took you on, and now I see it was fate. Do you think so?"

"I do."

Guthrum waved an arm down the length of the town. "In doing this you have made me a rival to Halfdan in a way he cannot ignore or dismiss. Word of it has spread too quickly. Because I helped spread it."

"My victories are your victories," Geirmund said.

"I know that, but I am pleased you still know it. You keep your oaths. I admire that, and I will reward it. You are a man of honour, Geirmund Hel-hide." His grin returned. "Did you know that's what the other jarls and their warriors are calling your company now?"

"What is?" Geirmund asked.

"The Hel-hides. They say you and your company defy death."

"No one can defy death."

Guthrum held out his hands towards Geirmund. "And yet here you are. But do not grow lazy or careless in your reputation.

Halfdan will hate you even more for what you have done here, and for now my protection has its limits. Any warrior may fall in battle, of which there are more to come."

"When?"

"Soon. Æthelred and Ælfred have withdrawn to a place called Bedwyn, to the south and west of Readingum. Halfdan and the jarls want to strike there. They have sent down the Thames and into East Anglia, calling for more warriors."

"My company will be prepared."

"I know they will," Guthrum said. "I would expect nothing less from the Hel-hides."

Geirmund heard pride in the jarl's voice, and in that moment he decided he liked the name.

16

For the next few weeks Geirmund and his warriors dwelt at Wælingford, and from there they made raids into the surrounding country seeking food and silver. In very few villages and farms did they find Saxons willing to fight them, and Geirmund wondered if some of them had been the same farmers who had fled Wælingford when offered the chance. If so, it seemed they still fled, for most raids found houses, churches, and stables empty, their people hiding in the hills and forests, leaving the Danes free to take what they wanted. When the Saxons did not run and hide, Geirmund's warriors stayed true to their oaths and only slayed those who raised weapons against them.

"Why did you set that rule?" Skjalgi asked one day as they rode back from raiding a small settlement west of Wælingford. "The Danes say it is not a common thing."

"There are two reasons," Geirmund said. "The first is that my grandfather and his warriors lived by that rule. There is no honour and no reputation in killing those who cannot fight."

"And the second reason?" the boy asked.

"After we defeat Wessex, we will have to manage the kingdom, and we will still need farmers to work the land. That will be difficult if we have killed or made an enemy of every Saxon we meet. It is better to teach them how they might live in peace with us."

Skjalgi nodded, and Geirmund studied him for a moment before risking a question about something the boy had avoided discussing in the past.

"Did your father go raiding?"

Skjalgi's gaze fell to the narrow, rutted, and grass-choked road they travelled. "No. He always said he wasn't good with a sword, and his axe was only meant to cut trees."

Geirmund had known others like that, and there were many in Rogaland who did not go a-viking. His own father would have found much in common with Skjalgi's. "I have heard that he was an honest and honourable man," Geirmund said. "Hard-working and strong as an ox."

Skjalgi went quiet for a long time, but he seemed restless, looking here and there as if fighting against a thought in his mind. Geirmund let him be, until the boy finally spoke. "He died under that tree without a weapon in his hand," he said. "Not even his axe."

Geirmund paused to think carefully about his words. "It is true that Óðinn is not easily pleased. He can be harsh and unforgiving, and not all will go to Valhalla. Many good men and women will not, but that does not mean they are undeserving of our honour and respect."

Skjalgi looked away, trying to hide the tears in his eyes.

"You have become a true warrior," Geirmund said. "A brave and honourable man. I believe your father would be proud of you, but wherever he finds himself, he cannot be any prouder of you than I am, or Steinólfur."

Skjalgi sniffed and nodded, squaring his jaw with the road ahead. "Thank you," he said.

Back at the hold, Guthrum summoned Geirmund to inform him that the march to Bedwyn would begin in three days, which were then spent preparing. On the third day they left eighty Danes to hold Wælingford and journeyed south to Garinges, where they met the Danes from Readingum under Halfdan and the other jarls.

From there the combined army marched hard and fast south of west along an old ridgeway, which carried the warriors over heath and bog as a rainstorm poured down on them. The forests there grew thick with birch and alder, and the rain filled those woods with mist.

At mid-afternoon the storm finally passed, and the Danes came to a high dun of chalky ground that towered over the countryside, stretching from east to west. Atop that hill ran a ridgeway, which the Danes followed west until it brought them within sight of the Saxon army encamped at the highest point on the dun. But Æthelred had built no walls there, which meant there could be no retreat behind them, and the battle would be waged over open ground as it had been at Ashdown.

The hill on which they stood offered commanding views of the land in all directions. The heavy clouds had moved south, draping the fields, pastures, duns, and dales that way in veils of rain, while vast, dense woodland grew behind them to the east, and ahead of them to the west. Geirmund and his company waited as Halfdan spoke with the jarls to form a plan of attack with the little daylight they had left to achieve it.

When Guthrum came back from his council, he did not seem pleased. "Halfdan orders me to flank the enemy."

"He's dividing our forces?" Geirmund asked, standing with Eskil and some of the other commanders. "What will Halfdan and the other jarls do?"

"They will charge Æthelred from the east. After they have engaged, we are to attack from the north."

"From the north?" Eskil said. "But that means we will be charging uphill."

"It does," Guthrum said, shaking his head. "I fear this will be a second Ashdown. But we have no choice."

He ordered his warriors back down the dun, and while Halfdan marched his forces along the ridgeway towards the enemy, Guthrum marched his along the base of the mount. Geirmund trudged through wet ground and kept himself and his company as close to Guthrum as he could, watching the Saxons on the ridge for any sign of movement.

Before long, and as soon as the Danes made clear their strategy, the Saxons did what they had done before and divided their force to meet the two fronts opposing them. Not only did Guthrum and his warriors face an uphill charge, but they also now faced a shield-wall, rather than the enemy's flank.

Geirmund could not help but question whether this was yet another way for Halfdan to be rid of Guthrum as a rival, along with Geirmund and his Hel-hides. He also wondered if this was the betrayal that Völund had foretold in his fate. He only knew it would not be his surrender.

When the moment came that Guthrum ordered his warriors to turn south and march back up the dun a second time, memories of the charge at Ashdown came unbidden to Geirmund's mind. He saw that place of battle, and he saw Jarl Sidroc's men. He heard them dying as if they were there at this battle also, and he remembered holding the warrior Keld as he coughed and gurgled on his blood. Geirmund's heart pounded, no longer with fear of the unknown, but because he knew battle now.

"Show no mercy!" Guthrum shouted. "Push the enemy hard!

Drive them back up the hilltop where we may slaughter them!"

When the Saxon line came within several acre-lengths of distance, Guthrum sounded the final charge and led the front line himself, his sword held high, his voice a bloodthirsty roar. The sight and sound of the jarl drove Geirmund's fear from him, and he ran to battle with his Hel-hides.

A volley of arrows shot up from the dun above them and came down hard, but the Danes did not slow. Some of them fell, pierced, but most collected arrows in their shields. Guthrum did not even raise his shield against that death-rain, but none of the arrows struck him.

At a dozen paces the Danes brought their shields down from overhead to hold before them, and so did the Saxons. At five paces the armies exchanged spears, and then they smashed into one another. Geirmund's boots slid in the wet grass, but he stayed upright and crouched, shoving hard against the enemy, his arm ringing from the impact.

The second and third lines behind him roofed the first with their shields, trapping Geirmund in shadow and the echoes of axes and swords on wood. When he could, he jabbed his sword between gaps in the shields, hoping to feel its point tear into yielding flesh. He felt the hammer of metal strikes on his shield. Steinólfur stood at his left, with Thorgrim beside the older warrior, and then Birna beside him. Beyond that distance, Geirmund could not tell Dane from Dane.

Guthrum shouted for his men to push against the Saxons, but the slope of the dun made it difficult for his warriors to hold their ground, and impossible to drive the enemy back. They were pinned to the side of the hill, and within moments Geirmund heard shields splintering and smelled blood.

He feared this battle would end in defeat as Guthrum had

predicted, but unlike Sidroc, Guthrum called no retreat. Geirmund stood near enough to the jarl to see the Dane's face growing redder in frustration and anger, until at last he let out a bone-rattling scream and threw down his shield. Then he charged through the gap in the Dane-wall he had just opened, pushed straight between two Saxon shields, and went behind their front line alone.

Geirmund felt too stunned by that action to take any of his own, but then he noticed the enemy shield on the other side of his weaken slightly, perhaps only in confusion at Guthrum, and perhaps only for a moment.

"Push!" Geirmund shouted. "Push, Hel-hides!"

They heaved, and the enemy line gave way, though not completely. The Saxons before Geirmund, Steinólfur, and Thorgrim fell back in disarray, some of them to the ground. Geirmund stumbled and trampled over them as he charged to join his jarl.

Guthrum fought with axe and sword, cleaving and slicing his way through many Saxons, whose blades seemed unable to touch him.

Geirmund turned towards Thorgrim and Steinólfur. "Open their shield-wall!"

Then he turned and rammed into the back of the enemy line from the side, stabbing and hacking with his Langbardaland sword and his seax. The Saxons either fell bleeding and took their shields with them, or they dropped their shields when they turned to fight him, both of which weakened their wall until the Danes succeeded in completely breaking it.

The battle then turned warrior-to-warrior, and Geirmund quickly slew three Saxons, his Hel-hides at his side. He saw Birna kill two of the enemy at once, and Vetr spinning like the wind with his spear. Skjalgi fought with sword and shield, holding his ground with his back to Steinólfur's. Geirmund could feel that the fight had shifted as a tide, and after that many of the Saxons pulled back and fled up the dun, as if to rejoin the larger force.

"Stand where you are!" he heard someone shouting, and then he saw their commander. The man wore a bright helmet with gold, and heavy armour. A dozen warriors surrounded him and kept close, engaging only those Danes who attacked them.

Guthrum saw the commander also, a ring-mound of bodies surrounding him as he pointed his sword at the Saxon. "Æthelred!"

Geirmund looked again at the enemy king. "To Guthrum!" he shouted, and he raced to join the fight even as more Saxons flocked to their leader.

The jarl reached the enemy first, alone, and Geirmund feared he would be cut down instantly, but somehow the Saxons failed to strike him as he fought his way through them, straight towards their king.

When Geirmund reached the enemy, he felt something bite into his thigh, but his leg stayed strong beneath him and he kept fighting. He slashed the nearest Saxon through the mouth and opened the side of his face, having aimed at his throat and missed, but the warrior fell away holding his jaw, perhaps believing he had been mortally wounded.

Geirmund looked up just then to see Guthrum hurl a spear, which struck Æthelred in the side, and the Saxon tipped back. A cry went up among his warriors and they swarmed around their king as though to shield him with their bodies, and while some turned to fight and die, the others bore him away.

Guthrum howled after them, but then he turned to his warriors. "To the summit! To Halfdan!"

The Danes roared in reply, and then they charged up the dun, arriving at the Saxon flank as they had been ordered to do. The surprise of that attack, and perhaps word of Æthelred's fall, broke the main Saxon line not long after. Enemy horns called for retreat, and the Saxons fled from the hill, surrendering the field to the Danes.

A victory cry went up among them. Geirmund howled and raised both his weapons to the evening sky. Had there been more light left in the day, Halfdan would have ordered his warriors to pursue the Saxons to slay as many as they could, but the Danes were too unfamiliar with that country to keep fighting at night.

Instead, they made a camp there and tended to their wounded. Geirmund went among the fallen, searching by the fading daylight for his warriors and for other Danes who could be saved, and helping them if he could. Some warriors would never leave that hill, and all that could be done was to honour them and speed them to Valhalla, if they wished for an end to their suffering. Geirmund showed many Saxons the same mercy.

It was after the sun had gone down that he found Rek. A grim Saxon blade had split his side and spilled his guts, and he lay on the ground unable to move anything but his neck and his head. Geirmund knelt on the heath next to him, wetting his knees with blood.

"I feel no pain," the Dane said. "Bastard chopped my back before he sliced me. But I think... I think I feel the life going out of me. My heart... it slows, I think."

Geirmund noticed Rek's hands were empty. He looked about, and nearby he saw his sword, Hámund's sword, given to Geirmund, and won by the Dane. He retrieved it, and then he put it into Rek's hands and curled the Dane's useless fingers around its grip. But when Geirmund let go, the Dane did also.

Geirmund put the sword back into Rek's hand, and this time he did not let go. "I will help you hold on to it," he said.

The Dane closed his eyes. "I thank you. I don't believe it will be for long."

"We won the battle," Geirmund said. "This night you go to—"

"I will stay," said a quiet, approaching shadow. A moment later, Geirmund recognized Eskil. "You may go, Hel-hide," he said.

Geirmund nodded, but before he went he said to Rek, "May you enter Óðinn hall this night." Then he rose to his feet and left one brother to die and the other to mourn alone.

At the hilltop camp he sought out his warriors, and he embraced Steinólfur and Skjalgi when he found both of them alive. Skjalgi had a deep gash on his hand, and Steinólfur had received a few cuts as well, but none of their injuries looked able to kill them.

That was when Geirmund remembered his own wound and looked down at his leg, where he discovered that a sword or spear point had stabbed him. It still bled, but not fast, and it wasn't deep. Despite Steinólfur's protests, he put off dressing it until he had accounted for all twenty-three of his warriors.

He found twenty of them that night, four of them dead or dying, and he found the remaining three the following morning, already cold. The Hel-hides had lost seven warriors in all, Muli among them, and Geirmund wished he had known the warrior better.

Before the Danes left that place, they built funeral pyres atop the hill for the fallen, and Geirmund helped to cut and gather wood from the forests at the foot of the dun. The strain squeezed blood from his thigh no matter how tightly he wrapped it, but he worked all morning, up and down, up and down. When it was time to burn Rek, Geirmund stood next to Eskil watching the flames, engulfed in meaty smoke.

For a while neither spoke. But then the Dane turned to Geirmund, his face and eyes empty. "I saw what you did."

Geirmund looked away and stared straight into the heart of the pyre.

"You could have taken that sword," Eskil went on. "But you put it into my brother's hand instead."

The thought of taking it had not even occurred to Geirmund. "The sword was his."

Eskil nodded. Then he looked back at the fire and sighed. "Too many died here, and Halfdan is to blame for it."

Geirmund understood the Dane's anger, but he wondered if the fault for Rek's death, and Muli's death, and the death of every other warrior lay with Halfdan, or if the Three Spinners had decided it all. He kept this question to himself, though, as he paid respect and honour to each of the dead warriors from his company.

When the Danes returned to Readingum, they all stopped there to drink ale to honour their friends and countrymen who now drank Óðinn's mead and feasted in Valhalla. But the empty tents and empty places around the cookfires were apparent to all and held the mood down. There were too few Danes left in the encampment, far fewer than when Geirmund had first arrived, despite Halfdan winning the last two battles, and that did not bode well for the final taking of Wessex.

"Muli is with his son now," Birna said, staring into her ale. "I am glad of that, at least."

"Did any of you see Guthrum fighting?" Aslef asked. His good-looking features had been ruined by a gash across his nose and cheek, right below his eye, which was swollen blue. "I've never seen the like of it. It is he who won the battle for us."

"He fought as if no iron or steel could touch him," Thorgrim said. "And none did."

Geirmund had seen the same with his own eyes, and when

he and Steinólfur shared a glance they also shared an unspoken thought that Völund's ring might have given the jarl more gifts than mere gold. But it was hard for Geirmund to say how he felt about that. He knew that no power nor craft could deny the Three Spinners the fate they had decreed, not even the might of the gods who would one day meet their doom, and surely not Völund's skills as a smith. Guthrum had lived because it was his fate to live, and if he had lived because of Hnituðr's power, then it was also fate that the Dane should have that ring.

"Guthrum will be made a king," Thorgrim said.

"You think so?" asked Aslef.

"He killed Æthelred," Birna said. "Many of the jarls would prefer to follow him than Halfdan."

"Did you see Æthelred die?" Aslef asked.

"If he lives, he won't for much longer," Geirmund said. "Guthrum's spear went into his belly."

"I would follow King Guthrum," Rafn said, and next to him Vetr nodded his head in agreement.

Eskil approached their circle then, carrying Geirmund's former sword, and all turned towards him. When he spoke, he spoke loudly, as though he wanted everyone there to hear him.

"I do not speak for my brother," he said. "I will make no apologies for him, especially now that he has gone to Valhalla. But I will speak for myself. My brother's sword has come to me but I chose not to burn it on the pyre. Instead, I say to you, Geirmund Hel-hide, that for your honour and courage this sword belongs to you and no other." The Dane then crossed the circle and presented the sword to him.

Geirmund hesitated. Then he rose to his feet and took the blade with a nod of respect. "I accept this gift, but not because I believe it is rightfully mine. This sword belonged to Rek. I accept it now to honour your generosity, Eskil, and with this blade I will slay many Saxons to honour Rek."

That brought cheers and raised ale cups and horns. Eskil returned Geirmund's nod, and then he left the circle to return to his own company, where he and his warriors dealt with their losses.

Geirmund sat and looked at the sword, and even though he hadn't been long parted from it, he saw the blade as though it were an acquaintance returning from a long absence. He studied its golden inlay of wheel patterns, which Eskil had cleaned of blood and polished. He pulled it free of its scabbard and, pointing it at the fire, looked down the length of its steel blade that rippled with reflected flames.

"A sword with the life it's had deserves a name," Steinólfur said.

"I was just thinking the same thing," Geirmund said.

"What will you call it?" Skjalgi asked.

Geirmund thought for a moment. "Both times this sword has come to me, it has been a brother's gift, so I will call it Bróðirgjöfr, to honour my brother and Eskil's brother."

"Not a name that will put fear into the hearts of your enemies," Thorgrim said, "but it is a good name."

The other Hel-hide warriors seemed to agree. After that, they kept drinking late into the night, and the next morning they learned that several of the jarls had rejected Halfdan and chosen Guthrum as their new king, just as Thorgrim had predicted. When Guthrum marched from Readingum back to Wælingford, he took most of his army with him, which now exceeded Halfdan's in number, leaving only enough warriors to keep watch over his ships, and on the march to Wælingford, Guthrum found Geirmund and travelled beside him for some time.

"I see you are carrying your sword once more," the king said.

"I see you are no longer wearing Hnituðr," Geirmund said, for he could no longer see the ring on Guthrum's arm.

"I wear it," the king said. "But it is under my sleeve."

"Why hide it?"

He lowered his voice. "Surely you have heard the rumours."

"I trust what I saw," Geirmund said. "Not what I hear. And I know what I saw."

Guthrum frowned and laid his hand over his arm where Geirmund assumed the ring to be hidden. "I know what you gave to me, even if you did not when you gave it. I also know how you fought yesterday, and I plan to give you rich reward, Geirmund Hel-hide. When the time is right, you will be made a jarl."

Geirmund blinked in surprise. As a jarl, he would be entitled to lands from Guthrum's conquest, perhaps some of the very Wessex or Mercian lands he had travelled through and admired. "I am grateful, my king."

"Ah, but I am a newly made king," Guthrum said. "I now sit equal to Halfdan, which means I can be his enemy as easily as his ally. For now we have a peace, for war between us would serve neither, and I doubt I would win such a war. To fight one son of Ragnar is to fight them all."

Once again, Geirmund realized that with greater power and wealth came greater danger and threat.

"Until my rule is sure," Guthrum said, "I do not want it said that I only became a king by virtue of a ring. My crown must be earned, and it must be mine."

"It is yours," Geirmund said, 'regardless of the ring. But I understand. I will speak no more about it, and I will see that my warriors do the same."

The king nodded. "On the subject of your warriors, there are more who wish to swear to you."

That surprised Geirmund. "But I lost seven of my twenty-three. The battle proved that neither I nor my Hel-hides defy death, after all."

"They know you fought by my side," Guthrum said. "They know you were there when I slew Æthelred. They believe that fighting with you will bring them great honour and reward."

Geirmund only hesitated for a moment. "I will accept them," he said.

"You would be a fool not to. Embrace your growing reputation, son of Hjörr, and your countrymen will hear of you not just in Rogaland, but the whole length of the North Way." He turned toward Geirmund with a wry grin. "At Avaldsnes, you told me I would one day fear the warriors that follow you."

Geirmund had nearly forgotten that boast. "And do you?"

"Not yet, Hel-hide." His smile faded. "Not yet."

17

One month after the battle at Bedwyn, word reached Wælingford that Æthelred had died and his brother, Ælfred, had been named king. The Danes rejoiced at this news, assuming the Saxons to be in a state of weakness, and they began to form a plan for the final assault against Wessex. By way of rivers, trackways, and Roman roads Guthrum's raiding parties had reached deep into the lands south of Readingum, and they had discovered a place called Searesbyrig, near the town of Wiltun, which lay less than a day's march from Ælfred's seat at Wintanceastre.

According to the Danes who had seen it, Searesbyrig must have once been a mighty stronghold. It sat atop a flat hill over two hundred fathoms wide, with steep slopes nearly fifty fathoms in height. A deep trench encircled the hill, adding to its defences, with a second inner trench to defend a great hall. The hilltop also bore the signs and markings of previous fortifications, perhaps belonging to the Romans or the Britons, though the Saxons had foolishly abandoned the place and now made no use of its fastness.

Guthrum and Halfdan decided to join their armies and march

to seize Searesbyrig, which offered their warriors a new site for an encampment that sat almost at Ælfred's gates. But they had to plan well and move quickly to take it, or else Ælfred might discover their intent.

Weeks passed before the time came to march. They left Wælingford and Readingum by the silver light of the moon in its fullness and journeyed south by night, making their way first to the ruin of a Roman city much like the one Geirmund had passed through with John the priest. The Saxons called it Calleva, and the Danes stopped there to rest during the day, hidden among its bones and broken foundations.

Geirmund's warriors made their camp outside the fallen town walls, at the bottom of a large bowl some thirty-five or forty fathoms wide and built from stones. Trees grew within and around it, partly hiding its true size and perhaps making it seem larger than it was. Even so, Geirmund couldn't imagine how such a building could be roofed, and he decided it must have been open to the air. The crumbling sides of the bowl climbed to its lip in large steps, as though made for the feet of an enormous jötunn.

Skjalgi looked up and around at the place, wide-eyed. "What do you think the Romans did here?"

"They held fights," Rafn said. "People would pay silver to watch them."

"How do you know that?" Steinólfur asked.

"Vetr and I have raided south into Frakkland," the Dane said. "There are many places like this. In Langbardaland they are said to be even bigger. Much bigger."

"Bigger than this?" Skjalgi asked. "How tall were the Romans?"

Rafn laughed. "Smaller than Danes."

"And Northmen," Steinólfur added.

"Those are seats, Skjalgi," Rafn said, "not stairs."

"And yet where are the Romans now?" Birna asked. "They are dead and gone because they were mortals like us."

"Real battle must have been far distant from them," Vetr said. "Why else would they build a place just so they could pay silver to watch it?"

That question put Geirmund in mind of the battle ahead. It seemed to do the same for his company, for they all turned silent and sombre after that, and then a drizzle of cold rain came through with slow and rolling thunder to match their mood. That storm made it difficult to rest, and it slowed their travel that night, darkening the Roman road they followed south-west to Searesbyrig.

The clouds finally scattered just after midnight, though the air and their clothing remained damp and chilled, and Geirmund was grateful for the heat their marching stoked in his legs and arms. The rain had swollen the streams and marshland through which they journeyed, but the Roman road kept them mostly on dry ground, only sliding below the water in three places that were easy to ford.

When dawn found the Danes, they had not yet reached their planned place of rest, a defensive mound similar to Searesbyrig and ringed by a trench, but not so steep, high, or broad. But it would serve well to hold their forces for the day, so they pushed hard to reach it before the sun could reveal their presence to the Saxons.

Yew, birch, and ash trees grew thick around that hilltop and held the heavy air close to Geirmund's chest. His sleep in that place was deep and filled with strange dreams of ocean waves that turned into waves of heath, and storms that rained blood and golden rings.

That night's march brought them at last to Searesbyrig well

before dawn, allowing them to take some rest before the work of strengthening the fortifications began the next day. Geirmund lay upon the ground amidst his warriors, looking up at the stars. There were times when those lights felt near, as if they knew him and watched him, and times when they felt distant, cold, and unconcerned with him. That night it felt as though they paid him no more mind than the sea would pay to a grain of sand. His brief sleep did little to renew him, and then the sunrise revealed the enemy.

The Saxon army had gathered less than three rests to the west, on a hilltop above the village of Wiltun. Several of the commanders and jarls joined Guthrum and Halfdan at the edge of Searesbyrig to discuss what the Danes should do.

"Ælfred somehow guessed our plan," Guthrum said. "He must have. Perhaps he is cleverer than his brother."

"Let him sit there on his hill," Halfdan said. "We have the stronger position. We will fortify this place, and they will never dig us out."

"We were expected!" Guthrum said, pointing at the Saxon army. "Ælfred will have moved all grain stores and livestock far from here, beyond our reach. We have food to last a short while, but we will need more soon, and we cannot count on raids to provide it."

"What do you suggest?" Halfdan asked.

"We thought Ælfred would be in Wintanceastre," Guthrum said, "hiding behind his walls. Instead, he is here, but perhaps that gives us an opportunity to finish this. I say we attack him now, this day."

Halfdan folded his arms. "That was not our plan–"

"Our plan depended on taking Ælfred by surprise," Guthrum said. "We failed at that, and we are now encamped in the heartland of Wessex. I swear to you for each day that we delay we will stand here and watch the enemy's numbers grow until we have no hope of victory. This is the time to attack." He turned to his jarls and commanders. "My warriors are ready. Are yours, King Halfdan?"

That question seemed to have the effect that Guthrum undoubtedly intended, for Halfdan unfolded his arms and lifted his chest. "My warriors are always ready."

"Good," Guthrum said. "Then let us put them to work felling Saxons instead of trees."

Halfdan glanced at his jarls and commanders, and then he agreed.

After that, the jarls and commanders ordered their warriors to battle, and the army marched from the high ground of Searesbyrig, across a river ford at Wiltun, through the abandoned village, to the hill where Ælfred had gathered his force.

The Danes faced the same uphill challenge that had almost defeated them near Bedwyn, but they possessed greater numbers and began their assault. Guthrum and Halfdan divided their forces as they had done before, with Guthrum attacking from the north, and Halfdan from the east. Geirmund and his warriors stayed close to Guthrum as the king led the charge, but the Saxons sent no wave against them, and they did not divide as they had done before. Instead, they tightened their position on their hill as if they meant to stand there until the last warrior had fallen.

As soon as the Danes came within the range of the Saxon bows, arrows fell around them in thickets that succeeded in slowing their advance. Geirmund and his warriors ducked under their shields, but he soon saw that one of Rafn's legs had been pierced at the calf. Vetr flew to Rafn's side and held his own shield over his companion.

"Can you march?" Geirmund shouted.

Rafn grasped the shaft of the arrow and wrenched it from his leg. Then he tossed it aside, looked at Geirmund, and nodded.

"Shield-wall!" Geirmund shouted, and his warriors closed their ranks around him to form a tight front. Arrows rained like hail on their wooden roof. "This is our Valhalla!" Geirmund yelled, laughing. "Raftered with spears and roofed with shields like Óðinn's hall!"

He then gave the command to step forward, and he called that same command for each step, and for each push up the hill after that. They advanced as one towards the enemy, one pace at a time, their line unbroken.

By midday Geirmund could no longer see Guthrum, but he knew the king would be unharmed so long as fate let him wear Hnituðr, and eventually the Saxon quivers emptied, and the arrowfall slowed until it was time to resume the charge in earnest.

"Are you with me?" Geirmund shouted to his warriors. "Today we take Wessex!"

They roared and rushed up the hill, but when they reached the top they found the enemy already falling back, retreating to the west before Halfdan's assault from the east. But Geirmund saw that their retreat was not disordered by fear. The Saxon line held, even as the Danes chopped at it and rammed into it again and again.

"It seems these Wessex devils have finally found their courage!" Guthrum yelled, suddenly at Geirmund's side.

"Do we let them go?" Geirmund pointed down the hill. "My warriors could move around them to block–"

"We let them go," Guthrum said. "But we do not make it easy for them."

Geirmund frowned in confusion. "My king, we have them. We could make an end to Ælfred and his–"

"Ælfred wishes to discuss terms of peace."

Again, Geirmund was confused, and shook his head. "How do you know this?"

"I spoke to him," Guthrum said, grinning. He held his arms out and looked down at himself. "Not even a scratch. I think the sight of me alone, behind their lines, would have turned the Saxons back."

Geirmund made no reply as the battle raged before him, too filled with amazement, fear, and envy. It seemed that Guthrum had become invincible, and it was through Geirmund that fate had given the king that power.

"I will make Ælfred pay dearly for his peace," Guthrum said. "You will be a rich man, Geirmund Hel-hide."

It was mid-afternoon before the Danes finally let the Saxons finish their escape, and then Guthrum and Halfdan ordered their warriors to return to Searesbyrig. Geirmund had lost no warriors in the fighting, though some had been wounded, like Rafn. After seeing to their needs, he sought out Guthrum, seeking answers to questions that had followed him from the battleground.

He found the king with Halfdan and their jarls, discussing the terms and compensation they would demand from Ælfred to secure the safety of Wessex. When Guthrum saw Geirmund approaching, he stepped away from the others to speak in private.

"You look troubled," the king said.

"I do not understand why we are discussing peace with the Saxons," Geirmund said. "Ælfred is a new king. He knows he cannot defeat us, so he is trying to buy time to rebuild his armies and gather his strength."

"Of course he is," Guthrum said. "He is no fool. I believe Ælfred is a man of cunning."

"But we came to take Wessex," Geirmund said. "When you came to my father's hall, that is what you said. Now that Wessex is almost ours, you would walk away?"

Guthrum sighed, and then he put his hand on Geirmund's shoulder. "Hel-hide, listen well to me. When you look at the warriors in this encampment, my warriors, Halfdan's warriors, your warriors, what do you see?"

Geirmund hesitated, unsure of the answer Guthrum wanted. "I see Danes," he said.

"And I see that our numbers are too few," the king said. "We could have taken Wessex today, but how long would we have held it? For now the Saxons care for nothing but their own shires, and their own fields, but that will not last. They will unite against us, and we are not yet strong enough for that. Do you understand?"

Geirmund had not considered that. "I believe I do."

"I can also see that my warriors are tired. They are wounded. They want silver in reward for their swords and their blood. In truth, many of them would rather be farming than fighting, and so would I." The king let go of Geirmund's shoulder. "Wessex will fall to us, I swear it, but only when we can be sure of our rule over it. Until then, we bide our time, grow strong, and make the Saxons pay for our upkeep. You must–"

"King Guthrum!" someone called from the tent. "Ælfred has sent an envoy. He stands at the entrance to the encampment."

"Bring him before us!" Guthrum called back. Then he turned to Geirmund. "Stay. Be silent and listen. You will see."

Geirmund put aside his misgivings and followed the king back to the tent. King Halfdan eyed him from the side, along with several of the jarls, perhaps wondering why Guthrum had invited his Hel-hide commander to their council, but none spoke against his presence.

A few moments later, two Danes brought a man into the tent that Geirmund knew well, and he called out before he thought better of it.

"Priest!" he said. "I have wondered if you live."

All the Danes in the tent turned to look at Geirmund. Some seemed surprised that he would know Ælfred's man, others confused, and still a few others, like Guthrum, amused. As for the priest, he may have been equally surprised to see Geirmund, but his nervousness made itself plainer by the way he held his cross, and the way his gaze darted around the tent.

The king looked at Geirmund and nodded towards John. "You know this envoy?"

"I do," Geirmund said.

Halfdan glared hard at the priest. "Can he be trusted?"

"He can," Geirmund said. "I would trust him with my life."

Some in the tent murmured surprise at such a statement, while the priest nodded his head to Geirmund in thanks and evident relief.

"I am pleased to hear it," Guthrum said. "You may speak, priest."

John cleared his throat. "Uh, yes, King Ælfred of Wessex wishes for King Guthrum and King Halfdan to meet the day after tomorrow, at midday, in the village of Wiltun, there to discuss terms for peace. Neither side shall number more than twelve."

"Why not tomorrow?" Guthrum asked.

John cast a quick glance at Geirmund before speaking. "Tomorrow is King Ælfred's weekly day of worship and prayer. He does not want to disturb the peace of that day with worldly matters of war."

A moment went by, and then the Danes in the tent began to laugh. The priest's cheeks flushed.

"Tell Ælfred we will meet with him tomorrow," Halfdan said. "His god can wait–"

"King Halfdan," Guthrum said, "with respect, I think we are the ones who can wait. We are quite comfortable here. But Ælfred should know that we do not wait for the sake of his god. We wait because we know that Ælfred will think more clearly about the price of peace if he has been allowed to pray."

John let out a deep breath as though from a bellows. "You are wise to see it, King Guthrum."

Geirmund watched Halfdan to see how he would respond to Guthrum's overrule of him. The Dane's blue eyes bulged, and he shook with anger. Then, without word or warning, he turned and stalked from the tent, followed quickly by his jarls. King Guthrum watched them go, his own face empty of any expression, and then he turned back to the priest.

"Is there anything else?" he asked.

"There is nothing more," John said.

Guthrum waved him away. "Then you may go."

As John turned to leave, Geirmund stepped forward, daring to speak now that Halfdan and his jarls had gone. "May I walk with the priest back to the edge of the encampment?" he asked.

That request raised one of Guthrum's eyebrows in surprise, or perhaps curiosity, but he nodded. "You may."

"Thank you," Geirmund said, bowing his head. Then he turned to John and gestured him in the direction they should go, and once they had left the tent, he smiled. "I am glad to see you, priest."

John wiped a great quantity of sweat from his brow with the sleeve of his robe. "And I you. If you can believe it, I actually prayed that you would be here, so that I would see at least one friendly face among the Danes."

"I can believe it," Geirmund said. "But I still see no reason to pray over what is fated."

They crossed the broad and open top of Searesbyrig as the sun neared its setting, and from that high place Geirmund could see acre upon acre in all directions, green and golden and rich, a country he had hoped would be Daneland that day.

"Once the terms of peace are settled," John said, "King Ælfred wonders if King Guthrum and King Halfdan will keep them."

Geirmund nodded. "Guthrum will. I believe Halfdan will also. You remember he has kept his peace with Mercia."

"For now," John said. "Guthrum seems to be a warrior of great skill. It is said no weapon can touch him. King Ælfred wonders if his power comes from a pagan relic, or from pagan devils."

Geirmund said nothing in reply to that. "What terms will Ælfred demand of Guthrum?"

John glanced out over that same sunset land. "He will demand that every last Dane leave Wessex. For that he will pay in gold and silver. He may also suggest that Guthrum and Halfdan be baptized."

"Baptized? To become Christian?" Geirmund laughed loudly. "That will never happen."

John smiled and shrugged. "The judgements of God are unsearchable, and his paths beyond tracing out."

"That is true of every god," Geirmund said. "But you must tell me before you go, what happened after we parted?"

The priest grew quiet. "I travelled with the wagons, as Jarl Sidroc ordered. Later, Danes came fleeing towards us, retreating from the battle, with Saxons in pursuit. They fought. The Saxons killed the Danes, and then they took me to their camp. After the battle, Ælfred sought me out, thinking that my brief time among you pagans might be of some use to him, and to God. I have served the king since." He allowed a brief smile. "And what of you?"

"I now command a company of warriors," Geirmund said. "We have fought in battles and fought well. But I feel I should tell you that I have slain many Saxon warriors."

"I have slain a few Danes," the priest said.

"You have fought in battle?"

"No, not battle." John looked down at the ground. "When I was with the wagons, and I saw the Danes fleeing, I thought they would try to kill me or take me with them. I... fought for my freedom."

Geirmund felt a conflict inside that the priest must also feel when hearing about his dead countrymen, namely that it angered and saddened Geirmund to think of Danes dying, but it pleased him that John lived.

"I think there is more to you than I realized, priest," Geirmund said. "Much more."

John held his open hands before him. "I make no claims to might in battle," he said, "for I am a poor soldier. But if I must be a soldier, I will be a soldier for Christ."

They reached the edge of the encampment, where Geirmund bade farewell to the priest. He then returned to his company, where his warriors shared in his confusion and frustration over the outcome of that day's battle. Geirmund did his best to explain King Guthrum's plan, and despite their misgivings, most seemed to welcome the thought of silver, and a time of rest to heal and enjoy it.

When the kings left the encampment two days later, they each took only a handful of jarls with them, and they returned from Wiltun that evening well pleased. Ælfred had agreed to pay them a vast weight of both gold and silver, and in return no Dane would cross the river the Saxons called Avon, and within that year the

Danes would leave Wessex altogether. Guthrum and Halfdan planned to withdraw from Readingum and Wælingford, after which they would bring their ships down the River Thames to Lunden.

Before leaving Searesbyrig, Geirmund gazed over Wessex from the top of that hill with Steinólfur and Birna beside him.

"Halfdan is on his way to being a powerful king," the older warrior said. "Some might say you and your Hel-hides made him so."

"Then let us hope he will be a good king," Birna said.

"He will be the king he is fated to be," Geirmund said. "Only the Three Spinners know what is to come. As for me, I believe my fate will bring me back here, and I swear that so long as I breathe, I will have Wessex."

PART FOUR

Jorvik

18

Geirmund had never before seen a place such as Lunden. It was not a town, but rather two towns sitting a rest apart from each other on the northern riverbank of the Thames, each with its own steads and fields that spread into the lands surrounding them. The first that Guthrum's fleet passed was an unwalled Saxon settlement called Lundenwic. From the river, Geirmund looked across its low wooden dwellings and high halls, its wharf a throng of ships coming and going, carrying travellers, traders, and wares, like bees coming and going from the hive.

Next to Geirmund, Guthrum nodded towards the town and said, "North of the river is Mercia, and there is a peace, at least for now."

"I passed through Mercia," Geirmund said. "From what I saw it would be easy to take."

"Perhaps," Guthrum said. "But that is for Ivarr and Ubba to decide. It is to them the king of Mercia pays tribute."

"Ubba?"

"Yes. A son of Ragnar. Halfdan's brother."

The name of that Dane reminded Geirmund of Fasti, the

kinsman of Ubba, and therefore perhaps Halfdan's kinsman also. He remembered the heat of the man's blood on his hand, and the sound of his kicking in the grass as he rowed away from Ancarig. "Where is Ubba now?"

"These days he is often found in the north fighting Picts, or raiding Irland to the west."

Geirmund nodded, feeling relieved, but kept his expression still.

They left Lundenwic, and a short distance on they arrived at the walled Dane-town of Lunden. Geirmund saw that Romans had built it, another of their bone-cities left empty by the Saxons, and therefore useful to the Danes, with stone fortifications three fathoms high already built and able to defend them. The town also appeared to be twice as large as Lundenwic, with twice the activity on its wharf, for traders undoubtedly knew who had the silver now.

The arrival of Guthrum and Halfdan's armies filled the river with enough ships to make a floating town to rival the two on land. Much of the encampment travelled from Readingum by road, but, even so, the unloading of those ships into Lunden took several days.

The town walls boasted six gates and enclosed an area well over three hundred acres in size. Most of Guthrum's army, including Geirmund's company, took up a place among the broken Roman columns, walls, and courtyards that lay between Lunden's easternmost gate and the gate that opened onto Earninga Street, a stretch of which Geirmund had travelled with John.

Guthrum planned to winter there, so Geirmund and his warriors worked to build roofs over their heads and walls where there were none, making Lunden into a town that looked half Roman and half Dane. A few weeks after Guthrum's army arrived, the commander of the town, a Dane named Tryggr, came to see the work those warriors had accomplished.

He was an older man, perhaps Steinólfur's age, with silver in his hair and the hardened leather skin of one who had spent much time with the sun, and wind, and salt, and spray of the sea in his face.

"This is all well done," he said as he strode through Guthrum's quarter of the town.

"I'm glad you approve," the king said.

Several of Guthrum's jarls and commanders trailed behind, including Geirmund, who did not understand why Tryggr's approval should be necessary. Guthrum stood above the town's commander in rank, equal to Halfdan. But Geirmund also knew both were kings without lands, and guests in Lunden, so perhaps that accounted for Guthrum's deference.

Tryggr turned around and nodded past Guthrum. "Your warriors have served you well." He looked over the faces of the jarls and commanders, but he stopped when he saw Geirmund. At first he seemed perplexed, but, a moment later, his eyes hardened, and his expression darkened. "Word of their deeds has reached us even here," he said.

"I could not ask for braver or stronger men," Guthrum said. "Now, Jarl Tryggr, please join me in my hall. There are matters we must discuss."

Tryggr's glare lingered on Geirmund before he broke his gaze and went with Guthrum, leaving Geirmund to wonder what had caused the Dane's apparent hostility. He was well accustomed to stares and suspicion, but Tryggr's eyes had seemed to contain more than that, and he hoped that did not bode ill.

When not working with wood and stone, Geirmund explored the town, carrying plenty of silver to enjoy it, since King

Guthrum had kept his promise and rewarded him well. Walking through the streets of Lunden, it seemed to Geirmund that it drew the world unto itself. He saw merchants and goods from all corners, and lands so distant Geirmund had never heard their tongue or their name. He drank wine from Spanland and bought himself a costly shirt of ringmail from Frakkland. He tasted the oil of olives from Langbardaland and Grikkland, and spices from Affrika and Indialand. Between his fingers he rubbed silks from Tyrkland, and Persiðialand, and places even further east, fabrics so soft and fine he had to use his eyes to know they were there, for his skin could barely feel them. After traders weighed his silver, they sometimes returned the excess to him in coins from Serkland marked with runes that curled like vines. He spent the night with a Frisian woman and learned to play dice and other new games from men with skin of many shades and hues. Unlike the Danes upon first seeing him, the travellers and traders gave Geirmund no second glances, and some even guessed that he had come from Finnland or Bjarmaland. To Lunden the world came, and then the clever left in their empty ships much wealthier than when they had arrived.

In this way weeks passed in Lunden as days and hours had passed in the battlefield, and those weeks turned into months with ease. Wounds healed, but Geirmund didn't want his warriors to grow soft, for still Wessex waited. To keep his company ready he asked daily work and training of them in the courtyard where they lived and slept.

Geirmund sat with Birna and Aslef one day, watching Rafn and Vetr sparring. The two men, fast and agile, one with a spear and the other with two swords, put Geirmund in mind of a dove and a raven wheeling and fighting in mid-air. Their combat took place over a colourful floor of small tiles, broken and set together in an intricate pattern of twisting and interlocking lines. A tiled man looked out of a ring at the centre of the floor, wearing a white tunic and a ring of leaves about his head. If he appeared as all Romans had appeared, Geirmund thought, he looked every bit a mortal and not a god.

"I could be content here for the rest of my days," Aslef said. The gash on his nose and cheek had healed, but with a scar that had almost, but not utterly, ruined his features.

Birna looked around. "It's a good place," she said, then elbowed him. "Eventually I'd want a change of company."

"I mean this town," he said. "Lunden."

Geirmund understood what he meant, and a part of him wished for the same thing, but another part could not imagine being idle for much longer. "You may not enjoy it so much when you run out of silver," he said.

Aslef nodded. "That's true."

"I would grow bored," Birna said. "Truthfully, I am bored already, but I'm trying to enjoy the peace before we return to war."

"I'm already tired of war," Aslef said. "I will fight if necessary, for honour or for kin, but I would rather settle down."

"What, to be a farmer?" Birna asked him.

"I don't know. I think I would like to have a wife and children, at least."

Birna turned to Geirmund. "What about you?"

"I want to have a wife one day, and children."

"Well, don't either of you look at me," she said, laughing. "Not until you pups have grown into your paws."

Geirmund smiled and went on. "I also want land to call my own, but not as a farmer. My brother will have a kingdom, and I would have the same."

"You want to be a king?" Aslef asked, sounding a bit surprised.

"I don't need to be called a king."

Birna smirked. "You just want to be seen as one."

"What I want is to live up to the honour and reputation of my forebears. I want to know I've earned my place at their bench in Valhalla."

Birna clapped him on the back. "Then you, my friend, are well on your way." She rose to her feet.

"Where are you off to?" Aslef asked.

"To find a wolf," she said as she walked away, and then looked back over her shoulder. "A fully grown wolf!"

Aslef called after her. "Would that wolf by chance be a Dane who fights with a bearded axe?" But she made no reply to him.

He and Geirmund laughed, but neither of them spoke again for a few moments, and the sounds of fighting by Rafn and Vetr took up the silence. Then Aslef said, "My father wanted to be a king."

Geirmund turned towards him. "Where is he now?"

"Valhalla, I hope. He died fighting for a crown in Jutland."

Geirmund gave him a slow nod of respect. "When I first met Guthrum, he said the Danes have seen much war."

"They have," Aslef said. "I came west to get away from my father's enemies. Away from war." He looked up at the square of sky visible above the courtyard. "Perhaps I shall stay here in Lunden. If you would release me."

"Release you? That is no small thing to ask."

"I know," he said. "But I am no oath-breaker. I will fight for you until I am released, or I die."

"You are a warrior, Aslef," Geirmund said, "and I would hold no warrior against fate and will. Only stay with us for now. When Guthrum marches, you can decide then whether to march with us or remain behind."

Aslef bowed his head. "I will do as you say."

"What do you two speak of?" Rafn asked, breathing hard. He and Vetr had finished their fight and stood huffing and sweating in the courtyard's middle.

"Fate," Geirmund said.

"Bah." Rafn waved them off. "Talking about fate is no more useful than talking about the weather."

Vetr wiped his shining forehead and face. "Come, Rafn. I need to wash."

"As do I."

The two warriors then left the courtyard to seek one of the Roman baths that could be found throughout Lunden. Many of those large basins remained empty and dry, but some Danes and other merchants had figured out how to fill and heat a few of them, for the use of which they asked coin and gained wealth.

"All we have here is ale," Aslef said. "I want some mead. Will you join me?"

"I will," Geirmund said.

They left the courtyard through an arched portal and walked down several narrow passages until they reached a wide road laid in stone. There they turned south and headed towards the town's wharf and market streets. Away to the west, above the ruins and roofs of wood and Roman tile, Geirmund could glimpse what remained of the flat top and straight walls of another stone bowl even bigger than the place in which they had camped at Calleva. He had learned from a Langbardaland merchant that such a building was called a coliseum by the Romans.

"When do you think Guthrum will march?" Aslef asked.

"I don't know," Geirmund said. "But I have heard him speak of unrest in Northumbria. We may be marching north to an encampment at Turcesige, on the River Trent."

A commotion in the road ahead drew Geirmund's attention, where it appeared that a wagon had tipped, causing a blockage of traffic. Merchants and Danes yelled, fists raised, while oxen bellowed, and some men tried to move the wagon out of the way.

Geirmund and Aslef stopped. Then Geirmund nodded his companion towards an earthen byway off the main road they could use to get around the din and trouble. It led them into a part of the town where the buildings stood closer together and the shadows climbed higher. They had only walked a short way when two Danes stepped out in front of them, blocking the road with their hands on their weapons in a way that seemed intentional.

"Stand aside," Aslef said. "This is Geirmund Hel-hide, one of King Guthrum's commanders."

"We know who he is," one of the Danes said. He wore a ring in his nose, and dark slithering lines marked his skin in the shape of a snake around his neck. "We've been watching him and waiting for a good long while."

Geirmund looked over his shoulder behind them and saw that two more warriors had entered the street, their weapons already drawn. He and Aslef carried weapons but had no reason to wear armour about the town, and so they were vulnerable.

"You know who I am," Geirmund said, turning to look at the leader who had spoken. "Who are you?"

"Krok," the snake-Dane said. "I am one of Halfdan's commanders, soon to be made a jarl."

"Why would Halfdan give a turd like you that honour?" Aslef said. "I've never even heard your name."

The Dane drew his sword and pointed it at Geirmund. "For slaying the Northman who murdered Ubba's kinsman, Fasti."

Before Geirmund could respond, they charged.

Aslef spun with a warrior's instinct and put his back to Geirmund's. Though outnumbered, they fought their attackers with enough ferocity to drive them back, but that reprieve would last only a moment. They had to reach the main road, where Geirmund hoped the presence of witnesses would stop the attack for long enough to make a true escape.

"Go north," he whispered.

Then he lunged to the south with a wild roar, swinging his sword and axe, putting the enemy on their back feet and taking Aslef's foes by surprise also. Then Geirmund spun and rushed with Aslef at the two Danes blocking the north passage, who regained their wits too slowly to react in time to stop them. But they did raise their weapons, and Geirmund fought the warrior on the left, who swung his axe at Geirmund's head. He ducked aside and slammed his elbow into the side of the warrior's head, sending him reeling as Krok and his warrior raced towards them from the south.

"Go!" Geirmund shouted.

Aslef had just given his opponent a nasty slash across his sword arm and broken free. Together, they ran back along the passage and turned west down an alley, then onto the main road, where another of Krok's Danes waited, keeping watch. Aslef put his shoulder into the man's chest and threw him aside like a boar tossing a hound, but the man had a knife and stabbed Aslef with it, then fell, sprawled on the Roman stones.

Some in the street took note of the fight, pointing as Krok and his warriors emerged from the byway, red-faced and snarling. But the enemy looked around and stopped short of attacking, as if weighing their choices. An open fight in the street could bring allies, as well as witnesses.

Aslef stumbled, and Geirmund grabbed him up, putting the Dane's arm over his shoulder to support him. "Are you going to attack an injured man?" Geirmund asked Krok, loud for all to hear.

Krok looked again at the crowd, which had now turned more of its attention on them, and he sheathed his weapon. His warriors did the same. "I swear I will kill you, Hel-hide," the Dane said.

"And I swear you will pay in blood for what you have done." Geirmund then turned north and hurried along the road. "Hold on," he said to Aslef.

"I'm holding."

They hobbled along together until they reached Guthrum's quarter, and then Geirmund called for help. As he reached the tiled yard, Hel-hides and other warriors came running to meet them. Thorgrim was there, with Birna, and they both hurried to Geirmund's side, helping to lay Aslef down upon the sun-warmed ground.

"What happened?" Thorgrim asked.

"We were ambushed," Geirmund said. "One of them stuck Aslef with his knife."

"Where?" Birna searched across Aslef's chest and belly. "How deep?"

"Deep." Aslef pointed to his wound with a grimace. "In my side."

Thorgrim gave Geirmund a worried glance, and then called for leeks and onions, out of which he boiled a broth as Geirmund and Birna pulled off Aslef's tunic. The wound was as small, narrow, and thin as the knife that had made it, and it poured out black blood in a slow and steady stream. When Thorgrim had made the broth, he gave it to Aslef to drink, and then they all waited as Birna kept pressure on the wound to slow its leaking.

King Guthrum came then, having heard word of the attack, and he pulled Geirmund aside to speak where none could hear.

"The attack was on you, I assume?" the king said.

"It was."

"Who?"

"He called himself Krok. One of Halfdan's warriors, but I don't know him."

"I know him." Guthrum's eyes turned dark as open barrows. "Halfdan will answer for this." He glanced again at Aslef, and then he stalked away from the courtyard.

A short while later, Thorgrim knelt at Aslef's side and smelled the blood coming from his wound for the odour of onions.

"Well?" Aslef asked. "Am I dead?"

Thorgrim looked up at Geirmund and Birna. "The blade cut into your gut," he whispered. "I'm sorry, Aslef."

The injured Dane went quiet. Then he sighed. "I thought it would end this way. Thought I could hide from it here in Lunden. But it found me." He looked up at Geirmund. "My father died of a gut wound. I don't want to linger that way for days and weeks, stinking of death."

"Quiet." Thorgrim laid a hand on his chest. "The gods may yet pull you through this. For now let us move you somewhere more comfortable."

They found a quiet room off the Hel-hide courtyard, where they made a bed of straw and furs. The sight of Aslef lying upon it reminded Geirmund of his brother lying on a similar bed back in their father's hall, and as with Hámund Geirmund felt responsible for what had happened to his warrior. It was Geirmund who had killed Fasti, and it wasn't right that Aslef should pay with his life for something his commander had done.

He stood over Aslef in shame, until Birna took hold of his arm and pulled him from the room, out into the courtyard. Rafn and

Vetr had returned, along with Steinólfur and Skjalgi, and they all stood with Birna, afire with vengeance.

"Where can we find these Danes?" she asked in quiet rage. "I will gut them cock to throat."

"Guthrum went to speak with Halfdan," Geirmund said. "When he returns, we will know more. Until then, keep your blades sharp."

Many in Geirmund's company took turns staying with Aslef, talking to him, or telling stories, or simply sitting by his side when he slept, sweating and groaning. That evening a fever came upon him that rattled his teeth together, and then Guthrum finally returned, and again he pulled Geirmund aside.

The king looked tired, eyes downcast as he said, "Tell me if it's true."

Geirmund did not need to ask what he meant. "It is true. But if I had not killed Fasti, it would have meant my death instead. That is the truth, and that is what I'll say to the Althing–"

"Althing?" Guthrum shook his head, almost laughing. "Where do you think you are, Hel-hide? This is Lunden, and we are at war. There is no Althing here."

"But the truth–"

"The truth does not matter. What matters is that Tryggr is a friend to Ubba. What matters is that word reached Tryggr of an ugly Northman named Geirmund who killed one of Ubba's kinsmen, and then that same Northman appeared in Lunden with Halfdan, who also knows of it now. This is a blood feud."

"I can pay wergild–"

"That will not satisfy them," Guthrum said.

"Then let Aslef's death satisfy the blood-price," Geirmund said, growing angry, "for he will not live much longer, and I would–"

"You are the Hel-hide." Guthrum growled in frustration.

"Halfdan has not forgotten you. Do you not see? This is the price of reputation, and it will not be the last time someone else pays it for you."

"Then let me fight Tryggr and Halfdan. A duel for–"

"That will not happen," Guthrum said. "They do not believe you worthy of that honour."

"Then what am I to do?"

"Leave Lunden."

"What?"

"They will not rest until you are dead."

Geirmund stammered in disbelief. "You–you would let them turn me into an outlaw? A beast of the forest?"

"Me?" Guthrum's cheeks and chest puffed in anger as he pointed at Geirmund's chest. "You did this to yourself! I did not kill that boy, and I will not make war with Ubba and Halfdan over you!" He inhaled and paused. "Do you know he demanded that I turn you over to him tonight? I put him off until tomorrow, but that is all I can do to protect you."

"I won't leave Aslef injured and dying. It is because of me that he–"

"And how many others from your company would you see dead? If you stay in Lunden, you will die, and it is almost certain you will take more of your warriors with you. Or you can leave, alone, and spare them the need to fight for you."

It felt to Geirmund as though the cracked and ancient walls of that city now threatened to collapse on him, for it seemed he had to choose between his honour and the lives of his friends and warriors, and faced with that choice he would take the path Guthrum offered him. "Where am I to go?"

"Seek your kind and kin," Guthrum said. "You can't rely on finding safe shelter among Danes, so go north. And here, take this." He gave Geirmund a small pouch of silver. "I will not always march with Halfdan. When you hear that our armies have divided, seek me out, and I will welcome you back. Together, we will take Wessex."

Geirmund bowed his head. "I thank you. I will gather my things."

"Be quick about it. You should be well away from this place before morning." Guthrum reached out and took Geirmund's arm in a firm grip. "Always be on your guard. Krok has sworn to take your life for Halfdan and Ubba, and I would see you come back to me in one piece."

Geirmund bowed his head again, and then Guthrum released his arm.

"Go," the king said. "Before it gets much darker."

Geirmund bade Guthrum farewell and went to the room where he slept and stored his things. He tried to avoid drawing attention, but almost as soon as he had pulled on his ringmail shirt, Steinólfur stood in the doorway scowling, Skjalgi and Birna behind him.

"Some might think you're going somewhere," the older warrior said. "But not me. I know you left us behind once before, and you'd never be fool enough to make that mistake a second time." He then spoke over his shoulder. "Isn't that what I said?"

Birna nodded. "That's what you said, but it looks to me like you were wrong."

Steinólfur stepped into the room and folded his arms, glaring at Geirmund. "Well? Are you going to make a liar out of me?"

Geirmund sighed and shook his head. "I am leaving," he said, and as the older warrior's face reddened with disbelief and anger, he added, "I must go. There is a blood feud between me and Ubba, and Halfdan."

"A blood feud?" Birna asked. "Over what?"

"After I washed ashore, before Ashdown, I killed one of Ubba's kinsmen. If I hadn't, it would have been my death instead. But there were no witnesses, and there is no Althing to give judgement on the matter."

"But why are you leaving?" Skjalgi asked next to her, appearing more confused than angry.

Though the boy had asked the question, Geirmund took a step towards Steinólfur and looked the older warrior straight in the eye. "Because Aslef has already paid the price for my choice, and I will not see that happen to another of my warriors. Halfdan will come for me tomorrow, and if I am here, there will be a fight. I will have no one else die for me."

Birna laughed. "I thought we swore to do just that?"

"I slew that man before your oaths," Geirmund said. "You are not bound by them in this matter."

"Then we will go with you," Steinólfur said. His voice had softened, he seemed to now understand the choice Geirmund faced. "The boy and me. We were sworn to you before."

"No, I can't allow that," Geirmund said. "Halfdan's warrior has sworn to kill me. If you travel with me, the blood feud will touch you–"

"I know that." Steinólfur unfolded his arms. "Of course I know that. You think I'm a fool?"

Geirmund smiled. "Only for asking to travel with me."

The older warrior snorted. "You're a fool if you leave me behind. And I'll follow you regardless."

"As will I," Birna said.

Geirmund and Steinólfur both turned towards her, and Geirmund at least felt somewhat surprised by her loyalty. "Why do you wish to come?"

"Because I swore to you," she said. "And also because I want vengeance for Aslef, and the shortest way to that will be at your side, if his murderer hunts you. And I've had my fill of Lunden besides."

Geirmund weighed his choices and realized he had few. Steinólfur would do as he threatened and follow him with Skjalgi, as would Birna, so it made little sense to try to leave them behind. "Very well," he said. "But what of Aslef? He is not yet–"

"Aslef would understand," Birna said. "You know this. And I know Thorgrim will wish to stay with him until the end. Thorgrim would also lead the Hel-hides until our return if asked."

Geirmund moved towards the door. "Then I will ask him–"

"Let me," Birna said. "This must be done quickly and quietly. And with Thorgrim… I have my own farewell to make."

"What of Rafn and Vetr?" Steinólfur asked, and then he and the other two looked to Geirmund.

"Offer them the choice," he said. "But tell no one else."

Birna nodded and left them, and then Skjalgi came fully into the room.

Geirmund resumed packing. "You should go and gather your things," he said, but after some moments neither the older warrior nor the boy had moved, so he looked up at them. "You have more to say?"

"You would have left." Steinólfur shook his head, and Geirmund knew the older warrior would not soon let go of his anger over it. "Not the others, us." He glanced at Skjalgi. "You would have left us."

"I had no choice–"

"Yes, you did." The older warrior pointed at Geirmund's chest. "This is the second time you have turned your back on us. If there is a third, I will surely know how little my oath means to you, and I will no longer be bound by it. Do you understand me?"

Geirmund paused to give Steinólfur's question the respect it deserved, for it was no small thing for a man of his honour to speak of breaking oaths. "I do, and I will not turn my back on you again."

"Good." The older warrior nodded. "We'll go and gather our things."

"I'll wait here," Geirmund said, and a few moments later Birna returned with Rafn and Vetr, who had decided to join their small war-band. "Thorgrim?" he asked the shield-maiden.

"He will make sure the Hel-hides keep their spears sharpened," she said. "Aslef sleeps for now, but if he awakens, Thorgrim will explain all."

"Then it is time to leave," Geirmund said.

And so, after Steinólfur and Skjalgi returned, they did.

19

Geirmund knew there would be many Danes on Earninga Street because he had seen them for himself when travelling with John, and that road lay too near the western border of East Anglia, which Ubba ruled. So, instead of taking a familiar way, he and his small war-band of five Hel-hides followed another Roman road north of west out of Lunden called Wæcelinga, towards the centre of Mercia, hoping to encounter fewer enemies.

The slender moon offered some light, enough to see the pale street of crushed rock that lay ahead of them, but not enough to be sure whether threats lurked in the shadows under the trees to either side of the road. For several rests they travelled through farmland that fed the towns on the River Thames, the lights and woodsmoke of the halls and houses there far distant from the road. Stretches of woodland soon broke apart those fields and pastures, until they came into a country of deep forest. Geirmund did not fear robbers at that mark of night, for it seemed doubtful that any would expect travellers to waylay, and would likely not attempt an attack against a group so heavily armed, but nevertheless he marched with his eyes open wide and his ears pricked.

At around midnight they entered a low-lying land of heath and marsh, with forests of oak and birch and thickets of hazel and hornbeam. Under the leaves of the trees the road finally sank into a darkness too deep to travel safely, and since they had put Lunden and Halfdan some fifteen rests or so behind them, Geirmund decided to order a stop for the night.

They stepped off the street some distance and headed for a gathering of three large oaks, each wider across than an arm span, and on the opposite sides of the tree trunks from the road they all settled down between twisted roots to sleep, taking turns at watch. They couldn't see the road from where they lay, but that meant anyone on the road could also not see them. Despite feeling hidden, Geirmund woke in alarm and discomfort several times before dawn, startled by noises in the blue early-morning light. He shivered, and his bones creaked like the branches overhead as his war-band set off again before the light had turned golden.

Before long, the land opened out of the heath and wood, and the sluggish sun finally rose over the ruin of another Roman city through which the road then carried them. Though large and impressive, its broken walls and buildings no longer struck Geirmund as such places once did, for he no longer imagined them to be inhabited by the dead, but they seemed to unsettle at least one warrior in his party.

Skjalgi's wide eyes never rested as they strode down the silent streets, past temples and a coliseum, and across an open square fifty fathoms wide. "At least the dead are quiet," the boy whispered.

"The Romans are not undead," Geirmund said. "They are gone. You have no need to fear them, Skjalgi. They came to England, they conquered it, and then they lost it. Now the Saxons possess these lands, but they will soon lose England to us."

That seemed to reassure the boy a little.

They soon left the ruin behind, and at midday they came upon a Saxon town. They passed its fields and farms, then a few houses that stood at its edge. Up ahead, Geirmund saw a crossroads at the heart of the village where several buildings stood close together, including what looked like a cold bakehouse and an alehouse, along with many empty market stalls. He saw few Saxons about, as if the people of that place had all gone into hiding, but then a man stepped into their path and held up his hand to halt them.

"There is a peace in Mercia," the Saxon said. He wore leather armour and a sword, and he looked past Geirmund at his companions. "What brings you here?"

"We are travelling north." Geirmund noticed three more men standing nearby, all carrying weapons, one of them with a bow and quiver at his side. "We have no plan to stay here, or to break the peace. We wish only to pass through."

"And where do you come from? Lunden?"

Behind Geirmund, Steinólfur chuckled. "This Saxon swine is bold."

"What does that matter to you?" Geirmund asked.

The Saxon shrugged. "It's my duty to know who comes and goes, where they come from and where they're going. Travellers often bring trouble."

The man's eyes narrowed as he spoke those last few words, and Geirmund noticed he had new bruises just starting to blush about his neck, and a bit of dried blood in the crevices of skin at his mouth, as if he had been involved in a recent fight.

"We are not the first Danes you've seen today," Geirmund said.

"What?" The man swallowed and frowned. "I don't–"

"Do not look," Geirmund said as the Saxon made to turn and glance back. "Keep your eyes on me, as though we speak about your crops. Betray me and I swear you will die on this spot, no matter what happens next."

"God's teeth." The man closed his eyes and let out a long breath through tight lips. "A curse upon all you pagan devils."

"Does their leader have a ring in his nose?" Geirmund asked. "A man called Krok?"

"I didn't ask his name," the Saxon said. "But yes, he has a ring in his nose, like an ox."

Geirmund's warriors murmured behind him, but they knew better than to draw weapons or react in a way that would warn Krok and his Danes, who undoubtedly watched and waited ahead to ambush them.

"How many?" Geirmund asked.

"Eighteen, perhaps twenty warriors." The Saxon looked at his boots. "They arrived at dawn, wanting to know if we'd seen Danes from Lunden."

"They must have marched past us as we slept," Rafn said. "When they discovered it, they decided to lay a trap for us."

Then Birna spoke. "Do not look, Saxon, but tell us, are we within reach of their arrows here?"

"Almost," the Saxon said. "A few more paces."

"Where are they?" Steinólfur asked.

"Some are in the alehouse." Sweat covered the man's forehead, despite the cool morning. "Some hide across the street from it. The rest are scattered with their bows."

Geirmund glanced along the empty street ahead, searching for weaknesses and opportunities, but saw none. "Why did you stop us? Why not let us walk into the trap?"

"He wanted you to think all is as it should be," the Saxon said.

"Where are your people?" Vetr asked.

The man gave a slight nod towards the east. "Hiding in the marsh until you Danes have all gone."

"We could go to the marsh," Steinólfur said.

"Retreat?" Birna scoffed. "Aslef's killer lies ahead. I will not–"

"They outnumber us three to one," Geirmund said. "And they control the ground. Vengeance can wait until we choose the battle."

"If you flee," the Saxon said, "he will know I betrayed him. They will kill us and burn our village."

"Why should that concern us?" Rafn asked.

The man paled. "You Danes are all–"

"What is your name?" Geirmund asked.

The Saxon hesitated. "Elwyn."

"Elwyn, where is the closest way into the marsh?"

"Just ahead. There's a road north of smithy. It leads to a path into the fens."

At the mention of the town's blacksmith a plan formed in Geirmund's mind. "Elwyn," he said, "these Danes are sworn to Halfdan, who is brother to Ivarr and Ubba, who have a truce with your King Burgred. They will only plunder your town if you give them reason, but if you do as I say, you and your town will be spared."

The Saxon shifted on his feet. "I'm listening."

"We will go to the blacksmith's shop and wait there. You will go to Krok, and he will ask what you and I have been talking about. You will tell him that we plan to stay in town for a day or two, and we've asked for the smith. That is your chance to convince Krok that you are still with him."

"What will you do?" Elwyn asked.

"We will wait," Geirmund said. "It is likely he will send one of his warriors here to act as the smith, and during that time he will move the rest of his war-band into position to attack us here, or his false smith will try to convince us to move where they can attack us. Either way, it is the false smith who Krok will blame when we make our escape, and Krok will likely leave your town to pursue us."

That seemed to reassure the Saxon enough that he gave a slow nod, then turned and gestured down the road. "I will lead you to the smith."

Geirmund glanced at his warriors, who nodded agreement, and they all moved down the quiet street. It remained possible that the enemy bowmen would try to shoot them, but it seemed more likely that Krok would want the honour of killing Geirmund with his blade, and would wait until the Hel-hides reached the place of ambush at the crossroads. Even so, Geirmund tried to walk without apparent alarm or concern, though he kept his ears alert to the twang of bowstrings.

When they reached the blacksmith's shop, they found it a bower, open to the roads running north and west, and walled with wooden planks to the south and east. A hot forge glowed in the middle, surrounded by several benches, and an anvil on which a pair of tongs gripped a heavy rod of iron hammered thin at one end. It seemed the smith had been at work when the Danes arrived, and had left in haste.

Elwyn gave Geirmund a last nod, and then he and his warriors went up the street towards the alehouse.

Vetr leaned against a bower post. "This is a good plan."

"Unless that Saxon swine betrays us to Krok," Rafn said.

"He might." Geirmund watched the alehouse door and the surrounding street for signs of movement. "But his choice and his fate are his. Either way, he will draw Krok to us."

"We could make for the marsh now," Steinólfur said. "Be done with it."

Geirmund turned to the older warrior. "Go. Take Skjalgi, Rafn, and Vetr. Scout the path to the marsh and keep watch down the town's backside. Birna and I will remain here a bit longer."

Steinólfur's frown said he didn't care for that task, but he and the other three left down the byway just north of the blacksmith's bower. Birna stepped up beside Geirmund to watch the alehouse with him, and for some time nothing happened.

"Why are we waiting here?" she finally asked.

"To keep my word to the Saxon."

"Even if the Saxon doesn't keep his?"

Geirmund smirked at her. "What was it you said about honour? Even when the gods alone will see it?"

She laughed. "Then let us hope Krok is as clever as you think he is, and no more."

"He showed a bit of cunning in Lunden," Geirmund said.

"Enough to catch you unaware."

"That will never happen again."

"One day you will fight someone more cunning than you," she said. "And you can be sure there–"

"Look."

The door to the alehouse had opened, and a shield-maiden with brown hair ducked out into the street. She looked around, fixed her eyes on the blacksmith shop, and strode towards them at a slow and even pace.

"She carries no weapons," Birna said.

"Nor does she wear armour." The corner of Geirmund's mouth turned up in a slight grin. "She's supposed to be a blacksmith, remember?"

"It seems Krok does have a bit of cunning. She almost looks like a Saxon."

As the approaching warrior drew up to the bower, Geirmund tried to match her calm air as he asked, "Are you the smith?"

The woman stepped into the shade of the workshop. "I am."

"Truly?" Birna made a show of looking her over from hair to hoof. "I didn't think Saxon men let their women do anything other than cook, pray, and whelp baby Saxons."

"I wouldn't know. I'm a Briton." The woman folded her arms, which looked strong enough for a smith. "Now, you need my work?"

"Yes," Geirmund said. "We have some armour and weapons that need mending."

She looked around the bower. "Where are the others?"

"Others?"

"There were six in your war-band. Or so Elwyn said."

"I don't keep my warriors on a tether."

The Dane hesitated, as if trying to decide what to do, then nodded her head towards the alehouse. "Come, let's talk over a drink." She moved as if to leave.

"We can talk here," Geirmund said. "It seems you were at work."

"What?"

He gestured at the tongs and iron left on the anvil.

"We don't want to keep you from it," Birna added.

"Oh," the Dane said. "It's no bother. Come, you–"

"What were you forging?" Birna asked.

Neither she nor Geirmund had moved, and a moment went by. The woman shrugged. "Pot hook."

"Seems a lot of iron for a pot hook," Birna said.

The warrior made no reply, but her hands tightened into fists.

"You are no Briton." Geirmund tipped his head to the side. "You are tall enough to be a Dane."

Nearby, Birna eased her axe free, and the other woman reached for a weapon at her waist that wasn't there. She looked down, and, having revealed herself, she abandoned her lie and let her lips curl in rage at Geirmund.

He drew his seax. "Tell me, what did Krok–"

The woman's head jerked sideways with a dull thud, bent at the neck by a thrown axe, which had split the top of her ear and lodged itself in her skull. Eyes open, the Dane slumped to the ground in a pile, her boots and fingers twitching as Birna marched over and wrenched her weapon free with a cracking and popping of bone. Blood and brain fell from the woman's opened head onto the dark and oily dirt of the blacksmith's shop.

"For Aslef," Birna said, wiping the edge of her axe clean with one of the smith's rags. "None of them shall see Valhalla by my hand if I have a say, and now they are one less. We should–"

"Geirmund!"

The voice belonged to Steinólfur, calling from somewhere east of the shop.

"They come!" the older warrior shouted.

Up ahead, the alehouse door opened, and warriors roared out into the street. Geirmund and Birna exchanged a glance, then raced from the bower down the byway. They passed a few outbuildings, the sound of fighting ahead of them, and rushed out onto a small green bordered by a tangled wood to the east.

Two Danes lay writhing and dying at Vetr's feet, his spear red. A third fell with a strangled cry before Steinólfur's sword as more enemies charged towards them from the north and west. Furious shouts went up throughout the town.

"Go!" Steinólfur pointed towards a break in the forest. "The path is there! Rafn went ahead to scout with Skjalgi."

An arrow hissed and struck the ground near Vetr. He spun around and knocked another arrow out of the air with his spear, then darted for cover in the trees, followed by Birna, Geirmund, and then Steinólfur. The four of them sped along the path, and as they pushed deeper into the wood the ground around them gave way to marsh, and soon they splashed through water and muck where the track dipped below the waterline.

Behind them, Geirmund heard the frantic sounds of pursuit, but knew the narrow trail and fen would keep Krok's warriors behind them and away from their flanks, at least for a time. The land there reminded him of the marshes around Ancarig, with mires and watery pitfalls, and islands of tall grasses.

"Where is Rafn?" he called, but his question was answered a moment later when the warrior stepped onto the path ahead of them, as if from nowhere, wielding his thin Miklagard sword.

"All here?" he called.

"All here," Vetr said as Birna, Geirmund, and then Steinólfur caught up to them.

"Can that sword give more than a scratch?" the older warrior asked.

"You would be surprised," Rafn said. "The eagle-eyed boy found a second trackway."

Then he turned and plunged into a wall of grass and bramble, and the rest of them followed, pressing and snapping through coarse reeds until they came out onto a much fainter trail made by animal hooves and paws. It wriggled off into dense marsh, where it seemed to vanish less than a hundred fathoms on.

Skjalgi stood there, waiting for them. "I don't know how far it goes," he said.

"It will do for now," Geirmund said, and he led the way, thinking that at the very least the trees would offer them good cover from arrows if Krok's warriors found them.

They followed that path into a region of marsh where the willow and alder trees grew closer together, and the air felt heavy and still, thick with the scent of rotting leaves and grass. Their passage scared birds with long beaks and long legs up into the sky, and sent frogs splashing into the water. Each time they halted to listen for Krok's warriors, the sounds of their enemies grew fainter, until Geirmund felt sure they had escaped, at least for the moment. When the trackway reached a small, dry island, he called for a rest and sat down upon the soft, worm-eaten trunk of a fallen tree to think.

"Krok just lost four warriors," he said. "If Elwyn spoke the truth, that means he is down to perhaps fifteen in his war-band."

"And you outwitted him." Vetr crossed his legs beneath him on the ground and began to clean and hone Dauðavindur, his spear. "He can't go back to Halfdan now. Not if he has any care for his reputation."

Geirmund agreed. "In Lunden he said killing me will earn him a jarldom."

"That is a rich reward." Rafn chuckled as he pulled a piece of dried meat from his pack and began to gnaw at it. "You can be sure he will hunt us with hatred to match."

"And he still outnumbers us two to one," Steinólfur added. "We had luck with us today, but that may not always be so."

"If it is my fate to die, I will die," Geirmund said. "But it will not be at his hand."

"Then let him die by yours," Birna said. "Or mine. They must all die."

Geirmund knew she spoke the truth, and that the only end to Krok's pursuit of them would be the Dane's death or his own. But he also knew he didn't have the tally of warriors he needed for an open fight and would have to rely on cunning to defeat his enemy.

"If we knew this marsh, we could make a stand here," he said. "But it would hinder us as badly as it would hinder Krok. We need to seek a new field of battle, where we control the ground, and stay clear of the enemy until we have found it."

Skjalgi slapped his own cheek. "A place without myggs, I hope."

That marsh did have an evil, unhealthy air, so Geirmund ordered them to keep moving, but it was not until late afternoon that they came out of the fen onto dry heath. From there they travelled off the Roman roads and Saxon trackways, through the wild places, and for the next two days they wandered in and out of forests thick with bramble that had to be cut through with axe and seax, and they sloshed across more marsh and fen and waded through cold streams.

At first they came by water easily enough, but food was more difficult to gather. Birna spied a few bushes of wild, sour berries, and they gathered some mushrooms Rafn recognized. They caught small fish in a stream using a cage Vetr weaved from willow branches, but the snares Geirmund laid for hare and squirrel lay empty. Then even water became scarce as they crossed longer stretches of bare heath, where there were few streams and no game above ground.

Geirmund shivered through the long nights, huddled close together with his war-band around small, weak fires only when they could gather enough dry fuel and knew the light of it would not be seen.

On the third day Geirmund's hunger became more than a pain, slowing his feet and his thoughts. He felt a weakness he could not banish with sleep and rest, though sleep and rest were all he wanted, but in the deep-night he imagined them stalked by the land-vættr of that lonely place and followed by a shambling draugr of Aslef seeking revenge for leaving him to die. It was only his duty to his Hel-hides that kept him moving, and it seemed their duty to him kept them from complaining.

On the fourth day they reached woodland again and smelled woodsmoke, after which they spread out and sneaked through the forest to discover the source, whether settlement or encampment. Geirmund peered through the trees, stepping as lightly as he could, until his war-band came upon a broad clearing in the wood, and in the middle of it stood a Saxon temple built of stone. It reminded him of the place he had seen at Medeshamstede, or what Medeshamstede might have been if it had escaped burning and destruction by the Danes.

The long hall of the temple before him rose fifteen fathoms high and stretched at least thirty fathoms long, with a peaked roof and a round tower at one end. A wall reached out from its southern flank to enclose several large outbuildings, while many byres and workshops lay outside those defences. Robed men worked in the fields and gardens that surrounded that place, the kind of priests that John had named monks. They carried no weapons other than tools for tilling and planting, and Geirmund watched them with his Hel-hides from the shadows for some time.

"If we can draw Krok here," Rafn said, "we could make use of such a place."

"If we can take it," Steinólfur said.

Birna laughed. "We can take it. Priests are weak."

"Many priests are weak," Geirmund said. "But I know at least one who fought and killed Danes at Ashdown."

"And there is a peace in Mercia," Skjalgi said.

The boy spoke up so rarely that they all turned to stare at him, including Geirmund and Steinólfur.

Skjalgi met their surprise with a calm sureness. "That's what the Saxon Elwyn said."

"Yes, it is." Steinólfur glanced at Geirmund with a wry smile. "But must we keep that peace?"

Geirmund considered that for a moment. "If we break the

truce, we give Ubba and Halfdan more claim to hatred of us. That could put us in even greater danger."

"Then what do we do?" Rafn asked. "I doubt we'll find a place more to our favour against Krok than inside those walls."

Geirmund looked again at the monks, recalling all he had learned about such men from the two priests he had met since coming to England, searching for some way to put their temple to use by his Hel-hides without breaking the peace. He thought back to the first time he'd met John, when the priest had offered him bread as hard as stone because his god commanded it, and then, as Geirmund looked into the faces of the monks there, he saw something that made him grin.

"I have a plan," he said.

20

A few fathoms apart from the walled temple and its buildings stood a large onion-shaped oven. Heat rippled the air above it, so Geirmund knew it to be in use, and his mouth watered at the thought of warm bread.

"I do not understand this plan," Steinólfur said.

The older warrior and the other Hel-hides watched Geirmund as he removed his armour and weapons, frowning at him in confusion, and some worry.

"You must trust me," Geirmund said. "We cannot simply walk up to them. I have tried that before, and they have too much fear and hatred of Danes. There is but one way to get what we want and still keep the peace, but they must believe I am in true need. And you must all swear to me that you will remain hidden, no matter what you see, and wait until I call for you."

His Hel-hides looked at one other in doubt, and finally to Steinólfur, who shook his head at them all and shrugged. "We will trust in your cunning," he said.

Geirmund nodded, then crept away to the south around the edge of the clearing, keeping to the woods until he was as close to the oven as he could get while remaining hidden. Even so, at least fifteen fathoms of open ground lay between him and the baking bread.

Just then, a broad-shouldered monk came out of a nearby building brushing flour from his robes. He went to the oven, opened it, and used a long wooden pole to pull dark loaves from inside it. These he bounced between his thick hands as he carried them to a bench and set them there to cool.

Geirmund waited until the large monk had gone, and until the other priests nearby had turned their backs. Then he darted for the hot loaves, racing through a field of turnips, their green leaves slapping against his boots and legs, thinking he probably looked a fool to his Hel-hides who watched him. He reached the bread, grabbed a loaf in each hand, and as he turned back towards the woods a pole struck him hard in the face.

Geirmund fell on his back with a loud grunt, eyes watering and nose bleeding, which was not part of the plan. The baker was quicker than expected, and Geirmund then felt the end of the pole jab him hard in the chest, pinning him to the ground. He let the loaves roll out of his hands.

"Weigh your next words and choices carefully, thief," the monk said, standing over him, "or I promise you'll regret them."

Geirmund believed the man could keep that oath. "Please," he said, "I've had no food in days."

"You should have started with that, instead of trying to steal."

Geirmund heard and saw other priests coming closer to see what had happened, and he searched them for a familiar face while the large monk kept the end of his pole wedged in his ribs. Geirmund swallowed the blood that slid down the back of his throat from his nose, hoping he wasn't mistaken about the man he'd seen from the trees.

"Who are you?" the baker asked. "Are you a Dane?"

"I am Geirmund," he said, and then the gathered wall of monks around him parted to let one of them through.

"Geirmund?" the newcomer asked. "Surely not–Brother Almund, get this man up. I need a better look at him."

The baker hesitated only for a moment. "Yes, Father," he said and pulled the end of his staff away from Geirmund's chest. Then he reached down with his large hands and hauled Geirmund to his feet with ease.

The other monk stepped closer to look in Geirmund's blinking eyes. Geirmund wiped the blood from under his nose with his hand and sleeve as he also studied the priest, pleased that he had recognized the man rightly, though he did seem younger than when they had first met through the window of a wooden tomb.

"Torthred?" Geirmund said.

The use of that name sent a murmur through the other monks, and they all turned towards the priest, who smiled broadly. "I was thirsty, and you gave me drink," he said.

"I am very glad to see you." Geirmund looked around them. "But I am surprised to find you here."

"I am here because the Danes at Ancarig left very suddenly, and in much anger. Not long after you departed, I might add. I do believe something caused them to forget about me in my anchorhold. But I am also here because of something you said to me."

"Oh?"

"Yes, and I decided you were right. God did not want me to stay and starve and die alone."

"This thief tried to steal bread, Father." The baker still gripped his staff as a weapon.

"I assume he is hungry," Torthred said. "Even were it not our Christian duty to feed the hungry, I would owe this man the kindness he once showed me. And I would also remind all my brothers that there is a peace with the Danes in Mercia. Now, please fetch him a loaf, Brother Almund."

The big monk relaxed and bowed his head. Then he bent to pick up one of the loaves that had rolled from Geirmund's hands, brushed it off, and gave it to him. Geirmund accepted it, but resisted tearing into it, hungry as he was.

"I still doubt my luck in seeing you here," he said.

"It is not so surprising to me," Torthred said. "I haven't travelled far. We are but forty miles from Ancarig. This monastery sits on land belonging to the abbey at Medeshamstede, and I am now the abbot here. But perhaps you have travelled further since I last saw you?"

"Much further," Geirmund said, "only to come back to where my journey in England began, it seems."

"Perhaps the hand of God has guided you here."

"Fate alone led me here," he said.

Torthred smiled. "You seem very tired, Geirmund. Would you like to rest awhile?"

Geirmund nodded. "I would."

"We have a small cottage for guests and travellers, which you may use."

"I can pay you," Geirmund said. "I have silver–"

Torthred held up his hand. "We ask for no silver." Then he lowered his voice and spoke from the corner of his mouth. "And, that is not because I fear how you might have acquired it. Come."

He ushered Geirmund west along the wall and then through an open gate, trailed by a few curious monks. They entered a small square that lay beneath the temple, where chickens clucked and pecked at the dirt in the building's shadow. Two doorways offered outlets from the yard, one into the temple, and another into the rest of the monk-hold. A stone well sat in the middle of the square, and a cottage not much larger than Torthred's wooden tomb had been leaned against the temple.

"You're not going to seal me in there, are you?" Geirmund asked.

The priest grinned. "Even were you baptized a Christian, I do not think you would belong in an anchorhold."

"Where does that lead?" Geirmund nodded towards the northern door.

"Our dormitory and refectory," the priest said. "We sleep and eat apart from the world. I would ask that you stay on this side of that portal, but you may otherwise come and go as you wish."

"Thank you," Geirmund said. "But I must tell you, I am not alone."

Torthred paused. "And what does that mean?"

"I have five Danes with me. They wait in the woods."

"What do they wait for?"

"Your leave for them to join me here. They are sworn to me and I to them. They are warriors of honour and will do you no harm."

Apart from some surprise at first, Torthred's face betrayed no other feeling or thought. He simply looked at Geirmund for several moments. "I would give you my leave, but I must first speak to some of my brothers about the matter. They may ask you to–"

"We will not be baptized Christian," Geirmund said.

Torthred smiled. "We will not ask that of you. Will you wait here?"

"I will."

The priest nodded and left the yard with his tail of monks through the corner door, and Geirmund went to the hut, where he leaned on the door frame and poked his head inside. The cottage had but one room that contained a wooden box-bed, long and narrow, filled with straw, and covered with woollen blankets and furs. The hut also held a small table, a stool, and above the bed hung a cross that reminded Geirmund of the hall where he and John had spent one night.

Geirmund decided to rest while he waited for the priest, so he went to lie down in the bed on his back with his hands behind his head. He looked up at the low roof of thatch, thinking that fate had surely guided him to that place, for the consequences of his many choices at Ancarig had not only driven him from Lunden but had also brought him to a place of shelter.

Torthred returned a short while later, looking pleased. "You and your warriors may stay," he said. "Our food and our ways are humble, but we will share them with you if you share in the work of growing and defending this monastery."

"Defending?" Geirmund knew well why he had chosen that place, but it surprised him to hear Torthred speak in similar terms. "Is there not a peace in Mercia?"

"There was also a peace at Medeshamstede and Ancarig. You and I both know there are those who do not respect it."

"I have fought such Danes, and I have made enemies of them. If any should come here, I will fight them again."

"Let us hope you won't have to."

Geirmund agreed to Torthred's terms, and then went to tell his Hel-hides, who all had deep misgivings about living with priests, despite Geirmund swearing they would not have to be baptized.

"They are weak," Rafn said. "I have no respect for monks. They are like– like…"

"Unfledged birds," Vetr finished for him, "with those bald heads of theirs. Or worse, fledged birds that never learned to fly or hunt, and choose to stay in the nest."

"The monks matter little," Geirmund said. "We agreed we would find no better place than this to stand against Krok. We also agreed to keep the peace with Burgred. This is the only way we can do both."

"He's right," Birna said. "I don't like it, but the Hel-hide is right."

"I agree," Steinólfur said, though his tone suggested he didn't, and after that Rafn and Vetr let go of their unwillingness.

Back at the monastery, the Hel-hides turned the courtyard around the hut into a small encampment, but only for the men. Upon realizing that Geirmund had a woman in his company, Torthred had insisted the cottage belonged to Birna alone. The priest had reacted with such shock and horror at the sight of the shield-maiden that Geirmund thought the monks may have refused the Danes if they had known about her. It seemed they lived by a law under which they seldom saw women at all, and almost never spoke to them. Only Torthred had that freedom as the abbot. Birna seemed little troubled by it, and even claimed to feel grateful that she would not have to talk to the monks, and Geirmund suspected she also liked having the hut and the bed to herself.

As for him, he slept well enough on the ground, but awoke after the middle of that first night confused, and it took him a few moments to remember where he was. Men chanted together as one nearby in a tongue he didn't know, their mournful voices rising and falling like the endless waves of the sea. Geirmund sat up rubbing his eyes with the heel of his palm and discovered Skjalgi awake nearby, the whites of his eyes showing in the darkness.

"Is that some kind of Christian galdur?" the boy asked.

"I don't know." Geirmund looked up at the temple and saw a faint warm light flickering through the tinted glass of its windows. It seemed the chanting came from inside. "Perhaps it is," he said.

"It does not sound evil," Rafn muttered, apparently awake, but not upright.

Geirmund agreed. The chanting even soothed him somehow, so perhaps it was a healing charm the monks worked. He and the others who had been awakened by it stayed up listening for a while, until the chanting stopped and the light in the windows went out. Moments later, the door to the temple opened.

Torthred emerged first. He carried a lantern, and the other monks all followed him in a silent line, the deep hoods of their cloaks drawn up, hiding their faces. When the abbot noticed Geirmund awake, he came over and crouched beside him as the monks glided onward across the yard to the north-eastern door.

"Are you all well?" the priest asked. He held the lantern up, his face and cheek aglow on the side near the flame.

Geirmund swallowed, his mouth dry. "We are well, thank you."

"What is that galdur you chant?" Skjalgi whispered.

Torthred swung the lantern towards the boy, tossing shadows that danced. "Our galdur?"

"Your spellwork," Geirmund said.

"Oh, you mean our prayers?"

Geirmund nodded. "What is it you pray for? This is an evil time of night."

"Perhaps that is why we pray at this time of night." Torthred stood. "We ask for God's mercy. What do you ask of your gods?"

"Full harvests and larders," Geirmund said. "Good seas. But mostly we ask for strength and glory in battle."

"Many Christian warriors pray for the same," the priest said.

"Then perhaps one day we will see which is stronger," Rafn said. "Our gods or yours."

"Perhaps," Torthred said. "But there are many kinds of strength." Then he bade them a good night and left the courtyard.

Over the next few days, Geirmund learned that the monks at

the monastery had come from many places, often as children and young men. Most were Mercians, but some were of Wessex and Northumbria, and one monk called Brother Morcant had been born in Wealas. It was their god and their prayer they held in common, though it also seemed that most of them were the youngest sons of ealdormen with many children, and they had long known they would inherit nothing from their fathers. Instead, their families had given them over to the monastery and the life of a monk, thereby preventing conflict, while also gaining favour from their Christian god.

Geirmund knew what it was to be a second son, and if Rogaland were a Christian kingdom, perhaps he would have become a monk himself. That thought made it easier for him to satisfy the terms of the bargain he had made with Torthred as he and his Danes worked beside the monks in their fields, and as they helped them to construct a wooden outer wall around their monastery to protect not just their temple but also their livestock pens and gardens.

In return the monks provided Geirmund's war-band with plenty of good food. They ate little meat there, but they had abundant eggs and cheese, and Brother Almund baked rich bread. Another priest, Brother Drefan, brewed a strong ale he flavoured with honey and yarrow that Geirmund grew to enjoy, and where Lunden had turned the days into weeks and months with all that it offered to delight his senses, the monastery did the same with simple hard work in which he took a measure of pride.

Rafn and Vetr scouted daily, reaching far, but they found no sign of Krok, though on a few occasions they did pursue thieves hunting in the monastery's forests, but word of the warriors' presence there soon seemed to frighten most poachers and other threats away.

The idea that the monastery and its monks owned land like jarls or ealdormen confused Geirmund. "In my country," he said to the abbot one day, 'seers do not rule as jarls or kings. I have never known a seer to even desire land or wealth."

They walked in the monastery's apple orchard, where the abbot checked the ripeness of the fruit, which would not be ready to harvest for several weeks yet.

"We do not desire any of this for our vain glory," Torthred said. "We are but stewards of the monastery's holdings, not its rulers." He stopped and spread his open hands wide. "Every apple on every tree is an expression of our love for God, and of his love for us. We are building the kingdom of God on earth."

"Why does your god need lands or a kingdom in Midgard? Does he not have his own lands? His own hall?"

"N-no." Torthred frowned, shaking his head. "God is in heaven."

"Is that like Valhalla?"

Torthred chuckled. "From what I know of Valhalla the two are very different. If it is Valhalla you seek, I think you would be very disappointed in heaven."

Geirmund shook his head. "I do not understand your god."

Torthred looked at Geirmund with a sudden smile. "Come with me."

"Where are we going?"

"You shall see," he said, and he led the way back to the courtyard where Geirmund's warriors idled, but the abbot went towards the temple. "You have never asked to come inside our chapel, Geirmund."

"It is often locked," Geirmund said. "I assumed you didn't want pagans like us inside it."

"I thank you for that respect," Torthred said. "But I am now inviting you inside, if you wish to see it."

Geirmund had been curious about the building where the monks prayed since he had arrived there, but not curious enough to sneak inside and risk offending his hosts. "Very well," he said. "I will go in."

The abbot nodded. They reached the door, and he unlocked it with a key he wore at his belt. Then they went inside.

The temple echoed with the sounds of their footsteps, and it smelled of damp stone and beeswax. The light that found its way in passed through coloured glass that softened it, casting the hall in a warm dim glow that kept the rafters overhead in shadow. At the far end of the temple an altar sat beneath a large window that held the figure of a man formed by the joining together of many irregular pieces of coloured glass. Upon the altar stood a tall cross either made from silver or clad in it, ornamented with carvings, and encrusted with jewels.

"If all Christian temples hold such riches," Geirmund said, his words loud and multiplied by the stone walls, "I see why the Danes plunder them."

"Silver and gold are meant to remind us of the spiritual riches that come from God."

Rows of wooden benches ran the length of the hall and flanked the altar. Geirmund imagined all the monks of the monastery chanting their prayers as one in that place, with its coloured glass and its imposing fortress walls, and he could admit he felt power there. Whether the abbot called it galdur or not, Christian magic in that temple seemed little different from seer magic done in a stone circle, other than the name of the god and what was prayed for.

"We are also blessed to have a sacred relic here," the abbot said. "A bone from the throat of Saint Boniface. I often think of the many prayers and sermons that passed through that bone as their holy speaker gave voice to them."

"Is that why you honour him? He talked?"

"His teaching brought many souls to Christ." Torthred leaned towards him. "And he even cut down an oak tree of Thór that the pagans worshipped."

Geirmund shook his head. "To risk the anger of Thór is foolish. What happened to Boniface after that?"

"He was murdered for his faith." Torthred seemed to feel a defiant pride in saying it. "His killers wanted gold, but all they found in his chests were sacred books."

"Books?"

"The holy scriptures, which are infinitely more precious than gold."

"Perhaps to those who can read them. The Danes will take your gold and burn your books."

The abbot sighed, his eyes downcast. He seemed disappointed, as if he had hoped the sight of his temple would cause Geirmund to become a Christian in that very moment. But then Torthred suddenly looked up again. "Let me show you something else, if I may."

Geirmund shrugged. "You may."

They left the temple, which Torthred locked behind them, and walked towards the north-east door on the other side of the courtyard. They stepped through that entry into the part of the monastery that Geirmund had never seen, where a roofed pathway surrounded a second, larger courtyard filled with flowers and bushes. Several monks stopped what they were doing at the sight of Geirmund there, but they moved on when they noticed he walked with the abbot. Torthred called that place a cloister, and he led Geirmund along one side of it, until they reached a second doorway.

"The work that goes on inside this room is costly and delicate.

It requires artful hands and eyes, and I would ask that you not disturb this work."

Geirmund nodded, his curiosity heightened. "I will respect your wish."

Torthred opened the door, and inside the room Geirmund saw four monks seated at slanted tables. The murmur of their voices filled the hall with the hum of a beehive, but it was difficult for Geirmund to hear just one alone, and it seemed they all spoke in different tongues. They leaned over books and parchment pages, reading, writing, and painting with brightly coloured pigments, and even gold. The markings they made upon the parchment appeared very fine, as the abbot had said, and included figures of men, women, children, beasts, and patterns so entwined the eye could not untie them. None of the monks there looked up from their work, so intent were they upon it, and their voices droned unbroken.

Torthred tapped Geirmund on the shoulder and nodded his head towards the doorway, and after they had stepped outside, back into the cloister, the abbot closed the door behind them.

"That is the monastery's scriptorium," he then said. "That is where we read and copy sacred texts, for ourselves and for others."

"What were they speaking?" Geirmund asked.

"They were talking with angels, apostles, and saints."

Geirmund looked again at the door. "I saw no one else–"

"They speak through the text on the page," Torthred said. "When we read the words of Saint Augustine, or Saint Paul, their voices pass through us and live once more."

"Your books hold voices?"

"All books hold voices."

"Even the voices of the dead?"

Torthred smiled and nodded. "Would you like me to teach you?"

"To read?"

"Yes."

Geirmund looked again at the scriptorium door, and he thought of John's ability to read for Sidroc. Such a skill could be useful. "Yes, if you are willing to teach me," he said.

That seemed to please the abbot, and for the next several weeks, every day, they sat in the courtyard after the night-meal, seated upon stools, the other Danes looking on in amusement as Torthred taught Geirmund to read. At first they used sticks to draw markings in the dirt at their feet, but after a month or so Torthred brought single fragments of old, worn parchment for Geirmund. The abbot praised him for how quickly he gained in skill compared to others he had taught, but to Geirmund learning was not a contest. He wanted to know how to read and write for himself because he found power in it.

It was during one of their nightly lessons that a priest arrived at the monastery gates. He was badly injured, with broken ribs and teeth, but he had nevertheless travelled some forty rests to deliver a message from the town of Tamworth.

The Danes, it seemed, had returned to Mercia, and the peace had come to an end.

21

Torthred returned to the courtyard sometime after the monks had taken the wounded traveller into their world beyond the north-eastern doorway. The abbot seemed very troubled as he explained that the Danes had put King Burgred of Mercia to flight. With no more silver to pay for peace, the axe had finally fallen. Ivarr and Ubba had attacked Tamworth, and since then Halfdan and Guthrum had also encamped at a place called Hreopandune to the north-west.

"Burgred fled?" Geirmund said. "After fighting Æthelred and Ælfred, I'd come to believe Saxon kings had more courage and honour than that."

"Some do," Torthred said. "Some do not."

Geirmund shook his head. "If the Danes are in Mercia, you and your monks are no longer safe here. The wall we built together will stand against a war-band, but not an army."

"Yes," Torthred said. He nodded along, but his eyes and mind seemed to be elsewhere, distracted by something. "Yes, I'm sure you're right."

Geirmund watched him for a moment. "Something more troubles you."

The abbot glanced at Geirmund. Then he looked downward and pressed his hands together below his chin as if in Christian prayer, the tips of his fingers against his lips. "I had a brother with me at Ancarig," he said. "Tancred. The Danes slew him."

Geirmund remembered then that John had once mentioned the name. "The loss of a brother is a hard thing."

"I also had a sister there," Torthred said. "Tova. But she managed to hide in the fens until the Danes had gone."

Geirmund had seen her face in the reeds. He had thought her a river-vættr. "Where is she now?"

Torthred closed his eyes. "She was at Tamworth during the attack. I have just been told that she fled to come here."

"When?" Birna asked.

The others in the courtyard listened, but Torthred suddenly sat upright and looked around at them as if he'd forgotten they were there. "Days ago," he answered, then nodded towards the corner doorway. "She left Tamworth even before the priest who has just come, and she should have arrived by now. I fear some evil may have befallen her."

Geirmund looked at Rafn and Vetr. Both Danes nodded without needing to hear his order aloud and gathered up their weapons. Geirmund turned back to Torthred. "My warriors will go and look for her. If she is to be found, they will find her."

The priest looked up. "I confess I'd hoped for such an offer but felt hesitant to ask."

"Why?"

"You–you are a pagan. And I feared–that is, with the peace now broken…"

Geirmund placed his hand on Torthred's shoulder. "It is true the peace is broken between our kings, but that does not make us enemies until we are called upon to fight one another."

Torthred sighed, short and almost a laugh. "As the Samaritan helped the Jew, so the pagan helps the priest." He dragged a hand down his face as if to wipe away his thoughts and his worry. "I am grateful."

"We're ready," Rafn said, and with another silent nod from Geirmund he and Vetr left the monastery.

Torthred watched the gate in the wall through which they had gone for some time, grasping the cross he wore about his neck in a tight fist, helpless. Geirmund pitied him, for, just as Vetr had said of priests months before, the abbot had never learned to fly and hunt, and so he could do nothing to protect his family. But Geirmund also knew that Torthred was no coward, and it was the god he worshipped who made him weak.

"Go and rest," he said to the abbot. "You can do nothing more tonight."

"I can pray," Torthred said, eyes unblinking.

"Then do that," Geirmund said, despite the little good he thought it would do.

The remainder of that night passed restless and heavy with threat, and Rafn and Vetr did not return until mid-morning the next day. They did not bring Torthred's sister with them, but they had found her, and in finding her they had also found Krok and his warriors.

"She is their captive," Rafn said, which caused Torthred great distress, but the Dane went on to say that she appeared unharmed.

"It seems they make their way here," Vetr said. "I think they know who she is and mean to ransom her. That is why they keep her safe."

"Why go to that hardship?" Steinólfur asked. "Why do they not simply take the monastery?"

"They lack the warriors for that," Vetr said. "We counted only thirteen."

"That means two more have died." Birna smiled. "And they have not yet returned to Halfdan. Krok must be in dire need of plunder, to reward his war-band and to please his king."

Geirmund agreed with her. "Were you seen?"

Rafn snorted.

"No," Vetr said.

Near them, Torthred paced about the yard, twisting and wringing his hands together. "If it is silver they want, they can have it. I will not–"

"Steady," Geirmund said. "There might be a way to keep your silver and also save your sister."

"How?" the priest asked.

"He has a plan," Steinólfur said, looking at Geirmund. "Isn't that right?"

He did have a plan. It would mean leaving the monastery behind, but that did not strike Geirmund as too great a cost, since they were not now long for that place with the Dane-kings close by and sure to burn it.

"Are you and your monks willing to abandon this place?" he asked the abbot.

"I–" Torthred blinked and shook his head. "Leave our monastery?"

"Yes."

"But–"

"Mercia is now Daneland," Geirmund said. "If you stay here, you will die, Torthred. Your monks will die, and their deaths will not be easy. You may give up your silver if that is what you wish, but after Krok's war-band has gone, there will be an army at your gate."

Torthred fell silent.

"How long?" Geirmund asked Rafn.

"If they are coming here, as we think they are, they will reach the gate tomorrow."

Geirmund turned back to the abbot. "I know you will need to talk with your monks, but you only have until sunrise to make this choice."

Torthred nodded and trudged from the courtyard, shoulders slumped, head hanging so low his chin almost touched his chest.

"Don't be surprised if they choose to stay," Steinólfur said, after the abbot had gone. "They're fools, the lot of them."

"Perhaps," Geirmund said.

He hoped that since Torthred had once decided to leave his wooden tomb, he would likewise decide to leave his monastery. The abbot did not soon return with an answer, and eventually Geirmund and his warriors gave up waiting and went to sleep, but not long after that the chanting of the monks in the deep-night awoke them. Geirmund stood by the temple door until they had finished praying, and he stepped in front of the abbot as soon as he emerged from within.

"Have you made a choice?" he asked.

Torthred blinked. "We have." He paused and looked over his shoulder at his monks. "We will leave the monastery."

"Good." The relief Geirmund felt upon hearing that surprised him. "Where will you go?"

"I am friends with the abbot at Cerne, in Wessex. Many of us will go there."

"I am pleased to hear it." Geirmund moved out of Torthred's path so the monks could return to their beds, and then he returned to his own.

At midday Krok finally appeared at the monastery's outer wall as Rafn and Vetr had foretold, but he had not come with his war-band. Geirmund peered through a thin gap between the wooden stakes and saw the Dane standing before the western gate with two of his men, who between them held Torthred's sister. Geirmund recognized her, barely, from the glimpse he had caught of her in the fenlands.

She looked to be Skjalgi's age, and though bound and gagged, she appeared unharmed apart from the dirt that covered her apron-dress, which must have relieved the abbot. He stood at the top of the wall as Geirmund and his warriors listened from below, out of Krok's sight. Geirmund had told Torthred what he must say, and how he must say it, but he worried whether the priest could make those words sound as if they belonged in his mouth.

"What do you want, pagan?" Torthred said.

"I am Krok," the Dane said. "Do you lead here?"

"I do. I am the abbot."

Krok pointed at Tova. "I am told you know this girl."

Geirmund had counselled the priest to hold a middle ground between fear and anger. If he showed too much fear for himself or his sister, then Krok might decide to attack the monastery, thinking it weak, but if Torthred showed too much anger, he might rouse Krok to anger also.

"I do," the priest said, his voice even. "She is my sister."

"Then let us keep this matter simple. You see what I have, and I think you know what I want."

"Silver," Torthred said. "You Danes are all the same."

Krok laughed. "Who doesn't want silver?"

"For the release of my sister," Torthred said, "we will give you silver."

"Good!" Krok clapped his hands together. "Now we must agree on a price."

"What price do you ask?"

"What price do you offer?"

"We are not wealthy." Torthred rubbed his chin as if tallying in his mind. "We can give you twenty pounds of silver."

Geirmund didn't know if the monastery even held twenty pounds of silver, but that was the amount he knew would please Krok without tempting his greed much further.

"Twenty-five pounds," the Dane said. "Not a penny less."

"We do not have twenty-five–"

Krok laughed. "I think you will find that you do if you look hard enough."

Torthred paused. "Agreed. Return tomorrow at dawn."

"Agreed!" Krok said. "Do I need to tell you what will happen if you fail to give me what I ask?"

Torthred paled, and Geirmund watched him, worried what he might say, but the abbot seemed to find his strength a moment later. "Do I need to tell you what you will get from me if my sister is harmed?"

Krok laughed again. "Until tomorrow, abbot-priest."

With that, their talk was over. Geirmund watched Torthred as he watched Krok's men drag his sister back into the woods, but the priest held his tongue and showed no weakness until he had come down from the wall. Then he began to shake, and his eyes watered with rage, pain, and fear.

"They will do nothing to her," Geirmund said, trying to calm him. "She is too valuable. You did well."

Torthred bent at the waist and blew several deep breaths, palms braced against his knees, and then stood upright again. "And now come the infernal hours of our waiting," he said, and while they waited, they prepared.

The monks went about loading carts with everything they

would take with them to Wessex, their books, their crosses and relics, some furniture, and food for themselves and the animals they planned to bring. Geirmund ordered his warriors to also pack up whatever they did not want to leave behind, and then asked Torthred for six of the monk-robes with deep hoods. The abbot seemed somewhat doubtful about that, but fetched them, and then Geirmund explained to Torthred what he needed to say when Krok returned. Lastly, Brother Almund brought forth a large empty wooden chest into which the abbot poured several pounds of shining silver coin, and with that they stood ready.

Dawn the next morning found them back at the western gate. Geirmund wore one of the monk-robes, as did Rafn and Vetr. Brother Almund had also insisted on joining them, and based on how well the baker had wielded his staff Geirmund did not object.

When Krok returned, Torthred led his true monk and three robed Danes through the open gate, which closed behind them, leaving Birna, Steinólfur, and Skjalgi on the inside of the wall. Brother Almund carried the chest of silver and set it down upon the ground several fathoms from the enemy, while Geirmund kept his face hidden within the deep shadow of his hood, the rising sun at their backs as he had planned.

"Where is your leader?" Torthred asked. "Where is Krok?"

Those questions caused Geirmund to risk lifting his head, and he saw that his true foe had not returned. Instead, four Danes stood before them with the abbot's sister, and Geirmund searched the treeline at the edge of the clearing beyond them for signs of Krok and his eight remaining warriors.

"He sent us in his stead," one of the enemy Danes said, a man with a forked beard. "Do you have the silver?"

"It is here." Torthred gestured towards the chest on the ground.

"We must see it," the forkbeard said.

Torthred gave a nod to Brother Almund, who lifted the chest and carried it a few paces, then set it back on the ground. After opening its lid, he slowly backed away without taking his eyes from Krok's warriors, and as the baker returned Geirmund's frantic thoughts searched for what to do now that his plan had gone awry. He needed to kill Krok, and kill him quickly, or else they would all be in greater danger than before.

The forkbeard approached the chest, looked down, and then gave it a kick that jangled the coins. "What is this?"

"It is five pounds of silver."

"You agreed to twenty-five–"

"So I did, but I do not trust you." Torthred pointed at the chest. "That wealth belongs to God, not to me. I will pay you silver for my sister's life, but I will not risk losing both. The other twenty pounds of silver are inside the gate behind me. I will give it to you only after you have released your prisoner and she is safe."

It seemed clear the Danes had not expected something like that from the priest. They said nothing for several moments, and then one of them near Tova pulled a knife and pressed its blade against her neck. Torthred took a step forward, but Geirmund put an arm out straight to hold him back.

"Ask yourself which is worth more to you." The forkbeard looked down at the chest. "We'll gladly take this silver and cut the girl's throat, but we'd much rather take the twenty-five pounds we came for and leave her with you."

Torthred opened his mouth but seemed to have no words to fill it. If Krok had come, the Dane would already be dead and done with, and now the abbot floundered. Geirmund needed to act before it all went utterly to shit.

"We will get your silver, Dane," he said, making his manner

of speech like that of a Saxon. Torthred looked over at him, and Geirmund gave him a nod, then glanced at Rafn and Vetr. "Come, my brothers."

The three of them moved towards the gate, and, as they walked, they spoke in whispers.

"Where is Krok?" Rafn asked.

"I don't know," Geirmund said. "Watching from the trees perhaps."

"This plan fails if he doesn't die," Vetr said.

"He will die." Geirmund resisted the urge to look back at the Danes. "But they die first."

They reached the gate, which opened before them, and on the other side Geirmund found Steinólfur had already brought a second chest much larger than the first.

"I thought you might need it when Krok didn't show," the older warrior said. "It looks heavy, so it will get at least two of you closer to them."

"Good." Geirmund glanced over his small war-band. "For now we get Tova free of them, then we deal with what comes after. Be ready."

They all nodded, and Geirmund picked up one side of the chest while Rafn took up the other. Then they lumbered back through the gate, with Vetr behind them, and made their way towards forkbeard and his warriors. As they passed Torthred and Brother Almund, Geirmund whispered, "Take your sister behind the walls the moment you have her," and on they walked.

The forkbeard grinned at their approach, but his expression turned to confusion when they walked right by him, towards Tova.

"Halt," the Dane said.

They ignored him for a few paces more, until he shouted at them.

"Halt, you flea-bitten rats!"

They stopped, the enemy now within reach of their weapons, Rafn the closest to Tova. The blade at her neck kept her body rigid, standing almost on her toes, and she looked at them with panic in her eyes.

The forkbeard stalked up behind them. "Are all priests as empty-headed as you? Put that silver on the ground."

Geirmund and Rafn lowered the chest and set it down. The forkbeard came around them to stand with his men, and all of them gazed at what they believed to be twenty pounds of silver. Geirmund wondered if they planned to betray Krok and steal it for themselves, and then thought they might have already slain their leader for his failures. That would explain why Krok hadn't come but did nothing to change the fates of the four Danes who were about to die.

"Open it," the forkbeard said.

Geirmund looked at Rafn, who nodded his readiness, and then bent towards the chest. He lifted its lid slowly, and, just as he revealed it to be empty, Rafn's robes flapped with a sudden lunge. The Dane holding Tova made a short choking sound and stood for a moment with his mouth hanging open, the sharp point of a thin Miklagard sword passing just above the girl's head through his eye. Then Rafn shoved the blade deeper into the man's head, and he collapsed.

"Run, girl," Vetr said.

Tova's shock lasted only a moment, and then she raced off towards her brother, hands still bound behind her back.

Almost as quickly, the forkbeard and his warriors recovered from their surprise and drew their weapons in rage, but Geirmund and his Hel-hides had the edge. Geirmund ran his sword through the forkbeard, and Vetr's axe cleaved the shoulder of one of the

Danes so deeply the man died as he fell, while Rafn's two swords slashed his enemy's arms and legs to uselessness. The fight was over quickly, and then Vetr pointed at the trees where several warriors had emerged, looking stunned.

"They come."

"To the wall," Geirmund said, and he grabbed the smaller chest of silver as they ran.

When they reached the gate, they found Torthred and Brother Almund had already taken Tova through and loosed her bindings. Steinólfur closed and barred the entry behind them, and they all turned to wait with weapons in hand for Krok's attack, but none came.

"He had but thirteen before," Birna said. "Now he has nine."

"He cannot take this place with only nine," Steinólfur said.

"He won't." Geirmund walked up to the wall and peered through it. The warriors in the forest seemed to have vanished, and he knew that Krok would soon be wondering how a few monks had slain four of his men. "He will be careful now, and I think he will soon go to Tamworth to seek the help of more Danes."

"We can't let him do that," Rafn said. "The fight is finally even."

"But how do we stop him?" Skjalgi asked.

"If he learns who defeated him," Geirmund said. "If he learns it was us, I think his pride will force him to forget the monastery and pursue us." He used the hem of his robe to wipe the forkbeard's blood from his sword. "We will draw them away," he said and glanced at Birna. "Then we will kill them all."

22

The Hel-hides had already packed their things and stood ready to march from the monastery, but before they went Geirmund tried to return the smaller chest full of coins to the abbot. Torthred refused it.

"Consider that silver a token of my gratitude," he said.

Tova stood next to her brother, and up close to them Geirmund could see the features they shared as siblings, the lively brown colour of their eyes, and the strong line of their chins. The girl reached out and took Geirmund's hand.

"I remember you from Ancarig," she said. "I am twice grateful to you for my brother's sake, and today I am grateful to you for my own."

Geirmund accepted the silver with a bow of his head, then handed it to Steinólfur to divide and pack away where it would not draw attention. "Do you and your monks still plan to leave?" he asked the abbot.

"We do, yes."

"Will you be safe on the roads?"

"We will use the ancient trackways and keep off the Roman

roads. It is not far to Wessex, and we should be safe once we cross the border into Christian lands."

"Wait a day or two," Geirmund said. "Be sure we have baited Krok and his warriors away. But do not tarry here longer than that. Other Danes will find this place, whether sooner or later."

Torthred nodded. "We have only a few more books to pack."

At the mention of books, Geirmund decided to ask something he had wondered about for several weeks. "I have one last question before I go."

"What is it?"

"Why did you teach me to read? I can't help but suspect you were hoping I would become a Christian."

Tova turned her attention on her brother, eyebrows up a little, while Torthred glanced elsewhere, his grin a bit sheepish.

"Well," he said, "I suppose that– yes, to be truthful, that was one of my reasons. I hoped that reading the word of God might soften your pagan heart." His smiled warmed. "But I can see now that is a hopeless cause."

"Do not fret," Geirmund said. "There are times we must all admit defeat."

Torthred chuckled. "That is both wise and true."

"But what of your other reasons?" Tova asked.

The abbot turned serious again, his gaze at Geirmund direct. "Should you and your warriors find a library, perhaps now you will not be so quick to destroy the treasure it contains."

"Perhaps not," Geirmund said with a nod of respect. "That was cunning of you."

"Geirmund!" Birna called from atop the wall. "I see movement in the trees."

"You must go," Tova said. "We will pray for you."

"Can I accept your prayers without accepting your god?"

"That depends," she said. "Can you accept the wheat of the field without accepting the sun and the rain?"

Geirmund chuckled and bade them both farewell, then left with his Hel-hides through the monastery gate. Brother Almund closed it behind them, and Geirmund strode to stand in sight of the forest, the hood of his monk-robe down, but out of arrow's reach. He said nothing and removed the robe as he stared into the trees so that Krok would know who had defeated his warriors before the wall. Then he turned, and his war-band marched eastward from the clearing at a slow enough pace the Danes could track them and follow.

"Do you think the bastard was watching?" Steinólfur asked.

"If not him, then his warriors." Geirmund pointed at a hill not far ahead of them. "Let's make for that high ground."

They quickened to a trot through a stretch of woodland, without care for the din they raised in snapped branches and kicked leaves, then charged up to the top of the rise. From there they could look west, back the way they'd come, and see the fields and roofs of the monastery among the trees in the distance, and they could also watch the breaks in the forest for any sign of Krok and his warriors coming after them.

"Do we make a stand here?" Rafn asked. "Seems as good a place as any."

"No," Geirmund said. "They still have almost twice as many warriors."

"What does that matter?" Birna already had her axe in hand. "We are twice as deadly."

"I do not doubt that." Geirmund glanced north, south, and east, searching the features of the land for good battleground. "But if they surround us, an open fight could prove costly, and I will not lose any of you to that Dane."

"Then what are we to do?" Birna asked. "Do we–"

"There." Vetr pointed down the hill with the tip of his spear.

Geirmund looked in that direction, and perhaps half a rest away he caught a glimpse of a few warriors sliding through the trees towards them. He knew that meant Krok's war-band would be there within moments, and he looked eastward again, where a river ran from south to north perhaps two rests away. He decided they could use that waterway to protect at least one of their flanks, and with luck they would find an embankment or low bluff to guard the other and force Krok into a narrow frontal attack.

He ordered his warriors towards the river, and as they reached the bottom of the hill Geirmund heard the first voices of the hunt behind them. His Hel-hides broke into a run across the land, and after they had covered a rest or so, they entered a dark grove of ancient, mossy oak, where they had to duck under heavy elbowed branches and leap over thick and tangled roots that reached up to trip them. When they finally burst from the forest onto the river's shore, they found a large ship moored in the water, up against the grass and reeds, its crew gathered on the bank around a fire.

The Hel-hides all halted in wary surprise, while the sudden appearance of Geirmund's war-band seemed to also startle the ship's crew, and a few of them called out and drew their weapons in alarm.

Geirmund glanced across their faces, trying to decide if he had rushed his warriors into a trap, but he quickly decided the strangers did not fight for Krok, and some of them even appeared to be Northmen, as well as Danes.

"Geirmund?"

One of the crew stepped out in front of the others, and Geirmund recognized her easily by her golden hair and the scars she bore.

"Eivor?" he said.

"By the gods, Geirmund Hjörrsson, it is you!" She strode towards him, grinning, her arms spread wide in astonishment. "What are you doing here? I'd heard you sailed with Guthrum. I have wondered what became of you."

"I–" His own startlement at seeing her there faded as shouts rose from the forest, alerting them to the coming of Krok's warband. Eivor also heard them, and she looked towards the woods as the Dane and his warriors charged out of the trees onto the riverbank, where the moored ship and its crew seemed to take them aback as it had the Hel-hides.

An uncertain moment passed, and Krok gazed along the shore, searching. When he saw Geirmund, he held up his sword.

"Hel-hide!" he shouted.

"Who is this?" Eivor asked. "Not a friend, it seems."

"He's nothing but an errand boy," Geirmund said.

Krok stalked up the shore towards him, still pointing his sword, his eight warriors marching behind him, while Eivor stepped up beside Geirmund, and her crew joined with his Hel-hides behind them.

"What is your purpose here?" the shield-maiden asked.

Krok scoffed. "Who are you to ask?"

"I am Eivor of Ravensthorpe," she said.

The Dane halted his advance so abruptly the ring that hung from his nose bounced, and he lowered his sword, making it clear he knew her name.

"My hall sits on this river, north of here," Eivor said. "What do they call you?"

He stood up a bit taller. "I am Krok Uxiblóð. I am sworn to Halfdan, who has a blood feud with the Hel-hide through Ubba."

"I know the sons of Ragnar well," she said. "I was with them at

Tamworth not long ago." Eivor glanced at Geirmund. "What is the price of the wergild?"

"Halfdan would accept no wergild," he said.

"That is a lie!" Krok raised his sword again. "King Halfdan set the wergild at eighteen pounds!"

"Eighteen pounds?" Eivor clicked her tongue. "Who did you kill? That is a high price."

Krok glowered. "The dead man was kinsman to Ubba."

"I swear, this is the first I've heard of any wergild." Geirmund folded his arms, confused that Krok did not seem to be lying about it. "If Halfdan is truly willing to speak of blood-price, then you may go back to him and tell him that I demand silver for the death of my warrior, Aslef."

"Or I could pay you that." Krok reached for a pouch at his waist in mockery. "What was he worth? A few pennies?"

Birna laughed. "Aslef was worth more than you and all the warriors foolish enough to follow you." She ran her thumb across the edge of her axe as if testing its sharpness. "We have taken half our blood-price easily, but only when the last of you is slain will the debt be fully paid."

Her words unsettled the Danes behind Krok, and he pointed his sword at her. "You are nothing but a cur, and I will–"

"Enough," Eivor said, rubbing her forehead. "Why are you here, Krok? This is not your blood feud. Where are the sons of Ragnar?"

"They have more important battles to fight." The Dane smirked. "Halfdan sent me in his stead to kill this coward, this argr boy."

The word stabbed Geirmund in the gut and stirred a murmur in the warriors behind him, an attack not on his pride but his honour.

Krok went on. "The Hel-hide fled from Lunden like a–"

"Hold your tongue!" Steinólfur bellowed, the cords of his neck tight and red.

"Or let it keep wagging, Dane," Vetr said, his voice like wind over frozen ground, "for I would gladly cut it out."

But every warrior who had heard Krok knew that silencing him would do nothing. The insult had already been given. The Dane had named Geirmund argr, and that could not be ignored, nor could anyone but Geirmund make a reply to it.

"I have kept my honour." He moved towards Krok, ignoring the Dane's sword, boring into his enemy's eyes with a fiery glare that Krok managed to hold, even as a few of his warriors took a step back. "I was willing to pay wergild," Geirmund said. "It is Halfdan who has forsaken his honour by sending a pile of ox shit to fight for him, but fight you I will, until one of us is dead."

Silence followed.

"I will fight you." Krok swallowed. "But it is you who will–"

"Steady, both of you." Eivor marched over to stand between Geirmund and the Dane. "I am jarl here and this holmgang will be done according to law. First, we must choose the day and the place."

"Here," Geirmund said. "Now."

Eivor looked at him as if she were seeing him anew, and he wondered how much he had changed in her eyes from the second son she had met in his father's hall. "And what say you?" she asked, turning to Krok.

"I will fight here and now," the Dane said.

"And you wish to fight until death?" She asked that question of them both but looked at Geirmund.

"Yes," he said, and so did Krok.

"Choice of weapon?" she said. "Axes? Spears?"

"Sword and shield," Geirmund said, to which Krok also agreed.

Eivor sighed. "So let it be done."

The warriors spread out to form the square in which the fight would take place, and Geirmund's Hel-hides drew close around him. They appeared worried, perhaps thinking of the last time he had fought in single combat with Rek and lost, but Geirmund chose not to take offence at their doubt and kept his mind on what he had to do. Krok was older than him, and possibly stronger, more skilled, and more deadly. Geirmund knew he would need to arm himself with more than his sword, but the laws of holmgang hindered the use of cunning to win.

"Expect a foul fight from this pisspot," Steinólfur said. "Be ready to fight foul in return. Dogs bite, horses kick, and cats scratch, but if he should deal that way, so must you."

Geirmund looked across the holmgang square at Krok, who had stripped off his armour and tunic to fight bare-chested. The Dane shook his head wildly and sliced the air with his sword in long, swift arcs to loosen his joints.

Birna watched him also, and then said to Geirmund, "I want you to do something for me."

"Name it."

She looked at Krok again. "Rip that ring from his nose."

Geirmund laughed, and then thought of something Birna had once said about warriors who fight with their pride. He believed Krok to be such a man.

"You will each have three shields," Eivor called from the middle of the square. "You will fight until a mortal wound is given, and every warrior here will accept the outcome. Should any refuse the outcome or interfere, the same shall forfeit their lives. Do you agree?"

"Agreed." Geirmund took his first shield from Skjalgi and strode towards Eivor and Krok with his sword in his hand.

Krok shifted his weight back and forth, from one foot to the other. "Agreed."

Eivor glanced between the two of them, and it seemed she looked a bit longer at Geirmund as she backed away from them. "Then let it begin. Now."

Krok struck hard and fast. Geirmund got his shield up to take the blow, but the impact stunned him onto his heels. The warriors around the square began to shout, some for him and some for his enemy, but all at once so that Geirmund couldn't tell their voices apart, and their words became one roar.

Krok charged again, but this time Geirmund returned a swing with his own blade after blocking the Dane's. They circled each other, striking and retreating, striking and retreating, searching each other for signs of weakness. Very quickly Geirmund's shield felt close to breaking, and he signalled for a halt, then went to Skjalgi to fetch his second shield before the first failed at the cost of his arm. Krok watched him and spat.

When they renewed the fight, the Dane struck even harder, three times, but Geirmund dodged the fourth and landed a blow that cracked off the top half of Krok's shield at the boss. The Dane halted the fight to get another.

When Krok came again, Geirmund chose to leap aside instead of taking the blow with his shield, and the force of the Dane's empty swing carried him forward, off balance. Geirmund tried to seize the opening with a slice at Krok's neck, but the Dane got his shield up in time and ducked away.

After that, Krok took more care with his sword-strikes, and Geirmund's second shield soon splintered apart. Sweat poured down his face, and his chest burned from hard breathing. His legs had strength left, but both his arms felt bruised to the bone. His sword felt heavy, and as he went to fetch his last shield, he worried that he had tired faster than his enemy. His warriors all looked at him as if they shared his fear.

"Hel-hide," Rafn said, "if you have a plan, I see no cause to hide it."

"Nor I," Geirmund said. His mouth tasted of iron.

Skjalgi handed him his third shield. "Do you have a plan?"

"You could always rip that ring out of his nose," Birna said.

Geirmund wanted to laugh but could not rouse his mirth, for he had no plan, but he wished that he could do as Birna said, if only to injure Krok's pride. Then it occurred to Geirmund that there were other ways to injure his enemy's pride, and that to wound his pride might perhaps weaken the warrior.

"Laugh at him," Geirmund said to his Hel-hides.

"Laugh at him?" Steinólfur asked.

Geirmund did not try to explain but turned to face Krok with all the confidence and strength he could gather, much of it false. "Tell me, ox-shit," he said as they came back together, "how many warriors have you lost trying to kill me?"

The Dane growled.

"I hope you are not as careless with your bastard children as you are with your war-band."

"Silence!" Krok shouted.

"Are your little ox-turds as ugly and cowardly as you?"

The Hel-hides laughed behind Geirmund, and so did several warriors from Eivor's crew, at which Krok looked around, then swung his sword hard, but it was a reckless move, and Geirmund stepped aside of the blow.

"Tell us, ox-shit," he went on, "were you watching from the alehouse when Birna split open the head of your false blacksmith? Unlike you, she had brains."

Krok roared and struck again, and again, each time more wildly, as Geirmund landed blows with words against the Dane's pride instead of a sword against his shield. His plan, to his surprise, seemed to be working.

"What was her name?" he asked. "She is not in Valhalla, and that is your fault. You were the fool who sent her to die without a weapon in her hand."

That caused Krok to glance at his war-band, perhaps in shame, before he turned back to Geirmund, "Stop your pissing and fight!" Spittle flew from his mouth. "I'll rip your throat out with my teeth!" He swung hard, missed, and the tip of his sword scraped the ground, flicking cut grass into the air.

"Were you there to see your warriors slain by monks?" Geirmund asked as he circled the Dane, keeping out of reach, searching for the right moment to strike. It was not a plan to be proud of, but unlike Krok he was not fighting with his pride. "We laughed at you behind the wall, you know. Even the Christians laughed at you."

Krok bellowed, then threw his shield away and took his sword in two hands.

"Think of that," Geirmund said. "Your name causes monks to laugh."

The Dane rushed at him with a berserker's rage, and Geirmund took a gash across his hand as he barely got away.

"Halfdan will know it," he said, then tossed his shield aside also. "He will know you are a fool among Dane and Christian alike, and that is how you will be remembered."

"Silence!" Krok charged, eyes bulging, and Geirmund saw his opening.

He spun out of the way, then swung back around and plunged his sword into the Dane's side, shoving the blade deep with both hands, feeling it tear through different layers of flesh as it went in near Krok's bare waist and came out higher up, from his back. The thrust staggered the Dane sideways a few steps. Then he looked down at his chest, seeming almost confused, and dropped to his knees with a single, bloody cough.

When Krok's sword fell from his hands with a ringing against the ground, every warrior there heard it and saw it. They all went silent, waiting to see what Geirmund would do, but in that moment he thought only of Aslef. Geirmund could not bring himself to send his friend's murderer to Valhalla, but for the sake of peace with Krok's warriors yet living he waved one of them over.

The man hurried to his commander's side and put the fallen sword back into his hand. Blood sputtered and bubbled from Krok's mouth, covering his nose ring, and his head lolled. His warrior eased him backwards onto the ground, but couldn't lay him flat because of Geirmund's sword point, and the Dane's head tipped sideways. A few moments later, Krok was dead.

Geirmund turned slowly to face Eivor and his Hel-hides, utterly spent. "It is over," he said. "Let this holmgang be an end to–"

"Look out!" Steinólfur shouted.

Before Geirmund could even turn, Eivor had thrown an axe that wheeled towards him with a thumping of the air and sank deep in the chest of Krok's warrior, who fell only a pace or two from Geirmund, a dagger in his hand. Then the last remnants of Krok's war-band drew their weapons, but Eivor's crew and Geirmund's Hel-hides cut them all down while he stood bewildered and tired in the middle of the holmgang square.

The fight lasted only a few moments, and Eivor walked towards him, then past him. "I thought that might happen," she said as she bent to pull her axe from the warrior's chest, after which the Dane groaned, shuddered, and died. "They had that look about them."

"What look?"

"Warriors whose pride and anger come before their honour. But I did warn them."

Geirmund still felt out of air, his body drained of all its fire, and a deep chill shivered through his limbs.

"That was not the cleanest of fights, Geirmund Hjörrsson," she said. "But it was lawful, and I am glad you survived it."

"So am I," he said.

She leaned towards him. "I do have questions about some of the insults you gave. But that can wait until we are underway."

"Underway?"

"Yes, aboard my ship." She nodded in the direction of the boat moored in the river. "You and your warriors will be my guests, as I was once yours at Avaldsnes."

"Where are we heading?"

"To my hall," she said. "We are going to Ravensthorpe."

23

Geirmund's sword did not come out of Krok as easily as it had gone in, but after cleaning and oiling the blade Steinólfur clapped him on the back and told him he was feeding it well.

Before leaving that place, they dug a shallow trench under a grey sky and covered the dead with earth, and then the river's current carried Eivor's ship north down the river. They glided through a rich low country of fields and pastures, and where the water slowed the crew dropped oars and rowed to speed the vessel along.

As they travelled, Eivor stood with Geirmund a little apart from his Hel-hides, near the sternpost. They spoke of what he had done since she had last seen him, specifically the killing of Fasti and all that had followed, from that death to the death of Krok and his warriors.

"If Halfdan has set wergild," she said, "you would be wise to pay it and end this blood feud."

"I would pay, but he set none. Guthrum would have told me."

"Guthrum is a cunning man." She glanced up the ship towards his Hel-hides. "From what I overheard your warriors saying after the holmgang, you also have a reputation for cunning."

"I make use of every weapon at hand," he said. "I have found that many of the deadliest weapons do not come from a smith's forge."

"I think that is true."

Geirmund thought she looked stronger than she had at Avaldsnes, and the way she moved suggested that she had gained much hard experience, like a good blade that had been used and sharpened many times. "I am surprised to find you here," he said. "I would have thought you in Rogaland."

Her expression darkened with anger, and she looked away, over the river. "I could never bend my knee to Harald."

"Harald of Sogn?" Geirmund knew of only one reason why Eivor would speak of bending her knee to anyone. "He attacked?"

She returned her gaze to him, frowning. "You do not know?"

"Know what?"

"That Harald–" She stopped, her brow creased. "Have you not spoken to Ljufvina and Hjörr?"

"How could I have spoken with them?" he asked, afraid of the answer he was already starting to guess.

"They are in Jorvik," she said. "They are in England."

He knew what that meant, but he still had to ask, "What of Avaldsnes?"

She said nothing for a few moments, and Geirmund listened to the oars stirring the river, and the water splashing and tumbling under the hollow of the boat.

"All the North Way has fallen to Harald of Sogn," she finally said. "Most kings and jarls willingly accepted his rule to avoid war with him. Those who did not accept either fled or died in defeat. That is how I came to Ravensthorpe, and how Ljufvina and Hjörr came to Jorvik."

Those words and that knowledge struck Geirmund more deeply than Krok's weapon ever could have, even had the Dane's sword run him through. When he thought of Harald in his father's high seat at Avaldsnes, he trembled with rage, but he could not say who he hated most. Harald had taken the hall that Geirmund's grandfather had built, but his own father had apparently surrendered it without a fight, and Geirmund had not been there to defend it.

He wondered what might have happened if he had not quarrelled with his parents and disobeyed them by leaving. He wondered if there might have been a different end, had he stayed, and he thought this must surely be the betrayal and surrender in his future that Völund had foretold.

Eivor sighed. "I wish you had heard it first from your kin."

"The truth is not changed by who speaks it." Then it was he who looked away at the river, but he was not beset by memories and regret, as Eivor was. He thought of his lost home, and he felt anger and doubt. "When I left Avaldsnes," he said, "I did not think it would be for the last time."

"Fate seldom gives such warnings. But would it have changed your decision if you had known?"

"I don't know."

"Sometimes that is the only honest answer we can give."

He brought his gaze and his mind back to the ship. "Have you seen them? Are they well?"

"They are well," she said, but with a slight hesitation. "Life is not easy in Jorvik, or anywhere in England. There are enemies everywhere. Some of them we see and know well. Others… they move in secret, and they hide their true purposes behind lies, masks, and the robes of Christian priests. It is difficult to know who to trust."

Geirmund moved his hand to his waist, touching the handle of the bronze knife Bragi had given him.

"Alliances here are fragile and hard won," Eivor went on. "But you should know I count Ljufvina and Hjörr among my most trusted friends. They have struggled, and they have faced enemies, but they are well. Will you go see them?"

"It seems I must."

She leaned away from him. "Do you not wish to see them?"

"We did not part on good terms," he said, remembering his argument with them in his father's council room. "I spoke in anger, and so did they."

"The gods know it is not for me to judge such things. But I will say this much. The wounds we ignore seldom heal well. They must be cleaned and bound, or they will fester." She put a hand on his shoulder and looked into his eyes. "Whatever you choose to do, I am glad to see you." Then she left him and moved towards the prow of the ship to speak with one of her crew.

Geirmund remained at the sternpost, and Steinólfur soon joined him there. When Geirmund told him what he had just learned, the older warrior seemed little troubled by it, but he was an Egðir, and not of Rogaland.

"It is a great loss for Hjörr," he said. "But you left that place to seek lands of your own."

"So I told my father when I turned my back, and yet I have no lands of my own."

"That need cause you no shame," Steinólfur said. "You are on the path to your destiny."

But Geirmund no longer knew that to be true, nor whether it had ever been true, and he felt suddenly lost and adrift, but he spoke no more about it for the rest of their journey downriver.

In the late afternoon the ship came to Ravensthorpe. The

settlement's blue hall rose high in the midst of two dozen buildings or more, all situated in the shelter of a low ridge on a gentle rise above the river, where a wharf reached out to receive ships and trade. It was a fine location for a town, with land to the north for planting.

As Eivor led them from the river towards her hall, Geirmund heard the hammer of a blacksmith somewhere in the town, and the bray of horses. They passed by the houses and workshops of several men, women, and children, who seemed to regard Geirmund with more curiosity than suspicion or fear. Not all of them appeared to be Northmen, and some even looked Saxon. One man even resembled the traders from Syrland that Geirmund had seen in Lunden, with dark skin and hair, and robes in a style neither Saxon, Northman, nor Dane. He stood outside his home, hands clasped behind his back, and he gave Geirmund a nod when their eyes met.

Then Geirmund and his Hel-hides arrived at the hall, with its dragon-prowed keeled roof. Eivor led the way inside, where they were all greeted by a woman whose hair shone with the colour of a red deer's hide, and though she wore no armour she carried herself as if her body remembered the fit of it well. Eivor introduced her as Randvi, her war-chief, and then Geirmund introduced his warriors in return.

"You must all be hungry and thirsty." Randvi motioned them towards a long table bearing food, drinking horns, and a pitcher of ale. "Come, sit, eat."

Eivor led the way, and though her hall was not the largest Geirmund had seen it possessed all the riches and comforts a jarl could desire. It was the sort of hall he wanted for himself one day, if that was to be his fate. "You have done well, Eivor," he said.

"I have been fortunate in many ways." Eivor glanced at Randvi. "But we have fought hard for everything you see."

"I do not doubt it," Geirmund said.

His warriors sat at the table and helped themselves to all that it offered, and after Rafn had taken a drink of ale he looked down into his horn with a grin.

"Your brewer has skill."

"I will share your praise with Tekla," Eivor said.

"Wolf-Kissed!"

Geirmund turned and saw the Syrland man had entered the hall.

"I come to introduce myself to your guest, if I may?"

"Of course." She moved towards the man, and Geirmund did the same, leaving his Hel-hides at the table. "This is Geirmund Hjörrsson of Rogaland," Eivor said. "Geirmund, this is Hytham, one of my advisers."

"It pleases me to meet you, Geirmund," the man said, bowing. He looked young to be an adviser, perhaps twenty summers in age, and he wore his dark hair cropped short, with rings in his ears. "Or should I call you Geirmund Hel-hide?"

Eivor looked at Hytham in surprise, then back at Geirmund.

"I answer to that name more favourably than I once did," Geirmund said. "How do you know it?"

Hytham held his fingertips together before his waist, pointed downward. "It is my duty to know what the Danes and Saxons are doing, and your reputation has reached me, even here at Ravensthorpe." He spoke in the manner of the other men of Syrland that Geirmund had met in Lunden. "I hear you are very clever," he added, "and that Guthrum especially owes you his gratitude."

"You honour me, Hytham," Geirmund said. "May I ask, are you from Syrland?"

"I am."

"What brings you to this place, so far from your home country?"

"I am a seeker of knowledge," he said, "wherever it may be found. Especially knowledge that has been lost or forgotten."

"Are you a seer?" Geirmund asked. "Or do you speak of books?"

"I am not the seer of Ravensthorpe," Hytham said, "and there are ways other than books to preserve knowledge and wisdom."

"But you have a völva here?" If Geirmund were at Avaldsnes, he would have sought Yrsa for wisdom, or perhaps even Bragi, but the seer of Ravensthorpe would do. "I would speak with her," Geirmund said. "If she will speak to me."

"She might," Eivor said. "She lives at the edge of the settlement, if you wish to find out."

"I can show you the way," Hytham said, gesturing towards the hall's door. "Would you go now?"

"I would." Geirmund looked at his warriors, who seemed content where they were, and then turned towards Eivor.

"Go," she said with a gentle smile. "We will speak more later, and tonight we will have a feast to welcome you."

"I'm very grateful," he said, and then he left the hall with Hytham.

They walked north under a few trees, above which Geirmund could see the tops of Roman pillars. He smelled the honeyed scent of wild flowers, and he heard a distant child laughing somewhere in the settlement, the first time in years that he had heard such a sound. A sense of peace and prosperity seemed to fill the air there, and Geirmund thought that in a short time it would be easy to forget that he still walked on Mercian ground, and not a land somewhere along the North Way.

"I have heard much of Guthrum," Hytham said. "It is said he killed Æthelred of Wessex."

"That is true," Geirmund said. "I saw him throw the spear."

"He has become a mighty warrior." Hytham strode with his hands behind his back, reminding Geirmund of Torthred. "But I believe he was not always so."

"What do you mean?"

"Only that it seems Guthrum has… obtained something."

Geirmund thought of Hnituðr and regarded the Syrland man with suspicion. "Such as what?"

Hytham's shoulders lifted with a slight shrug. "Bravery? Perhaps a new fire of ambition burns within him?"

"King Guthrum was never a coward," Geirmund said. "Perhaps you are simply speaking of his fate."

Hytham smiled. "Perhaps you are right." Then he gestured towards a hut that had emerged from the trees nearby. "The seer is just ahead."

That was something Geirmund did not need to be told. He could now smell the potent smoke in the air, and he saw the cats prowling around that place, the herbs and mushrooms drying in the sun, the bones and skulls of humans and animals fixed to posts before it and hanging from its walls, and he knew it to be the dwelling of a seer.

"I will leave you now," Hytham said. "But before I go I would say one more thing to you, Geirmund Hel-hide. If you ever find something lost or forgotten, and you wish to understand it, seek me out. I will be here." With that, the Syrland man turned and left.

Geirmund watched him, wondering again what he knew about Hnituðr, and how he knew it, before turning his attention back to the seer's hut. He approached its door with some reluctance, for seers spoke with the gods, and it was no small thing to go where gods had been.

He raised his knuckle to rap on the door, but it opened before he could knock, and a young woman peered out. She wore a loose dress the colour of deep water and woad paint across her pale brow, nose, and cheeks. Her long hair fell in thick cords as black as the deep-night, woven with bits of bone, antler, and metal, while her eyes shone up at him with a depth and brightness that had nothing to do with their colour. The combination of her youth, her beauty, and her fearsome power as a seer struck Geirmund silent for several moments, during which she looked into his eyes, trapping his gaze, and waited.

"I–" he began, and faltered. "My name is Geirmund Hjörrsson, sometimes called Hel-hide."

Still she said nothing.

"If I may, I would speak with you," he said. "I wish to know what fate you see for me. If you wish, I have silver, but little else to offer you."

"That is not true," she said, her voice like warm rain trickling down Geirmund's spine. "So long as you have something to lose, you have something to give."

He looked down at himself. "What you see is all I own."

"I see a Saxon blade."

She eased the door open and stepped through, closer to him, and he resisted the urge to back away from her. She reached down towards his waist, still staring into his eyes, and gently laid her palm over the plain pommel of the seax. Then she slid her hand and fingers around its handle, and Geirmund flinched as she pulled the weapon from its sheath.

"If you would know the will of the Three Spinners," she said, "you must offer this blade."

"Why?" Geirmund asked, then realized he sounded unwilling and sputtered, "You–you may take it; I give it freely. But… why the seax? It is a common weapon."

"You would rather I take your fine sword?"

"No, that's not what I–"

"The gods do not tell me why. They only tell me it offends them and does not belong with you." She turned the weapon over in her hand and looked up and down its blade. "Whose blood has it tasted? How did it come to you?"

Geirmund understood then why the gods demanded it, and he also knew the seer heard their voices, for she could not have possibly known. "It was given to me by a Saxon priest," he said. "I had no weapon then, and it has served me well in–"

"It is a Christian blade." She spat and sneered at the seax in disgust. "From this day you will be stronger without it."

"Take it, then." He moved to untie its sheath from his belt, but she put her hand on his to stop him.

"No," she said. "Save a place for the weapon you will find to take its place."

He paused, but nodded, leaving the empty sheath on his belt, and the seer disappeared into her hut with the seax.

"Come inside," she called.

Geirmund swallowed, then followed her, but could see little of her dwelling in the dim light and pungent haze of smoke that hung in the air. A post of sunlight stood in the middle of the room between the dirt floor and an opening in the roof, leaving the rest of the dwelling in shadow. Geirmund thought he glimpsed things moving in the corners, but he tried not to look too closely, fearing to see what a mortal should not.

"Sit before the fire," she said.

Geirmund blinked and noticed a ring of stones resting upon the ground within the footprint of the light-beam. He took a few steps and sat down in the dirt before the circle, where he felt the glowing heat of the red coals upon his face. His heart pounded loud and fast in fear and awe as the seer sat opposite him on the other side of the hearth, almost hidden in the shadows until she leaned forward into the waterfall of sunlight. She looked at him, the vast gleam in her eyes as fierce as an empty and sweltering summer sky, and she tossed the seax into the fire. Nothing happened for a moment or two, but then the wooden handle began to smoke and smoulder, until it finally caught fire and burned.

"Perhaps if you had killed the priest to claim it," the seer said, "the gods might have allowed you to keep it."

"I understand," he said as he watched the seax blacken, feeling some grief at its loss. He would never have killed John for it, and he remained grateful for the priest's trust and kindness, but that was in the past, not Geirmund's future.

"What about your fate would you know?" the seer asked.

He watched the flames dancing along the blade, turning it red beneath a crust of cinder. "I was told once that my fate would lead to betrayal and surrender. I have seen both, and I wish to know what now lies ahead of me."

"Are you certain you wish to know that? Before you answer, remember that the gods care nothing for whatever it is you hope to hear. They speak only the truth, and only the truth they choose to speak."

Geirmund took a deep breath. The air in the hut tasted of ash and dried blood. "I am certain."

She nodded, and then she leaned back, out of the light and into the shadows, but Geirmund could still see the soft glow of her eyes. She stared at him for a long while, until she no longer seemed to see him, and it felt as though her eyes looked through him, inside him and beyond him, to a treacherous place he would never dare go, where madness and wisdom became waves over the same sea.

"Betrayal and surrender," she said. "They are yet a part of your fate."

Geirmund sighed, having hoped that both were behind him.

"But," the seer went on, "you have already been given the way to overcome them."

"What way?"

"That is for you to learn," she said. Then she closed her eyes, and when she opened them again, she leaned back into the light and looked at him as she had through the doorway to her hut, seeing much, but not as the gods see. "You have your answer," she said.

"I do." His own eyes burned and watered from the smoke. "But, as you warned me, it is not the answer I hoped for."

"You have a war inside you, Geirmund Hel-hide. In that way you are much like Eivor Wolf-Kissed." She glanced down at the seax in the fire. "But the gods can favour you now as they would not have favoured you before. May they watch over you."

He nodded. "I thank you," he said. Then he rose to his feet and stumbled across the hut, through the doorway, and out into the sun, where he blinked and rubbed his eyes and sucked the clean air deep into his chest until he felt steady on his feet. Then he wandered back to the hall, where he drank more ale and rested with his warriors until evening fell. Then Eivor held the feast she'd promised, where Geirmund ate his fill of meat, almost more than he had seen during their entire stay with the monks at the monastery. He devoured boar, and goat, and goose, along with so many horns of ale and mead that he lost the ability to count them. He laughed and played toga hönk with the folk of Ravensthorpe, but quickly learned that the winning side of the rope would always be the one anchored by Tarben, a bear of a man who had been a feared berserker before becoming a baker and turning his paws to bread-kneading for Eivor and her settlement.

As guests of the feast grew drowsy, some staggered home to their beds, while others fell asleep where they were, on the benches and floor of the hall. Eivor found Geirmund and sat next to him with a contented sigh, something he thought might be rarely heard from her.

"A good feast," she said.

"It is the closest I have felt to home since leaving Avaldsnes," Geirmund said. "I do not know where my home is now."

"What of Bjarmaland?"

"I've never been to Bjarmaland. My mother says they have towns and halls by the sea, and they are much like Finns, but they do not look like Finns. Some of them make offerings to our gods, but they also pray to a god called Jómali."

"Have you ever thought of sailing there?"

"My father has never given me a ship to sail anywhere," he said. "But I would like to go there one day."

She looked at him for a moment. "Is it true?"

"Is what true?"

"What they say about you and your brother? Did Ljufvina trade you both for the son of a thrall?"

Geirmund could not remember the last time someone had dared ask him about that, though he had often known that question to be on many minds whether asked or not. "I see your tongue is still free," he said.

"I've had much to drink. And you do not have to answer if—"

"Yes, much of the story is true. But not as it is often told. It began when my brother and I were born too early."

"It is often so with twins," she said.

"It is, but that frightened my mother. She was young and newly married. She spoke little of my father's tongue, and he was often away at sea. He was still almost a stranger to her. She feared what he would do when his sons looked nothing like him. She feared he would think she already carried us by another man when she married him."

Eivor nodded with gradual understanding. "And the thrall? Is that true?"

"Her name is Ágáða." Geirmund felt his throat tighten at the thought of her. "She had just given birth to her own son, and she understood my mother well enough to know the root of her fear. She wanted to help. But I do not think she meant to offer what my mother demanded."

Eivor shook her head. "Gods, then it's true."

"My mother would tell you she wasn't in her right mind. She would tell you it was a hard birth, and she let her fear and pain make the choice." Geirmund looked upwards into the smoke that curled around the rafters, while his mind's eye turned towards his memories. "If she were here, she would say she never planned to leave us with Ágáða for so long. She would say that she only wanted to keep us safe, and that she regretted her choice the very next moment and every moment since. She would tell you she should have trusted my father, but by the time she realized this it was done."

"How long were you–"

"Four summers." He felt a cold hollow forming inside him as he said it. "We lived with Ágáða for four summers."

"Do you remember her well?"

The hollow in Geirmund grew wider as more of him fell into it. "I do."

"And is it true that a skald revealed the secret?"

"No," he said. "Bragi was simply the first person with the boldness to say what everyone else could see."

"Even Hjörr? Could he see it?"

"My father is no fool. I think he had to know the truth. There are times I think he only forgave my mother's lie so easily because he knew that by leaving it unchallenged all that time he had been party to it."

"Why would he do that?"

Geirmund shrugged. "He loved my mother. He saw what he wanted to see. Until Bragi made him see his sons."

"And what happened to the thrall's boy?"

"Three summers after he returned to his home, he died from weak lungs. It is said that he was born frail and often sick."

"And his mother? What of her?"

"When the truth came out, my mother released her from bondage. My father gave her and her husband land. My parents said they wanted to make things right, but I think they wanted her away from us. I wasn't allowed to see her again for a long time."

"Did you miss her?"

The hollow inside ate the last of him. "I looked to her as any son would look to his mother."

Eivor said nothing else for some time. "The truth may not change by who speaks it, but I am glad to know the truth of all this from you."

"There are very few people with whom I have spoken of it so readily."

They kept drinking, until Geirmund could drink no more, and then Eivor guided him towards a comfortable corner stuffed with blankets and furs. He leaned on her as they walked.

"A ship leaves for Jorvik tomorrow," she said. "Would you like to be on it?"

"I would," Geirmund said. "But I am drunk, and you might need to remind me of that in the morning before the ship departs."

She laughed. "I will."

"And I will go to see Hjörr and Ljufvina," he said.

They reached his bed, and he collapsed into it, his limp arms and legs twisted like roots.

Eivor stood over him, grinning and shaking her head. "So the name Hel-hide no longer bothers you?"

"It does not," he said. "Guthrum gave it new meaning."

"Many things only ever have the meaning we give them," she said. Then she laughed again and gave him a gentle kick. "Sleep well, Geirmund Hel-hide."

24

The ship rowed up the River Ouse through a cold rain, approaching Jorvik from the south. Clouds draped their tatters of mist so low to the ground they almost became a fog that hid much of the town, but their gloom matched Geirmund's mood well.

He had left his warriors behind in Ravensthorpe, feeling strongly that he had to make this journey on his own, and for once even Steinólfur had agreed with him. Geirmund did not know what he would say to his parents, or to his brother, as his shame and his anger fought for control of his heart and his words. He had left his family in pride and anger to meet his fate, and he returned to them without lands and without much silver, carrying only his reputation, which now accused him of slaying the kinsman of a Dane-king. But he also raged inside at his father for claiming he could not spare a single warrior of Avaldsnes to go with Geirmund, only to later surrender his kingdom without a fight and land in England himself.

At Jorvik the River Foss flowed down from the east to join the Ouse and the town rose up on the wedge of land that lay between the two waterways, defended in the same way that Readingum had been, but it had also spread its buildings to its western bank. Geirmund noticed Jorvik's walls had been built by Romans, like the walls of Lunden, and the Danes had strengthened them further, making Jorvik the most impressive stronghold that he had yet seen in England.

The ship rowed up the Ouse and soon moored at one of the town's wharves near a stone bridge, and Geirmund found a wet, unhappy Dane there overseeing the loading and unloading of cargo. His name was Faravid, and he told Geirmund where he could find Hjörr and Ljufvina, in their house at the top of the hill near the inner Roman walls to the north.

Geirmund thanked him and made his way in that direction through the town, keeping the hood of his cloak up as much to stay dry as to avoid being recognized, for if word of him had reached Lunden, it may have also reached Jorvik. The wooden planks that lined the roads flexed beneath his boots and kept the streets passable despite the rain that collected in flowing channels beneath them. Where there were no planks, the ground was a mire that smelled of piss and shit, both animal and Dane. Geirmund crossed a large market emptied of merchants and trade by the foul weather, travelled down narrow byways, and slowly worked his way up through the jumble of Dane-houses and Roman ruins towards the cloud-covered hilltop.

When he reached the ancient, inner fortifications above the town, a house of dark wood emerged from the fog and rain. Its steep roof touched the ground and rose to a sharp peak where dragons perched, and Roman pillars surrounded it like the dead trunks of a stone forest. It was not a hut but a humble building compared to a king's hall or a jarl's longhouse, and Geirmund wondered how it could be that his parents had willingly traded the strength and beauty of Avaldsnes for such a place. A second, lower roof fronted the house over its door, and he strode towards it in trepidation, pausing before finally shaking his head and calling a greeting as he knocked.

A moment later, the door opened, and his mother stood before him.

Instant recognition opened her eyes wide. "Geirmund!" she cried out and pulled him into her arms, where she repeated his name against his chest several more times, weeping and squeezing him hard. "Can this be true? Is it really you?"

"I am here, Mother." He couldn't stop his own tears from rising at the sight of her and the feeling of her embrace. "I am here."

She leaned back to look up at him, smiling, laughing, crying, and shaking her head. "Hjörr!" she called. "Our son has come back to us!" Then she took his hand in hers. "Come, come inside!"

She pulled him through the doorway into the house, which was warm and dry after his journey on the river and his walk through Jorvik in the rain. Thick rugs covered the wooden floor, and a calm, steady fire burned in the hearth. Geirmund looked up at the sound of footsteps above, and saw his father coming down a narrow flight of wooden stairs from the upper floor, looking thinner than Geirmund remembered him.

"I don't believe it," Hjörr said, and then he rushed towards Geirmund and hugged him the way his mother had done. "We feared we had lost you, boy."

"Hello, Father," Geirmund said.

"By the gods." Hjörr stepped back and wiped his eyes with the back of his hand. "Thank the gods."

"It is good to see you both." Geirmund bowed his head, his earlier anger nearly forgotten in the presence of their joy and his own surprising happiness at seeing them. "Where is Hámund?"

"He took to the whale roads," Hjörr said. "He trades and forms alliances. He said he wanted to make his own way."

Though Geirmund felt some disappointment that he would not see his brother there, it gladdened him to know that Hámund had struck out to find his path, rather than accepting a life in Jorvik, but he hoped that Yrsa had spoken the truth, and that their entwined fates as brothers would one day bring them back together.

"I wish him well," Geirmund said. "I will make offerings to Rán to keep him safe upon the seas, and Njǫrd to favour him with luck and wealth."

"Let me hang your cloak where it can dry," his mother said, and after Geirmund had removed it she shook it out and laid it over a bench near the hearth. Then she motioned him towards a nearby table. "Sit, sit."

Geirmund let her usher him into a chair, and then he watched her as she set a pitcher of ale, cheese, bread, and smoked fish before him. He thought she looked older, with more silver thread in her black hair and more creases around her eyes than when he had last seen her. She eased into the chair at his right, and then his father took the seat to his left. Hjörr also seemed older, his eyes duller, his chin and shoulders lower. A moment went by, and no one touched the food.

"Is that a scar?" His mother suddenly leaned towards him and reached to touch his temple. Geirmund smiled and tipped his head closer, then felt her fingers gently pushing his hair aside to better look at his injury.

"A Saxon warrior gave me that at a place called Garinges," he said, 'right before he sent me for a swim in the River Thames."

"This was an evil wound." Her poking and prodding turned a bit rougher. "And the healer could have done better work with the scarring." She withdrew her hand, frowning.

"I am certain you would have done better," Geirmund said. "But I am healed, Mother. You need not worry."

She reached for the pitcher, still frowning, and poured them each a cup.

"You were in Wessex?" his father asked.

"I was." Geirmund took one of the ales.

"With Halfdan and Guthrum?" his father asked.

Geirmund nodded and took a drink. "There is much land there. Good land."

His mother pushed a cup towards his father. "There is good land here also," she said.

"I don't doubt it," Geirmund said. "But Wessex will soon fall to Guthrum. I was at his side when he slew Æthelred. Now that he is a king, he has said he will make me a jarl and give me lands."

"Then it seems you were right to go with him," Hjörr said. His voice held bitterness, and also anger, but it wasn't clear what he was angry about, or who he was angry with. Geirmund's mother looked at her husband from across the table, eyebrows raised in concern, and it seemed she wanted to catch his eye, but Hjörr stared into his ale.

"But Wessex hasn't fallen yet," Geirmund said. "Æthelred's brother is king now, Ælfred, and he is a cunning man."

"Cunning often wins the day," his father said without looking up. "More than strength, and more than honour, it is cunning that holds the field and makes a king."

The house had lost some of its warmth as outside the rain fell harder and rattled louder against the roof. A damp chill settled over Geirmund's shoulders, mostly caused by his wet clothing, but also by the mood at the table. A stranger listening might think Hjörr had just foretold Ælfred's final victory over the Danes, but Geirmund hoped his father hadn't meant his words in that way.

"I have just come from Ravensthorpe," he said. "Eivor sends her friendship and her high regard for you both."

"We are lucky to count Eivor as an ally," Ljufvina said. "She has been a great help to us and to the people of Jorvik."

"How so?"

She shook her head and waved off his question. "Nothing to go into now. But I'm glad you visited her settlement. I hear Ravensthorpe is a–"

"I must go." His father stood, knocking his seat to the floor with a loud clatter. Cheeks reddened, he then stooped to right his chair and push it up against the table. "There are council matters I must deal with," he said. "But I shall return before dark." Then he placed his hand on Geirmund's shoulder. "It is good to have you returned to us, son."

"It is good to be here," Geirmund replied.

With that, his father marched from the house, and after he was gone Geirmund's mother sat back in her chair with a deep sigh. "Eat, Geirmund," she said.

He did as he was told and ate, and while he ate they spoke little. His mother sipped her ale, and he chewed his food, and the rain fell. Unlike the empty silence between strangers who have nothing to say to each other, the silence at that table bore the oppressive weight of too many unspoken things, and, as with summer floodwaters held behind a melting glacier, Geirmund felt it best to leave those words undisturbed for now.

"What council does Father go to?" he asked.

"King Ricsige's council," she said.

"Ricsige?"

"The king of Northumbria."

"But I thought Halfdan ruled Northumbria."

"He does, through Ricsige." With her fingertips she slowly spun her cup of ale upon the table. "The Danes have learned that to rule the Saxons in peace it helps to have a Saxon king on the throne, so long as that king understands who truly rules. Before Ricsige, a man called Ecgberht was king, but he became obstinate. Hjörr is part of a council put in place to make sure Ricsige does what Halfdan and the Danes want him to do."

"So my father serves a Saxon king."

"Yes, I suppose he does."

"Would he consider leaving Jorvik?" Geirmund asked. "Would you?"

"Where would we go?"

"Wessex," Geirmund said. "If Father fights for Guthrum, we–"

"For Guthrum?" She sat up straighter, her eyes alight with a fire he knew well from Avaldsnes, but which he realized he had not yet seen in her there until that moment. "You would have us fight for the Dane who took our son from us?"

"He didn't take me," Geirmund said. "I chose to go–"

"You forgot who you were. Who you are. Your father is Hjörr Halfsson, the rightful king of Rogaland, and you are his son."

"I have never forgotten it," Geirmund said in quiet resentment.

"But you speak of fighting Wessex for Guthrum. Does this mean you plan to return to him?"

"I am still sworn to him," Geirmund said. "I have warriors sworn to me. As soon as Guthrum parts ways with Halfdan, I will return to fight for him."

If she wondered why he had to wait for the two Dane-kings to divide, she said nothing. Instead, she tucked her arm close, like a wing, and rested her chin and lips in the heel of her palm. She shook her head. "I thought you had come home."

"This is not my home." He glanced around the house. "Jorvik isn't my home."

"Perhaps it could become–"

"No."

"But we are here," she said. "That makes it your home–"

"No, it doesn't. In truth, Avaldsnes was never even my home. It was simply where I was raised."

He saw a rim of tears form in her eyes. "If not us… where is your home, Geirmund?"

"I don't know."

"Was it–" She paused for several long moments, as if struggling to speak, before she finally managed to simply whisper, "Her?"

"Who?"

She had begun to tremble. "Ágáða."

Geirmund could not remember the last time she had uttered that name, nor allowed anyone else to say it, and the pain and regret he could hear in her voice seized him by the throat. That she would mention Ágáða now spoke to how far from Avaldsnes she had fallen.

"No," he said.

She closed her eyes, pressing out her tears, and he knew that was the answer she had hoped to hear him say, but that was not why he'd said it.

"Mother, I left Avaldsnes to seek my fate," he said. "I seek it still."

She nodded and wiped her cheeks and her eyes with both palms. "I would not hold you from that."

The rain had lessened by the sound of it, and Geirmund decided he needed to breathe in the open air. "Jorvik may not be my home," he said, "but if it is to be yours, I would like to know it better. I think I'll walk now and see more of it."

She nodded again, and then she left her chair to fetch his cloak. "You will need this," she said. "Jorvik can be cold even without the rain."

The coarse wool remained damp but felt warmed by the fire as he pulled the cloak around himself. "Thank you, Mother."

"Go on." She turned away from him and busied herself with clearing the table. "Try not to get into too much mischief."

He smiled as he left the house, and once he stood outside he looked up into the grey sky and inhaled deeply several times. He had tried to avoid the flood of unspoken things, but a few of them had broken free, and now that they had been said he felt relieved of their weight and burden. Much still remained unsaid, perhaps more than could ever be fully told, but he would take them in their time.

From that vantage he could look out over most of Jorvik, much of which remained hidden by the mist. The Ouse crawled out of the fog to the west and turned south where it met the northern wall of the town. The shadowy ruins of a Roman coliseum towered over the buildings to the south, while elsewhere a Christian temple and a great Dane-hall each stood watch over half of the city, one on each side of the river.

Geirmund assumed the hall to be that of Ricsige, and he decided to wander towards it, thinking he might meet his father there. He passed back down some of the same streets he had already walked, but with the rain's easing he found more people about, especially in the market. In Jorvik it seemed that Danes and Saxons lived, worked, and traded alongside each other, and if that peace resulted from Northumbria having a Saxon king, then Geirmund began to understand what his mother had meant.

He had to cross a stone bridge to reach the hall, and then pass under the pale and broken statue of a Roman woman wearing thin robes, her features somewhat worn away by age, wind, and weather. When he finally reached the hall of Ricsige, he found it to be as high and great as his father's hall had been at Avaldsnes, and perhaps even larger. A strong stake-wall surrounded the building, and warriors stood guard at its entrance, both Saxon and Dane. They hailed Geirmund as he approached to learn his purpose.

"I am Geirmund Hjörrsson," he said. "I am told my father is here."

"Hjörr?" one of the warriors said. "I haven't seen him today."

"Are you sure? He said he had to meet with the council."

Another warrior shook his head. "Not today. There is but one way in, and we would have seen him."

Geirmund nodded, feeling confused and frustrated. "I thank you," he said and turned back towards the bridge.

"You might find him at the river," one of the warriors said. "Just outside the north wall." He pointed off towards Geirmund's right. "He often goes there."

"Thank you again," Geirmund said.

He walked the way the warrior had directed him and found his way down to the river, which he then followed north along its embankment and wharves until he reached the Roman wall. He saw no gate there, but a section of it had fallen near the waterline, not enough to weaken the town's defences against an army, but wide enough to climb up, over, and through.

Geirmund slipped past the wall, then down and up the sides of a deep trench, and found himself outside the town, facing a rugged land of hills and valleys broken by the winding of the wide river as it came down from the north. Forest and woodland reached only as close to Jorvik's walls as the Danes allowed for defence, creating a broad meadow of grass that turned thick and reedy near the water. Not far from Geirmund, an old stubby wharf still clung to the riverbank, and his father stood upon it looking north, as unmoving as the Roman statue.

Geirmund sighed and cut across the edge of the meadow towards him, and he called a greeting when he drew close enough for his footsteps to be heard. His father turned.

"You said you had council matters," Geirmund said, but his father made no reply until he'd joined him on the wharf, which wobbled and creaked over the lapping and gurgling of the current beneath.

"I did," his father said, turning again to face upriver. "I needed counsel with myself."

"May I ask what about?"

"I'm sure you can guess," he said. Then he inhaled a long breath through his nose and lifted his chin. "This place. Right here. It almost reminds me of a narrow fjord, as if I am back in Rogaland."

Geirmund looked again at the river and the hills, and he saw what his father meant. The features of that land shared just enough in common with Rogaland to stir memories, though they could never fully imitate or replace the North Way. "There is beauty in England," he said.

"Yes, there is." Hjörr sighed, then turned his back to the water and faced Geirmund. "You may ask me now."

"Ask you what?"

"The question that has been on your mind since you spoke with Eivor."

Geirmund's father still knew his mind well, and Geirmund knew which question his father meant.

"Why did you surrender?" he asked.

"Yes, that's the one." Hjörr looked south, towards the walls of Jorvik. "That is the question I often come here to ask of myself."

"And what do you answer?"

His father said nothing for several moments. "Harald is cunning. More cunning than any of us knew. The other kings and jarls, we tallied our warriors and thought we could defeat him. But then he surprised us by sending all his warriors and ships into the Hafrsfjord for a single battle." He held up his finger, pointing it at the sky. "A single victory. In the end that was all Harald needed. The Hafrsfjord gave him Stavanger, the Boknafjord, and the entrance to the Karmsund. After that, he controlled all trade."

Knots tightened in Geirmund's gut. "He cut you off."

His father nodded. "He had already secured the loyalty from several kings and jarls to the north and the east, with promises of silver, marriage, and trade. Others swore to him the moment they heard of his victory, hoping to gain his favour."

"Could you have fought him?"

"A warrior can always fight until death."

"But could you have defeated him?"

Hjörr turned and gazed north again, and for some time he said nothing. "What sort of king surrenders his kingdom?" he finally asked, quietly. "Does a good king fight a hopeless war until the last of his warriors has fallen? Or does a good king choose to be a king no more to avoid needless bloodshed and death?"

Geirmund did not know how to answer that, but he realized that he had twice faced a similar dilemma, first on Guthrum's ship and then in Lunden, and both times he had sacrificed his own life and honour for the sake of his warriors. He realized then that he may have been too quick to judge his father's choice.

"I assume you will return to Guthrum." Hjörr glanced at him sidelong. "Your mother will not like it."

"She knows I am still sworn."

"And you are a man of honour, as you have always been."

Geirmund studied his father as he stood on that wharf in regret and longing for the land that he had lost, and he found he was no longer angry, or, at least, his anger had been tempered by a greater understanding.

"Come with me," he said.

"Where?" His father turned to face him. "To Wessex?"

"To Guthrum," he said. "Fight with me. You are Hjörr Halfsson, and you are meant to be more than a minder for a Saxon king."

It seemed that thought appealed to his father, for his shoulders lifted a little, and he grinned as he said, "Your mother would not like it."

"She is as much a warrior as you or me," Geirmund said.

Hjörr chuckled. "That is true."

"You came to Jorvik in defeat," Geirmund said. "Let Wessex be your victory, a chance to reclaim the honour you fear you have lost."

A few moments passed in which it seemed they both imagined what it would be like to fight together in battle, to stand shoulder to shoulder in the shield-wall, but then his father's thoughts appeared to shift as his smile faded.

"I would be proud to fight at your side, my son. But if it is my choice, I would be done with war. I want what Guthrum said he wanted when he came to Avaldsnes. Lands and peace. Your mother and I have found both here."

"I understand," Geirmund said, and he did, though it saddened him to see his father diminished. "Will you seek to prevent me from going, as you once did?"

"I was wrong before," his father said. "Even were it not a matter of honour between you and Guthrum now, I would not try to hold you back from your fate."

Geirmund bowed his head. "Thank you, Father."

"But that doesn't mean I've stopped worrying about you being a reckless fool."

Geirmund smiled. "I know."

The clouds had finally begun to clear, leaving the air and the dome of the sky rinsed and polished. They stood together upon the wharf, watching the light of the setting sun turn the river to gold, and before the day had turned fully to night they walked back through Jorvik, across the bridge, towards the house where Ljufvina waited.

PART FIVE
Wessex

25

Geirmund stayed with his mother and father for several days, and during that time he learned more about their life in Jorvik. In many ways, Hjörr led the people there by fulfilling the same duties he had performed at Avaldsnes. He negotiated trade with merchants, he oversaw matters relating to the town's supply of silver, food, and ale, and he acted as lawspeaker for lesser disputes and crimes that did not need to involve Ricsige. Ljufvina worked at many of the same tasks, but it seemed she also came and went from Jorvik, sometimes answering Eivor's calls for help and allies.

For Geirmund's part, he spent much of his visit working with his father, taking on responsibilities that before had only ever been given to Hámund. In doing so, he began to see more of what the burden of high office demanded, and he understood better why warriors like Halfdan and Ubba preferred to leave such daily governance to others under their control.

When word reached Jorvik from Ravensthorpe that Guthrum and Halfdan had divided their armies, and that Halfdan would soon return to Northumbria, Geirmund finally told his parents about Fasti, and about his blood feud with Halfdan through Ubba because of it. Though he would be leaving, he worried what it would mean for them upon the Dane's return, but they seemed unconcerned.

"Halfdan will not turn against us," his father said as they sat together at the table, eating their night-meal. "If not for us, there would be no Jorvik to which he could return."

"If not for Eivor, you mean." Ljufvina raised an eyebrow at Hjörr as she tore a piece of bread from a loaf.

"What did Eivor do for Jorvik?" Geirmund asked.

His mother handed him the piece of bread and broke another for herself. "She came here to hunt members of an order hidden among us. Some were even Ricsige's trusted advisers, but they secretly worked to further their own plans. They would have destroyed Jorvik from within."

"What kind of order?" Geirmund asked.

"That we still do not fully understand." She dipped her bread into the porridge of barley and beef in her bowl. "We know only that they are powerful, and their reach is long, from as far away as Egiptaland, and before the time of Nor."

"By the gods." Her words reminded Geirmund of the ancient lands beneath the sea that Völund had described. "And you stopped them?"

"It was Eivor who stopped them," Hjörr said, giving Ljufvina a slight nod. "We simply did what we could to help her."

"We owe her a debt," Ljufvina said. "So does Halfdan, and he also owes us a debt. Our service to Northumbria will more than satisfy the demands of the blood feud, or any wergild he may have set."

"But that may not satisfy Ubba," Hjörr said. "Be wary of him."

"I will."

"Halfdan has been away fighting for many summers," his father went on. "His jarls and his warriors are tired. When they return, they will expect their rewards, and Halfdan will give the greatest among them lands."

"And you?" Geirmund asked.

Hjörr nodded and glanced at Ljufvina. "We will have a hall again."

Geirmund looked down at his porridge. "Peace and lands," he said, and then ate a mouthful.

His mother leaned towards him. "You have a place here, should you choose to stay."

Geirmund knew that to be true, and a part of him wished he could remain with them in Northumbria. Hámund would return one day, and together they could build a lasting legacy for their family, their children, and their children's children. But the greater part of him knew he could not stay, or that he would not choose to stay.

"I swore to Guthrum," he said. "I am sworn to my warriors, and they to me. I hear they have gone to Hreopandune to find Guthrum, and they will wait for me there. And I swore to myself that I would take Wessex."

His mother said nothing, but she seemed disappointed as she accepted what he had said with a nod.

"You must do what you will," his father said, "for honour and destiny. I assume you plan to leave soon?"

"Yes. I would leave tomorrow if I could."

Hjörr took a drink of his ale. "Can you not?"

"I thought you might have need of me before I go. I don't want to leave you as I did before–"

"This is not like that," his mother said. "Do not delay for us. We will be well."

Geirmund bowed his head to both of them in thanks, and after they had finished eating, they helped him gather food for the road, along with everything else he would need. The rest of the evening they spent talking, drinking, and playing hnefatafl, and when they finally went to their beds, Geirmund lay awake restless. Thoughts of his return to Guthrum and his warriors kept sleep away until the deep-night, and then it was sunrise.

Unlike the last time Geirmund had left his parents, stealing away as a thief, he ate a morning meal with them, and afterwards they surprised him with the gift of a warhorse, a Saxon stallion with a shining chestnut coat, a pale mane the colour of straw, and a burst of white across his brow.

"His name is Enbarr," Hjörr said. "He comes from the Picts."

"He is breathtaking." Geirmund looked the horse over, noting the strength in his muscles and form. He then let Enbarr smell him, and he stroked the stallion's muzzle and mane, sensing the animal's will and sureness of temperament. "Has he seen battle?"

"He has," Hjörr said.

"May he serve you well," Ljufvina said.

Geirmund thanked them both for such a kingly gift, and then they walked with him as he led Enbarr down through Jorvik's streets to the city gate. There he bade them farewell with quiet words spoken while embracing, then mounted his new horse and set off down a south-westerly Roman road.

He and Enbarr came to better understand each other as they travelled. With each passing rest, the stallion seemed to feel more at ease with Geirmund upon his back, while Geirmund learned the kinds of guidance and command the horse answered to best. Together, they covered twenty rests a day, making their way first down the Roman road, and then along the course of the River Trent towards Hreopandune. Enbarr carried his own feed, but Geirmund made sure to allow him plenty of time for grazing each day, and in the evening on their fifth day of travel they came upon a vast field of new burial mounds over which no grass yet grew.

The light of the falling sun set ablaze the haze of dust and smoke hanging over that place, casting shadows against dozens and dozens of barrows. They rose from the ground, some high, some low, and Geirmund could tell by the offerings left there that the mounds had been raised by Danes to honour their fallen warriors. He knew some would contain the ashes of the victorious dead, but others would be empty of remains, the warriors they honoured having been left behind on the field of battle where they fell, either as food for the swans of blood or burned on the pyre.

Geirmund wondered if one of those barrows belonged to Aslef.

The air there felt restless, as though the dead had not yet settled, and even Enbarr rolled his eyes and seemed anxious to move on, but before Geirmund left he poured out the last of the ale in his skin upon the ground with a prayer to honour those now drinking mead in Valhalla.

From that high field, he looked down into a river valley, where he sighted a town in the distance to the west, and he descended the rise towards it. He had seen no army encamped there from the hill, but as he drew closer, he knew that place to be Hreopandune. The town's Christian temple had been put to good use as a fortified gate in a new wooden wall, which stretched to the east and west until it reached the shores of the river, enclosing a well-defended Dane-hold. As Geirmund approached those defences, he found that some Danes still remained within, and he learned from them that King Guthrum had marched his army south-east to a place called Grantabridge.

He stayed there that night and paid in silver to buy food for himself and his horse before setting off again, following directions given by the Danes for a Roman road they called Wæcelinga, a day's travel to the south. After another two days of riding, past the smoking ruins of several Saxon farms and towns, he came to a crossroads and turned from Wæcelinga onto an old trackway leading east.

For the next three days, Geirmund made slower progress on the winding and rutted trail than he had on the even Roman road, covering only ten or fifteen rests before stopping each night to sleep and let Enbarr graze, but on the fourth day he came at last to the outer walls of Grantabridge.

A large and thriving Dane encampment filled the land within those defences, and a Roman ruin on the banks of the River Granta formed the heart of the town. Though not quite as busy with trade as Lunden, Geirmund saw many of the same wares from distant lands for sale in the town's markets, and the smiths and other craftsmen there seemed to have no shortage of work. As he made his way down the roads and byways, the sharp smells of forging, tanning, burning, and cooking surrounded him, mixed with the scents of human and animal waste.

He rode in search of Guthrum and his army, and eventually he found them on the north side of the encampment, where his Hel-hides welcomed him back with joy, and some fresh sorrow over Aslef. The young warrior had died just a day after Geirmund left Lunden, having never truly awakened again from his last sleep, but Thorgrim had been with him at the end. The Hel-hides all drank to Aslef, and after word of Geirmund's return spread, Guthrum summoned him, and Steinólfur walked with him on his way to speak with the king.

"Hjörr and Ljufvina are well?" the older warrior asked.

"Well enough," Geirmund said. "But they have lost much." Then he told Steinólfur all that his father had told him about Avaldsnes and Harald of Sogn, none of which seemed to surprise him.

"The rings of kingship can be golden shackles," he said. "Perhaps there are times it is better to be free of them. Did you make peace with your parents?"

"I am no longer at war with them," Geirmund said.

The older warrior nodded. "That is something, at least."

When they reached the Saxon building Guthrum had claimed for his hall, Steinólfur waited outside while Geirmund entered, where he found the king a changed man. Guthrum had more grey in his hair, and it seemed that a weariness had begun to hound him, biting him ragged at the edges and cutting his temper short. He invited Geirmund to sit, and then he poured him wine into a silver goblet that reminded Geirmund of the cup he had seen in the temple at Torthred's monastery. The Saxon wine tasted of leather and metal, and though it was doubtless of high quality, Geirmund would have preferred the ale brewed by Brother Drefan, or Tekla's ale at Ravensthorpe.

"I'm glad to see you, Hel-hide." The king poured wine for himself in an ale horn and sat in a high seat draped with a wolf's pelt, the animal's empty head and eyes laid over one of its armrests. "When you left Lunden, I feared you would not return."

"There were times I shared that fear. Halfdan sent a war-band after us."

The king leaned an elbow on the arm of the chair and plucked at the fur between the wolf's ears. "What became of that war-band?"

"They are dead."

"All of them?" Guthrum sounded surprised, but also pleased. "Your reputation grows."

It was not reputation Geirmund cared about in that moment,

nor even the king's approval, but rather the truth of the wergild. "I slew their commander in single combat," he went on, "witnessed by Eivor of Ravensthorpe. A man called Krok."

The king's hand went still. "I know the name. You spoke with him?"

"I did. Before we fought, he told Eivor that Halfdan had set wergild. Eighteen pounds."

Guthrum stroked the wolf's ear with his thumb. "That is not true."

"Then why did he say it?"

The king threw his hands up. "He said it because Halfdan asked for eighteen pounds."

Geirmund opened his mouth, then shook his head. "Then why–"

"It doesn't matter what Halfdan asked for. Only the Althing can set wergild."

Geirmund knew then that Guthrum had lied to him back in Lunden, or had at least withheld the truth, and he took a drink of wine to cool his rising anger at the Dane. "Althing or not," he said, "if I had known, I would have paid–"

"No, I could not allow that. Eighteen pounds?" Guthrum leaned forward, his voice rising with irritation. "The boy you killed, Ubba's kinsman? He was no jarl, nor even a landed karl! He was not worth half that weight in silver. Halfdan wanted to punish you, one of my most cunning warriors, and enrich himself while doing it."

That did not answer Geirmund's anger and confusion, and he still doubted whether Guthrum had even spoken the full truth, but he felt unsure of how to press the king on the matter, so he turned to a greater goal that mattered more. "When do we march on Wessex?" he asked.

"Wessex." Guthrum sighed and sat back deep into the wolf pelt.

"Yes, Wessex. When do we march?"

"Soon."

"What do you wait for?"

The king downed the wine in his horn in several large gulps, and then leapt to his feet with a suddenness that almost caused Geirmund to flinch. Guthrum stalked over to the table and poured himself more drink.

"Ivarr is dead," he said.

For Geirmund, and for his blood feud with Ubba, that meant one less son of Ragnar to worry about. "What does that mean for Wessex?" he asked.

"Nothing for Wessex." The king began to pace around the room, which reminded Geirmund of a Saxon hall more than a Dane's, with its carvings, hangings, tableware, and benches. "It means there is much land to be ruled in East Anglia and Mercia. I could see to it that some of that Daneland is yours."

Geirmund pushed his goblet of wine aside. "What are you saying?"

"Halfdan and Ubba are now the last two sons of Ragnar." Guthrum tipped his horn back and wiped his mouth with the back of his hand. "When Halfdan learned of Ivarr's death, it seemed that a fire went out in him. He took his warriors and returned to Northumbria to enjoy his wealth before he dies. Wessex no longer matters to him. His days of war-making are at an end. Only Ubba remains." He looked around the hall. "I have wealth and land that I won in hard battle. I have been made a king, and I have my honour. So, I ask myself, if it is my fate to die, what shame is there in dying here?"

"What shame–" Geirmund worked to keep his anger from raising his voice. "Are you now content to rule here and leave Wessex standing?"

The king stroked his beard, clinking the silver beads woven into it, as if he had to think about his answer, before finally waving away Geirmund's question. "No, of course not. Wessex must fall."

Geirmund could only hope that Guthrum meant what he said.

Over the next few weeks, the king sent scouts south and west into Wessex, and as they returned with knowledge of the enemy, Guthrum and his jarls planned their final attack. The loss of Halfdan's warriors meant they needed both cunning and care if they were to win against Ælfred. Some warriors from the north would answer the call to battle, including Eivor and her allies, but not enough that their tally alone would secure the Wessex crown.

The Danes coming from Northumbria and other distant places would travel quickest by sea-road, and Guthrum needed to offer them a safe harbour in which to land their longships. He chose the town of Wareham on Wiltescire's southern shore, which would give the Danes a firm foothold in Wessex, raiding distance from Ælfred's high seat at Wintanceastre, with a second hold as a fallback in a Roman ruin on the River Exe some sixty rests to the west of Wareham, near the shore of Defenascire. Geirmund knew this much when the king summoned him again to his hall for a private council.

"I will send some warriors by sea," Guthrum said. They sat together at the table, and this time Guthrum drank wine from the silver goblet, while Geirmund drank ale from a horn. "But I will march most of the army overland to Wareham."

"How long will that take?" Geirmund asked.

"At best, four days, possibly five. Longer if we have evil weather."

"Ælfred will be ready."

"He is ready now. My scouts tell me he has the fyrds of Wiltescire and Bearrocscire under his command, and he watches the River Thames and the Icknield Way. He expects we will attack that way. That is why we will march by night, south down Earninga Street to Lunden, then west over the Roman road to the ruin of Calleva, which you may remember from our march to Bedwyn. From there, we march to Wareham."

"That is a long way. If Ælfred learns of your plan–"

"He must not learn of our plan. We must slip past the Saxon army unseen. That is why I have summoned you." Guthrum poured himself more wine. "I need the eyes of Wessex turned northward, away from the roads we will use, and I want you to draw their gaze."

"How?"

"The Thames marks the border between Mercia and Wessex. I want you to take your Hel-hides, cross the river, and raid the towns and villages there as you drive south into Ælfred's kingdom."

Geirmund sipped his ale. "That will surely draw their gaze."

"You must be quick, and you must strike hard for five days. Ælfred must believe you are more than a single war-band."

"Our tally will be small against Ælfred's army. If he should catch us–"

"He will not catch you." The king reached out and gripped Geirmund's shoulder. "He must not catch you. I ask this of you because I know you alone have the needed cunning."

Geirmund paused to consider what Guthrum wanted of him. To follow the king's order would mean marching his Hel-hides deep into enemy lands, without friends or defences to which they could fall back, and rather than hide from the Saxons, Geirmund was to draw Ælfred's full wrath down upon himself and his warriors. Death seemed certain, and he knew that fate, not cunning, would decide the outcome of such a task, though speed might help them.

"Each of my warriors must have a horse," Geirmund said. "Some of them will need new weapons and armour."

The king nodded. "You will have whatever you need."

"And you will pay ten pounds of silver to every warrior who returns."

Guthrum's eyes opened wide. "What? Are you–"

"That is, ten pounds on top of the silver they are owed already."

The king laughed in disbelief. "That is many times the weight I would pay–"

"They will be facing many times the danger, and they are giving you Wessex. Each Hel-hide who returns from this should have wealth enough to buy land and livestock, if they wish it." Before the king could argue, Geirmund said, "This is not greed, my king. We will not have time to plunder. If you need my warriors to accomplish this, then I must give them a reason to accomplish it. The matter before you, then, is how badly you need this."

The king scowled, and Geirmund took a drink of his ale, waiting.

"What about you?" Guthrum finally asked. "What do you want for yourself?"

"To be a jarl in Wessex," Geirmund said.

A moment passed, and then the king nodded. "Ready them quickly. Ten pounds to each who returns."

Geirmund bowed his head and left the king's hall. When he returned to his Hel-hides, he chose to tell them first about the silver, which seemed to stir and heat them like a hot stone dropped in the pot.

"Óðinn's eye, ten pounds?" Rafn turned to his pale companion. "A warrior could stop raiding and settle with that."

"What does he want from us?" Vetr asked. "I doubt the king is simply being generous."

Geirmund inhaled and explained the task that Guthrum had allotted them, after which his warriors cooled, falling silent and still.

"Now I understand," Birna said. "Guthrum doesn't plan for any of us to return."

"It doesn't matter what the king plans," Geirmund said. "If it is our fate to return, we will return. All of us."

"Then let us empty the bastard's hoard," Steinólfur said. "When do we leave?"

"Soon." Geirmund looked across the faces of his warriors. His company still had a tally of forty-two, but many were in need of gear. "Sharpen your swords. Get yourselves fresh shields and armour. The king's smith will give you what you need. Rest and be ready, for when we ride, we will not stop until Wessex is taken."

26

The Hel-hides left Grantabridge three days before Guthrum planned to march on Wareham. Geirmund's warriors would reach the river-border between Mercia and Wessex on the fourth day and begin raiding the towns there. On the ninth day, they were to ride south towards the Roman ruin on the River Exe to meet more than two hundred longships under the command of the Dane-kings Oscetel and Anwend, who sailed from East Anglia, there to wait until Guthrum called for them. That would give the Danes two holds in Wessex from which they could raid the lands of Defenascire and Wiltescire, and take Ælfred's seat in Wintanceastre. It was even said that Ubba might return from raiding in Irland and Wealas to join the attack, and though Geirmund worried what would happen if he should meet him, his warriors believed the presence of a son of Ragnar to be a good omen.

They journeyed down the Icknield Way, a road Geirmund had already travelled with Jarl Sidroc and John, but they left that path some distance from Wælingford and rode west to avoid Ælfred's scouts. On the evening of the fourth day, they came to the edge of a birch wood and looked down into a valley, where a large market town sat on the River Thames with a monastery and a bridge.

"This is where we cross into Wessex." Geirmund dismounted from Enbarr. "We'll attack after dark and burn it. Then we ride on."

"There is silver to be had down there," Thorgrim said. "Those monks—"

"We can spare no time for plunder," Geirmund said. "Think instead of your ten pounds when we return."

Thorgrim turned to Birna, shaking his head, and she shrugged. A few other warriors grumbled, and Geirmund turned to face his Hel-hides as they sat slouched on their horses among the pale trees.

"Hark, all of you," he said, putting steel in his voice. "Remember what we are here to do and remember the oath you made to the other warriors of this company. The time to balk has long passed. If your lust for plunder is greater than your honour, you should have stayed in Grantabridge with the other cowards, where your fate would have found you drunk in a cowshed or taking a piss."

His warriors stood up straighter at that, as though a wind had come through and lifted them like a field of grain. Steinólfur folded his arms close and covered his mouth to hide a grin.

"You are here now," Geirmund said. "It is here your fate will find you, and I will have no Hel-hide meet it with dishonour. Now, get off your horses and take what rest you can." He turned and pointed at the distant town. "In the deep-night we become trolls and put a fear of more than death into those Saxons." He looked into the eyes of every warrior within reach of his gaze, catching nods of agreement after that.

"You heard him," Thorgrim said, climbing down from his horse, and the rest of the company followed.

Geirmund led Enbarr away from them for a short distance, and a few moments later Steinólfur sidled up next to him.

"Trolls?" the older warrior asked.

"Or devils." Geirmund leaned against a birch with peeling bark. "Whatever the Saxons see when their dreams turn evil." He looked at the tree, and then he tore off a large piece of its bark, which he turned over in his hands, thinking. "They fear trolls. There were beasts in the books Torthred showed me."

"I know that cast in your eye," Steinólfur said. "You have a plan."

Geirmund unrolled the curl in the tree bark. "You know why we are here. We must do something Ælfred cannot ignore."

"You think he'll ignore us when we torch his towns?"

"Not at first." Geirmund nodded towards his warriors. "But if the people of the towns we visit tell him we are but a single warband, he may not come after us with his army. He might even realize Guthrum's plan and look for the true Dane army elsewhere."

"What are you saying? That we should kill all the witnesses?"

Geirmund shook his head. Then he poked his thumb through one of the black knots in the white bark. "I'm saying the witnesses should not know what they have seen." He raised the wood to his face, like a mask, with one eye peering through the hole he had made. "Ælfred will hear of a howling pack of troll-Danes and devils harrowing his people in the deep-night, and that is a riddle the cunning Saxon king will have to solve."

Steinólfur nodded, but slowly, as if seeing the plan come into view. "Some might say there is no honour behind a mask."

Geirmund lowered the piece of bark. "To hide behind a mask in fear or shame is not honourable, but we are neither afraid nor ashamed. Against these Saxon townsfolk, a mask is simply cunning, and when we go to battle, we will face the enemy without them." Geirmund handed the bark to Steinólfur. "Spread the word that every warrior is to become a troll that would frighten their own children. Their horses also."

The older warrior looked at the piece of bark, and then gave it a tap with his knuckle. "I'll see it done."

He walked away, and Geirmund used his bronze knife to cut off another piece of bark from the tree. He carved holes for eyes and a jagged mouth that turned his mask into a kind of skull, which he fitted with a leather cord to tie around his head. He then cut a few more strips of bark, which he rolled and bent to give Enbarr horns, and he fashioned both of them bark-skin where he could attach more pieces of wood.

By the time he finished the moon had risen, and he turned to find his Hel-hides had almost vanished in the darkness, replaced by pale fiends and trolls with branches for antlers and fangs, and faces shaped like wolves, wyrms, and other nameless fears. They stood ready and restless in the forest, clad in twisted bark the colour of old bones, as though the birch trees had torn free of their roots and come to dreadful life.

"Now your hides are of Hel," Geirmund said. "Your own fathers would shit themselves at the sight of you, and tonight we make these Saxons soil their beds."

A low rumble of pleased laughter rolled through his warriors, and they set off down into the valley, walking their horses in the treacherous darkness. As they crept closer to the town, they could hear the distant, deep-night chanting of the monks, and they halted at the edge of the settlement's fields until the priests had finished praying and returned to their beds. Neither the town nor the monastery had defensive walls, and only a few warriors had been set to watch.

"When will these Saxons learn?" Skjalgi asked. His mask reminded Geirmund of a snow-fox, and it muffled the boy's voice.

"We could wait here until the fools have built defences, if you prefer," Birna said from behind a draugr-like face.

"Their temples needed no walls before the Danes came," Vetr said. "But they will learn."

"That is why we must take Wessex now," Geirmund said, and pulled out his fire-flint. "Light your torches. Spread out and put fire to all that you see. Howl and wail like beasts in the wind. Fight them only when you cannot break away." He pointed south, in the direction of the river. "Make your way to the bridge. I expect it will be defended, so prepare for arrows and a battle there. Then we cross."

"And those who do not reach the bridge?" Steinólfur asked. "What of them?"

Geirmund looked across the masks leering at him out of the night and tried to see past them to the warriors beneath. "I will leave none behind, but the Hel-hides must ride on without me, for Guthrum and for Daneland. All who make it to the bridge must be gone before the town raises its defences."

That did not seem to sit easily with his warriors, but none refused.

Geirmund then struck sparks from his fire-flint into his torch and blew the embers into a blaze. He climbed onto Enbarr's back, and when his warriors had all lit their flames, he raised his torch and charged out across the field towards the town with a roar. A moment later, hooves thundered at his back, and his warriors raised a shrieking squall that could freeze blood and turn even the bravest warrior pale with fear. Geirmund's howl turned to laughter that echoed inside his mask.

An acre-length from the nearest hut, a cry finally went up from the warrior at watch, but he turned and fled, rather than staying to fight, and Geirmund held his torch under the first building's thatch.

The Hel-hides galloped past him into the town, swinging

axes and lighting fires along the way, and when they reached a crossroads near the monastery, some warriors rode down a byway to the west, while others drove southward, and a few went to see what harm they could do to the Christian temple. Geirmund watched the doors and windows of the buildings they had already set alight for enemies that might try to defend the town, but the only villagers who appeared seemed intent on fleeing and nothing more, mostly women and children.

Geirmund spurred Enbarr into a trot down what seemed to be the town's market road from the river. A thick grey smoke soon choked the air, a glowing red haze filled with rushing shadows that turned it into Muspelheim, and Geirmund's Hel-hides into fire jötnar. Animals squawked and bellowed, and somewhere in the direction of the monastery a bell rang.

Two hundred paces on, he entered the market square, where stalls and wagons burned, and several of his warriors raced through shouting curses. Another two hundred paces or more brought him to the river, where it seemed many of his Hel-hides had already gathered. Geirmund rode up to the front and found Steinólfur.

"Let us hope all towns in Wessex are so easily dealt with," he said to the older warrior.

"We're not across the river yet. Look."

Geirmund turned towards the bridge, where he saw a single boy standing guard, wearing a plain helmet that sat low and tipped sideways on his small head, and holding a sword and shield that seemed far too heavy for him.

"Who will clear the bridge?" Steinólfur asked, but Geirmund understood the true meaning of his question. No Hel-hide would enjoy killing such a boy.

"I will see to it," Geirmund said.

He climbed down from Enbarr and strode towards the bridge, whereupon the boy widened his feet and made sure of his grip on the sword. Geirmund chose not to draw his own weapon, but he halted a few paces from the young warrior in case the boy knew more about using his blade than it seemed.

"What is your name?" Geirmund asked, making his voice harsh behind his mask.

The boy said nothing.

"Your name, whelp!"

"Es-Esmond," the boy said.

"Esmond, we were not sent here to kill you. If we had been, my warriors would already be sucking the juice from your eyes and gnawing the gristle from your bones."

The boy's thin neck bobbed as he swallowed.

"We are sent from Hel," Geirmund went on. "We come to clear the way for a great Dane army that marches down from the north." He took a step towards the child. "What is this place called?"

"Abingdon," Esmond said.

"And where are the warriors of Abingdon?"

"They fight for the king, Ælfred, who is God's king, and–" Esmond raised the point of his sword. "And he will destroy you."

Geirmund looked around. "I see no king here. Are there none left but you to defend this place?"

His eyes held spite and boldness. "They all fled."

"But you did not." Geirmund took another step towards him. "You would make a strong Hel-hide, Esmond of the iron will." He looked at the boy's sword, the hilt of which glinted silver in the moonlight, alive with birds and other animals inlaid in black. "That is a fine weapon. Know that if you raise it against me, I will have to kill you, and my warriors will feast on your flesh. But if you give it to me, we will pass you by and you shall live. What say you?"

The boy said nothing and held still.

"Neither your god nor your king want you to die this night, boy, and I do not want to kill you. Do you wish to die?"

"You—you say Danes are coming?"

"I do, and they are."

Another moment passed. Then Esmond spun and tossed both his sword and his shield off the bridge, and before they had even splashed into the water, he raced away from the town, and into the night. Geirmund looked down at the river and almost grinned.

By then it seemed the Hel-hides had all gathered, watching him and waiting as the town burned behind them. Geirmund felt the hot wind of the flames against his face as he returned to Enbarr, hoping that most of the guiltless townsfolk had fled, and climbed back into his saddle.

"That was a waste of a good sword," Steinólfur said.

Geirmund shrugged. "Better than to waste a good warrior."

"Even a good Saxon warrior?" Thorgrim asked. "Boys most often grow into men, if I am not mistaken."

"When that boy grows into a man, he will remember that his life was spared, but before that, perhaps Ælfred will learn of what I said to him." Geirmund turned to Steinólfur. "Are all here?"

The older warrior nodded. "All are here."

"Then let us move on."

They crossed the Thames from Abingdon into Wessex, following a trackway south until the first hint of dawn sent them towards a forest to the east. They pushed deep enough into that woodland of alder and oak that they could camp without being seen, but to be sure none would find them they lit no fires and ate their food cold and dried. Then Geirmund set watches so his warriors could take some rest, and he went to Rafn and Vetr.

"We need to know when Ælfred is near," he said.

"You want us to scout?" Vetr asked, and Geirmund nodded.

"We will take Skjalgi with us," Rafn said. "The boy has sharp eyes."

Geirmund agreed. He thought Steinólfur might worry over it, but Skjalgi had proven himself a warrior, and in truth was no longer a boy, though out of affection it would likely be some time before the Hel-hides called him otherwise.

Rafn and Vetr went to find Skjalgi, and Geirmund found himself a quiet place under a giant yew to rest. Its branches touched the ground like the woven green walls and roof of a hut, and it was old enough that time had hollowed out the tree's trunk. A gap in the wood spread almost wide enough for a warrior to squeeze through, but inside the yew was too dark for Geirmund to see, and he kept away from the opening. It was a tree to which seers would listen and make offerings, a tree that remembered the gods, and upon which a god might hang for nine days and nights. Red berries grew on its branches like splattered droplets of blood.

The air beneath the yew felt heavy with its smell, and Geirmund sat down in the cradle between two roots where the soft needles of countless summers had gathered. He leaned his back against the rough bark, closed his eyes, and dreamed of Völund.

The smith was not in his forge under the sea, but in a place that looked like Wessex, with its green duns, wooded vales, and white, chalk ridges. Völund stood before the doorway of a long barrow, flanked by standing stones. He said nothing, but he looked at Geirmund, and then he was gone, and Wessex turned to fire and ash. Geirmund's Hel-hides fought against an army of burning beasts made of birchwood, and children with fangs. Then he was alone, fleeing before the draugar of Aslef and Fasti. The fires went out, and the ground turned slippery and hard with frost.

Geirmund's breath joined a thick mist over which a blood moon rose, and then he awoke.

At first he thought night had fallen while he slept, but quickly realized the deep shadow under the yew only made it seem that way. It was evening, and the sun had not quite set.

Geirmund left the tree, blinking and scratching his head, and went to see if Rafn and Vetr had returned. He found them with Steinólfur, feeding their nickering horses, and Skjalgi looked pleased with himself for having gone with them.

"Where were you?" the older warrior asked him.

Geirmund nodded in the direction of the tree. "I fell asleep under an old yew."

"I have heard that a yew gives strange dreams to those who sleep beneath it," Vetr said.

Geirmund chose to say nothing about that. "What did you find while scouting?"

"No sign of Ælfred," Rafn said. "But there is a town perhaps three rests west of these woods. We could attack there tonight, and then fall back here."

"I agree," Geirmund said. "But we should move on after that. A forest like this would be the first place I would go hunting for raiders of nearby towns."

So they used what light remained to cross the woods, and then halted at its western edge to make new torches and wait for night to fall. The town they planned to attack had no monastery, so no monks would be awake chanting, and just after midnight, the Hel-hides donned their masks and moved from the forest, over fields and under stands of elm. When the town came within reach of their voices, they lit their torches and charged, and, as with Abingdon, there were no warriors there to fight them. The village was small, with a lowly hall, and it burned easily, but there seemed to be few townsfolk left within it. Geirmund watched a handful of women and children as they fled westward, frantic and crying, like wild game that expected the Danes to run them down.

"Someone warned them," he said.

"That whelp from the bridge?" Thorgrim said. He sat on his horse alongside Geirmund and Birna, watching them go.

"It seems they flee somewhere," the shield-maiden said. "There must be another town that way, and not far."

"Perhaps we should press on," Thorgrim said. "Make a second attack."

They had plenty of night left before sunrise, so Geirmund agreed. They rode west, ignoring the frightened townsfolk they passed, and followed the road over a hundred acres or more of farmland, which brought them not to a town but to a stead with a large hall surrounded by several byres and other outbuildings. No fires or lanterns burned there.

"An ealdorman's land?" Skjalgi asked.

"Seems so," Steinólfur said. "Do you think he's away with Ælfred's army?"

Geirmund spurred Enbarr forward. "Let us find out."

They charged towards the stead, but not all of them had torches left, so those that did rode in front. The Hel-hides roared, and two hundred paces from the hall, the shadow of a man broke away from the buildings ahead of them. Geirmund expected the Saxon to run, but instead he stood his ground, and Geirmund squinted, trying to see what manner of man faced them.

A moment later, an arrow whistled, and a horse near Geirmund screamed as it fell and threw its rider. Geirmund couldn't see who it was in the darkness, but the Hel-hides were all within reach of the bowman's arrows, so their attacker had to be dealt with quickly. The man let two more arrows loose before a warrior could reach him. The first struck the ground, but the second took down another rider.

Thorgrim got to the bowman first and swung his axe as he charged past. The blow shattered the Saxon's bow and struck his shoulder, which sent the man reeling into Birna's path, and he fell beneath the hooves of her horse.

The other Hel-hides galloped among the byres and circled the hall until they felt sure there were no other warriors lurking in the shadows. Geirmund sent Steinólfur and a few others back to see to the fallen, while he climbed down from Enbarr and stalked towards the Saxon.

He found the man folded and broken, unmoving but still alive, and older than he would have expected. The bowman had a hoary beard and spotted bald head, and with the last of his strength he cursed the Danes for pagan devils.

"King Ælfred will send the lot of you to hell!" he hissed with blood between his teeth.

Geirmund crouched down next to him. "I have already been there. For that I am called Hel-hide."

"Then Ælfred will send you back where you belong." The man laughed, but it sounded wheezy and pained. "You are fools, the lot of you. Ælfred was born in these lands, and you dare defile them? He will slay you and plough you under like pagan shit and none shall remember you."

"Who are you?" Geirmund asked.

"I am Sæwine. I fought with–" A sudden cough racked him, and he spat a great gout of blood onto his chest, but he kept speaking. "I fought with Æthelwulf of Bearrocscire when he thrashed you Danes at Englefield." The Saxon closed his eyes. "Now that I am dying, my only regret is that I was too old to fight for Ælfred a second time and thrash you again."

A few of the Hel-hides who had gathered around chuckled at that, but their laughter held some admiration, and Geirmund shared it. "Where are your people?" he asked.

The man clamped his mouth shut.

"You were warned, yes?" Geirmund said. "By a whelp called Esmond?"

The Saxon opened his eyes, and they were full of tears and hatred. "One boy of Wessex is worth more than a war-band of Danes. And now I will say no more."

Geirmund knew the old man meant it. "Then I have no more use for you." He pulled out his knife and stuck the man in the chest, right to the heart, to end his pain and quicken his death. The Saxon's eyes widened in shock, and his open jaw worked a bit as he let out one last ragged breath.

Geirmund wiped his blade on the man's sleeve and stood. "Do not burn this place."

"Why not?" asked one of his warriors.

"This Saxon loved his king," Geirmund said. "He may be known to Ælfred. Tie up the corpse before the door of the hall."

Then he went to see about his fallen Hel-hides and found that luck had favoured the first warrior, who had lived through his bruising tumble, though his horse had not. The second warrior, a man named Løther, had taken an arrow to the chest, which would have been the end of him within a day had he not broken his neck when he hit the ground. Geirmund ordered the dead horse left in the road after stripping it of its saddle and tackle, and he gave the dead warrior's horse to the Hel-hide who had lived.

"Bring Løther's body with us," Geirmund said. "We will bury him away from this place."

He then returned to his Hel-hides at the hall, where the corpse of the Saxon now appeared to stand before the doorway, head drooped, arms outstretched as if he waited to greet his visitors with an embrace.

"Well done." Geirmund hoped that the old man's loyalty to Ælfred was widely known, so that all would see the cost of that loyalty. "Let the ravens begin their harvest."

Then they left that place and galloped back towards the forest, racing the dawn, and after they had reached the heart of the wood, Geirmund went to Rafn and Vetr to send them scouting once more.

"Take some rest," he said to them, "but then I need to learn something, if you can find it out."

"What is it?" Vetr asked.

"That dead bowman said Ælfred was born in these lands. I would know where."

Vetr looked at Rafn, who narrowed his eyes, and then nodded. "I think that is something we can learn, no matter how unwilling the Saxon."

27

Before Rafn and Vetr returned with Skjalgi, a hard rain set in that raised a fine mist from the forest floor and soaked Geirmund's Hel-hides even under the shelter of the trees. They buried Løther near the old yew and made offerings to the gods. The storm clouds pressed down all day and into the evening, and when the scouts finally returned, they looked like sea-dwellers come ashore. One of Rafn's sleeves had torn, and blood seeped through a linen binding around his arm.

"You fought?" Geirmund asked them.

Rafn glanced at his arm and shrugged. "It is nothing."

"It is deep," Vetr said, scowling.

Skjalgi looked at the ground, appearing shaken.

"What happened?" Geirmund asked.

"We met with a few of Ælfred's scouts," Vetr said. "There were five of them, so we thought we could slay them easily enough and keep one alive for questions."

"We did slay them easily," Rafn said. "But the one we spared had more claws than we thought. And he was also… strong-willed."

"Did you learn anything from him?" Geirmund asked.

"Yes." Rafn looked down at his hands. "My will proved stronger."

Geirmund noticed blood under the Dane's nails, but thought better of asking what tortures Rafn had used on the Saxon prisoner.

Vetr glanced at Skjalgi. "There is a hall south-west of this wood that belongs to the king," he said. "Five or six rests from here. It stands near the foot of a great ridgeway. It is called Wanating, and Ælfred was born there."

"What of Ælfred's army?" Geirmund asked.

"He marches up that ridgeway from Readingum," Rafn said.

That news pleased Geirmund, for it meant Ælfred had perhaps taken the bait the Hel-hides had offered, but it also brought dread. If the Saxon army caught them, there could be little doubt they would all be slain.

"How far?" Geirmund asked.

"Two days," Vetr said.

"Guthrum should reach Wareham in three." Geirmund wiped away the cold rain droplets that had gathered in his eyebrows. "We need Ælfred to keep his march this way."

Rafn chuckled. "An attack on the place where his mother shat him out should catch and hold his anger."

"That is the plan." Geirmund looked again at the warrior's wounded arm and thought of something Steinólfur had said to him back in Rogaland. "Take care of that limb. I think your Miklagard sword would miss it, and none of us know how to feed that blade."

"He will take care of it," Vetr said.

"Go and see Steinólfur." Geirmund pointed off into the trees towards the older warrior. "He has some skill with healing, but I warn you now the scar will be ugly."

"Ugly scars are better for bragging," Rafn said, and then he and Vetr walked away into the forest drizzle, leaving Geirmund with Skjalgi.

The boy was sitting on the trunk of a fallen tree, leaning against a thick broken branch that stood upright like a post.

Geirmund sat down next to him. "Are you well?" he asked.

Skjalgi nodded. "I am well."

Geirmund knew he was not well, and he guessed the reason had to do with the way Rafn had learned what he needed to learn from the Saxon. A moment passed, and he asked, "Did you keep your oaths? Did you slay any who raised no weapon against you?"

Skjalgi shook his head.

"Then you have kept your honour and need feel no shame. No man answers for the deeds of another. See to your fate alone and let Rafn see to his. Understand?"

The boy looked up for the first time, and his shoulders seemed to lift a bit. "I understand."

"Good. Then I will leave you to rest," Geirmund said, and he allowed all his Hel-hides to do the same until the storm seemed to lift, and the rain slackened, though leaden clouds remained. They moved out of the wood when they still had some light, and then they rode south with their torches lit against the darkness of the moonless and starless sky. The mud and water in the road slowed them further, for no warrior wanted to risk laming a horse, and after travelling four rests, the rain returned as heavy as it had fallen all day, soaking and chilling them from skin to bone.

When they finally reached the hall at Wanating, they found it a hold with high walls of wood, surrounded by a deep ditch that had gathered a foot or two of rainwater at the bottom. It was a large enough fastness to house a small army, and Geirmund watched the tops of the walls for movement, but saw none, nor any light, nor did he smell any woodsmoke.

"It looks empty," Birna said.

"It's too wet to burn," Steinólfur said. "The rain will put out any fire we manage to start."

Skjalgi pointed. "The gate is open."

Geirmund tried to peer through the dark and the slanting sheets of rain to see if the boy was right but couldn't quite say. "Are you sure?"

"I'm sure," Skjalgi said.

"Perhaps they heard of us and fled," Birna said.

"Let us go in and find out," Thorgrim said.

Geirmund found that tempting, if only to get out of the rain. Returning to the woods made little sense, for they weren't much dryer than the road, and he had wanted to be gone from that forest.

"Let us go in," Geirmund took off his mask. "But remember that Saxon bowman and be wary of traps."

So they rode on, and when they reached the hold, Geirmund led the way across the wooden bridge over the ditch, his gaze upon the tops of the walls. Through the gate he saw a hall standing back and to the north an open yard. Smaller buildings, byres, and sheds surrounded it, built into the defences, and there was a well against the western side. Rainwater poured from the roofs in runnels, past shuttered and darkened windows, to make mires in the corners of the hold. Geirmund saw no one and heard no sound above the rain.

He dismounted. "Rafn, Vetr, see if you can find anything amiss in these outbuildings. Thorgrim, Birna, come with me. Everyone else, be ready to fight or flee."

He slogged across the yard towards the hall, and Birna and Thorgrim got down from their horses to follow. Before he entered the building, he drew his sword, and the two warriors with him freed their weapons also. Across the way, Rafn and Vetr entered the nearest hut through a low doorway, seaxes drawn, and Geirmund pushed the hall door inwards.

Without the torch Thorgrim carried they could have seen nothing inside, where the darkness lay thicker than it did out in the yard. The silence within felt heavier also, the rain a distant pounding on the roof.

Geirmund pressed ahead by the limited light of the torch, past tables and benches, and a hearth with cold ashes. Nothing about that place spoke of threat, whether seen or unseen.

"It seems they are truly gone," Birna said.

Firelight swelled from a brazier Thorgrim had found and lit with his torch, showing more of the hall. A high seat stood at the far end, and there seemed to be rooms behind it through two doorways to either side, and also above on the second floor.

Thorgrim moved up the hall, past the high seat, and through the doorway to the right. A few moments later, he returned through the doorway on the left, holding a loaf of bread and shaking his head.

"The larder back there is full," he said.

"That's what a fear of Danes will do," Birna said. "They left quickly."

That was how it seemed, but Geirmund took Thorgrim's torch and found the staircase leading upwards along the northern wall to make a sweep of the upper rooms. He found beds, chairs, and tables, but nothing of any great worth, and no Saxons in hiding. From the windows facing south, he could peer down into the yard, where his Hel-hides waited in the rain, looking cold and miserable.

He returned to the lower floor. "We will stay here for tonight," he said. "Close and bar the gate. Use the byres and sheds to get the horses somewhere dry. Then have everyone come in."

Birna and Thorgrim nodded and left, and Geirmund found a woodpile near the hearth to build a fire. Then he went to the larder to see what Thorgrim had seen, and he found shelves sagging under the weight of cheese-wheels, bread-loaves, eggs, baskets of dried mushrooms and fruits, and barrels of ale and wine. A smoked and salt-crusted hog's leg hung from the ceiling.

He couldn't think why the Saxons had taken everything else with them and left such stores behind, but his mouth already watered at the sight of so much food, and his Hel-hides would not let it go to waste as the Saxons had apparently been willing to do.

He took the ham down and carried it out into the main hall as the first of his warriors came in stomping and shaking rain from their heads and their beards. They looked up at him as he flipped the leg onto the middle table with a loud thud, breaking away some of its shell of salt.

"We eat well tonight," he said, and they did.

Long before sunrise, the larder stood empty, and every belly in that Saxon hall was full of food and drink. The rain departed, and the clouds parted before the stars, which meant they could burn that place when they left it behind, but Geirmund decided to wait until morning and allow his Hel-hides a few hours to sleep off their ale.

Sunrise found him upon the hold's wall looking out over rich Wessex lands of field, pasture, and timber. Many of the oak trees Geirmund could see grew straight and tall, worthy of the shipbuilder's axe, waiting to be hewn into keel, rib, and strake. On the southern horizon, a green ridge ran from east to west, the slanted light of dawn upon its brow, and misty shadows in its folds.

Unlike the Christian temples and monasteries, the Wanating fastness had strong defences, with arrow slits, peepholes, and a narrow, sloped opening above the gate through which defenders could attack enemies on the bridge. Geirmund heard footsteps coming up the wooden stairs from the yard and turned as Skjalgi climbed onto the wall to join him. Together, they leaned against the wood, which was still damp from the rain, and folded their arms across the tops of the timbers. The rich, golden dawn filled Skjalgi's blue eyes, and Geirmund could see by the boy's frown that he had a weighty matter on his mind.

"We'll be marching soon," he said. "It may be some time before you can ask what you wish to ask."

Skjalgi chuckled and rubbed at the scar over his eye. "You know me well."

Geirmund waited for him to gather his words.

"Back in the wood," the boy said, "you told me that no warrior answers for the deeds of another."

Geirmund nodded. "I did."

"But what of oaths? If a warrior is sworn to a king, and that king asks the warrior to do something without honour, what is the warrior to do? Is it worse to break an oath, or to do the dishonourable thing?"

Geirmund turned his gaze again towards the southern ridge, unsure of how to answer. "If you are worried about your place in Valhalla," he said, "I do not know how Óðinn would look upon the matter. Only a seer can tell you that. But for myself, I know what kind of shame I can live with. To break an oath is no small thing, but I think it is worse to do something dishonourable and blame another for it."

"Even a king?"

"Especially a king. If every warrior chose honour, there would be no dishonourable kings."

"I think that is true. I think Guthrum–" Skjalgi stopped and pointed to the south-east. "What is that?"

Geirmund looked, squinted, and stepped back from the wall. A dark line had appeared on the ridge, and it grew thicker and longer with each passing moment. "That is an army," he said.

"Ælfred?"

"Keep watch!"

Geirmund turned and thundered down the stairs, leaping several at a time, and then marched across the yard towards the hall. Inside, he rushed the length of the floor to rouse his sleeping Hel-hides, bellowing and kicking when they struggled to climb out of their stupor.

"Ælfred comes!" he shouted. "Gather your weapons! To the yard, all of you!"

"Ælfred?" Thorgrim sat up, bleary-eyed, and pushed away a basket of apple cores that someone had dumped over him as he'd slept. "I thought he was two days away."

"As did I," Geirmund said. "He must have marched through the night."

"Or that Saxon had a stronger will than I thought," Rafn said from across the room, wincing as he belted on his swords.

That had also occurred to Geirmund. "It matters little now," he said. Then he turned and left the hall, and out in the yard he called up to Skjalgi. "What do you see?"

"No end to their line!" the boy yelled back.

Geirmund cursed himself for a fool. He had entered Wanating looking only for hidden enemies, but he wondered now if the food left behind by the Saxons had been the true bait, meant to keep the Danes there until Ælfred came to slay them. If so, then Esmond's warning had spread even quicker and further than Geirmund had planned. Some might now question the wisdom of letting the boy live, but Geirmund would have made a different choice had his task been other than it was. He and his Hel-hides had been sent to draw Ælfred's gaze, a task they had done well, and the dangers of which they had known well.

The sun had not yet risen above the walls, and his warriors blew clouds into their fists as they emerged from the hall into the blue shadow of the cold morning. When the Hel-hides had all gathered, Geirmund climbed halfway up the stairs and turned to face them and speak honestly.

"We will make our stand here!" he said. "To the last warrior! If we try to flee, Ælfred will see us easily from the ridge, and he will know our true tally. He may then give chase to slay us, but that is not what I fear. When Ælfred sees we are no army, I fear the cunning Saxon king will know that he has been tricked." Geirmund pointed south. "Guthrum needs only two days more to take Wareham! For those who had fallen, and for those who still fight, we must hold Ælfred's army here!" He pointed at the ground beneath him, which was still sodden from the rain. "You may think we are few, but the Saxons do not know how many warriors stand behind these walls. They do not know what manner of Danes they are about to fight!" He drew his sword, Bróðirgjöfr, and held it high. "After today, they will know us! After today, all of England will quake at our name, for we are Hel-hides!"

His warriors let out a roar in reply, and many of them shook their weapons above their heads. Geirmund descended the stairs and ordered the gate shored up and braced with the heaviest beams that could be found within the hold. He then ordered the fires in the hall built up with any and all wood, down to the tables and benches, and had every stone thrown into the flames to heat.

Steinólfur soon found Geirmund, nodding his approval at the preparations, and pointed at a large kettle. "We don't have much fat to boil, but we could fill that with water."

"Stir in some horseshit and mud," Geirmund said. "Something to cling to their Saxon flesh. But melt what fat we have also."

The older warrior nodded again and went to see it done, while Geirmund returned to the yard, where he found the gate had been strengthened well enough to withstand a great deal of battering. He didn't know if it would hold up against two days of attack, or even one, but he knew that fate would decide it. With little food and few warriors, only the Three Spinners knew who among the Hel-hides would live through the coming battle.

Geirmund called for the few bowmen in his company and ordered them into place before the arrow slits on the walls. Then he went up to look out over the enemy and saw the mounted leaders of Ælfred's army now lay but a rest from Wanating, having turned north and come down from the trackway towards the hold. The line of Saxons behind them marched shoulder to shoulder, five or six warriors in width, and stretched nearly a rest in length, almost to the ridge from which they had come.

"How many?" Skjalgi asked.

"At least three thousand," Geirmund said.

"By the hand of Týr," the boy whispered. "I think there can be little doubt Ælfred has turned his gaze on us."

"Word of a Dane army must have reached him, so he brought an army of Saxons." He looked over his shoulder, down into the yard. "We are no army, but we must do our best to give the king of Wessex what he came for."

Skjalgi smirked. "We would not want to disappoint a king. Even a Saxon king."

Geirmund chuckled, and together they watched the enemy draw nearer, until the riders halted their horses a quarter-rest from the walls of the hold. The warriors marching up behind them spread out to either side, forming a line at least a hundred fathoms wide and six warriors deep, followed by a second rear line of the same size and strength.

"They can't think we'll ride out to fight them, can they?" Skjalgi said.

"They would welcome us gladly if we did," Geirmund said. "But I think they simply want us to know we cannot flee."

"Do you think Ælfred is with them?"

"I do," Geirmund said. "He is no coward."

Not long after that, several of the Saxons on horseback led a group of warriors away from the body of the army towards a copse of elm, where Geirmund knew they would cut down a tree to make a battering ram, and it galled him to do nothing but watch and wait for his enemy to act against him. He listened to the distant bite of their axes, and when the riders eventually returned, they dragged the trunk of a tree behind their horses, and Geirmund knew the battle would soon begin.

"To the wall!" he shouted. "Bring fire! Bring stones!"

His Hel-hides came forth from the hall carrying dampened, steaming buckets filled with glowing embers and rocks, followed by two warriors who lumbered under the weight of the bubbling, stinking kettle, which hung between them from a sagging pole upon their shoulders. When they reached the gate, they tied a cradle of rope around the heavy pot, and as they raised it up to the top of the wall, a large force of Saxons marched on the gate with their ram, each step slow and hard won.

Before the enemy came within reach of any Hel-hide arrows, they raised their shields over their heads, but Geirmund's bowmen drew their weapons and took aim, ready to fire through any weakness or opening the Saxons offered them.

"Steady!" Geirmund shouted.

A shield-wall a dozen warriors wide followed behind the battering ram, guarding enemy archers and a second wave of Saxons, who stood ready to take the place of any fallen. The bridge before the gate groaned as the heavy ram crossed it, and then the shield-wall split apart, just wide enough to allow the bowmen behind them to loose their arrows.

"Take cover!" Geirmund shouted.

He and his Hel-hides dived behind their defences as the enemy's arrows whistled around them, and then the whole fastness seemed to shudder with the first thunderous charge of the ram.

"Arrows!" Geirmund shouted.

His bowmen stepped before slits in the wall and released their arrows, taking aim at the shield-wall to force those Saxons into hiding for the next moment or two. In that gap Geirmund held up his hand to signal the boiling kettle, and just as the ram came again, he gave the order, and three Hel-hides tipped its scalding contents down the sloped hole above the gate.

Men screamed below as the hissing sludge poured between their shields and armour. Many of them fell into the ditch, where they writhed in the water, and without their strength the front end of the ram tipped forward into the ground. Saxons rushed up from behind the shield-wall to right it, and Geirmund knew he had to push them back.

"Rain fire!" he shouted.

His Hel-hides tipped their buckets of hot coals and rocks over the walls and tumbled their burning rubble down the hole above the gate, pounding flesh and bone and striking shields aside. His bowmen shot arrow after arrow into the warriors on the bridge, sending more of them into the ditch, but Ælfred's bowmen returned in kind.

Geirmund knew he had lost warriors. He could hear their cries, and at the edge of his eyes he had seen some of them fall from the wall into the yard below, but he could not yet stop to name them or mourn them.

When the Saxons on the bridge had finally lost too many warriors to bear the weight of the battering ram, the rear end of the tree trunk fell with a loud thud and a crack, and those enemies still standing quickly retreated from the bridge, back behind the shield-wall, leaving the ram where it lay.

"The oil!" Geirmund shouted. "Pour it on the battering ram!"

The warriors nearby looked confused, no doubt thinking the hot fat would be wasted without an enemy to burn below, but that was not why Geirmund had ordered it done. The oil would make the ram slick and harder to carry for the second wave that Ælfred would surely send to take it up, though Geirmund knew that would not save his Hel-hides for long.

The king of Wessex had just lost perhaps thirty or forty Saxons, almost the whole tally of Geirmund's war-band, but still led an army of three thousand. Ælfred's first attack had likely been but a test of the hold's defences. His second attack would be in earnest.

"More fire and stone!" Geirmund shouted. "Fill the kettle!"

His warriors sprang down from the wall with their buckets, and they lowered the heavy pot to the yard, but Geirmund feared it would not be enough. The little wood they had for coals would soon be spent, and his bowmen would run out of arrows. It seemed likely the Saxons would breach the gate before the sun set, and Geirmund needed a plan for the bloody fight that would surely follow. Until then, he looked for a way to slow down the enemy, perhaps by destroying the bridge.

Geirmund strode along the wall to the gate and looked down, where he saw the bodies of Saxons piled in the ditch on either side of the bridge, blistered and stuck with arrows, some of them still moving. He decided the battering ram should stay in place on the bridge. It was too green to burn, and even if his Hel-hides could roll it off the bridge into the ditch, the Saxons would simply cut down another. But if Geirmund could burn the bridge beneath the ram, it would not matter how many trees Ælfred felled.

"The Saxons flee!" one of his warriors shouted.

Geirmund looked to the south, where Ælfred's army did seem to be in sudden retreat, falling back towards the ridge in a quick march, but Geirmund doubted the truth of it even as a wild cheer went up among his Hel-hides.

Steinólfur joined him on the wall, his chest covered in blood, but before Geirmund could ask about it, the older warrior shook his head and said, "It's not mine."

"Skjalgi?" Geirmund asked.

"He is unharmed."

"Then who–"

"Thorgrim," the older warrior said. "He isn't likely to live. But I am not sure any of us are. What is Ælfred doing?"

Geirmund shook his head. "It seems he is leaving."

"Leaving? After a few pebbles and some horseshit soup? He can't frighten that easily."

"Perhaps he hopes to draw us out."

"I doubt it." Steinólfur gazed at the ridge through narrowed eyes. "Ælfred knows these walls can hold no more than a thousand warriors, and such a tally would stretch it at the seams. That means he also knows his army is at least three times larger than ours. He would have to be a fool, or think us fools, to hope that we would pursue him."

"Perhaps word of Guthrum has reached him."

"Perhaps," Steinólfur said. "But he seems to be marching west, not south."

"I must know where he goes," Geirmund said as he watched the Saxon line withdraw. "I do not like this."

"I like that I'm alive," the older warrior said. "It seems that luck and the gods are still with you."

Geirmund wanted to agree with him, but he did not feel the presence of the gods or luck in his war-band's twist of fate. Instead, the dread that lingered in his chest seemed to whisper in his ear that his warriors should all have died, but had somehow swindled death, and for that Geirmund feared there would be a heavy price.

28

The Hel-hides had lost three of their warriors to bowmen during the Saxon attack, and several more had been wounded, two of them so badly that Geirmund feared they would not live much longer, especially Thorgrim. The stout Dane had taken an arrow between two lower ribs on his right side, deep into his liver, but in his battle-rage he had snapped off the arrow's shaft to keep fighting, leaving the barbed head lodged within him. Steinólfur's attempts to pull it out had covered him in Thorgrim's blood, and after speaking with every Hel-hide skilled in the least bit at healing, the older warrior had decided to risk no more effort until Thorgrim lay with his sword in his hand, ready to die, for that would likely be the outcome.

Birna had stayed with the wounded warrior every moment of the day since the end of the attack and Ælfred's retreat, and that evening Geirmund sat with them both in one of the rooms behind the high seat in the hall. Thorgrim lay upon the ground in a bed of furs and blankets, his skin pallid and his breathing short and quick. A basin of red water sat nearby him, with bloody rags and metal tools beside it. The warrior held himself still against the pain caused by the slightest shift, and he kept his eyes closed, but he had not yet fallen into the sleep of blood loss.

"Do one thing for me, Hel-hide," he said, grinding his teeth.

"Name it," Geirmund said.

"Make Guthrum give my ten pounds of silver to my bed-bear."

Geirmund glanced at Birna, who reached out and took Thorgrim's hand in hers. "I do not care about that," she said to him. "I do not want it."

"But I want you to have it." Thorgrim opened his eyes and looked at Geirmund. "Will you do that for me, Hel-hide?"

Geirmund hadn't been aware of how close the two warriors had grown, nor even that they shared a bed. As their commander and friend, he felt that as a shortcoming, but he gave a nod. "I will do my best to see it done."

At that Thorgrim seemed to slacken and settle deeper into his bedding, and he closed his eyes again. "Any word of Ælfred?"

"Rafn and Vetr have not returned," Geirmund said. "We know only that he marched his army west."

"What lies west of here?" Birna asked.

"Saxons," Thorgrim said. "And more Saxons west of those Saxons. Then Britons, then the sea." A low growl rumbled in his throat and chest. "I wish I could have lived to see Wessex and England fall. But fate had another plan."

"They will fall," Birna said. "But you may yet live to see it—"

"I am a dead man." Thorgrim opened his eyes to look at her. "You know I am."

She seemed about to argue, but she stopped herself and nodded. "If you are, then I will shout your name at the last battle so you can hear it in Valhalla."

"You are the only woman who has ever frightened me," Thorgrim said. "I think that is why you are the only woman I have loved. My bed-bear."

Birna squeezed her eyes shut and bowed her head.

"I am ready, Hel-hide," Thorgrim said. "You will need to march soon, and I gain nothing by lingering."

Geirmund moved to rise. "I will fetch Steinólfur–"

"No," Thorgrim said. "Give me the tongs. I'll do it myself."

Birna glanced up at Geirmund, and he hesitated, then reached for the tool.

"I'll need you to take hold of it," Thorgrim went on. "After that, leave it to me."

Geirmund nodded, then peeled the linen binding away from Thorgrim's side to look at the wound. It appeared that in Steinólfur's hunt for the arrowhead, the older warrior had made cuts to open the flesh wider. As gently as Geirmund could, he spread the skin, causing fresh bleeding, which Birna wiped away without the need to ask her.

Thorgrim winced and grunted. "Do you see it?" he asked.

Geirmund peered into the wound, and he glimpsed the ragged end of an arrow's shaft just barely poking out between the white of two ribs. "I see it."

"Get a good grip on it with the tongs."

Sweat had gathered on Geirmund's brow, and he held his breath as he pushed the tool into the warrior's side. Thorgrim let out a gasp, then snarled with a grimace as Geirmund worked to get the teeth of the tongs around the thin piece of wood. When he had a tight hold of it, he leaned back a bit to allow Thorgrim to take the tool.

"When you are ready," he said.

Thorgrim reached up and gripped the tongs. "I have been honoured to fight for you, Geirmund Hjörrsson."

"The honour has been mine," Geirmund said.

Thorgrim opened his other hand, and Birna placed his bearded axe in it. "I have been honoured to fight at your side, Birna Gormsdóttir." A few tears leaked from his eyes and trickled down his temples. "I will hold a place for you on the bench beside me."

"I will join you," she said, "when fate wills it."

Thorgrim looked up at the ceiling, took a deep breath, and then let out a roar as he wrenched the arrowhead from his chest. The barbs pulled out tatters of soft liver with their hooks, and then blood welled in the wound as if from a spring. Birna leaned forward and pressed a rag against the opening to stop the flow, which Thorgrim seemed not to notice. Instead, he held the arrowhead up before his eyes.

"I wish I could return this gift to the Saxon who gave it to me," he said.

Birna whimpered, her hands soaked in blood, unable to dam the river.

Thorgrim's arm slowly went limp and dropped to his side, and the tongs clattered free of his grasp, but he held on to his axe as sight left his eyes and breath left his chest. It was some time after he had died before Birna leaned away, staring at the body, and it was longer still before she spoke.

"You will not ask Guthrum for his silver," she said.

"I told him I would."

She looked down at her hands, and then she turned to dip them in the basin. She rubbed her palms and fingers together in the water, twisting and wringing them as if to clean them of more than blood. "He had a plan," she said.

"What plan?"

"He wanted to use our silver, his and mine, to buy a big farmstead and build a hall, where we would live together as husband and wife." She pulled her hands dripping from the basin. "He spoke of it often."

"Did you want that life?"

Birna sighed and pressed the back of a wet hand against her forehead. "I had not decided. Perhaps I did." Then she looked down at Thorgrim. "I let him think I wanted it."

"A skald at my father's hall once told me that war and farming are much the same. But I must tell you, I cannot see you happy milking goats and cows, or gathering eggs."

She laughed, but it was half-sob. "I said almost those same words to him."

"We talked of farming back in Lunden, you and I, with Aslef. Do you remember?"

"I do. I left you pups to go and find Thorgrim." She smiled to herself. "That was when I first took up with him."

Geirmund had not known that, and he felt again his shortcoming. "Now I understand why he wanted you to have his silver."

"And that is why I will not take it, so do not ask Guthrum for it. Even if I had wanted that life, it is gone now, and I will have it with no one else but him."

Geirmund bowed his head. "So be it."

"I will ask you for another thing instead."

"Name it."

"Give me Saxons to kill. Many, many Saxons."

He nodded again. "That I can do. Perhaps we–"

"Geirmund!" Steinólfur came into the room, but he halted just inside the doorway, and his gaze landed on Birna, the body of Thorgrim, the pooling blood, and the tongs. He let out a short, sharp sigh. "I am glad his pain is ended," he said. "And better now than later."

"Why do you say that?"

"Rafn and Vetr have returned."

Geirmund glanced at Birna, worried to leave her, but she gave him a nod, and he touched her shoulder before rising to his feet. Then he crossed the room and returned to the main hall with Steinólfur, where his two scouts waited.

"What did you find?" he asked.

"An army of Danes," Vetr said.

"What?" Geirmund thought he may have misheard. "Who leads them?"

"Ubba," Steinólfur said. "It can be no one else. He must have come back from Irland."

"We think it is Ubba, yes." Rafn sounded short of breath, and his face looked pale. "Ælfred's army had already attacked when we reached them, so we kept our distance."

"How far?" Steinólfur asked.

"Six rests from here," Rafn said.

"How many Danes?" Geirmund asked.

Vetr hesitated before answering. "Perhaps six hundred. No more than eight."

Silence followed, and then Steinólfur turned to Geirmund. "What will you do?"

Geirmund took a few moments to think. "It will be a dark night for a march that far through unknown country, but ready every able Hel-hide to ride before dawn. The wounded can follow behind. If the outcome of the battle is still undecided when we reach the field, we will fight with Ubba against Ælfred."

"Is that wise?" the older warrior asked. "Ælfred has almost four Saxons for every Dane. Our small tally will do nothing to sway that fight." He leaned in closer. "And do not forget, there is still the matter of your blood feud with Ubba."

"I have not forgotten it," Geirmund said. "But only the coward believes he will live forever if he avoids the battle. They are Danes fighting Wessex, and it may even be that we brought Ælfred to them. Their battle is our battle."

Steinólfur frowned, but he accepted Geirmund's decision with a bowed head. Then he went to spread word of the plan, and Geirmund turned to Rafn. "You do not look well, my friend."

"It is nothing," he said. "A chill from the rain last night."

"His arm festers," Vetr said.

Geirmund looked at the linen wrappings. "Show me."

"Perhaps later," Rafn said. "You have heavier matters to deal with before you worry about a scratch on my arm."

"Then see to it." Geirmund glanced at Vetr. "Before it becomes a heavy matter."

The white-haired Dane nodded and glowered at Rafn as if they had already fought that same argument many times.

Geirmund left them and went to tell Birna that she would soon have an army of Saxons to kill. He then helped her wrap Thorgrim's body and bear it out into the main hall, where they laid it beside the corpses of the other dead warriors. For much of that night the Hel-hides honoured the fallen with stories and songs, after which they slaughtered the horses of the dead as offerings, and before they left the next morning, they set the Wanating fastness ablaze for a pyre.

Instead of moving south to use the same ridgeway that Ælfred's army had travelled, Geirmund marched his warriors west along a low-lying road that followed the course of the hills, and which offered them forests and groves for cover. Rafn and Vetr led the way, and the Hel-hides rode hard, reaching the field of battle before midday.

Geirmund smelled the death before he saw it, and he heard nothing but the flapping and cawing of gleeful ravens as his war-band came into a broad and shallow dell soaked in blood and strewn with the bodies of hundreds and hundreds of Danes. Heaps of smoking cinder and ash marked where the tents of an encampment had stood, not far from the banks of a narrow river, and it seemed the Saxons had already marched on, leaving the silent dead to rot in the sun where they had fallen.

"The doors into Valhalla will be crowded this day," Steinólfur said.

Geirmund stared at the slashed, pierced, and sundered corpses, and the dread he had felt at Ælfred's retreat came back with its cold touch across his neck and deep in his gut. He had known there would be a price for their luck, and the dead before him had paid it. "Ubba has fallen," he said.

"How can you know?" Skjalgi asked.

Birna answered him. "No son of Ragnar would flee from a battle. He would fight to the last and die with his warriors."

Ubba's death meant Geirmund's blood feud with the Dane had come to an end, but its manner of end brought him no gladness or comfort. "Guthrum will take this loss hard."

"Will he?" Steinólfur asked.

"What do you mean?"

"Was this his plan? Do you think he knew that Ubba would be here?"

The other Hel-hides glanced at him with angry scowls, and the older warrior drew himself up in defence.

"I cannot be the only one to think it," he said. "Guthrum sent us here to bring Ælfred looking for a Dane army." He nodded towards the battlefield. "Ælfred found a Dane army, and now Guthrum is one of the last Dane-kings left in England."

Geirmund hoped that Steinólfur was wrong, but as he thought about Guthrum, he remembered the doubt and mistrust he had felt at Grantabridge. The nearest Hel-hides shifted in their saddles, glancing at one another in discomfort, but said nothing.

Then Birna spoke. "Guthrum is cunning, but he would never betray a son of Ragnar. He needed Ubba to take Wessex."

"Where is Ælfred now?" Vetr asked. "The Saxons must have marched from this place before the blood had dried."

Geirmund spurred Enbarr out into the field. The horse snorted at the sights and smells of death, and within a few paces they had passed many dozens of corpses stretching away to the north and south. Geirmund gazed over them, unsure what he was looking for, aside from the meaning or reason for such loss that he knew would never be found. If the Three Spinners had reasons that guided their fingers and shears, they did not share them.

The Hel-hides followed Geirmund into the bloodbath, and as Enbarr plodded down the field, Skjalgi spoke up behind him.

"What is that?" he asked. "Is that a horse?"

Geirmund glanced back, then looked in the direction the boy pointed, where high on the slope of a hill above the dell, someone had carved a giant horse into the earth. It gleamed white against the green turf of the dun, at least fifty fathoms long from nose to tail, frozen in the act of galloping over the land. The size and beauty of it made Geirmund think of Óðinn's horse, Sleipnir, and its great presence overlooking the field almost made him forget the corpses through which he trod.

The white horse so distracted the Hel-hides that they almost failed to notice a gang of Saxon thieves and scavengers picking over the dead, but Birna ran them down and brought four of them to heel with help from Rafn and Vetr. Before Geirmund let her have the pleasure of killing them, he learned what they knew about the battle that had taken place there, and it seemed they knew quite a lot.

The thieves knew the burnt encampment had been under the command of Ubba, for the Saxons had taken his raven banner. They also knew that Ubba had fallen, because the Saxons had afterwards spoken of how hard it had been to kill the Dane-king, and how many warriors Ubba had slain with his bare hands before he had finally died. The scavengers did not know where Ælfred marched, but they said his army had gone down the ridgeway in great haste to fight more Danes. When Skjalgi asked them who had carved the white horse into the hillside, they said it was the work of giants who dwelt in those lands long before the Romans came to England, and they said that up on the ridgeway lay a smithy that belonged to a giant named Wayland. Then Birna slit their throats and split their heads open with Thorgrim's bearded axe, which she carried now to honour him.

"Ælfred marches on Wareham," Vetr said.

"Whether he does or not," Geirmund said, "we have fulfilled our task, and must now ride for the River Exe and the fleet. We will use the Saxon ridgeway."

"And halt at Wayland's smithy?" Steinólfur asked, keeping his voice low enough the others would not overhear him.

That name had struck Geirmund as well, thinking perhaps it was what the Saxons called Völund, and he glanced around before answering, "We will see what is there."

They waited for the wounded Hel-hides to catch them up, and then Geirmund led his war-band out of that dell of the dead and the white horse, up the ridge to the south, and onto the trackway, from which height they could see for several rests in every direction. The winds up there blew hard and strong as they followed the ridgeway south of west, until they came into a thin forest of scraggy beech wood that Geirmund knew from before.

"I have seen this place," he said to Steinólfur.

"How?"

"I dreamed it under the yew."

A short distance into that wood, they came to the same long barrow Geirmund had seen, and before which Völund had stood, though in his dream the standing stones had appeared more newly hewn. Under the waking light of day, with his warriors at his side, that place seemed older by far than any ruined Roman town or coliseum, and more lasting. Geirmund pulled Enbarr's reins towards the mound, where the dark, low opening into the barrow led down into the earth, while most of the Hel-hides moved to the other side of the ridgeway from it as they passed, looking askance at it. None but Steinólfur and Skjalgi followed him closer, though Birna halted nearer to the barrow than the others.

"What are you doing?" she asked.

"Ride on," Geirmund said, knowing that the wounded among them would slow their march. "We will catch you up later today."

She leaned and looked behind him at the mound and stones, frowning in confusion, but eventually nodded and moved on. Geirmund waited and watched until the Hel-hides had passed out of sight in the trees, and then he climbed down from Enbarr. Steinólfur and Skjalgi did the same, but Geirmund stopped them when they moved with him towards the barrow.

"I will go alone," he said.

Steinólfur peered into the darkness of the barrow's mouth. "Are you sure?"

"I am sure."

The older warrior pointed at the nearest tree. "You'll want a torch for–"

"If this is truly another of Völund's forges," Geirmund said, "I won't need it."

Steinólfur blinked and shook his head, then said, "Take this, at the least." He drew his seax, flipped it in his hand, and offered its handle to Geirmund. "You might need something shorter than your sword for a tight fight, and your sheath has been empty since Ravensthorpe."

"Thank you." Geirmund accepted the blade, not because he shared Steinólfur's fear but to calm it.

"That won't help you against a draugr," Skjalgi said.

Geirmund grinned. "There is no draugr here." Then he turned and strode towards the barrow opening, and he paused only a moment to check his footing before he took his first step down into the darkness.

The step-way of stone did not sink far into the earth before it brought Geirmund into a narrow corridor in which the low rock ceiling forced him into a stoop. Down that passage, just beyond the reach of outside sunlight, he came into a cramped, empty chamber, and despite the darkness there, he could tell it looked nothing like Völund's hall under the sea. Geirmund smelled the damp earth and felt the rough stone that had been shaped by Midgard hands, not the hands of Æsir, trolls, or elves, and he knew it was no smithy of the gods.

He sat in the silence feeling thwarted, but also could not say what he had hoped for when he had entered, and he wondered at the meaning of his dream, for he knew he had seen that place.

"Völund?" he whispered, and the stone walls spun his voice to make it louder. "Are you here?"

The smith appeared before him, as sudden and bright as a flame in dry tinder, standing upright in the midst of the rock floor, as if he burned within it. He wore a different tunic to before, and had no helm or plates of armour, but Geirmund recognized his eyes and the shape of his long face.

"It is you," Geirmund said. "And you are also called Wayland."

"By some," the smith said.

Geirmund glanced around the small chamber. "And this is your forge?"

"This is not my forge," he said. "This mound of earth and stone is much too young, but it sits within the borders of my forge."

"Then where is your forge?"

"It is here, but deep underground. The way is shut to you." He moved closer, sliding through the stone. "How do you know me?"

The smith's question baffled Geirmund into a moment of silence. "I am Geirmund, son of Hjörr, whose father was Half, whose father was Hjörrleif. You brought me to your forge under the sea. Do you not remember me?"

"No. I am not the Völund you met."

Geirmund struggled with the meaning of that. "You share the name with another?"

"Yes. We are different memories of the same being, but I have not been able to hear the voices of the others for a very long time."

"Why?"

"That is difficult to explain. I am… dying. But slowly. The children of your children will be dead long before I am utterly gone."

"I do not understand your kind," Geirmund said.

"It would be highly unexpected if you did."

"Do you know of the ring, Hnituðr?"

"I know all the rings I crafted, but none by so new a name. Why do you ask?"

"You–no, the Völund under the sea, he gave that ring to me."

"Did he?" The smith paused. "Do you have it with you?"

As Geirmund opened his mouth to answer, a pang of sudden shame surprised him and kept him from speaking for a moment. "I do not."

"Where is it?"

The question made Geirmund feel that he had somehow failed the smith, or himself, and he looked down at the barrow's floor. "I gave it to my king."

Völund raised one of his eyebrows. "Why?"

"I believed it was his fate to wear it."

"Fate is made by the mind," Völund said. "The ring is law. If it was given to you, it was yours to wear. To give up one of my rings is to give up great power."

Geirmund made no reply to that because he knew it to be true, though he had needed Völund's words to see it so clearly. A part of him had always regretted giving the ring to Guthrum, whether fated or not. His honour had kept him from admitting that to himself, because he had sworn to the Dane, but now he saw that the matter had little to do with his honour but instead his power, which was always his to give or take, and the more he doubted the Dane-king, the more he wanted to take the ring back.

"Why have you come here?" Völund asked. "My forge is buried and cold. I can give you nothing more."

"That is not why I came," Geirmund said. "I dreamed of this place."

"That is because you have been inside one of my forges. When you came near another, the deeper parts of your mind felt it and rose up to meet it."

"That may be, but I think there is more. I think I needed to hear you speak of the ring."

"That may be also," Völund said. "Your kind often hears what you want and need to hear, when you want and need to hear it. Is there more you wish to speak about?"

If the Völund before him had been more like the Völund under the sea, Geirmund may have lingered, but it seemed he had come to the end of his fated purpose there, and he knew Steinólfur and Skjalgi would be starting to worry. "No, but I thank you," he said. "I will take my leave now."

"I have no power to send or keep you, but you are welcome, Geirmund, son of Hjörr, whose father was Half, whose father was Hjörrleif."

Geirmund bowed his head, and when he looked up, the smith had gone, and he was alone again in the small, dark barrow. He left the chamber and crept back up the narrow stone passage into the harsh and blinding sunlight. For a moment he had to shield his eyes with the flat of his hand and squint at Steinólfur and Skjalgi.

"Well?" the older warrior said. "You were in there long enough for something to have happened."

Geirmund gave him back his blade. "I talked with Völund."

"What did he say?" Skjalgi asked.

"Less than he said the first time he spoke to me. But he said enough."

Steinólfur sheathed his seax. "Enough for what?"

"Enough to know what I must do." Geirmund moved towards Enbarr and climbed onto the horse's back. "But first we must take Wessex."

29

The march to Defenascire and the River Exe took five days. Geirmund could have pushed his Hel-hides harder to make it in four, but the wounded in their company needed a slower pace. They kept to the ridgeway through Wessex and into Dorsetscire, until they reached the River Lym, from which place they followed the coast west until they came to the Exe and the Roman town Guthrum wanted them to take. Geirmund had expected to see a fleet of two hundred longships or more, carrying an army of four thousand Danes but found barely a few dozen vessels moored at the riverbank.

Upon entering the town, Geirmund learned that a storm at sea had sunk one hundred and twenty longships, drowning over three thousand warriors, including both kings Anwend and Oscetel. That disaster had so overwhelmed the surviving crews that many had sailed back to where they came from, believing the storm an evil omen, and the Danes that had stayed in Defenascire were not eager for battle.

The loss of the fleet also struck the Hel-hides hard, especially after finding Ubba's army slaughtered, and the mood about their encampment held little hope. Only a fool would fail to wonder if luck, fate, or the gods had turned against the Danes and sent them all to their doom.

"How can Guthrum take Wessex now?" Steinólfur asked late one night when there were few to hear him, staring into the fire. "Without Ubba, and with the fleet at the bottom of the sea, the Danes cannot defeat Ælfred."

"Guthrum is cunning," Birna said. "He will find a way."

Steinólfur spat into the embers, which hissed in reply. "Ælfred is also cunning."

Geirmund might have agreed more with the older warrior, were it not for Hnituðr. So long as the Danes had the ring on their side, they could still take Wessex, despite the heavy losses that befell them.

"Perhaps Ælfred has already fallen," Vetr said. He sat near Rafn, who lay next to the fire, weakened and fevered. "Guthrum may have defeated the Saxons at Wareham."

Steinólfur shook his head, as if he did not believe that possible.

"We can only wait for word of the outcome," Geirmund said. "And hope that it is so."

Word came a few days later, carried by Eskil, who Geirmund had not seen since Lunden. The warrior had ridden hard from Wareham sixty rests to the east, almost laming his horse, and the Hel-hides sat him at their fire to give him meat, drink, and rest.

"Guthrum took Wareham easily," the Dane said. "But Ælfred came with an army shortly thereafter, and for now... there is a peace between them."

Geirmund struggled to believe it. "A peace?" he nearly shouted. "After everything we have risked and lost for Guthrum's plan, he would make peace with the Saxons?"

"He did." The scowl Eskil wore said that he shared Geirmund's frustrations with their king. "Ælfred made Guthrum swear to it on the cross of his god."

"Then Guthrum's oath is empty," Birna said. "The cross means nothing. He must have a plan."

Eskil made no reply to that, and then looked hard at Geirmund. "What is it?" he asked.

The Dane ran his tongue around his teeth, as if he disliked the taste of the words in his mouth. "Guthrum also swore on the ring you gave him. Ælfred knew of it somehow, and he demanded an oath upon it."

"And Guthrum agreed," Steinólfur said, sneering in disdain.

"Guthrum is changed," Eskil said, then shook his head. "He is no longer the man I swore to in Jutland. He took Ubba's death harder than the loss of his longships, and now swings from grief to rage in moments, without thought and without his past cunning. But Eivor came to Wareham as I left, and it seems he listens to her, so all is not lost."

Knowing Eivor counselled the king brought some comfort, but it troubled Geirmund that Ælfred knew of Hnituðr. He did not know how the Saxon king had heard of the ring, but rumours of it had also reached Hytham in Ravensthorpe, and Geirmund remembered the priest John asking if Guthrum drew power from a pagan relic, so perhaps Völund's handiwork was not quite the secret Geirmund had thought it to be.

"What does Guthrum ask of the Hel-hides?" Rafn said, his voice strained as he lay near Vetr.

Eskil seemed to hesitate before answering. "By now Guthrum and Eivor have ended the peace and burned Wareham."

"He would break his oath?" Skjalgi asked.

"I would not be bound by any oath to a Saxon," Birna said.

Geirmund wasn't sure he agreed with that as a matter of honour, but especially for an oath that had been sworn on Hnituðr. "Where is Ælfred now?" he asked.

"At a place called Cippanhamm," Eskil said. "It has no walls, and Ælfred has few warriors with him. He is there for a Christian feast, and that is where Guthrum plans to attack. He calls every axe and sword to his side for the battle."

"What swords?" Steinólfur said. "The fleet is sunk and scattered. Ubba is dead."

"Not all Saxons are willing to die for Ælfred," Eskil said. "Word has spread of an old oath-man broken in two and tied to the door of his ealdorman's hall. Wulfere of Wiltescire has already sworn to Guthrum. And Eivor has many allies across England, and rivals in her debt, who will fight under her banner." He turned to Geirmund. "I have heard that Hjörr and Ljufvina will answer her call."

"All is not lost," Geirmund said.

Eskil nodded. "All is not lost."

"When do we attack?" Vetr asked with a downward glance at Rafn.

"In four days," the Dane said, 'during the feast the Christians call the Twelfth Night."

"Guthrum did not give us much time to march," Steinólfur said.

Eskil hesitated again. "The king did not send me. I came to you of my own will because you are warriors of great courage and honour. I knew you would want to fight beside your fellow Danes and kinsmen."

The Hel-hides around the fire fell silent in confusion and anger at Guthrum's slight against their war-band.

"We have fought and died for him," Vetr finally said. "And he wishes to forget us."

"Is it for the silver he owes us?" Rafn asked. "Perhaps he–"

"It isn't that." Steinólfur looked around the circle. "Or, it isn't only that. It is much simpler than greed." He turned to Geirmund. "The Dane-king does what he does because he fears you. Guthrum sees in you what I saw all those years ago. You are a king, Geirmund Hjörrsson. It is only a matter of time before you realize that and take a kingdom for yourself."

Geirmund felt a heat in his cheeks that did not come from the fire, and he waited for at least one of his Hel-hides to speak against the older warrior, in defence of Guthrum's honour, but none did, not even Eskil.

"Do we march?" Skjalgi asked.

Geirmund did not have to think long about his answer. "Yes, we march. But we do not fight for Guthrum. We fight for Muli, for Aslef, for Thorgrim, and for every Hel-hide who has fallen. We fight for Eivor, and for our kinsmen who march to Cippanhamm at her call. Are you with me in this?"

"You are forgetting someone," Vetr said.

Geirmund felt the gaze of the circle upon him, but he could not think what the warrior meant. "Who?"

Steinólfur let out a growl. "It's you, you horse's ass. We fight for you."

A moment passed, and then the warriors all broke into laughter that lasted for some time, after which the Hel-hides went to prepare for battle, and then Eskil came to Geirmund.

"Where do you ride from here?" he asked the giant Dane.

"I will march with you," Eskil said, "if you will have me."

The offer surprised Geirmund. "Do you worry Guthrum will name you oath-breaker?"

Eskil shook his head. "I do not care what an oath-breaker might name me."

"Then I welcome you to march with us," Geirmund said. "And

I will be honoured to fight at your side once more."

They left the River Exe the next morning and travelled by way of a Roman road. A day of hard riding brought them to the edge of a vast wetland of marshes, rivers, meres, and islands, which reminded Geirmund of the fens he had crossed when he first washed up on England's shores. The raised Roman road moved them northward and kept them from getting mired in those lowlands, which stretched to the westward horizon and beyond, but another full day passed before they put the marshes behind them and climbed up into dryer hill country.

From that high place they could see a great, seemingly endless forest to the east, which Eskil called Selwood, and which loomed alongside the Roman road for another full day. When they halted to rest that night, they did so almost in the shadows of its trees, near a large, jagged rock that may have once been a standing stone raised by the same giants who had carved the white horse.

Geirmund found it hard to sleep there, knowing that the next day would bring them to Cippanhamm and battle, where he would fight beside his father and his mother. He rose early the next morning, his blankets and the ground around him covered in a thin rime, teeth clacking in the cold, and almost as soon as the Hel-hides had mounted their horses to leave, Rafn toppled from his saddle and fell to the ground, landing hard on his side.

Vetr leapt down and flew to him, and soon Geirmund and a few others stood over both Danes. Rafn mumbled, but not in words that fitted together, and his lips had turned blue.

"It is his arm," Vetr said. "The fever in his wound has spread."

Steinólfur knelt down next to him. "Let me look at it."

Then he and Vetr removed Rafn's armour, tunic, and linen, a task made difficult by the limpness in the warrior's body, and when they pulled the binding from the wounded arm, Geirmund's stomach turned over. Rafn's flesh had gone putrid, and dark lines crawled beneath his skin like poisonous serpents.

"You proud, bastard fool," Steinólfur said.

The memory of Thorgrim's death still pressed on Geirmund's mind, and he raged at the thought of now losing Rafn. "What must be done?" he asked.

Steinólfur leaned back, hands on his thighs, and looked up and down the arm. "This limb must come off," he said, "and it needs to come off now. He'll die if we don't. But even that might not be enough."

Though Geirmund had expected as much, he found it hard to speak. To a warrior like Rafn, the loss of an arm would be akin to death. Vetr laid a hand on his companion's forehead and leaned in close, searching Rafn's face as if seeking his leave to do what needed to be done, but the mind of the black-haired Dane was lost and utterly unaware of what was happening to his body. Vetr looked at Steinólfur, closed his eyes, and nodded once.

"I trust he will forgive me," he said.

Geirmund looked away from Vetr to his Hel-hides, many of whom had stayed on their horses, and he thought about the day still ahead of them. "How long will this take?" he asked Steinólfur.

"To gather what we need and do it well?" Steinólfur said. "Half a day, at least."

"That will bring us late to the field of battle," Eskil said.

Geirmund hoped that would not mean an outcome like that which had befallen Jarl Sidroc and his warriors at Ashdown, and to avoid that he ordered his war-band to march as planned. "I will stay with Rafn," he said. "I swore to you at Abingdon that I would leave no man behind, and I will not break that oath now. Vetr will stay, I am sure, and so will Steinólfur and Skjalgi. All others will–"

"I will also stay," Eskil said. "I march with you, Hel-hide."

Geirmund looked up at the Dane and nodded. Then he turned to Birna. "I said I would give you Saxons to kill."

"Yes," she said, "you did."

"I would trust few others to lead our warriors into battle," he said.

"Nor would I." She grinned and went to her horse, and after she'd climbed into the saddle, she said, "I will try to leave some Saxons for you to slay, but I cannot swear to it."

"Do what you must," Geirmund said. "May Óðinn and Týr go with you."

She gave him a nod, then called the Hel-hides to her, and away they galloped. Geirmund turned back to Rafn before they had passed out of his sight, and he asked Steinólfur, "What do you need?"

"Clean water," the older warrior said. "A hot fire and hot steel. Plants for healing. Linen for binding."

"We will see it done," Vetr said, and they moved as one to make it so.

By midday they had gathered water from a clear stream and plants from the woods, and they had buried the blades of several axes and knives in red embers. Rafn had stopped muttering and now drifted in and out of sleep, but Steinólfur said he would still fight like a bear the moment they made the first cut, so they tied him down and pulled a leather strap tight between his teeth. Then they all looked away, then watched, then looked away again as Steinólfur went to work butchering the warrior.

He cut through the top layer of skin first, all the way around Rafn's upper arm, with a cold knife so the flesh would bind together again later, and he rolled the Dane's hide up like a sleeve. Then he used a hot knife to cut through the deeper cords of flesh, filling the air with sounds and the smell of charred meat that Geirmund remembered instantly from his ordeal with Hámund in the mountains. The searing by the hot steel slowed much of the bleeding, but not all of it, and the ground beneath Rafn turned to mud. Through it all the Dane howled, eyes bulging, neck as tight as a ship's rope under sail.

When Steinólfur reached bone, he traded his knife for an axe, and he placed a flat rock beneath Rafn's arm to strike against. The older warrior dripped with sweat, and he breathed in and out a few times before he brought the axe down. There was a dull thud, and another, and then a ringing when the blade hit stone and the bone cracked in two. The arm fell away.

"It would have been better with a saw," Steinólfur said as he picked and peeled away loose chips of bone.

The older warrior then washed the torn flesh at the stump with heated water and rolled the skin and tissue back down, which he then gathered and sewed together like a pouch, but he left it partway open so it could weep, and he packed the opening with the plants they had gathered.

Rafn had stopped screaming and fallen into dazed whimpering, and after they had untied him, Eskil lifted him as easily as a child and carried him into the woods a short distance. Vetr told the giant where to put Rafn down, and then Steinólfur set blankets and furs around and over his whole body.

"The shock from that alone can kill a man," Steinólfur said. "Keep him warm."

"I will," Vetr said. "And no matter what happens, I am grateful to you."

"I hope it was enough." The older warrior bowed his head and backed away.

"I am grateful to all of you," Vetr said. "But now you must ride to Cippanhamm. I will bring Rafn there as soon as I can."

"I am not leaving you behind," Geirmund said.

Vetr placed a hand on Geirmund's shoulder. "There is nothing more you can do. It is up to fate now, and if Rafn is to die, I wish to be alone with him before he goes to Valhalla."

A few moments had to pass before Geirmund could agree. "If I don't see you at Cippanhamm soon, I will come back for you."

"If not there, we will be here," Vetr said. "Now go, before Birna kills all the Saxons."

Geirmund glanced down at Rafn, and then he moved away, out of the woods towards the horses. He went to Enbarr, and his Hel-hides crossed to their mounts, while Vetr took his horse and Rafn's to lead them back into the trees.

"Burn that arm," Steinólfur said. "Otherwise, the hugr in it will torment Rafn with pain and itching he can't scratch."

"I will see to it," Vetr said.

With that, Geirmund spurred Enbarr north, but he left behind a plea for the gods to grant Rafn the strength he needed to heal.

30

They had travelled ten rests up the Roman road towards Cippanhamm when Skjalgi sighted a mounted war-band racing south along a ridge to the east, and Geirmund halted his warriors to see who the riders might be. The strangers galloped hard, perhaps thirty strong, and they flew no banners.

"They're Saxons," Steinólfur said. "That much is plain by their shields and helms. Beyond that, I can't–"

"It is Ælfred," Eskil said.

Geirmund strained to see the warriors better. "Ælfred?"

"Yes, Ælfred." He spat upon the ground from his saddle. "I saw him at Wareham, and those same warriors were with him. I know the colours of their horses."

"What is he doing?" Skjalgi asked.

"He flees the battle," Steinólfur said. "Perhaps it has already turned against him."

"Perhaps," Geirmund said.

He had a choice to make, and only moments to make it, whether to chase the war-band or to ride on towards Cippanhamm. He had only himself and three warriors with him, too few to fight the

Saxons. But if Eskil was right, then Ælfred had slipped away from the Danes, which meant the battle at Cippanhamm would not be the end of Wessex, no matter who held the ground at the end, for Wessex would only fall when Ælfred was taken and slain.

"Are you sure that is him?" Geirmund asked.

"I would swear it on my brother's sword," Eskil said. "That is Ælfred."

"Can they have seen us?" Skjalgi asked.

"They haven't slowed or changed course," Steinólfur said, then looked around them. "We're lower here, with a few trees for cover, and we are only four. They may have missed us."

"We must follow him," Geirmund said. "We cannot fight that many, but we can see where he goes, and perhaps find a way to slay him. If not, we'll know where he is, and we can return later with more warriors."

They all agreed with that plan, so they turned around and rode after the war-band, keeping hidden as best they could while marking the enemy's path. The Saxons followed the ridge until they reached the northern edge of the Selwood, at which border they came down from the high ground and rode south along the Roman road. Geirmund and his warriors kept back as far as they could without losing track of the king, trusting that even if they were seen, the Saxons would not assume four riders to be enemy Danes sent after them by Guthrum.

Eventually, they came to the stone that marked the place where earlier that morning they had taken Rafn's arm. Geirmund saw the bloody patch of ground as they galloped by and wished he could have stopped to see if Rafn still lived, but they had no time for side-paths.

When the sun dipped low a few rests on, the Saxons halted for the night and made a camp off the road. Neither company lit fires, and Geirmund kept his warriors at a safe distance to avoid any scouts that Ælfred set to watch.

Before the sun had risen again, the enemy moved on, and that day rode into the upland country of duns and dells that had earlier lifted the Hel-hides above the fens. For six rests they travelled through woods of ash and maple, beneath grassy hills and cliffs of pale stone. When the Roman road dropped from the uplands to the marshes, the Saxons rushed southward for nearly another twenty rests before halting again for a night's rest. The next morning, they broke west from the road and pushed into the level wetlands.

"It seems they know ways through the marshes," Steinólfur said.

"I think they have known their path since they left Cippanhamm," Eskil said. "This flight seems planned to me."

"To what goal?" Skjalgi asked. "Where do they go?"

"We will know soon enough," Geirmund said.

Then he and his warriors pressed their chase into the fens, through tall grasses and thick stands of alder wrapped in fog, and they kept their feet dry only because the Saxons who led them needed firm trackways for their horses. Even so, the going was often narrow and treacherous, and at midday they came to the end of their hunt and could go no further.

They crouched in the grass, peering between the reeds as Ælfred and his warriors rode out onto a fastness of small islands chained together by a wooden causeway over a broad mere. A modest village stood on the island nearest the shore, bustling with small ships and defended by a gate and many warriors, but on the second island beyond it the Saxons had raised high stake-walls and a hold among the trees that grew there.

Eskil shook his head. "It is as I said. This was planned."

"I think you are right," Steinólfur said. "That hold is strong, and it looks newly built."

"Can it be taken?" Skjalgi asked.

The older warrior glanced over his shoulder, back the way they had come. "No army could march over that ground."

"Longships could reach it." Eskil pointed at the water surrounding the island. "That lake must surely meet the sea if–"

"But Guthrum has no fleet," Geirmund said, letting his frustration sharpen his voice. "And I am sure Ælfred knows it. He chose this place because he knows the Danes cannot take it, and because it has everything he needs. There is water, and there is food, and it is beyond our grasp. Ælfred could sit on that island and go on calling himself the king of Wessex until he dies of old age."

"He can call himself king," Steinólfur said, "but a king of what? This forsaken marsh?"

"He is a king of more than land to his Saxons," Geirmund said. "You must think like a Christian. Ælfred is the king of their god. While he lives, there will always be ealdormen in Wessex who follow him, even from his fen-hall."

"Then what can we do?" Skjalgi asked.

"I do not know," Geirmund said. "But we must leave that plan for another day. For now we go to Cippanhamm, to fight and to tell Guthrum and the other Danes what we have learned."

His three warriors seemed reluctant to leave, and Geirmund understood why. The isle to which Ælfred had fled lay before them, almost within reach of an arrow, and it was maddening to stand so close to their enemy and yet have no power to take him and slay him.

"Let us be off," Geirmund said.

They tried to leave the marsh by the ways they had come, but they became lost several times in the fenland maze of forest, grass, and mire, which further showed the strength of Ælfred's hold. When they finally emerged from the marsh onto the Roman road, mygg-bitten and tired, the day's light was spent, and they had to rest for the night before marching north again.

Two days later, they reached the Selwood standing stone, and Geirmund stopped there to see if Vetr remained in the forest nearby, and what had become of Rafn. They went on foot, leading their horses into the trees, and they found the wounded Dane lying in the same place they had left him. His eyes were shut, and he looked almost as pale as Vetr. It did not seem that his chest moved with any breath beneath the furs. Geirmund saw no sign of Vetr, but he knew the other warrior would be somewhere close, and as he moved towards Rafn, he wondered if the Dane had ever awakened from the fever and shock in which they had left him.

Just then, Geirmund heard a low thrust of wind and turned as the head of a spear sliced at his throat from behind a tree, but it pulled away when the warrior wielding it saw who had come.

"Geirmund!" Vetr planted the end of Dauðavindur in the ground and bowed his head. "Forgive me, I should have looked."

"You did look," Geirmund said, "which is why I still have my head."

"Hel-hide?"

The voice came from the ground. Geirmund glanced down at Rafn, amazed to see the Dane looking back, and then dropped to his knee beside him. "You are alive?"

"I hope I am alive," Rafn said, his voice soft and his smile weak. "Because I know I'm not in Valhalla."

"You have the strength of Thór," Geirmund said.

"And the luck of Týr." Rafn glanced down at his stump. "But instead of losing my limb to Fenrir's teeth, I lost mine to a Saxon blade and my own foolishness."

"I am sorry," Geirmund said. "If we could have saved it–"

"I know." Rafn looked up at Vetr, and an unspoken meaning passed between them. "It is my own doing. And my undoing."

"Nothing is undone," Geirmund said. "You are still a Hel-hide, and even with one arm, you are twice as deadly as any Saxon."

Rafn snorted. "That is no feat, but I thank you for saying it."

"How is your arm?" Steinólfur asked.

"I think Vetr burned it."

Skjalgi laughed, but Steinólfur did not. "You know what I mean," the older warrior said.

Rafn looked again at his stump. "There is pain. But it heals."

Steinólfur turned to Vetr. "Fever?"

"He burned for two days, but then it broke," the pale Dane said. "The wound still weeps, but the stream is almost clear."

Steinólfur grinned. "That is good to hear. He needs to eat lots of cheese, meat, and honey, and drink plenty of ale."

"I can do that," Rafn said.

"Can you ride?" Geirmund asked.

Vetr seemed about to say no for him, but Rafn spoke first. "I will ride. I grow bored of these woods, and there has been little more to eat than squirrel."

"Then let us ride," Geirmund said.

They moved quickly to pack up their camp, and then they helped Rafn to his feet. He shivered as the furs and blankets fell away from him, and he was less steady on his feet than Geirmund had hoped he would be. The Dane would need someone to ride with him to keep him in the saddle, and since Enbarr was the tallest and broadest mount in their small herd, Geirmund offered his horse for Vetr and Rafn to ride together, while he took Vetr's animal.

Despite Enbarr's strength and easy stride, the sway and hitch in his gait caused pain in Rafn's stump, which drew sweat and grimaces to his face, though he refused to complain. They halted often to give him rest from it, stretching out their journey and forcing them to spend one more night camped aside the Roman road.

When at last they arrived at Cippanhamm, they saw the leftovers of battle upon the surrounding land. The town sat on a hillock, and a thin morning mist lurked in the low hollows at its feet. Heaps of rotting Saxon corpses offered bloody harvest to the ravens, foxes, and other animal scavengers, and the faint smell of smoke from the pyres of the honoured dead still lingered in the air. Geirmund tallied the charred stacks of timber and offered his silent gratitude to Óðinn that there were far fewer of them than Saxon bodies, and that, though Ælfred may have fled, it seemed the Danes had taken the field.

As Geirmund's small company climbed the hill towards the town, they passed Danes and Saxon thralls digging deep trenches and raising high walls.

"Guthrum plans to stay and defend this place," Eskil said.

"He should be marching on Wintanceastre," Steinólfur said, and Eskil nodded his agreement.

After finding an alehouse where Rafn could rest, Geirmund went to seek Birna and his Hel-hides to see how they fared, and it thrilled him with gladness to find her unharmed in body. In her heart and mind, she still mourned the loss of Thorgrim, a cold basin that she had not been able to fill with hot Saxon blood, no matter how much of it she had spilled, though her mood lifted when she learned that Rafn yet lived, and she went looking for him. Of Geirmund's other Hel-hides, twenty-seven remained, and he greeted each of them before going to look for his parents.

He tried asking a few Danes in the town where he could find Hjörr and Ljufvina, but each time, upon hearing those names, the Danes cast their eyes downward and simply pointed the way. When Geirmund reached the dwelling to which they had sent him, he learned the reason for their silence.

His mother sat alone in the shade of an elm tree, on a bench against the wall of the hut where she had been sleeping, and Geirmund watched her without her noticing him. She stared off somewhere beyond the village borders, and her face and her eyes held no feeling and no thought, as if her hugr had left her body. When she did finally look up and see him, a moment passed in which she seemed not to know him, and in the next she awakened and came back to herself.

"Geirmund," she said, rising to her feet as he drew near.

"Mother."

They embraced, holding on to one another tightly for some time, saying nothing, for Geirmund did not want to hear what he knew she would soon tell him, and he knew she did not want to say it. He felt as though he stood at the threshold of some doorway of fate, and once he stepped through it, he could not go back.

She felt thin in his arms, and her hair still smelled of the smoke from the pyre. "Father?" he finally whispered, ready to know.

She squeezed him more tightly, saying nothing for several moments, and then she pulled away, her eyes red but dry, as if she had cried until no more tears would come.

"All colour is dimmed," she said and touched a silver brooch she wore. "I feel my heart in my chest, but I cannot make sense of it. How can a heart that has ended keep beating?"

"I am sorry I wasn't there," Geirmund said, thinking of his father on the battlefield, alone, surrounded by Saxons, in need of another sword, and how Geirmund would have raced to his side, but it felt as if he was trying to outrun a wave breaking inside him. "If I had been there, perhaps I could have—"

She covered his lips. "Silence, my son. There is nothing you could have done. It was fate."

He pulled her hand away from his mouth. "I asked him to fight Wessex with me. We stood together by the river in Jorvik, and I asked him—"

"It was fate," she said. "The coward believes he will live forever if he avoids the battle, but there can be no truce with death. Is that not what Bragi always said? Be proud that your father met his death with courage and honour."

In that moment Geirmund felt himself step over the threshold in which he had been lingering, into a darkened hall with an empty high seat, and the emptiness in that seat robbed him of breath. Little else had changed, and yet everything around him had become unfamiliar, as if it only made sense against the thing he had lost.

"Wait here," his mother said, and she stooped to pass through the low doorway into the hut. A few moments later, she came back out carrying a seax. "This was your father's. Something told me to hold it back from the fire, and now I see that you lost a weapon."

She gave him the seax, which had a grip made of polished antler and a blade of Frakkland steel, and it so pleased Geirmund's hand when he held it that he knew it also pleased the gods. It seemed to be of the same length and width as John's seax that he had given to the völva to burn, and he found that it fitted into the empty sheath he still wore at his belt, as if they had been made together.

"The seer in Ravensthorpe told me I would find another," he said.

"Kingdoms will pass," his mother said. "Wealth will pass. Warriors will pass. I will pass, and you will pass. One thing alone will never pass, and that is the honour and fame of one who has earned it. Always remember that you are a son of Hjörr."

"And a son of Ljufvina," he said.

She smiled, something it seemed she had not done in days. "I am proud to be your mother, and I know your father was proud of you also. He wanted Wessex for you. And now it is won."

Geirmund froze, unsure of how to speak the truth without taking away some of his mother's comfort. "It is almost won," he said, and when she questioned his meaning, he explained what he had learned of Ælfred. His mother agreed with him that the Saxon king could not be left in his fen-hold.

"Have you told Guthrum?" she asked.

"I have not seen him yet."

"Go now," she said. "Ælfred must not be given time and freedom to plan his return. But choose your words with care. Guthrum is now a Dane of many minds, and you may not always know which one you speak to."

She pointed him towards a Christian temple sitting atop the village hill, and he left her to seek the king there, but on the way he met Eivor as she came down from the rise. He was glad to see her again, and they clasped hands in greeting, standing together in the temple's shadow. She spoke briefly of her respect for his father, and her mourning for him, though it seemed she felt her sadness most strongly on behalf of Ljufvina, for which Geirmund was grateful. He knew his mother would need friends in the lonely days and years to come.

"I hear Guthrum owes you a great debt, Eivor," Geirmund said.

"I do not think he could have won this battle without you."

"I am sorry you missed it, my friend."

"I missed a fight," Geirmund said. "I have not missed the war."

She gave him a puzzled smile. "What does that mean?"

"Wessex has not yet fallen."

"Have a look, Hel-hide." She gestured around them, taking in the town. "We have struck them a mighty blow–"

"Ælfred lives," Geirmund said.

Her mood darkened, as if a shadow had passed over her eyes. "He slipped from our grasp; it is true. He is a cunning one, that Saxon king."

"We saw him flee," Geirmund said. "Me and a few of my warriors. We tracked him to a fastness in the fens to the south."

"He is in Sumorsæte?" she asked.

"I do not know the name of that place, but he is behind the walls of a hold on an island in the marshes."

She nodded slowly, as if thinking to herself. "Ælfred has been laying his hidden plans for a great long while. He had great ambitions for all the Saxon kingdoms of England, and he has them still."

"There are no more Saxon kingdoms," Geirmund said. "There is Daneland, and there is Wessex, but Wessex will soon fall." He looked up the hill towards the temple. "I go to Guthrum now, to make plans for–"

"He will not see you," she said. "I was just there, and he refused me. I have not spoken to him since we set fire to the pyres of the fallen. He talked of the Christian cross in a way that…"

"What?"

She shook her head. "He is a changed man, Geirmund. That I will say."

"I see your tongue is not as free and honest as it once was."

"Perhaps not," she said. "But I hope it is wiser."

"He may be changed, but he will not refuse me." Geirmund moved to march past her. "I will make him hear me–"

She pressed a hand against his chest to stop him. "Tread with care, Hel-hide. Your tongue could make use of more wisdom." Then she released him. "There are many trackways in life, and many whale roads. If ever the day comes when you are no longer sworn to Guthrum, you have a place in Ravensthorpe."

"I thank you, Eivor." He looked down the hill towards his mother's hut. "I hope Ljufvina has a place there also. I hate to think of her alone in Jorvik."

"She has a place." The shield-maiden's smile was sad and gentle. "And she knows it. But you know she goes where she will."

Geirmund smiled also. "I do."

"I am leaving Cippanhamm, but I hope that I will see you again." She glanced up the hill, and her smile fell away. "A Northman in England will always have need of allies."

They embraced and then parted. Eivor went on down the hill, and Geirmund climbed it until he reached the Christian temple, which looked much like the temple of Torthred and his monks, if smaller. The beams of the door in its side hung sundered by their ironwork and hinges, and as Geirmund stepped around them, he spoke out.

"My king? Are you here?"

"I am here," came a reply within. "Is that Geirmund Hel-hide returned from the dead once more?"

Geirmund moved deeper into the dim temple, careful of his footing. Some of the windows held coloured glass, but others had been broken out of their frames, allowing in sharp blades of light that crossed the room like clashing swords. Geirmund felt the grit of the shattered glass beneath his boots.

"I have returned," Geirmund said. "With news of Ælfred."

Guthrum was silent for a moment, and then he simply repeated the name. "Ælfred."

The king's voice came from one end of the temple, and Geirmund pushed through the shadows, light, and dusty air towards him. "Yes, Ælfred. He hides in a hold to the south and west. Eivor named the place Sumorsæte. It is a treacherous land of deep marshes, but I think we can make a plan to root him out of it."

Guthrum made no answer, and Geirmund found him standing before the Christian altar.

"Did you hear me, my king?" he said. "Ælfred is–"

"I heard you. Ælfred is in Sumorsæte."

The way he spoke it said to Geirmund that he may have already known it.

"I have been thinking of how we might go after him," Geirmund said. "The task will be hard, but it can be done. Not with a large army, but I would need more warriors than just my Hel-hides. If you give me–"

"You will leave Ælfred where he is," Guthrum said.

"But, my king, it can be done. And Wessex will never–"

"You will leave him where he is!"

The swiftness of the Dane's anger sent Geirmund back a step. "Guthrum, I mean you no dishonour. I only speak to you in this way because the fight for Wessex is not yet over."

The king appeared to calm himself. "It could be over."

"How?" Geirmund frowned, thinking of the many possible meanings behind Guthrum's words. "What are you saying?"

Guthrum sighed, heavy and deep, and it seemed he almost shrank in size. "I am saying I am more tired of war than I was when I first came to your father's hall."

"We are all tired of war!" Geirmund shouted, his anger and grief raising his voice before he could bridle them. "Do you wish to hide from it? Here in this Christian temple?"

"Hide?" Guthrum turned away from the altar for the first time to face him. "You dare name me coward?"

"I hope not a coward." Geirmund held himself still, thinking of what Eivor had said, weighing each word with care. "I see you are building defences here, and that is wise. There are times it is wise to retreat and gather strength. But a retreat for strength can easily last longer than it ought because of fear. You can be sure Ælfred is not idle in his hold. Every day that we leave him there gives him time to gather his strength also."

"What of it?" Guthrum said. "He cannot take Mercia or East Anglia from us. He cannot take Northumbria. They are Daneland. He knows this."

"For now," Geirmund said. "But if we leave even one Saxon king standing, especially Ælfred of Wessex, they will one day take back their lands. You know this."

Guthrum turned back towards the altar. "Perhaps there is a way to make a lasting peace with Ælfred."

"A lasting peace?" Geirmund said. "What is this talk? What has happened to the Dane that came to Avaldsnes? You swore England would be ours, but only after we take Wessex. That is what I sailed to these shores to do, and that is the oath I swore to myself. That is why I swore to you! I turned my back on my father, my mother, my brother." Geirmund pressed his fist against his chest as if stabbing it with a knife. "My father died here! I have lost warriors and friends! Their deaths will not be for nothing."

The king sighed again. "I thank you for your honesty, Hel-hide. I will think on what you have said. But for now I am finished speaking of it. Leave me."

Geirmund stood there for several moments, stunned into silence, trembling with rage. He could see he would get nowhere with the king, and he worried what his anger would drive him to say and do. He turned and stormed away.

31

"You should kill him," Birna said.

Her words surprised Geirmund, and they seemed to surprise the other Hel-hides gathered around the evening fire. Several days had gone by since they had come back together at Cippanhamm. Eivor had left, and Geirmund's mother had gone north to await Hámund's return in Jorvik. The king had refused to hear Geirmund since the last time they had spoken, and aside from the town's defences, had made no move or plan against Ælfred or Wessex. Even so, for Birna to speak openly of killing Guthrum did not seem to fit with her honour, and it also did not seem to sit well with the other warriors.

"Take care with idle words," Eskil said. "Some might mistake your meaning."

"My words are not idle," the shield-maiden said. "And I do not speak of murder. Geirmund should challenge the king openly. Many would follow him."

"The time is not right for that," Steinólfur said. "Guthrum is still too strong."

Geirmund knew the older warrior spoke of Hnituðr, but there

were only a few in that circle who understood his full meaning. Eskil knew of the ring's power, and so did Skjalgi, but the others did not. They knew only of Guthrum's feats in battle, how he had slain Æthelred, but that seemed to be enough for them to agree with Steinólfur, even if Birna scoffed.

"If Guthrum is so strong," Skjalgi said, "why does he not slay Ælfred? What does he fear?"

Geirmund had asked himself the same question many times. Hnituðr gave the king power to march on Sumorsæte almost as an army unto himself. For Guthrum to hold back at Cippanhamm suggested to Geirmund that the king had either lost trust in the ring, or he had a hidden and bewildering plan unknown to anyone but him.

"Fear comes from many places," Vetr said. "I have seen mighty warriors brought low by fear of a small spider."

"It was a poisonous spider," Rafn said next to him, sounding irritated. The Dane was able to sit up now, and he had more colour in his cheeks. He still slept for most of the day, but Steinólfur said he had crossed the strait of greatest danger and would heal. "A deadly spider," Rafn said.

"I think the spider Ælfred is spinning a web," Eskil said.

"Perhaps Guthrum spins a web of his own," Skjalgi said.

"To spin a web," Vetr said, "a spider must leave its lair and risk climbing out on the branch."

Geirmund looked up at the silhouette of the hilltop temple against the night sky, its windows a deeper black, except for the single faint light that flickered at one end. He did not know why Guthrum stayed in that place but it troubled him. Völund and the völva had both spoken of betrayal in Geirmund's fate, and he was beginning to see what that meant. Guthrum had betrayed him and the Danes, but not fully, and not yet to utter defeat, though at times it felt that way. Geirmund often had to remind himself that the seer had also said that he had been given the way to overcome, if only he knew what it was. He rose to his feet.

"Where are you going?" Steinólfur asked.

Geirmund nodded up the hill. "To try again."

"Go, then," Birna said. "Keep talking. But the moment will come when words fail and there is nothing left but to act. Do not put that moment off, and do not hide from it, if you want warriors to follow you."

Geirmund gave her a nod, not in agreement but to let her know he had heard her. Then he left the fire and trudged up the hill. A wind blew that night, wrenching the treetops and dragging thin clouds across the stars, and the higher he climbed, the rougher it scoured the hill. He walked hunched against it with downcast eyes, and barely noticed the two figures slipping away from the temple door as he crested the rise.

They did not look like Danes. Though only shadows, Geirmund could see the robes of a priest flapping about one of them in the wind, while the other wore strange garments with tassels, and a cap. They scurried like thieves over the far side of the hill, away from the town, and Geirmund dropped low to give chase, but he soon lost them to the darkness among the trees and the flocks of sleeping sheep.

He thought of Guthrum, and rushed to the temple, fearing the king may have been slain, and he pounded on the newly hung door with his fist.

"Guthrum!" he shouted. "My king, can you hear me?"

A moment later, the door opened, but only partway, and the king looked out at him through the gap. "I was sleeping," he said. "What do you want?"

Geirmund did not hear sleep in Guthrum's voice, nor see it on the king's face. He glanced in the direction the thieves had gone, and he almost mentioned them but stopped himself.

"Well?" the king asked.

"I am sorry for waking you," Geirmund said. "I must have heard something in the wind."

Guthrum grunted and shut the door, leaving Geirmund outside in the cold, wondering about the two thieves. He realized, as he thought back to what he had seen, that they had come from inside the temple, and the king was awake and unharmed, having lied about being in his bed. Geirmund knew if he had asked about the strangers, the king would have lied about them also, and perhaps taken steps to keep him from finding out the truth.

After that, Geirmund lay in hiding each night among the sheep near the foot of the hill, watching the woods and the slope for their return. He told no one, not even Steinólfur, and for eight nights he watched, and for eight nights he saw nothing and crawled into his bedding aching and cold each morning before sunrise, but on the ninth night, the thief in the priest robes returned alone.

Geirmund sneaked up on the stranger and threw him easily to the ground, scattering the mewling sheep, then pinned him down with his father's seax at the man's throat. Only then did he see who he had taken.

"John?"

The terror in the priest's eyes faded. "Geirmund, praise God."

"Do not praise him yet." Geirmund left the edge of his blade where it was. "What are you doing here, priest?"

"I-I'm here…" He sputtered and stammered. "I come to see how the Danes are treating the people of Cippanhamm that they have enslaved."

"Is that what brought you here nine nights ago?"

The whites of John's eyes grew a bit larger in the moonlight. "I–"

"You were in the temple with Guthrum, and you had another with you. Who was he?"

The priest hesitated. "He was a minstrel."

"What is that?"

"A storyteller, a–a kind of singer."

"A skald?"

"A Dane might call him that."

Geirmund noticed a leather satchel about the priest's shoulder. "What do you carry?"

"Nothing," John said. "Some food. That is all."

"Give it to me."

"Geirmund, please–"

"Give it to me! Or I will take it from you."

Instead of cowering, some of John's fear seemed to fade, as if he had been feigning it. His eyes narrowed, and his body relaxed despite the weapon at his throat, and Geirmund caught a glimpse of a man inside the priest that he knew nothing of, and had not seen in all the days they had spent together.

"Will you kill me, Hel-hide?"

"Do not call me by that name." Geirmund bent down, grasped the leather satchel, and ripped it from the priest's arm. The tussle sliced the seax against John's neck and left behind a thin ribbon of blood. Geirmund pulled the blade away and stepped back. "You are much changed, priest. What has Ælfred made of you?"

"He has shown me the kingdom of God."

"I have had my fill of kingdoms. Get up."

John stood slowly and wiped the blood from his neck with two fingers while Geirmund looked inside the satchel. He saw several pieces of parchment, rolled up and folded and realized John was simply the messenger, but now Geirmund had the message, and the priest did not know he could read. "Go," Geirmund said. "Go back to your marsh-king."

"What will you do with my satchel?"

"I will take it to Guthrum."

John nodded, and it seemed in the darkness that he smiled. "What if I choose not to go?"

"I will not kill you, priest." Geirmund sheathed his blade. "I wonder now if I ever knew you, but for the sake of our past travels together I will not kill you."

John bowed his head. "I am grateful for–"

"But the other Danes will kill you, when I call them, and it will not be a quick death."

The priest glanced up the hill. "You would do that?"

"I will," Geirmund said. "I do not know why you are here, but I give you your life as a parting gift, along with a warning. If we meet again, it will be as strangers, Northman and Saxon, pagan and priest."

John did not move or speak for several moments, and then he bowed his head again. "I will still pray for your soul, Geirmund Hjörrsson."

Geirmund shrugged. "It is your breath to waste."

John smiled, and then he turned and walked away without hurry. Geirmund watched him go until he vanished into the shadows beneath the trees, and then he climbed the hill towards the temple.

He did not go straight to Guthrum, but went back to the Helhide campfire, and by the light of its flames he read the messages in John's satchel. He found some of the words difficult, but he understood enough of the writing to finally see the depth of Guthrum's dishonour and betrayal, and he knew that part of his fate had been fulfilled. With that knowledge came peace, but it was the bitter, unforgiving peace of winter over a frozen land. He knew what he would do, and he roused Steinólfur to share what he had learned.

The older warrior might not have believed Geirmund, were it not for the pieces of parchment in front of him, and his mouth hung open in shock. "I do not understand," he said. "Guthrum and Ælfred work together?"

"Yes."

"For how long?"

"I don't know. But there is to be another battle between the Danes and the Saxons, and Guthrum will surrender there. He will be baptized a Christian, and he will receive the lands east of the Roman street called Wæcelinga. Ælfred will keep Wessex."

"Why would Guthrum do this?"

"Only he can know that. I have learned there are unseen forces at work in England, ancient brotherhoods and orders. My father and mother fought them in Jorvik, and it seems that Ælfred has had some part in it all."

"And now he has snared Guthrum," Steinólfur said. "Perhaps Ælfred really is a spider."

"There is one more thing," Geirmund said. "Ælfred demands that Guthrum give up the ring. I will not let that happen."

"What will you do?"

"I am going to take it back."

"How?"

"I do not know yet. But the seer said I already have the way."

"When?"

"Tonight. Now. Ælfred's messenger will tell him I took the satchel of messages, and he will surely act on it."

The older warrior moved to rise. "Then let us–"

"No, my old friend," Geirmund said. "I do this alone. You must rouse the Hel-hides and be ready to lead them from this place, no matter the outcome. If it is my fate to fall, all who followed me will become enemies to Guthrum. But I do not think it is my fate to fall."

Steinólfur grabbed Geirmund and pulled him into a fierce embrace, something he had never done. Geirmund felt the older warrior's frustration, and pride, and love. "It is not your fate to fall," Steinólfur said. Then he pulled away, thumbing the tears from his eyes. "I will rouse the Hel-hides, but we will not ride without you, because you will lead us."

Geirmund gave him one last nod before setting off towards the hill. He had no plan, and he knew that no cunning could defeat Guthrum while he wore the ring. Only a few years ago, back at Avaldsnes, he might have been called reckless and a fool for what he was about to do, but to be reckless was to chase fate while fearing it, but also to hide that fear behind scorn. Geirmund had done that before, but no longer. He did not fear his fate, and he would not chase it, so he did not charge up the hill to meet it. He marched.

When he reached the temple door, he rapped on it with his knuckles, and he heard Guthrum's distant voice within.

"Come!"

Geirmund opened the door and stepped inside.

"You are late," the king said, facing the altar at the end of the temple hall where a soapstone lantern glowed, but as Guthrum turned, he flinched in surprise. "Geirmund? What are you–"

"Who did you think would come?"

The king paused. "What do you want, Hel-hide?"

Geirmund strode up the hall towards him. "I want the ring."

Guthrum laughed. "What?"

"Völund's ring, Hnituðr. I have come to take it back, and then I am leaving with my Hel-hides."

"At last you admit you are an oath-breaker. I knew that one day you would betray me. It was you who warned me I would fear you."

"Is that why you sent me to die? Twice?"

"Yes." The light behind the king threw his long shadow over Geirmund, and across the floor and walls, seeming to swell him to the size of a jötunn. "But each time I also hoped you would return."

Geirmund halted a few paces from the altar. "I am here. And you are the oath-breaker."

The king snorted. "How?"

"You deal secretly with Ælfred. You would become a Christian and betray your gods, and you would betray your warriors by surrendering to that Saxon spider."

Guthrum said nothing for a moment. "You are cunning, Hel-hide. But you are wrong. I cannot be an oath-breaker, for I am a king, sworn to no one."

"What of honour?" Geirmund asked.

"What of peace!" Guthrum shouted. "The sons of Ragnar and the warriors sworn to them have all been taken to their grave-beds by the sleep of swords. What comfort is their honour to them? We Danes have had our fill of raiding and war. My warriors want to settle on the lands they have won. They want to drink, hunt, hump, have children, and grow old telling lies about their youth. Would you have me tell them to go on fighting and dying instead?"

"They will die humping, or they will die fighting, but they will die, for there can be no truce with death. Only the coward–"

"Do not speak to me of fate!" Guthrum's hand went to the grip of his sword. "Did fate sink my fleet and drown my army? Did fate slay Ubba, and Ivarr, and Bersi? Did fate give Ælfred and his brother victory at Ashdown?"

"Yes," Geirmund said. "But fate also gave you Cippanhamm."

"Cippanhamm?" The king laughed, full of bitterness and defeat. "We did not come for Cippanhamm! What is Cippanhamm without Ælfred, but a hovel covered in sheep shit." He drew his sword and pointed it at Geirmund. "We came here for the king of Wessex! We chose this place so we would only face his hirð, but still he slipped away. We cannot fight the ealdormen's fyrds, we do not have the strength, and now we are surrounded by the warriors of Wiltescire, Bearrocscire, and Defenascire. If you say that is fate, then I say we are cursed."

"But you have the ring," Geirmund said.

"The ring is war!" Guthrum bellowed. "And I want peace. So I say there is no fate, and no curse. We are but straw dolls who must make our own peace, and our own destiny."

Geirmund knew then that the king's mind could not be changed by anyone but a powerful seer. Guthrum denied the power of the Three Spinners because he lacked the courage to meet the fate they had cut for him. That kind of cowardice seldom changed to courage.

"I surrender the fight for Wessex," Geirmund said. "I will leave you to your peace with Ælfred, but only when I have the ring."

Guthrum sighed. "You will have to come and take it, Hel-hide, if you can, for I will not give it to you."

"Why?"

"Ælfred wants it destroyed." He shrugged. "The price of peace."

Geirmund drew his sword, Bróðirgjöfr, and he charged at the king. Guthrum stood his ground without moving, and he barely lifted his blade as Geirmund brought his sword down from over his head with the strength of both arms.

Before the strike landed, Geirmund felt his blade slow, as if slicing through water. Then it seemed to hit stone, and it glanced off the Dane with a force that rang the bones in his arm like bells and sent him reeling.

"Now you see," the king said, moving towards him.

Geirmund found his feet and turned to face the Dane again. He did not know how he would break through the ring's power, but this was not a battle from which he would surrender, no matter the end. This fight had been fated from the moment he had given Guthrum the ring.

He howled and charged again, still holding his sword with both hands, this time up near his shoulder, blade up, point forward. When he reached Guthrum, he felt the same slowing of his weapon, pushing back against his arms and his shoulder, and then the king swung his sword and swept Geirmund's aside with more than a man's strength.

Bróðirgjöfr lurched and dragged Geirmund's arms with it, spinning him as it flew from his hands and chimed against the temple stones a dozen paces away. At the edge of his eye he saw Guthrum's sword swinging around for a second strike, and he dropped to the ground and rolled away to dodge it.

Guthrum chuckled. "Did you know what it was when you gave it to me?"

Geirmund leapt to his feet and pulled his father's seax from its sheath. Guthrum stalked towards him, swinging his sword in the air like a herdsman driving sheep. Geirmund changed his stance and his grip, using one hand to better control his strikes and keep his footing. Even the strongest armour had gaps and places of weakness, so he stabbed and ducked, sliced and leapt away, searching for an opening. But the power of the ring surrounded the Dane like a wall, a headland of swords, and

Geirmund only tired and weakened in throwing himself against it.

He pulled back a few paces to catch his breath, forehead dripping, and he knew his death would come within moments. If Guthrum were a younger, stronger man, or a better warrior, Geirmund would have already fallen. He needed to weaken the Dane within his unseen armour, in the same way he had weakened Krok.

"After you become a Christian," he said, "I hear Ælfred will give you a new name. You will be like one of his dogs, sniffing his cock and begging from scraps."

Guthrum laughed. "You know nothing, Hel-hide. Any Christian in England would be honoured to have Ælfred christen them."

He rushed at Geirmund, swinging his sword fast and hard. Geirmund fought to keep his grip on the seax as the Dane's blows flung it from one side to the other, until the sweat on his palm turned slick against the polished antler, and the blade flew out of his sight.

The king grinned, a troll in the dim lamplight, and butted Geirmund's face with his forehead, smashing his nose. Geirmund stumbled backwards and fell, blood coating his lips, blinded by sparks and tears. He blinked up as Guthrum came towards him, flipping his sword around in his hand for a downward thrust.

He knew that in the next moment that blade would pierce him, but he had no weapon in his hand, no way to join his father in Valhalla. He only had Bragi's bronze knife, just as he had when he was sinking in the sea. He pulled it from its sheath, but unlike when he had thought he would drown, he refused to surrender, so long as he had one more claw.

Geirmund clutched the knife close until the Dane came within reach.

"Farewell, Hel-hide," Guthrum said. "You–"

Geirmund lunged from his hands and knees, like a wolf. He expected to be thrown aside, but instead he heard a grunt. Then his chest hit the cold stone floor as the king staggered backwards. Geirmund looked at the knife still in his hand, saw blood on its blade, and he realized that he had stabbed the Dane.

Guthrum realized it also. He looked down at his thigh, where a stain of blood grew, and then looked back up at Geirmund, and at the knife, in true fear. The wound did not look fatal, so that was not the source of his terror. The king now knew that Geirmund had a blade that could kill him, and he knew Geirmund could do it. The king could see his fate.

He dropped his sword, which clattered to the temple floor, and limped towards the altar as Geirmund rose to his feet.

"Where did you get that knife?" Guthrum asked.

"It is a common thing," Geirmund said. "It was a gift to remind me where to look for true enemies, and true danger."

The king bumped up against the altar and put his hands back to steady himself. "If I give you the ring, will you let me live?"

Geirmund laughed. "You still believe there can be a truce with death?"

"There can be a truce between us."

Geirmund looked again at the bronze weapon and thought of Bragi, who had last used it to cut his meat, the night they spoke of weapon-weather. At that memory Geirmund made his choice and looked up at the Dane. "Toss me the ring."

"How do I know you—"

Geirmund raised the knife, holding the blade between his fingers as if he meant to throw it at the king. "The ring," he said. "I will not miss."

Guthrum reached up his sleeve, wedging his hand up high, and then slowly tugged the ring down his arm until it came free of his hand. He looked at it for a moment, and then he threw it towards Geirmund.

The metals glinted in the light, spinning their colours around the temple walls, and then Geirmund caught it out of the air. He had not seen it in years, and he admired it anew, its craft and beauty, and the glow of its runes, thinking that Hytham would likely wish to see it, and may know more about it. He slipped it over his hand and pushed it up his arm, outside his sleeve.

"Do not trouble yourself, Dane," he said. "I will not kill you. A wise man once told me that come winter, neither king nor thrall can expect to harvest anything other than what they sowed in summer. I was not sure I believed that then, but I believe it now. England has taught me well that war grows only more war."

Guthrum sneered. "So now you want peace?"

"Not your peace," Geirmund said. "Not the peace of the coward, and not the peace between kings who ask warriors to die for them. Never again will I swear to king or jarl. I will make my own peace, with honour."

Guthrum swallowed and winced, holding his hand to his bleeding thigh. "Will you leave England?"

"Do you fear I will stay?" he asked, but he did not wait for the answer. "I will go freely where my will takes me," he said. "Kingdoms will pass. Wealth will pass. Warriors will pass. I will pass, and you will pass. One thing alone will never pass, and that is the honour and fame of one who has earned it. And you, Guthrum the Christian, will never forget that I am Geirmund Hjörrsson, called Hel-hide."

EPILOGUE

There are kings of the land who rule patches of ground and wage war over the size and shape of their borders. They live as prisoners behind the walls of their holds and fastnesses, their freedom and their wealth bound to the land. There are also sea-kings, whose halls are longships that sail the whale roads and grow no roots. The waves and the currents are their kingdom, where the only borders they know are beaches and shores, and the limits of their courage.

Before Geirmund Hel-hide became a sea-king, and before he settled the reaches of Island far to the west, he fought for the Danes against the Saxons in England, winning many battles through his cunning and courage. When Guthrum, king of the Danes, made peace with Ælfred, the king of Wessex, Geirmund and his Hel-hide warriors rode north, and after some time there they took to the seas with Geirmund's twin brother, Hámund.

With them were Steinólfur and Skjalgi, Vetr and Rafn One-Arm, Eskil the giant and Birna the shield-maiden, Thrand Spindle-Shanks and Kjaran, along with as many warriors as would take the oaths required of every Hel-hide. They raided and traded to the edges of the world, performing many feats that are well known and often told, and gaining much fame and riches until their longships were feared by all.

It was sometimes said that Geirmund wore a ring made by Völund the smith, which turned his skin to iron so that no weapon could pierce him, but upon his death no ring was found in any of his halls, nor was it on his arm, nor was it buried with him in his barrow, and it was generally agreed that he needed no ring to become a king, and that his fame was well earned.

TEN QUESTIONS WITH
MATTHEW J KIRBY

Assassin's Creed Valhalla: Geirmund's Saga is an original story set within the game world, though not directly linked to it. What made you decide on this specific route to take for the first Aconyte-published Assassin's Creed novel?

That is the creative direction Ubisoft generally takes with their novels, comics, and other publishing projects. One of the many things that made writing in the *Assassin's Creed* universe so appealing to me is the fact that the Ubisoft team didn't want me to write a novelization of the game. In a way, that story has already been told, and I'm not sure it would benefit from a simple retelling in the form of a book. Instead, Ubisoft wanted an original story that would be connected to the world of *Assassin's Creed Valhalla*, while offering a new story to give readers and gamers a different perspective on some of the game's characters, locations, and events. That way, the book can be enjoyed whether a reader has played the game or not, and if they have played the game, the book will hopefully add another layer to that world to enrich the experience.

Why did you choose Geirmund Hel-Hide and his story specifically?

When Ubisoft approached me to write a story in the world of *Assassin's Creed Valhalla*, they provided a list of possible figures from history and the game to focus on as the protagonist, and they invited me to send them any ideas I had. Geirmund was on their list, and I was immediately drawn to him. He was the son of a Norwegian king, but his mother was not from Norway, so he appealed to me as an outsider character. His mother was said to be from Bjarmaland, a region that was likely situated in northern Russia, but we don't know much about the people there, and they seem to have migrated and assimilated into neighboring territories by the 15th century. The fact that Geirmund's father likely lost his lands to Harald Fairhair added another dimension of drama to his story. I'd never heard of him before, but he is briefly mentioned in some of the historical sources and texts, such as the *Landnámabók*, and I knew I wanted to give him a proper saga of his own.

Valhalla follows the story of Viking invasion in England in the 800s. What sort of research goes into creating a story that is both exciting and historically accurate?

For me, that process does involve extensive research, but it helps that the material is already incredibly exciting and doesn't need any help from me to make it more so. What I do when I write historical fiction is to first read as much as I can to understand the time, people, and events that I'm writing about. That's somewhat difficult when we're talking about Vikings in the 9th century, because the Vikings from that time period didn't write anything down until a few centuries later. All we have are sources like the Anglo-Saxon chronicles, which are not exactly unbiased in their account of the invasions. We do have archeological evidence, which is helpful, but ultimately the process of writing about Vikings from this time involves some degree of extrapolation and intuition. For me, writing historical fiction, especially about a time so far removed from our own, is a balancing act between accessibility and accuracy. For example, a completely accurate story would be written in Old Norse, which would make it completely inaccessible to anyone but scholars. I don't speak or write Old Norse, so simply by writing this story in English, I've already taken a step away from historical accuracy. As best I can, I try not to contradict what we know from the record, but when I do knowingly contradict something, I do it intentionally because it's necessary either for the story, or for accessibility. For *Geirmund's Saga*, I also made some choices in the interest of continuity with the game, a medium that balances accuracy and accessibility differently than a book.

Can you recommend any further reading for readers who have enjoyed this story and want to learn more about Geirmund, Hamund, and the skald Bragi?

I mentioned the *Landnámabók* above, but Geirmund is also mentioned in the Sturlunga Saga, and his ancestor, Half, has a saga of his own that is a fantastic read (called *The Saga of Half and His Heroes*). Bergsveinn Birgisson has written an entire book about Geirmund, but it hasn't yet been translated into English. If and when it does get a translation, I would love to read it. If readers want to know more about the Anglo Saxon side of the conflict, I highly recommend *Alfred's Britain* by Max Adams (which has also been published with the title *The Viking Wars*, but they're the same book).

What is the most surprising thing you discovered while writing Geirmund's Saga?

I think the thing that surprised me most, that I tried to reflect in the book, and which is also portrayed well in the game, is how complicated the Viking invasions were. I knew that it was likely a highly dynamic process, but I was nevertheless surprised at just how nuanced and layered it was. Prior to the period modern historians have demarcated as the start of the Viking age, Scandinavians were already well known to the Saxons, and some of the first invaders may well have started out as traders. One need only look at the similarities between the famed Sutton Hoo helmet and those buried at Valsgärde in Sweden to see that significant cultural exchange had been established for a few hundred years prior to the events depicted in *Geirmund's Saga* and *Assassin's Creed Valhalla*. Not only that, but the Saxons were a Germanic people, and they shared cultural and linguistic roots with the Vikings, such that their spoken languages seem to have been at least somewhat mutually intelligible, and despite the religious divide between pagan and Christian, they shared some of the same mythic figures, such as Wayland the Smith.

How do you develop your plot and characters?

That depends on the book I'm writing. For me, the heart of any story is the change that takes place in the character, so when I'm developing a book, I'm trying to figure out how the character will be different at the end from the character who began the journey. Ideally, the plot of a book serves that change in some way, by compelling it or making it harder, pushing the character toward the resolution. When I'm writing a wholly original story, I have the luxury of adjusting the plot to suit the needs of the character's change. When I'm writing historical fiction, the plot is somewhat predetermined by the record, and my job is then to locate my protagonist's story within those events in a way that makes them active, rather than a passive observer or historical tour guide. For Geirmund, his change as a character is directly tied to his purpose in joining the Viking invasion of England, which is one of the reasons I chose to write a book about him. It was a natural and obvious fit.

What would you say is your most interesting writing quirk?

I don't know if it's an interesting quirk, but I do write in an extremely linear way that sometimes surprises people. I write my books in rigid order, from the first page to the last, and I do not move on from a page until it is working as well as I can possibly get it. When I realize I need to make a revision, as when I discover that, say, I need to set up a plot twist better, I stop writing and go back in that moment to make the adjustments. It's a slow, methodical, and plodding way of doing it. Consequently, my books don't have drafts in the way many people think about them, and I don't go back to reread them before I send them to my editor. Some scenes may have been rewritten a dozen times, while a few rare scenes may remain pretty much the same as the day I wrote them, if it was a particularly good day. I've tried writing scenes out of order, and I've tried making revision notes to myself and just moving on, but I have found both to be disastrous to my process, creating far more work for me in the end.

On a typical day, how much time do you spend writing?

I still work as a school psychologist, so during the school year I'm usually writing for a few hours in the evening most weeknights. On the weekends and during the summer, I try to put in six to eight hours, but sometimes I'll call it a day at four if it's been a good day or I need to step away to figure some story things out. When I'm under deadline, I work hard to get into a zone where I can put in twelve hours or more, if I need to. When I wrote *Geirmund's Saga*, I went away for a retreat in the woods of north Idaho and did nothing but write and research for about three weeks. Those sorts of stretches become a blur where I never fully leave the book, mentally.

What, in your opinion, are the most important elements of good writing?

For me, it all begins with character. If I don't feel like I know my protagonist, if they don't feel like a fully formed person, then I don't have a story yet. It's the same when I'm reading a book or watching a show. I don't necessarily need to know a character's favorite color or pizza toppings, but I do need to have a sense that they are a real person driven by the same fundamental needs that drive me and everyone else (and if not, then I want to understand how their needs differ). Character manifests in a book not only through choices, but through the style and voice of the writer, which is also really important to my enjoyment of a story. A fully realized setting is also essential, but is often somewhat invisible, and the heavy work it's doing can be overlooked. But a well-chosen, careful detail can bring a story to life for me and ground me fully in a book, usually by showing me something that is unexpected but feels completely true. For example, I remember reading a book on the Renaissance that described the period as one where the smell of blood mingled freely with the perfume of roses, and boom, I was right there in it. The final thing I find essential is a sense of direction. I have to feel like the story is taking me somewhere. So, if a story has a living, breathing character, a compelling setting, and the promise that it's taking me on a journey, I'll follow it anywhere.

Which books or authors have most influenced your own writing?

This question reminds me of something the inimitable children's author Richard Peck once said: "We write by the light of every book we've ever read." I think that's true. The single book and author that made me want to be a writer was *A Wizard of Earthsea* by Ursula K Le Guin. I was twelve-going-on-thirteen when I read it, and in retrospect, it isn't an exaggeration to say I was a different person afterward. As a young reader, I loved the historical fiction of Elizabeth George Speare, and the fantasy works of Natalie Babbitt, Lloyd Alexander, and Susan Cooper. A bit later, Tolkien was a huge influence on me. As an adult, I've continued to have formative experiences reading Octavia Butler, Gene Wolfe, Philip Pullman, and M T Anderson, to name only a few. The list could go on and on, and I'm always adding to it. I take much consolation from the certainty that I will never run out of good books to read, and new writers to discover.

Watch an exclusive interview with Matthew J Kirby on world expanding fiction in Assassin's Creed Valhalla:

ABOUT THE AUTHOR

MATTHEW J KIRBY is the critically acclaimed and award-winning author of the middle grade novels *The Clockwork Three*, *Icefall*, and the Assassin's Creed series *Last Descendants*, among many others. He has won the Edgar Award for Best Juvenile Mystery, the PEN Center USA award for Children's Literature, and the Judy Lopez Memorial Award.

matthewjkirby.com
twitter.com/writermattkirby